The Cuckoo

V. R. Nelson-Watts

Stuart Tartly Press

The "California Cuckoo" or Brown Headed Cowbird, may lay up to 30 eggs each season. These birds are called parasites because they lay those eggs in other birds' nests. They are brown in color and related to blackbirds. They pose a serious threat to native species. The word "cuckoo" is also used to describe someone who is not quite sane.

Chapter 1

JACK'S WIFE Lily was with him the last time he was in the San Jacinto mountains. She loved going with him to pick up firewood. That was a long, hard year ago. She laughed when she dropped an armful of pinecones in the truck bed where he was about to carefully place the last log. She knew he wanted to keep the wood stacked precisely, so it wouldn't shift on the sometimes steep and bumpy road back down. He looked at her, and then, with exaggerated care, he collected up the scattered pinecones and put them in the empty picnic cooler so they too would be protected on the drive home. That made both of them laugh. She grabbed his sleeve and said "Come look – I found a bird's nest!" Eyes shining, she pulled him towards an uprooted oak tree. And there, among the tangled roots, was a tidy little nest carefully woven together and lined with moss, fine grass, and pine needles.

"I think it's a Junco's nest, Lily. We can take it home if you like. They don't use them twice, and this one's not a new one. I think you can claim it as one of your 'nature gifts'."

She lifted it carefully and placed it in a bag with some of the other treasures she'd collected. Acorns, rocks, sticks,

1

anything that took her fancy was carried home and incorporated into her collection. Her 'nature gifts' had become a passion, and although it was hard for him to live with the kind of chaos they created, he celebrated them with her. He knew then that he wouldn't have her much longer.

He remembered how warm it had been that day. But today it was cold, and an almost icy breeze made it hard to move as easily as he had a year ago. He felt that year had aged him, made him slow, and filled him with a deep and lonely grief.

The wind shifted a bit and a welcome breath of warm air carrying a familiar scent lifted his heart. He remembered Lily's face again and smiled. He finished loading the firewood he had come for and leaned against the truck to catch his breath.

The warm breeze disappeared, and with it the lovely scent. Suddenly the intense blue of the sky, the sharpness of the oak and mesquite in the biting air were all too much. The firewood wasn't stacked precisely, but he was ready to go home. Home without Lily, but still, home. He drove carefully down the winding road back to the broad desert.

———

Kitty left town on a bicycle that didn't belong to her. She had no idea where she was going, but she had been peddling along a flat stretch of back road for about half an hour when the front tire popped. Now she was pushing the bike slowly, trying not to notice the very painful blisters on her heels. Her shoes were not the right size. She had pulled the shoes and a bright pink sweater out of a box of nearly new clothes left outside the Salvation Army collection box. The sweater fit perfectly. "*Just my color*," she thought.

She was hoping some kind soul would give her a lift back to the homeless shelter, so every time she heard a vehicle approach, she stuck out her thumb. Her head was pounding, and she could not remember how she had gotten to a homeless shelter from the nightmare she'd been through in Tijuana with Gray and that other creep Ron. She had a vague memory of being at a Casino in San Diego. But was that before or after Tijuana? And even with the perfume on the sweater she picked up, she could still smell the two men all over her, though she had showered at the shelter. She was bruised, too, meaning it wasn't only her feet that hurt. Not being able to sit on the bicycle seat was probably what gave her the blisters on her feet. *Where was Gray? Did he leave me at the shelter? Or did he send me here and stay in Baja? I really hit bottom this time. I should throw myself in front of the next car that comes along and hope to god it kills me.*

Then she heard the crunch of tires on gravel behind her and turned to see if someone was really stopping.

An older man with a shock of white hair leaned out of the pickup. "You need some help there?"

"Oh my god. How kind of you! My tire went flat and my feet are killing me!" She pushed away thoughts of turning him down, and tried to smile.

The man got out of the pickup and went to open the tailgate and lift the bike onto the truck. Then he turned and looked at Kitty. "Name's Jack, by the way." He opened the passenger door.

"I'm Kitty! Well, Catherine, but everyone calls me Kitty."

Jack hesitated a moment, and then walked to the driver's side and got in. "Where were you headed, anyway? There's not much up ahead." He could see a faint bruise under her left eye now that they were seated so close together, and her hands were trembling.

"I don't really know!" She smiled at him. "I was desperate to get out and get some air. Something kind of suffocating about where I'm staying." She lowered her eyes. "Could you drop me off near a gas station? I think the tire is just flat. I can make my way back from there."

Jack eased the pickup onto the road. Kitty was nervous. She knew he would ask more questions, and she could hardly tell him she was a fugitive from a homeless shelter. Maybe she needed to switch to the sweet, somewhat helpless mode that had worked for her before.

"Thanks so much for stopping. I don't think I could have pushed that bike another ten feet!" She turned her head towards the side window.

Jack noticed she'd clenched her hands to keep them from shaking. "You been walking that bike for long?"

"Oh, I don't know -- about an hour. What time is it, anyway?"

"Almost noon. Starting to warm up, too." He really wanted to ask about that bruise under her eye but thought better of it. "It's lunch time. You hungry?"

"Are you asking me out to lunch?" she laughed.

"Why not? Aren't you hungry?"

"As a matter of fact, yes. No breakfast this morning!"

Jack laughed. "That's too bad! Let me take you to one of my favorite places."

He pulled into a strip mall parking lot and stopped in front of the Snowbird Café.

Chapter 2

"COME ON, I'll buy you a burger." He noticed she had no purse, no pockets in her sweater or pants. He thought that she had the same kind of vulnerability Lily used to have – and there definitely was something else – something he couldn't quite name. *"The color of that sweater? Lily had worn one like it. She loved it, I never thought it suited her. Sometimes I think she wore it to annoy me. It certainly did make her stand out, which was probably why I didn't care for it. Or was it Kitty's voice? When she spoke, there was something in her voice..."* he thought.

The little café was one of his favorites. The food was better than good, and he went often. They knew him by name and remembered his favorite menu items. Since Lily died, he was there several times a week.

Kitty knew that confidence was the best cover, so she threw her shoulders back and looked Jack straight in the eye when he opened her door. "All right then! Thanks! This is a cute place! I'll just duck into the restroom for a minute and freshen up." He smiled at her and took his favorite booth in the corner by the window.

A waitress appeared at the table with a cup of hot coffee in her hand. She lifted it towards Jack without a word, and he just nodded.

He took a sip. "Perfect! As always, Jess."

"Of course, Jack. Nothing but the best for you. Hey, you gave me a start there for a second when you walked in with that woman. I thought it was Lily! Must be the sweater...and something about the way she looked at you."

"Yeah — that sweater mystifies me a bit, too. Looks so much like the one Lily had."

"Well it IS the one Lily had! I'd recognize it anywhere! That rose she stitched at the neckline makes it one of a kind. Where'd this woman get it, anyway?"

Jack scowled. "That can't be right! I sent that one to the thrift shop. You must be mistaken."

"Well, maybe. I've just never seen another one like it, though. You want me to bring some waters? She gonna eat here with you?" Jess looked like she disapproved.

"Yes, Jess, she's joining me for lunch. And you're wrong about the sweater. Bring some water and menus, please. And don't look so worried! It's just lunch."

"OK...if you say so." Jess looked doubtful.

KITTY TOOK her time cleaning up. She was shaky, and her head was pounding. She washed her hands and face and did what she could with her hair. With no comb, the best she could do was remove her hair band and make a messy ponytail with her dark brown and gray curls, leaving a few escaped tendrils around her face. She pinched her cheeks to bring some color and realized the black eye hadn't faded as much as she thought when she had looked in the mirror of the dark bathroom this morning. She hoped Jack hadn't noticed, and wished she had some makeup to cover it. Oh well, if he asked any questions, she'd think of something.

She beamed at Jack as she slid into the booth, picked up her water glass carefully and drained it. "Thanks for this. I thought I'd have to walk all the way back to town. So many cars just drove right by. I guess an old lady with a busted bike can be invisible."

"I wouldn't call you an old lady, Kitty! Now tell me where <u>were</u> you going, really? You weren't just out for the exercise, am I right?"

She looked around nervously to see if anyone was listening and saw that they were alone at that end of the café. A tear slid down her cheek, and she reached for a napkin. She leaned in close to Jack and he caught the sweet scent of roses. Lily's favorite perfume. Was that what the warm breeze carried on the mountain? Impossible. He pulled back and picked up the menu.

"What would you like? They do a great corn chowder bowl, and the burgers are fantastic."

"I don't mind – you order for me. I'll eat anything."

He motioned the waitress over and told her to bring a sourdough bowl of corn chowder and a burger.

———

"Okay, Jack, who gets what?" Jess was balancing two heavy platters on one arm.

"Just put them down – we'll sort that out. Thanks, Jess. Kitty? Your call – I like them both!"

She couldn't remember when she had eaten, and she was so

shaky she was afraid she might not be able to manage the soup. "The burger looks good. I'll take that! Thanks so much!"

Jack stirred the soup to cool it. He could see that Kitty was in no shape to have been riding a bike in the first place, and that bruise under her eye puzzled him. She needed help.

They ate in silence for a while, Jack lost in thought, Kitty trying to figure out what might be next.

Jack looked up from his plate. "You know, Kitty, I can easily repair that bike. Why don't I take you back to my place? You can take off those shoes and put some band-aids on those blisters, so you won't be in so much pain. Shouldn't mess around with blisters, you know. They can get infected."

"I don't know. You shouldn't go to all that trouble. I should figure this out myself."

"It's no trouble! I'm pretty good at fixing things like bicycle tires. And since you were feeling suffocated where you were, why not take a breather? I can run you and the bike back later this afternoon when you've rested, and I've fixed that tire. My place isn't that far away."

Kitty smiled. "Well...if you're sure. But only if you're sure, Jack."

They were quiet as they drove to Jack's house. Kitty knew she would have to be careful about what she told Jack about her life. He didn't look like the type who was easily taken in. And there were a lot of things about her situation that she would like to forget, not have to reveal. Jack was right, she did need to rest. She was bone tired, and though she was a little less shaky, she was hurting, and not just from the blisters.

Jack finished repairing the bicycle tire and went to check on Kitty. She had fallen asleep during the short ride to the house after lunch. He had taken her to the guest room and told her to finish her nap.

When he looked in, he could see that she was sound asleep. He pulled the door to and let her rest. She must have been exhausted – and the way she ate her burger made him think it had been more than just one or two meals she had missed.

Chapter 3

Kitty woke up when she heard Jack in the kitchen.

She went into the bathroom and found he had left her some antibacterial soap, medication, and bandages in a basin with a note that said "for your blisters!" There was also a comb and a new toothbrush.

She filled the basin with warm water and the liquid soap and gingerly tested the water with her toe. The blisters had burst when she pulled her shoes off, so the pain was intense when her feet touched the water. She knew it was wise to get them clean. She put the medicated cream on the bandages and felt immediate relief when the raw skin was covered. Jack also left her a pair of terrycloth scuffs and some white socks. *"This man thinks of everything."* she thought. It took her awhile to make some order out of her neglected hair. The best thing was being able to brush her teeth. She just might start to feel human again.

When she came into the kitchen, she saw Jack was grinding pepper into a pot on the stove.

"Smells great, Jack! You a good cook?"

"Hey there! Well, you look perkier! Have a good nap?"

"Yes, thanks. How long was I asleep?"

"Oh, about three hours, I think. So, I thought we could have dinner and then maybe talk about getting you back where you belong. Do you need to let anyone know where you are?"

"No. I'm not going to be missed. But are you sure you want to feed me again? After all, you've done so much already."

"Well, firstly, since you ask, I am a pretty good cook — and secondly, it's no trouble. Your bike is good to go again, but it will be dark soon. So, I can drive you wherever you need to go after dinner."

"You really have been kind, Jack. Most people would never have stopped to help me. Most people didn't, in fact. I am grateful. And thanks for the stuff for my feet. They feel so much better. I'd like to stay for dinner. What are we having and what can I do to help?"

Jack smiled. "Good. Well, we are ready here with the chili. You can take the salad out of the 'fridge if you like. We'll eat here at the kitchen table."

The table was set, and there was a bottle of red wine waiting to be poured, as well as a frosty carafe of water. Kitty took the salad out and put it on the table. "Anything else I can do?"

"Nope! We're all set." Jack sat down and so did Kitty. "Would you like some wine?"

"I'll have some wine," she said, while reminding herself to go slow on the alcohol. She had finally begun to feel more grounded and knew she needed to stay that way.

"Here's to making new friends, Kitty!" Jack raised his wine glass.

"Is that what we are, Jack? Here's to new friends!"

They turned their attention to the salad and the chili.

"Everything tastes wonderful. You are a good cook! Tell me, is that the guest bathroom in there? It doesn't look much like one a man would use! So much pink – and, well, girl things!"

"Yeah, well my wife used to keep it ready in case our daughter Jenny came for a visit. She didn't come that often, but Lily always wanted to be prepared."

"Your wife? I thought you were single."

"Lily died six months ago. She had a massive coronary while she was in chemo for cancer. Very quick."

"I'm so sorry!"

"We'd been together for 45 years. That's a long time sharing."

Kitty thought "He's lonely. Loneliness can kill you, too, or at least make you wish you were dead. I know that much."

"How old is Jenny? Why doesn't she visit much?"

"Jenny is 43. She's got a husband and two teenagers. Busy life in Los Angeles. She and her mom didn't get along all that well, frankly, and it was probably better that they didn't see too much of one another. You know how it can be."

"Yeah. I do. I've got a 34-year-old daughter I haven't seen for ten years. I don't even know where she lives, now. Last I heard she was marrying a guy much older who had two kids, but I wasn't invited to the wedding – if they had one," Kitty sighed. "This chili has a little extra something in it, doesn't it?" She needed to change the subject. "Is it cinnamon?"

"Yes! You guessed it! That's my secret! I like a little sweetness with my spice!" He winked at her.

Is he flirting with me? Surely not. She ducked her head and took another bite.

Half the time she felt on the edge of the shakes from alcohol withdrawal, and half the time she felt like she was in a dream, so she couldn't be sure of anything.

"No worries, Kitty. I'm just talking about the chili. So, what brought you and your bike out on that lonely back road? Just out for exercise, or bird watching?" Jack helped himself to more salad.

She took a deep breath, and another sip of wine.

"No," and she took another deep breath. "I was running out of a homeless shelter, and I don't even know where I thought I was going. And the bike isn't mine. I just took it. Now you know."

Jack looked at her but said nothing for almost a minute. Kitty lowered her eyes to her plate and clasped her hands tightly in her lap. Jack said "That must have been a difficult place to be. Had you been there long?"

There was a sharp ping from the timer on the oven. Jack jumped up from the table and pulled a round, crusty loaf out of the oven and placed it on the table next to a dish of olive oil and rosemary.

"We'll let that cool for a bit. So, again, have you been in the shelter long?"

Kitty took another sip of wine, another deep breath. "I must confess I'm not entirely sure. I woke up in a shelter this morning feeling like shit – sorry, but that's how I felt – and couldn't seem to get my bearings or remember why I was there or how I got there. The last thing I remember was sitting in at a poker game at some Casino."

"Has this happened to you before?"

She knew she needed to keep this as honest as she could. "I've had black outs before and found myself in a drunk tank or on someone's couch a couple of times. I'm not a full-time drunk, but I sometimes have what they call lost weekends."

Chapter 4

JACK SAID NOTHING, just broke off a crusty piece of bread, dipped it in the oil, and handed it to her. "You might want to eat this before you drink any more wine."

"Thanks. I think the wine I've had is making it easier for me to get back to normal, oddly." She took a bite of the bread.

"I'm not surprised. That's often how it works. I know. But too much – well too much is always too much."

"I know that too. And I've known it for a long time."

Jack didn't press her for any more details. They finished dinner, and she finished her glass of wine. He corked the bottle and put it in the cooler. "That'll keep for tomorrow, I think. No need to go overboard tonight. How about some tea? Or coffee?"

"Can't do caffeine after 3. Makes me jittery and then I can't sleep."

"So – some herbal tea? You name it, I've got it!"

She settled for chamomile, with some honey and lemon.

"What about you, Jack? What's your life like now that you are alone?"

"I'm alone, and lonely. You can probably tell. I've been trying to sort things out for six months. Lily collected a lot of things, and sorting all of that out and sending it where it might do some good has been emotional. Hard work, and slow."

"Not surprising. It looks like your guest room is sorted through – very tidy and very clean!"

"Ah. Well, that was the easy part. But she did a lot of thrift store shopping and on-line impulse buying – most of it was new. There's a lot of clutter in most of the rooms of this house. I've made a start, but I am by no means getting the better of it all yet. I did take a box to the Salvation Army yesterday. In fact, the shoes you were wearing were very much like ones I left in that box. And your pink sweater was, I think, in that box too."

Kitty was silent, picking at her salad, and wondering how to respond. She shivered.

"Were you in that shelter that's close to the Stager Brother's market on Pine? Because that's where I left the box."

"You might as well know I took the bike from there too. There was no lock on it, and it seemed like an opportunity to get away." Her eyes welled up, and she dabbed at her face with her napkin. "I'm a terrible person. You should take me back to the shelter, Jack. You've been so kind. But you've done enough."

He knew that was the sensible thing to do. But he was a fixer. A fixer of broken things, broken hearts, when he could be. *"I should be careful. Go gently with this. She touches me the same way Lily did when we first met...vulnerable, and beautiful."* Jack smiled at her and thought that surely there would be no harm in letting her stay in the guest room for one night until she had recovered more of her equilibrium. He could take her back to the shelter tomorrow, couldn't he?

"Why don't you stay here, Kitty, for tonight. We can talk about getting you where you need to be tomorrow. For now, let's clean up this kitchen. Then you can find whatever you need to make yourself comfortable in that guest bathroom and tuck yourself into bed for a good night's sleep. There's some aspirin in the medicine cabinet in there – you may want to take a couple."

"Are you sure, Jack? Really? I haven't told you anything that would make you think I was worth any more of your time. Why would you want me to stay?"

"I think I can trust that you are not going to run away with the family silver in the middle of the night. Not with those sore feet! Really, Kitty, it's fine if you want to stay tonight. I'm tired and not sure I want to go out again. I don't much like driving in the dark."

"I guess you've got me for the night then. Thank you. I'm very grateful." She started to clear the table. Her hands were shaking again, and she was on the verge of a crying jag, but she pulled herself together long enough to help him load the dishwasher and then told him good night.

"Look in the bathroom cupboard for towels and pajamas. I think you'll find what you need. Good night, Kitty."

Jack poured himself another glass of wine and went out onto the back porch to drink it. He could watch the stars come out. It was what he always did.

――――――

KITTY TURNED the tap on in the bathtub, opened a cupboard and found towels and some worn flannel pajamas. *"Guess I'll have to get used to wearing other people's clothes for a while," she thought.*

She added a tiny bottle of bath salts to the water, grateful for the smell of lavender, also knowing that might help her sleep. So many little bottles – looked like free samples collected here and there – or brought back from hotels. Some of them were ancient, the liquid inside dark brown and thick, the labels faded and peeling.

Her feet were throbbing and putting them in water again wasn't pleasant. She washed quickly, put more medication and bandages on her heels. *He was right. I do need that aspirin.*

She slid under the covers, pulling them tight around herself, hoping, praying, that she would sleep through the night and not wake up with a terrible craving for the rest of that bottle of wine.

―――――

JACK WAITED until the light went out in the guest room before he locked up and went to bed himself. His room was on the other side of the house, and he probably wouldn't hear her if she got up during the night.

"If I start worrying about that I won't sleep at all. She's got to do this on her own. She very well may not be here in the morning. I must let it go. She does runners, she said so herself. Maybe those sore feet will make her think twice, at least until tomorrow. Funny – I'm not worried about her stealing anything, even though I know she's done that before too," He drifted off.

Chapter 5

JACK WAS ALWAYS UP before the sun. This morning was no different. He pushed his feet into his slippers and padded into the bathroom and then to the kitchen to turn the coffee on. He heard the thump of the newspaper being tossed onto the porch and went out to get it. Before he settled at the kitchen table with the paper and his coffee, he went to check on Kitty. He opened the door just a crack and saw that she was still asleep.

Kitty heard Jack open the door to her room. She closed her eyes to let him believe she was asleep, but she had been going over what she remembered of the last few days.

She did remember how and where she got so beat up. She'd been with Gray at Ron's fancy hacienda in Tijuana, and it was a horrible night that she tried to push out of her mind. But she couldn't remember how she got from there to that Casino. Was she with Gray? She couldn't remember who, or why they were there – or how long. She did remember having tequila shots – lots of tequila shots – and then there was just nothing until she woke up on a cot in the shelter with the stale smell of sick, tobacco smoke, and skunk weed in her hair.

She remembered taking a shower in the cement bunker of a

bathroom, washing her hair with something left in a plastic bottle which she hoped was shampoo, and pulling on the jeans and t-shirt that was at the foot of her bed along with information about some social service she could contact for assistance. There was a note explaining that her personal items were at the desk in the office.

She remembered feeling trapped, suffocating in the stale air. She remembered walking out the front door, the clerk calling after her, and running down the street as fast as she could in her bare feet.

She remembered sitting down on a bench at a bus stop to catch her breath and seeing the collection box for the Thrift Store in the parking lot of the grocery store behind her. Someone had left a cardboard box full of clothes too big to shove through the pull-down opening. She remembered finding shoes and the pink sweater, stealing the bike, and riding off. Her head had been pounding, and she needed water.

She remembered turning onto a paved road from the dirt path that ran along the foothills of the San Jacintos, and that the fresh air was helping. She remembered the punctured tire and walking the bike until her feet were blistered and she was exhausted.

And then, along came Jack in his beautiful blue pickup.

By the time Kitty came into the kitchen, Jack had finished the paper and picked some grapefruit from the backyard tree. He was rummaging in the kitchen drawers looking for the grapefruit spoons when she came through the swinging door.

"Good morning! You sleep okay? Want some coffee?"

"I am surprised after that nap yesterday, but I slept very well. I'd love some coffee. Let me get it – you're busy there."

"Are you a breakfast eater or just a morning coffee drinker?"

"I'd love some breakfast. But just toast would be fine. Don't fuss."

"No fuss – this is the day of the week I allow myself the full breakfast spread. We'll start with grapefruit, and then go from there. I've got some Canadian bacon and I make a mean omelet. Shall I just do my usual, or do you have any preference?"

"No – I'm happy with whatever your usual might be!"

"Good. I'll let you slice what's left of the bread from last night and make us some toast."

He noticed she had pulled on a pair of sweats and a long sleeved t-shirt. He thought they both were Jenny's – Lily never wore sweats or t-shirts with any kind of slogan. This one said SAVE THE WHALES. Yep, Jenny's.

"I hope it's okay if I borrow these things? I found them in the cupboard with the towels," Kitty pointed to the whale.

"Nobody owns those anymore — I think Jenny wore them when she was a teenager! You can keep them if you want."

"Maybe I can find a whale to save!" she smiled. "Did I hear a rooster this morning? Or in the night?"

"I'm sure you did. Somebody has one as a pet – I never could figure out why that was a good idea, but there you are. To each his own."

He broke four eggs into a bowl and whisked them until they were foamy.

"Looks like you have spent a lot of time in the kitchen, Jack. You beat those eggs like a pro."

"My wife wasn't much of a cook. She could do a good salad, and she did make a mean meatloaf. But that was about it. So yes, I guess I have spent a lot of time cooking. Especially since I retired."

Kitty put two slices of bread in the toaster and sat down at the table with her cup of coffee.

"How long have you been retired?" she asked.

"Going on five years now. I retired early when we got this house. We'd lived in the San Fernando Valley most of our married lives. When we first moved there it was kind of like this area is now – lots of agriculture -- orange, walnut, and pomegranate groves – peaches. Lots of ranches too, and small family farms. That's what we liked about it. Room to breathe. Too many big houses there now, eating up the little ones."

"I don't think this area will be much different in a few years, do you? But you're right, it is nice to have some peace and quiet – and space." She poured herself another cup of coffee. "You want a refill?"

"Sure. Thanks."

The omelet was ready to flip, and he picked up the pan and gave it a sharp tip and pull. "Perfect."

They ate in a comfortable silence – she poured more coffee, he brought some marmalade to the table.

"That was great, Jack."

"I'm glad you liked it. Now let's talk about what's next. I have to ask, because I am a bit of a compulsive – when was your last tetanus shot?"

"Wha...what?? Why?"

"This is horse country, Kitty, and if those blisters you've got on your feet have broken, they are primed and ready for an infection. So, tell me."

"You're right about the blisters. They are a mess. I can't remember having a tetanus shot as an adult. Do grown up people actually do that?"

"Yes. Especially when they live around horses. So, our next stop is going to be the clinic where they can give you what you need and look at those feet."

She started to laugh. "You're kidding, right?"

"Not at all. We are going, and that's not an option. After that, you can do what you like. But first stop is the clinic. No questions, no arguments." Jack looked determined.

Kitty wondered why he had suddenly been so firm with her. Was his request unreasonable or only cautious? Seemed like ordinary blisters to her, but if he was worried and she wanted to keep on his good side, maybe she should agree.

"Okay. But I don't have any identification or anything, including money as you know! Are you sure they'll see me?"

"Yep. I've already made an appointment. It's a free clinic, and they don't ask a lot of questions."

She knew, from experience, that wasn't entirely true. They would ask a lot of questions. She would have to give them some information so they could check to see if she had any kind of insurance. She'd have to tough it out. She wasn't covered, and hopefully nothing else would show up when they ran her name.

Chapter 6

Jack put the bike in the back of the pickup. Kitty picked up the clothes she had worn the day before. They would no doubt want them back at the shelter.

"I thought we'd just leave the bike where you found it. Probably best, don't you think?"

"Of course. Do you want to put the sweater and the shoes back too?" Kitty asked.

"No. I'll deal with those another time."

The clinic was clean but crowded. Even though she had an appointment, they had to wait almost an hour before they called her name. They handed her a two-page form and asked her to fill out her medical history.

While they waited, Jack kept handing her magazines and telling her "Hang in there, it won't be long now." She was about to bolt when they called her name.

"Catherine Somers?"

Jack smiled. "You're up, Kitty!"

The nurse told her to take off her scuffs and socks and asked her to put her feet in a basin of water so she could remove the bandages without causing too much discomfort. Kitty was glad to comply – the last time she changed them, it hadn't been easy or painless.

"Doctor will be in soon. She'll want to look at your feet, so we won't rebandage yet."

Kitty thought "Oh great. More waiting."

It was only a matter of minutes when the doctor came through the door. She stopped for a moment, then checked the intake sheet.

"Oh! Hello! Do you remember seeing me a couple of nights ago? At the shelter?"

"Gosh -- no. I don't remember much about the last few days. Were you the doctor at the shelter?" Now Kitty was really nervous.

"Yes. I saw you the night you were brought in. Crazy time to be called out, but there it is. You were not in good shape at all."

"Well, I'm better today, thank you." Kitty bit her lip and watched as the doctor reviewed her medical history, ordered a tetanus booster as well as a blood test. "It's routine for all patients at the clinic. We want to identify any other potential medical need. You need to keep your feet clean, and the blister area covered during the day. At night you can remove the bandages to help speed up the healing. I'm going to put you on a quick course of antibiotics just in case. You don't indicate any allergies to medication. Is that right?" She looked at Kitty. "Have you been in an accident recently? How did you get that black eye and the other bruises I found when I examined you the other night?"

Kitty squirmed. "I don't really remember. Sorry. I may have fallen down. And I am allergic to penicillin."

The doctor raised one eyebrow. "Well, if you don't remember, you don't remember. I think I need to do a little more thorough examination than I did when you were brought to the shelter. I'm concerned about some of those bruises. The nurse will bring you a gown and take you to x-ray. You said you'd had some unexplained bleeding? Have you gone through menopause?"

"I said that? I don't remember. Yes. I'm done with all of that. How odd."

"I think it will be important to get that checked out, so I'll do a pelvic exam as well. Come back here after you're done in x-ray." The doctor left the room.

Kitty had turned bright red, she could feel her cheeks burning.

JACK KEPT CHECKING HIS WATCH. It seemed like Kitty had been in the exam room longer than necessary. He started to pace. When Kitty came back out, she looked so small and scared. All her confidence seemed to have drained away. She looked at him with tears in her eyes.

"What's wrong? Did something happen in there? Why were you in there so long?" He reached out and took her hand. It was freezing. "Come sit down and tell me what happened."

They sat down and Jack waited for Kitty to explain. She took a deep breath and gave him a little smile. "I'm just a big baby. Can't handle shots! And they wanted x-rays because of some bruising on my back. That turned out fine, just bruising is all it is. She thought I might have cracked a rib or something, but I haven't really had that kind of pain. Sorry it took me so long. I'm supposed to pick up some medication at the counter. I have to take some antibiotics as a precaution with these blisters,

I guess." She knew that wasn't the real reason, but it would have to do. She wasn't going to tell Jack any more than she had to. Not now, maybe not ever. "They took some blood tests, too, and want to see me back in a week."

"Good. I'm glad they are being thorough. That's good." Jack sighed with relief. "And don't worry about where you can stay until then. You'll just stay with me until you get through these pills and keep that appointment. Maybe that will give you some time to figure out what you want to do next."

"You've already done too much. I really can't keep imposing on your generosity, Jack."

"Nonsense. I've got the space, and I've got the time. Maybe you can give me some help sorting through some of the chaos in my house while you are waiting. I could use it."

What else was she going to do? She was homeless, she wasn't feeling all that great, and she couldn't even begin to think of another option. "Are you sure? Truly?"

"I am. And that's an end to it. Let's pick up the medication and get you back home."

"Could we stop by at the shelter and see if my purse is there? I'd like to know if I still have my wallet, at the very least."

Chapter 7

J ACK HEARD the pharmacist tell Kitty she should take her medication with food to prevent stomach upset. He suggested they get a snack before they went to the shelter. "Shall we go back to the Snowbird Cafe?" He asked as they walked back to the truck.

"We'll get a bite so you can take one of your pills. Then we can get your things and maybe drop off the bike where you found it."

Jack opened the passenger door.

"I don't think I'm dressed very well to go anywhere, Jack. Do you?"

"Nobody will care at the Snowbird."

"But I'm not even wearing shoes! Just these slipper things!"

"I've seen worse, believe me. You're fine."

Kitty sighed. "If you're sure. I feel terrible about the way I look."

"You look just fine, Kitty. Just fine. But if you're really uncomfortable, I can pick up some pastries and we can eat in the park. That make you feel any better?"

"Yes! It would. If you don't mind."

Kitty waited in the truck while Jack went into the Snowbird. This was going to have to work. It had to. She had to pull herself together, or she might never have another chance to set things right. She was tired of living so close to the edge of disaster, so close to despair. Maybe he was right. Maybe Jack could help. God knows she needed help...all the help she could get.

Jack appeared with a container of food and coffee and handed it to Kitty through the window. "You okay, Kitty? You look worried." Before she could answer he went around to the driver's side and got in.

"I'm as good as I've been in a long time. I'm just so grateful for everything you've done. How can I ever hope to repay you?"

"Let's see. First you can cheer up and have a little picnic in the park with me and take your first pill. Second, we will drop that bike off and go to the shelter and get your things. And third, we will go back to the house and get you settled in so you can find out what you want to do next. You can stay with me while you're making a plan. I think those three things are about enough for one day, don't you?"

"If you say so, Jack. Yes. I think that will be quite enough."

THE STOP at the shelter was hard. Kitty asked Jack to wait in the pickup.

The woman at the desk was on the phone and motioned for her to take a seat. Kitty looked around at the reception area and shivered. It was cold, and it smelled of disinfectant.

"How can I help you?"

"I think I left some of my things here. I came in sometime over the weekend, I guess. I really don't remember."

"Name?"

"Catherine Somers. I hope you have my purse. My driver's

license should be in there along with my credit cards. At least I hope they are in there. It's a gray shoulder bag with black trim."

"I'll go check. Wait here."

The woman came back with a plastic bag as well as a gray shoulder bag.

"You're lucky it's still here. Things and people," she looked hard at Kitty, "seem to disappear with great regularity."

"I can imagine. Were you on duty when I came in?"

"I was. The guy you were with seemed in a big hurry to get you off his hands as fast as he could. You hook up with him again, or what? I never believed his story – that he found you wandering around outside the Casino at 3 in the morning. He said he was a security guard there and didn't want to call the cops. Thought you might be better off here to sleep it off. He didn't look like much of a security guard to me. Gave us quite a generous donation to take you, by the way."

"*Gray,*" thought Kitty. "*It had to be Gray. That son-of-a bitch!* "I am grateful you took me in. I don't remember anything about last weekend, unfortunately. Last thing I remember was tequila shots and a poker game."

"Looks like you've cleaned up a bit, but you're gonna need more than a bath to get whatever monkey you've got off your back. Drunks aren't pretty – especially at your age.

"Here's your stuff. The clothes are the ones you wore when you came in, and we haven't washed them. I'll let you decide if they are worth keeping or not. We can't throw anything out that belongs to you. Sign here." She shoved a form at Kitty.

"I brought back the clothes you provided. They aren't washed, but I thought you might be able to use them again."

"Probably. You were in such bad shape when you were brought in we had a doctor take a look at you. She wanted to see you again before you left. Said she had some questions. Her number is in the bag with your things."

"I don't remember any doctor. You sure that was me?" That part was true, she didn't remember.

"Yeah, I'm sure. You were pretty out of it, though. So I'm not surprised you don't remember. We've also got social services you can contact if you really want some help. I put the information in the bag. I hope we don't see you back here again."

"I'll see my own doctor when I get back home." Kitty picked up her things and went out the door, the heat of the pavement and the bright sun stunned her for a moment.

Chapter 8

JACK WAS PACING around by the truck. She saw him and started to cry. She looked humiliated and pitiful. In fact, the tears were more from relief than humility. Jack put his arm around her and took the plastic bag. "Please put that in the back of the truck. I'm sure it doesn't smell very nice. It's got my things from when I was brought in." She opened her purse and found her wallet, car keys, and some cosmetics still in it. "Well, I guess I dodged that one. My driver's license is here, and my credit cards."

"You'd better cancel those. They may have been used without you knowing it."

There was an envelope in her purse with a note and a key taped to a business card for a storage locker.

All your things are out of the apartment and in a storage locker. The car has been returned to the dealership. The locker is paid for through the next month but get that stuff out of there quickly or I'll just trash it all.

She knew Gray's printing well enough. Well, at least she knew for sure there was no going back now.

Jack watched Kitty's face as she read the note. "Bad news? You've gone pale. You okay?"

"I'm okay. Everything I own has been moved out of the apartment and into a storage locker. And if I want any of it I'm instructed to get it as soon as possible or it will be gone for good. What a mess."

"Well, maybe it's a mess, and maybe it's not. At least you know that returning to that apartment is not an option. Where's the storage locker?"

"It's in Perris. That's an odd place to put my stuff. Where is that, anyway?"

"It's not too far from here. It's about halfway between Riverside and Hemet. I suppose the rental fee might not be as high there. Maybe that's why?"

One thing had gone missing from her purse. Her cell phone. But it was a cheap pay as you go. So, no real loss. She had only used it to contact Gray, anyway, and she had no interest in contacting him again, ever. Her own phone had been left in her desk at the apartment. Maybe it had been put in storage along with everything else.

Jack was having a hard time not asking questions. He could tell she needed time to process this new information. He started the truck and headed home. She would talk to him when she was ready.

After they had been driving for a while, Kitty realized she'd been back in her own darkly complicated world, and flashed Jack a smile. She couldn't afford to lose his good will right now.

"I don't want to be a burden, Jack. But I do seem to be stuck for resources right now. I lost my job two weeks ago. Got fired. And I have no idea if my bank account has been cleared out of what little was in there."

"It's settled then. If you are willing to help, I'll make sure you have food to eat and a roof over your head. No other strings attached." He needed to make that last part clear. Lily had only been gone six months.

"I'm not a bad housekeeper, and although cooking isn't my gift, I can do a few things in the kitchen. And I do know how to do laundry. You got an iron? If you show me what you want done, I'll do my best. I do have a talent for sorting and organizing, that I will admit."

There was a warmth about her that she obviously tried to hide, but he could see it when she looked at him. Her blue eyes were a different shade than Lily's – but that deeper blue seemed to hold a kind of sweet vulnerability. She also had a way of gesturing with her hands, much as his mother had done. And she was good company. A good listener. He needed that.

She could feel a slight shift between them – he was a safe bet, for now, she knew that. Maybe this could work for longer than a week. He obviously was well off, drove a high-end truck, lived in a great house on a big chunk of property. He was a thoroughly nice guy. Could she tolerate a thoroughly nice guy?

"Yes, I've got an iron! And, miraculously, I also have an ironing BOARD!" He laughed as they turned into the driveway. They were home. And he wasn't alone, at least for now.

The one thing that was worrying Kitty was the warning that she needed to retrieve her things quickly or they'd be gone. What was the hurry if the place had been rented for a month?

The one thing that was worrying Jack was how to tell his daughter Jenny that he had a woman staying with him. He'd have to think of something fast to make that go down well.

Chapter 9

Jenny opened her suitcase, releasing the scent of both lavender and sage, a strong reminder of place and process. She was home from a retreat where she had been surrounded by wildflowers, peace, and loving counsel for an entire week. She only wished the peace had returned with her as well. But one week is a short time to try to rebalance all relationships after a loss. The woman who was assigned as her advisor had helped her deal with the death of her mother, but now she was worried about her dad. He must be going through his own painful process, but she doubted he would seek out or want any kind of counseling. She called him when she got to the airport, but there was no answer. She called again when she got home, but there was still no answer. She left another message, knowing she hadn't been able to keep the concern out of her voice. That wouldn't go over well. He never wanted her to be concerned about him, maintaining that she needed to focus on her own life, her own family, and let him take care of himself. She sighed, unpacked the case, and carried her laundry downstairs. She would add it to the pile that Kevin and the kids had accumulated while she was gone.

Kevin was sitting at the kitchen table making a grocery list.

"Still no answer when I call dad. Where could he be? He always picks up."

"He's fine, Jenny. He's probably just out shopping or running errands. You know he's trying to clean out that mountain of stuff your mom collected. Maybe he's taking your advice and really digging in."

"I've got to go down there, Kevin. I can't rest until I know he's okay," Jenny started sorting colors from whites. "Are we taking in washing? Looks like you guys wore every piece of clothing you own last week!"

"I'm sure you would have heard if there was anything to worry about. He does have friends, Jenny. They know how to reach you – and if he were ill you are the only one listed as an emergency contact. Relax. He's probably just sorting through stuff, and maybe that's harder than you know. He'll call, I know he will. You need some help here? I guess we didn't stay on top of the laundry."

"Just go to the store and do the shopping. We seem to be out of everything. What happened while I was gone? Did you feed the neighborhood?"

"The kids brought a lot of friends home. They cooked, I cleaned. At least you didn't come home to a kitchen full of dirty dishes! It was kind of fun to see what they put together – vegetarian lasagna – pasta primavera – salads with quinoa and dried berries -- it was all pretty tasty! Amazing how food has become a political statement. If it's not vegetarian, it had damn well better be local."

"Well go on and get out of here. And get a rotisserie chicken. I'm ready for some normal food. I had enough of vegan cuisine when I was on retreat. It was good, but I think my tastes are more eclectic."

"Thank god! Sure – and I'll pick up a pizza from Joe's so we won't have to cook tonight."

"Good – oh and get some wine. We seem to be out of that too."

She poured herself a cup of tea and settled at the kitchen table and went through the stack of accumulated catalogs. Consumerism run amok – but mom would have loved some of this stuff. Lots of pink and polyester, some Hummel figurine knockoffs, machine made lace curtains, doilies, and kitsch. Lots of kitsch. I wish we had more in common – it might have been nice to really know her. She had a lot of power; dad loved her without question or criticism – even though his life was so often made miserable by her extremes.

Jenny often felt sidelined. Her mother held center stage, always. And her dad was the biggest fan, most loyal supporter, expecting Jenny to understand that her mom had special needs even when Jenny was only a child with some pretty big needs of her own.

Move on, reconfigure. Live in the moment. Jenny sighed. How could I be so tired when I've just had a week of quiet rest and contemplation? That was, though, hard work. Digging up the past led to regret, anger, lots of heavy emotions. Now that I've unearthed all that stuff I have to make some sense of it, put the pieces together.

Her counselor said, "Go gently, Jenny. Don't look for the big picture until you've spent some time with the little pieces. All you've brought back from the past are snapshots, really. They can be sorted and stored however you like, but there is no way to make sense of all of it until you've accepted what you see as real, as part of your past, and worthy. This is slow work. Don't push. Let it sit for a while, and then, when you're ready, you'll be able to see past the layers of drama and that will help."

Jenny put her cup in the sink and went upstairs to lie

down. She never could sleep during the day, but right now she could barely keep her eyes open. The sun was shining through the half-opened shutters making a pattern of light and dark on the wall. *Looks a bit like prison bars.* And then she was asleep. A mail order catalog fell from her hand onto the floor.

Chapter 10

"This truck have air conditioning?" Kitty was hot, and her arm where she'd had a tetanus shot was beginning to ache. Her stomach was upset, and she was longing for a drink.

"Sure! I just love the fresh air." He closed the windows and snapped on the air.

"Thanks. I'm not feeling well. Little queasy."

"Could be the antibiotics. You didn't eat much when you took those pills, and those can be hard on your stomach. I'll get you some ginger ale and ice when we stop for groceries."

She kept her eyes focused on the road ahead, hoping that would steady her.

They pulled into a parking lot in front of a huge shopping mall, a supermarket at one end.

"I can get the groceries. Anything in particular you fancy?" Jack asked.

"That ginger ale sounds good – but I can't think about food right now. Just get what you're used to."

"You want to come in? They've got a section of clothing and cosmetics. Not a lot, but maybe enough that you could find something so you had a change? Maybe better than SAVE THE WHALES? And it is air conditioned in there."

"I hate to put you out like that. I already feel you've done too much."

"Just don't spend more than 75 bucks – my budget can handle that for the week, I think!" he winked and helped her out.

She grabbed her purse, thinking she might see if her credit cards would work. If they did, she could probably assume they hadn't been compromised. And she might feel like she had a window out if she needed it. Right now, she was beginning to feel a little hemmed in.

"I'll meet you at the front by the checkout stands in about 20 minutes. Go see what you can find, Kitty."

She took a cart and headed towards the end of the store where she could see a couple of racks of pants and shirts. There was also an end cap with scarves and wrap-around skirts marked SUMMER CLOSEOUT 50 – 70% OFF. *This is the end of summer? Sure doesn't feel like it.*

She found a package of panties in her size, not so sexy, but serviceable, and a couple of cotton bras. A pair of drawstring pants should work – the fabric was cool, and would dry quickly. She chose a block-print wrap skirt, and a couple of tops. She made a quick total in her head - $65 bucks. The scarves weren't on sale – more like pashminas than scarves, really, and there was one in a deep blue she knew would look great on her. The fabric was so light and soft, but it was $18. She slipped it off the hook and put it in the cart. This would push her past her limit – she'd just have to see if Jack would spring for it.

Or maybe...

"Excuse me, where's the restroom?" she asked a clerk who was restocking greeting cards.

"End of aisle 12, back of the store."

"Thanks."

When she came out of the restroom there was no sign of the pashmina in the cart. She had tucked it into her purse, thinking she could explain it, when she wore it, by telling him she'd had it when she went to the shelter. He wouldn't know, he hadn't seen those clothes, and she wouldn't let him touch that bag.

She tossed some deodorant and hand cream into the cart – as well as some free samples of moisturizer. It would make the total a bit over $75, but she was pretty sure she could get away with it.

Now if she could only get some shoes that she could wear while those damn blisters healed.

"All set?" his cart was almost completely full.

"Wow – you planning on company?"

"I just want to be sure we've got what we need for the week. I don't like to make daily trips to the store for groceries."

"That lot ought to last you for a month!"

They stopped at the deli after they checked out for a ginger ale and ice, even though she said she was feeling better.

He put the things she had selected into his cart without even checking the price tags. She probably could have just put the pashmina in there too, but she didn't want him to think she was taking advantage.

He put the bags in crates he kept in the back of the truck. "Boy are you organized!" she said.

"Well, this way they don't fall over and spill out – better safe than sorry, I learned that lesson a long time ago."

By the time they got back to the house she was exhausted. She grabbed the things from the shelter from the back of the truck and was about to lift one of the grocery bags out. "Don't worry about that Kitty – I'll get them. It's so hot and you look like you need to lie down for a bit. Go on."

He unlocked the door for her and went back to the truck. He preferred unloading the groceries – he had his own way of doing that. He'd been very efficient about bagging all of them himself, making it easy to put things away when he got home.

KITTY WENT STRAIGHT to the guest bathroom, locked it and unpacked the bag from the shelter. It wasn't as bad as she feared – although everything did reek of cigarette smoke. She put some shampoo in the bathtub and ran some warm water. All of the things from the bag went in. Then she shook out the pashmina from her purse, ran some cold water into the basin and rinsed it out. She hung it to dry on the shower curtain rod. *There. He will never suspect.*

She turned on the ceiling fan and lay down on the bed. She was exhausted, and her arm did hurt. She took a sip of the soda, longing for some whiskey to put in it. She knew she wouldn't sleep, but she needed to be alone and this was about the only way she could make that happen. *Maybe this wasn't such a good idea. But what choice do I have?* Was Jack a little too concerned, a little too much of a watcher? She wasn't a child. When she was feeling stronger, she would prove that to him.

THE VOICE MAIL alert was blinking. Jack looked at the machine and saw there were three messages. He knew they were all from Jenny. He should call her, she was such a worrier. He'd find a way to do it later, maybe after Kitty had gone to bed for the night or was running a bath. For some reason he didn't want her to hear him talking to his daughter. Right now, he didn't want to have to tell Jenny about Kitty, and the few times he had mentioned Jenny, Kitty had quickly changed the subject. No need to upset her when she was so fragile.

Jack moved around the kitchen as quietly as he could. He put the flowers in a vase on the table. It didn't take him long to stow the groceries. He put the bag with Kitty's new things by her door. She must be resting; he wouldn't disturb her.

Now was a good opportunity to make sure she had no access to the alcohol he had on hand. He knew she'd be wanting something, anything, and eventually would find it if he left it in a cupboard or the refrigerator. He put the bottles in a cardboard box and carried the box to the storage shed. The door had a padlock, and he kept the key on his ring. Not only was it secure, but after she had gone to bed he could have his usual nightcap on the patio.

HE PUT some chicken thighs in the slow cooker with a jar of tomatillo salsa. It was about as easy at cooking could get. They could simmer for a few hours and be ready to put over rice, or black beans. He'd let Kitty decide which. The salad was a little more complicated. He cleaned and chopped some romaine lettuce, tomatoes, cucumber and green pepper. The dressing was the tricky part – had to get the right balance of chopped onion and garlic, olive oil, red wine vinegar, mustard, paprika, salt, pepper and some sugar to mix with tomato soup to make the perfect French dressing. It was a recipe he used often, but if the balance was off, so was the dressing. He mixed and tasted until it suited him, then sealed it in a glass jar and put it in the refrigerator to chill along with the salad.

The wood he'd collected in the park needed restacking, and the patio plants needed watering. Even though it was hot, he would be working in the shade of the trees in the yard. There was an Albizia his father had planted, and three seedlings had sprung up the first year he and Lily had been there. She insisted on carefully moving them strategically so that almost the entire yard was shaded. Now they were as tall as the original tree. They gave a nice lacy shade and thrived in the desert heat. The fuzzy pink and yellow blossoms gave off a sweet, intoxicating smell. He knew the seeds and pods were poisonous but had heard that some people ate the leaves and flowers. Fascinating that something so beautiful was also so dangerous—nourishing but poisonous – attracting hummingbirds, butterflies, and people.

That wood won't stack itself. I'd better get to it.

Chapter 11

KEVIN HAD ALMOST FINISHED the shopping when he saw his daughter and a boy he didn't recognize. She hadn't seen him, and he didn't want to embarrass her, but he thought she told him she would be with a girlfriend this afternoon. He ducked back into the frozen food aisle, and they walked past him. The boy had a six pack of beer, and a bag of potato chips. Maybe he wasn't such a boy, after all. They stepped up to the check stand, and he produced some identification that seemed to satisfy the clerk. Deena grabbed the chips as they walked out of the store, and she also grabbed the guy's hand.

Confrontation was not Kevin's strong point. He would do anything to avoid it, as Jenny had often reminded him. But Deena was only just eighteen. This other guy had to be at least twenty-one, or have fake id. Either way it made him nervous. If Deena wasn't home by dinner time, he would have to tell Jenny what he'd seen. If she did get back for dinner, he'd have to risk a serious talk with his daughter. He knew kids her age were testing limits and figuring out who they were – but Deena had never given them any reason to question her behavior.

He stopped to get the pizza and took the long way home. He hoped by some miracle his daughter would be there when he got back.

He was disappointed. Her car was not in the driveway.

Kevin put the pizza in the oven to keep it warm for dinner. They usually ate at five, which was early, but with the kids' schedules, and homework, that seemed to work out best. He would have preferred that the kids eat early and he and Jenny have a leisurely dinner at seven with a glass of wine and some conversation. But maybe it was just as well for now. She wasn't in a talking mood. Right now her worry could be a distraction from her grief. So much unresolved with her mother, and now so many questions about her dad's ability to make a life on his own – and not just a life, a happy one. Something Kevin certainly couldn't fix.

He had his own problem right now – who was that guy buying beer and holding his daughter's hand? Where were they headed? He could call her cell, but he knew the minute she saw who it was, she'd let it go to voicemail. No point. Best to wait until dinner and see if she showed up as agreed this morning when she left.

Kitty couldn't rest. She went into the bathroom and drained the soapy water from the tub. She refilled it and rinsed the clothes that had been soaking. There were empty hangers in the closet, and she used those to hang them over the bathtub to finish drying. In the heat, it wouldn't take long.

The 7-up was warm, and too sweet. She went to the kitchen for some water, and saw that Jack was stacking wood in the backyard. This was her chance to do a little careful snooping. Is it possible that there might be some left-over wine or a couple of beers in the 'fridge? No. Nothing. Nothing in the cupboards, either. Hoping she might find a liquor cabinet somewhere else in the house, she started to explore.

The living room was very different from the rooms she had seen so far. The kitchen and the guest room and bath were stripped down, almost bare. But the living room was a horror. *"Kitschy, cheap, and cloying,"* she thought. *"How did he stand it?"*

Jack told her he was clearing things out, but obviously had left this room untouched. Kitty picked up a cheap Hummel knock-off, thinking that this room would be a challenge for anyone to sort through. She knew some things would bring in cash if there happened to be a thrift shop that would take them on consignment, but most would just have to be donated. She wondered if any of them had sentimental value for Jack or his daughter.

There was a liquor cabinet, of sorts. It had elaborate laminate wood designs on the doors of the upper cabinet. When she opened it she saw it had once held a television or stereo – the back had large holes crudely cut for cable connections. There were some pressed glass cocktail glasses and heavy red wine goblets, but no alcohol. Plastic shot glasses and champagne flutes, collected from some party or cruise ship, filled one shelf. She closed the doors and walked back into the kitchen.

Salsa and chicken were simmering in the crock pot. The delicious smell was tempting. It was too early for dinner, though. She filled a glass with water and went back to the guest room. Jack was still organizing the wood pile. The digital clock on the bed stand said 3:25. Kitty moved the drying clothes into the bedroom and hung them on a curtain rod. She decided to take a long bath since there was nothing better to do. She would explore the rest of the house another time. She'd seen enough in the living room to know Jack really did need some help to make order out of chaos. And she knew she could be the person to do that. This whole set-up was looking more and more appealing.

Chapter 12

Kitty decided to wear the new clothes she had bought rather than put on any of the things she'd been wearing when she got to the shelter. They needed to shake off some of the bad vibes. In fact, she wished she could just get rid of them completely, but that would be foolish this early in the game. Best to behave and not do anything that would raise an eyebrow. She chose the skirt and a gauzy white top with sleeves that would cover her bruised arms. The skirt had block print shades of green, blue, and purple – faintly reminiscent of a water color painting she had seen once in a museum. Was it a pond with waterlilies? She couldn't remember, but even though the fabric was cheap, the colors pleased her. She knew they suited her, and the blue pashmina would deepen the blue of her eyes. That she'd save for later, maybe after dinner, when it cooled off a bit. She rebandaged the still-oozing sores, using the medication and large bandages they had given her at the clinic. The only shoes she could stand were the flip-flops Jack had given her. Now, what to do with that mess of hair. She found a hair dryer under the sink, and straightened it as best she could, then pulled it back from her face with one of the hair ties she always kept in her purse. She smiled at herself in the mirror and slicked her lips with some lip gloss she found in the drawer, then went to see if Jack had finished whatever he was doing in the yard. Surely the wood had been stacked by now. She thought she heard water running somewhere – was he showering or watering the yard?

The patio had that damp, just rinsed smell. The plants looked perkier. She recognized the bright geraniums and hanging spider plants – but there were others she couldn't name. The dust had been washed from the collection of rocks and shells that lined one of the shelves. There was a round, red table with two matching chairs in the center of the paving stones that formed a wide half-circle against the back of the house. Humming birds had begun to hover and dip into one of the feeders hanging by the kitchen window. She sat down by the table to watch them, figuring Jack would find her eventually.

JACK TOOK a quick shower and then set the kitchen table. He saw Kitty out in the yard and poured them each a glass of sparkling water, adding a slice of lemon and a dash of bitters.

"Hey there – how are you feeling? Still queasy?"

"No. I feel pretty good, on the whole. My feet are still killing me, but I guess that's to be expected. I saw you re-stacking the wood you cut. You are a perfectionist!"

"Yeah – I guess I am pretty fussy. I like things tidy. Makes life simpler. That wasn't a priority for my wife, sadly. Lily didn't even recognize chaos."

"Thanks for the um...drink!" she sipped a bit and raised her glass. "Not the real thing, but very ---- refreshing."

"Well – until you've finished those pills, that's the best I can do, drink-wise. Chicken is ready. Would you prefer to have rice or black beans? I've got both."

"How about some of each? I like both – it's hard to choose." She sipped her drink.

"Sure! No problem. I'll go and start the water for the rice. Back in a minute."

He turned on the outdoor speaker and chose a jazz station. He put the beans in a pan to simmer, measured the rice and poured it into the boiling water. She looked so at home, sitting there watching the birds and sipping her drink. He watched her for a moment before he went back out – just for the pure pleasure of it. There wasn't anything he would have changed – even the reasons that brought her here. *I feel like a kid again. I haven't felt this way about anyone except Lily – and that was a long, long time ago. Kitty's voice, her hair, her eyes – everything about her seems just about perfect. I don't know anything about her, really, and what I do know isn't exactly reassuring. Still...*

"I think we're ready, here Kitty – do you want to eat on the patio? Or would you prefer to come inside?"

"Oh let's eat out here. It's lovely – starting to cool off, and it's nice to be outside. Let me help you carry."

And so they sat, under the trees, and shared another meal. He reminded her to take her medication and while she went to get it, he went in to make coffee. When he came back he noticed she was wearing a soft wrap that matched the color of her eyes almost exactly. "You are a lovely picture, Kitty. I'm glad you're here."

"I am so grateful, Jack, for all you've done. I don't know what would have happened if you hadn't come along when you did." Her eyes started to fill, and she turned her head away.

"It's nice to have some company. Found myself eating out of a can the other day, standing over the sink. This is better."

She ducked her head to wipe her eyes and smiled into her napkin. Maybe she could figure out how to make this work long enough to figure out what she would do next.

Chapter 13

"Would you give me a tour of the house?" Kitty said. "I haven't really seen anything but the kitchen and the guest room. You always use the back door – are you hiding something up front?" she laughed.

"Nope, nothing to hide – but you realize I'm still recovering from Lily's death – sorting things hasn't been easy. I've only just got a handle on the rooms you've seen. But if you want to see the rest, of course, let's do it."

She learned that his father had designed and built the house. His stepmother wanted a design that was more pragmatic than pleasing, so Jack had made some changes when he inherited the place to suit Lily. Beige linoleum covered the floors in all the rooms when they moved in, and he had just finished replacing most of it with wood or Mexican tile. The guest room was next, but then Lily got sick, so that was never started. They went through the kitchen to the living room. Kitty caught her breath when he opened the door (as if she hadn't seen it before) and then smiled at him. "This must be the kind of décor your wife liked, right? It certainly doesn't look like your taste!"

"Lily was a collector, and she loved pretty things. Always going for lace trim, that sort of thing. It made her happy. I just …. lived with it… for her sake. She had some problems, and it felt like that was the least I could do. Choose one's battles, right?" and he winked.

"Of course. But now? What are your plans for this room?"

"I intend to enlarge that tiny fireplace, give it a real rustic feel. The room is actually quite big – you can't tell because it's full of so much stuff, but once I sort through all of it and get rid of things, I think there will be room for a big farm table. I have dreams of sitting in front of a decent fire and working on my models in the evening. Want to put in a really good sound system, too, for the music I love."

"I don't see a TV anywhere – you not a fan?"

"I have a small one in the bedroom – usually watch something before I fall asleep. Lily used to have one in the kitchen, but I don't like to be distracted when I'm cooking. I moved it to the shed. Would you like me to put it in the room you're using? There's a cable connection in there."

"We'll see – we don't know how much longer I'll be here, yet."

"You'll be here until your feet have healed, that's for sure! No debate about that. So if you'd like me to move the TV in there, just say the word."

"What I do need is to find something to do so I can contribute. I have a little money in a bank account in Riverside. Maybe we can go get that so I can at least buy some groceries while I'm here. And I want to reimburse you for these clothes!"

"We can see about that in a few days. Let's say we'll make a trip out when you've finished your medication and those heels are better. You go back to the clinic on Wednesday, right? We can talk about it after that. In the meantime, let's just take it easy."

He walked her through the rest of the house – another small bedroom which was full of boxes and storage bins. The master bedroom had another bathroom and an adjoining office space which contained a drafting table and a desk. There was a bay window that looked out on a side yard and a fire pit. "Boy, I can see why you needed to collect some wood! You love your fires, don't you?"

"Yep. Always have. Something about sitting by a fire with a drink or a cup of coffee – no matter how bad things might be. I've spent a lot of time out there watching the flames and looking at the stars. Might do it again tonight!"

"Sounds perfect. Let's do it. I'll get you some coffee and make myself some tea while you build the fire!"

The temperature had dropped and the cool, pale evening air settled around them. The fire caught the carefully laid logs and set some sparks flying towards Kitty. She laughed and waved them away. "I've never seen a fire catch that quick without some kind of starter. You only used twigs and sticks. Amazing!"

"If you know how to build it so there is room for the burn, it's easy. Most people stack wood so tightly the fire doesn't have a chance. The trick is to leave some space for it to breathe."

Space to breathe. That's what she needed too. Could she get it here?

They watched the fire settle. Jack wanted to ask questions, get to know all about her, but he sensed she was not ready to talk. Not yet.

Chapter 14

"WERE you happy when you were a kid, Jack? I know you loved Lily – but it sounds like she was a challenge from the start. What gave you the sticking power?"

Jack thought if he told her a little bit more about himself, she might share her story too, so he said, "My biggest fear as a child was being abandoned. My dad left when I was very young, and my mom raised me on her own. I can remember being terrified whenever she went anywhere that she would never come back. She had to work full time. My grandmother lived with us and she was always there to look after me, but my mother had an independence of spirit that always frightened me. When we rode on the streetcar I would sit as close to her as I could, and secretly grab onto her coat. The idea of leaving anyone was just not something I could do. Like most of us, I suppose, I developed coping skills. My compulsive behaviors used to drive Lily crazy, but that's one of the ways I stay grounded, in control."

"Coping skills. Yes. Some of mine, I'm afraid, haven't been very healthy or ultimately helpful."

THE FLASH of headlights coming up the driveway startled both of them. Kitty jumped up immediately and started to retreat into the house. "Please don't let anyone know I'm here Jack! Please!"

"It's okay, Kitty. I won't. You're safe. Stay out here by the fire. I'll go see who it is."

He hurried into the house, and before anyone could ring the bell he was on the front porch. His friend Steve was just coming up the walk.

"Hey there! What's up?"

"Well you might ask! What's up with YOU? We had a lunch date today, remember? Then I saw you at the Snowbird with some woman waiting in your truck – sneaky old buzzard!" Steve punched him gently on the arm.

"Oh my god – I totally forgot! I'm so sorry," Jack grinned. " – uh, ah – one of Lily's old friends found herself in a bit of a bind and asked if she could come and stay for awhile. So, for Lily's sake, I said sure. She's going to be staying in the guest room for a bit. Had a bit of bad luck, it seems."

"Well you should let somebody know! They're constructing all kinds of interesting stories at the Café – Jess said this woman was wearing Lily's sweater?!"

"Oh, that wasn't Lily's. She had it on when I picked her up!" *Not quite a lie,* he thought. "It all happened so fast, I didn't have time to think about letting anybody know. But I should have called to cancel lunch. I'm sorry."

"Oh – and just to let you know, Jenny called me to see if you were ok. She says she's called several times. I told her I saw you today at the Café, but that's all I said. You feel like a beer? I've got a cold six pack in the car."

"Not tonight. I'm pretty beat. And I don't think my guest is up to company just yet. Another time?"

"Another time. Huh. OK, well, take care – and let's reschedule that lunch soon. I've got some new Rail King HO catalogs I want to show you."

"GREAT! WE'LL MAKE A DATE." Jack watched him until he got into the car.

"Hey -- call Jenny! She's worried!" Steve slammed the door and backed down the driveway.

Now everybody at the Café would know that Kitty was staying here. There would be more gossip for sure.

"You want some more coffee?" Kitty asked.

She looked tired – maybe they had both had enough for the night.

"No, I'm fine." She looked tired.

"I heard your friend tell you to call Jenny – that's your daughter, right? You talk to her every day?"

"Usually, just to check in. She worries. And since her mother died, that seems to be worse than ever. Not sure why all the focus is on me – she's got her own family to take care of. I'll call her later." Jack held the door open. "You said you have a daughter too, won't she be concerned about you?"

"We haven't spoken in ten years. We never really got along, anyway. Too much alike, I guess. Strong opinions!" she laughed and picked up their coffee cups. "I don't even know where she lives. I heard from one of her friends when she was getting married. I wasn't invited to her wedding – she asked her dad, but not me. That ended it as far as I was concerned. Sad, but there you are. I suppose I understand – I put her through some rough times after I divorced her dad. She never really forgave me."

"I've heard divorce can be harder on older kids than young ones. How old was she when your marriage broke up?"

"The first time, she was ten. Then I dated for a while, married again, divorced that one a couple of years later. I remarried her dad when she was sixteen. Divorced him when she was twenty. I've got a dicey past, Jack – best not get involved!" she smiled and then put her hand on his arm briefly. "I can only imagine how all of this sounds to someone who was married to only one person for forty years plus!"

"I'm not worried," he said and patted her hand. She pulled away and put the cups on the counter.

"Were you warm enough last night? Kitty? It can get cold in that room."

"Yes – I was fine. And I think I'll head that way now. I'm tired, and you need to call your kid, right?"

"Right. See you in the morning."

Maybe maintaining the fiction he'd spun for Steve was the best way to let Jenny know Kitty was staying with him. He hated to lie, but he also didn't want to alarm Jenny about having taken in a stranger, especially a homeless one. She'd be down here in a flash. That was the last thing he needed right now.

He went to his study and punched in Jenny's number. Relieved that it went to voicemail, he said "Hi honey – just wanted to let you know I'm fine! Just been real busy lately. I'll call another time and maybe find you home! Tell Kevin and the kids hello." Relieved, he went to clean up the kitchen.

Chapter 15

AFTER TWO DAYS of sorting through all the knick-knacks and odd pieces of furniture in the living room, they had a truck load of items for the consignment shop in town. While they were there, Jack insisted on finding Kitty some suitable shoes.

Walking shoes that protected rather than irritated her feet were not easy to find – at least not if they met Kitty's need for a bit of style, but they finally found some sandals with an open heel that would suit. She decided she could live with them – and was glad to have something besides the flip-flops and her dressy heels that weren't suitable for much besides sitting on a bar stool. Jack insisted on paying for them, as well as for a pair of jeans and a couple of blouses. Kitty told him she was keeping track of what he was spending and fully intended to reimburse him when she could access her funds.

"Tell you what, I will consider whatever we get for the things we dropped off as payment. I appreciate your help. And, you do have an eye for what might sell. Deal?"

"I think you'll get more than the shoes are worth – so I'd be fine with that. Some of those pieces may not be valuable, but right now they are in demand."

"Well, anything over what the shoes cost will be yours. It would have taken me at least a week to get through what we did in two days. You made all the decisions about what to keep and what to get rid of much easier."

"I hope your daughter will want some of the things we saved – and that she didn't have her heart set on anything you are selling!"

"No, Jenn isn't sentimental that way. And her mother's taste was nothing like hers."

"Still, things can have an emotional value over personal taste or actual worth."

"I'm not worried. There's still plenty of things for her to choose from for sentiment's sake. She and her mother really didn't get along that well, sadly."

There was a message on the answering machine reminding Kitty of her follow-up appointment at the clinic.

"Did you remember you've got an appointment at the clinic at 10 tomorrow?"

"Yes. I don't really see the need, my feet seem to be healing pretty well."

"You still have some soreness – I want to be sure all of the infection is gone – something like that can hang on. Better be safe."

"You're a 'safety' kind of guy, aren't you Jack?" Kitty smiled at him and flicked an imaginary speck off his shoulder.

"Guess so. But, you know, better safe than...." He laughed.

The living room had been stripped of all the decorations and all that remained of the furniture was a couch, a coffee table, and a desk that Kitty thought worked well under the windows. It wasn't valuable, but it had good lines and could be a good place to hook up a computer, if Jack would permit it. It would be nice to reconnect with the world at some point, although she wasn't really in any hurry. They had even removed the huge area rug, revealing the beautiful wood flooring Jack had installed. The room, now it was relieved of all the knick-knacks and extra pieces of furniture, could be made into something beautiful. Kitty had already improved it by putting fresh flowers on the desk. She had Jack move a mirror so that the window and the desk with the flowers were reflected on the opposite wall. It opened up the room, filling it with light.

"You have experience as a home decorator, Kitty?" Jack asked when he saw the effect of the mirror. "This room never looked so good!"

"As a matter of fact, I have a passion for it! But no real training and no work history. I've always enjoyed making the most of living spaces. Turn me loose and I could make this place into something very special....not that it isn't already... though, Jack!" she realized she was sounding as if she had a right to do what she liked.

"I might just let you do that if you're serious! It needs something, that's for sure. And I don't have the eye for it. Oh, I can manage the kitchen because that's like a workplace to me, but living spaces always confounded me. And my wife liked to have lots of stuff around, as you know. I never felt like there was a comfortable place to sit!"

"Interesting challenge. I'm hungry, speaking of your 'working space'...have you got any plans for dinner? Can I help?"

"I thought we'd do pasta and salad tonight – and maybe have some of that melon for dessert. Sound okay to you?"

"Yes – better than okay."

"Why don't you relax in a tub while I put things together. Should take me about half an hour. I'll give you a shout when everything is ready."

"Tell you the truth, I'd love that. I'm feeling hot and dusty. Can we eat outside on the patio again tonight?"

"Sure."

There was another message on the answering machine from Jenny. She sounded worried. He called her back and got her machine. And again, he breathed a sigh of relief.

He heard the bathtub draining, and thought he'd have time for a quick shower before dinner. The pasta would cook in minutes, and he had already grated parmesan and chopped some basil. The salad was chilling. Maybe, just maybe, he could coax a little more information out of Kitty over dinner.

Chapter 16

THE SAN JACINTO VALLEY was home to the migrating "Snow Birds" – not actual birds, but retired people who spent winters where they could count on temperate weather and relief from the snow and cold of the north and east. There were still many rural areas, with small farms or ranches, and a few agribusiness incursions where huge areas were devoted to cattle, dairy, and poultry. The oversight of these developments looked, to an outsider, to be very haphazard and unplanned. Often a dairy farm was located very near a residential area, and the impact of handling waste products and manure a constant irritation. Like any area that was ripe for change, there were people with opinions and organizations that fought to maintain the old way of life. Jack had been lucky so far. His grandfather had chosen a good spot, far off the main roads even in the beginning, and close enough to the mountains to be unattractive to those wishing expansive farms or business enterprises. He was safe, if he was able to hold onto his acreage, and he felt sure that nothing would really threaten his area for some time. For one thing, some of the most vociferous and wealthy people were his close neighbors, and none of them were about to give up their way of life, even for more money. They loved their homes, the weather suited them, and the area permitted any number of variances for those who wanted to use their land as family farms or rent space to artists looking for affordable studios and facilities to paint, sculpt, or write. The area had become unofficially known as Colony Arts Spring, and one enterprising young artist had done an installation created from bed springs, garage door hinges, copper coils, old sprinkler heads — anything that could channel water and create the concept of not one, but several springs. The structure had a pump which circulated water up the center to the top where it dripped through a pipe full of holes. The sound of the water falling and pooling in various areas of the structure was a refreshing sound on hot days, and a relaxing one at night. No permit had been obtained to build it, and an obliging neighbor had taken on the job of making sure the water was replenished. It had become a community gathering place, and a few garden benches appeared along with some logs to serve as seating or tables. Several pepper trees provided shade, but not so much that you couldn't see the stars at night.

Jack had helped build a fire pit, and often supplied wood from his trips to the mountain. What more could a gathering of friends want? The sound of water, the warmth of the fire, and starlight – perfection. Maybe he would take Kitty there one night once her situation had been settled and he could feel comfortable. Not tonight, though. He still needed more information and a better plan in place. Although the community was open and receptive, he knew gossip could make lives miserable. And as in any other group, gossip always found a conduit, like the water in the carefully constructed Canyon Springs.

Chapter 17

KEVIN PACED THE FAMILY ROOM, waiting for Deena to finish her text message. Jenny was upstairs getting ready for bed, and Ben was in the shower.

"So, Dad – what's up? What's so serious that we need a private talk?"

"Where were you this afternoon, Deena... really. You weren't doing homecoming stuff, were you?"

"What do you mean? I brought Ben home, didn't I? Where do you think I was?"

"Come on, Deena! I saw you at the market. Buying beer, with some guy I don't know and who looks much too old for you! What's going on?" God, he hated this. Hated suspecting his kids of anything – usually they were pretty reliable and on track. Deena was especially trustworthy – or had been.

"Oh, so now you are spying on me? I was just picking up the pizza for the homecoming crew and Mike gave me a ride! He wanted to pick up some beer, FOR HIMSELF, Dad, FOR HIMSELF, so we went to the store! Why is that such a big deal? Don't you trust me?"

"Who is this 'Mike'? I've never seen him before and he's certainly NOT in high school!"

"No, he's not in high school! He goes to Cal Poly, and he's helping Ben with the hydraulics for the float. He is Carol's cousin, and he's staying with her folks. He's taking a semester off so he can earn money to pay his tuition. He feels topped out with student loans, and needs to start paying his own way, especially since he wants to go to grad school in a year. And no, he didn't take the beer to the float, and in fact it's probably still in his trunk because he had to get to work." Deena spit all of that out like it gave her a bad taste. "Who do you think I am, Dad? I can take care of myself!"

She picked up her phone and left the room, pounding up the stairs and slamming her bedroom door.

Kevin went up to check on Jenny, but apparently, she had heard nothing. The shower was still running. He went back to the kitchen and finished the cleanup. He loaded the coffee machine for tomorrow. *Now what? Should he apologize to Deena or just let the whole thing drop? He knew they would have another conversation. Deena never let anything drop. She was like her mom that way.*

He went into the family room and turned on the TV. Jenny wouldn't want any more interaction tonight – he could tell that for sure. She left the dinner table even before he had finished his wine, announcing she was exhausted. She had poured herself another glass and taken it upstairs. Best to let her get to sleep before he went up.

Chapter 18

THE CLINIC WAS ALMOST empty when Kitty and Jack arrived for her appointment. They only had to wait five minutes before she was called in. The examination room was cold, and she shivered.

"I know it's not a warm and cozy place – would you like a blanket? The exam rooms are always freezing." The nurse opened a cupboard but Kitty told her not to bother, she'd be okay. No need to prolong this any longer than necessary.

"Let me just get your temp and blood pressure and the doctor will be right in. Your lab results came in yesterday and she'll share those with you."

Jack couldn't settle in the waiting room. He was up, down, pacing and finally decided to walk outside for some fresh air. He could see well enough through the window so he'd know when Kitty came out. He felt nervous about this visit, but he couldn't logically explain it to himself. Her feet seemed well on the way to healing, she had finished the antibiotics, but something was making him edgy. Maybe he was just flashing back to all those doctor appointments with Lily. He never liked waiting for test results. He liked to know, but he always dreaded getting unwelcome information.

Kitty was coming out, and she had a worried look. He opened the door and she walked to the truck without saying a word.

He opened the passenger side door and she got in. "What's up, Kitty? Everything okay?"

"My feet are fine, but the test they took showed some 'slight irregularities' – the doctor said it wasn't anything to worry about at this point, but I need to take another test, this time going in without eating for eight hours. I have to admit I haven't had any kind of physical for a long time, but I've never had to retake a test. Makes me feel uneasy." She wasn't going to tell him about the other things the doctor had talked over with her. He didn't need to know anything about that. And there wasn't much she could tell him that she remembered, in any case.

"Did they tell you what the concern was?"

"Just that my kidney function seemed a bit off, and that could be because I had been somewhat dehydrated. It isn't uncommon, I guess, for people over a certain age. Have to keep my fluid intake up!"

"Well that shouldn't be a problem. When will they retest you?"

"I've got an appointment for the day after tomorrow, at 8 a.m."

"Well let's make sure you are good and hydrated by then! For now, let's celebrate that your feet are better. You feel like some fresh fish? I know where they have wonderful seafood delivered every day from San Clemente!"

"I guess. I hate it that I need more blood work. Makes me feel so defective and kind of ---- angry."

"I had to have three separate blood tests last time. And I

know what you mean, I hated it too. I'm sure you'll come through just fine next time! Did they give you any restrictions between now and then? Anything you can't eat or drink?"

"No, although she did say if I wanted anything alcoholic to take it easy. No more than one drink today and tomorrow. So maybe we can have something tonight? I've been looking forward to that, you know!"

"Sure! I put a bottle of prosecco on ice before we left. And I can certainly pour you one glass! I think you deserve that much."

"Where is this seafood place?"

"It's about 45 minutes away – in Riverside. The Market Grill – have you been there?"

"Never. People I used to know weren't big fish eaters. Do they make a good clam chowder? Or shrimp cocktail?"

"Yes, but the best thing to try is the catch of the day. Sometimes they have halibut and they do a wonderful sherry sauce. Hmm. You look doubtful."

She smiled. This man was not like any she had known before. His willingness to trust her, to take care of her, was something altogether new. And she was confused about what she was feeling for him. A bit out of control? Why was she so willing – even hopeful – that he could continue his kindness even after she told him about her long and complicated relationship with Gray? She didn't even like to admit to herself what had gone on between them personally and financially. Owning up to her part of that sordid relationship was hard admit to herself, let alone reveal to someone else. But she knew she couldn't keep that part of her past secret for long, or Jack would lose the trust he had that she would, at the very least, tell him the truth about herself. She closed her eyes and allowed herself to drift. Maybe drifting was what she needed to do for a while. Just drift on this good man's kindness and care. She could think about next steps when she regained more balance. But for now, she did feel safe. And safe felt very good.

Chapter 19

Jenny was up before Kevin. The coffee pot was half empty by the time he came down for breakfast. She was not in the kitchen, so he poured himself a cup and went out to the backyard. She wasn't on the patio, either. He went through the house to the garage to see if her car was still there. It wasn't. She must have gone to work early. Probably lots to catch up on after a week off.

"Where's mom?" Ben was dressed for school, but his hair hadn't been combed and his feet were bare. "I can't find any clean socks."

"There's a basket of underwear and socks in the laundry room. I'm sure you'll find something in there. Wear mine if you can't find some of your own. We need to catch up on the laundry. Your mother has gone to work, I suppose. She was already gone when I got up."

"Really? That's not like her!"

"Is your sister up?"

"Yes, she's been in the shower forever – I came down here to use the guest bathroom. We should get going."

Kevin made two omelets and folded them in tortillas. He

poured two glasses of orange juice. Deena came downstairs as Ben was pulling on his socks.

"Hurry up Ben! We're going to be late again."

"I'm ready – drink your orange juice. Dad made us egg burritos to take. You got lunch money? I'm out."

Kevin pulled out two tens and handed one to each kid. "Tomorrow you pack your own lunches, okay?"

"Yeah sure...thanks Dad...." And Ben was already out the door.

"Where's mom this morning? She wasn't in the bedroom."

"She left for work early, I guess. She wasn't here when I got up."

"Huh. Well I guess I'll see her later tonight. By the way, Dad, I'm sorry for yelling at you last night. I know you just want to keep me safe. But you have to trust me to make some decisions for myself. I'm not a child anymore."

She gave him a quick peck on the cheek and grabbed her breakfast. She was out the door before he could think of a good response.

His relief was so great he almost wept. He was dreading a long, painful silence from Deena after their confrontation, and apparently he had dodged that one. He fixed himself an omelet and took it out on the patio with his coffee. Peace. For now.

JENNY DROVE CAREFULLY – her head was pounding. Too much wine last night, and not enough sleep. The pain killer she took hadn't started to work, and she was queasy from taking it on an empty stomach with nothing but coffee to wash it down. *Maybe I should stop and get some breakfast before I get to work. Might calm me down and help me focus. Should have let Kevin fix me breakfast but I couldn't face him this morning. His sweet cheerful face was the last thing I wanted to see.*

She had a favorite café not too far from work, so she stopped there. Her usual waitress came over to take her order and said "Whoa, Jen – you okay? You don't look too good!"

"I've got a killer headache and the medication I took upset my stomach. Thought I'd try to eat something. Oddly enough I'm kind of feeling like Huevos Rancheros with some extra hot sauce. Am I crazy to think that would help?"

"Crazy – or pregnant!? Hah!"

"Well pregnant isn't even possible, so I must be crazy. Make those eggs poached."

"You got it."

"And bring me some coffee."

"Drink that water I brought you. It can work on a headache quicker than coffee."

Jen made a face at her but picked up the water and sipped at it. Why did other people sound so confident about what to do? Water did seem to help. Maybe she was dehydrated. Kevin and Deena had a fight last night. I heard Deena come pounding up the stairs like she does when she's mad at me. One more family dynamic I don't know how to deal with, and don't want to deal with, and don't want to think about. I've got enough dealing with my mom's death and my dad's health – why can't I catch a break from more drama in my own home?

"Here's your eggs and coffee. And hot sauce. Eat up!"

"Yes ma'am," Jenny smiled. Her headache was dissipating, and the food tasted good.

Chapter 20

AFTER THE CALM of Jack's place and the quiet of the community, Riverside was overwhelming to Kitty. She had forgotten how much pressure could come just from being in a place with so many people and so much going on. There was a time when she loved all of that, feeling at the center of it, being almost frantically busy. But not now. Jack had a hard time remembering where the Market Grill was until he recognized a familiar bank building. He circled the block and pulled into a parking space.

The bank reminded Kitty that they were close enough to where she had her own account. Maybe she could see what funds were left. Maybe close that account. Seemed prudent, and she needed to feel she had some money of her own to live on and to reimburse Jack.

Lunch was fine, although Kitty was not as fond of the halibut as Jack. She did like the shrimp cocktail. They spent some time deciding on whether to have dessert and settled on two cappuccinos instead.

"Jack, could we drive over to the Chase Bank near the University before we go back to your house? That's where I have my accounts. I need to make sure I've still got some funds there, and maybe close out. Would you mind?"

"No, I wouldn't mind! I think it's a good idea. I need to go to my Credit Union over that way. I could drop you off and be back to pick you up in twenty minutes or so?"

"That would be great."

Kitty found that she had only $4500 left in her savings account, and that her checking account was down to $12.73. She asked for a printout of the account activity for the last three months, and then took a cashier's check and $200 in cash to close both accounts out. It took longer than she thought, and Jack was sitting in the lobby when she turned to leave the teller's window.

"Sorry if I kept you waiting!"

"I've only been here a few minutes. You have any luck?"

"Some. I closed my accounts and I have a cashier's check so I can open another account."

"You should put it in my credit union. Anyone can open an account there – and the rates are good. Would you like to do that?"

"But I have no permanent address or phone – won't I need that?"

"I have no problem with you using my address and phone for now. Do you?"

"It seems like another imposition. Are you sure?"

"Yes. I'm sure. Come on, let's go do it. You can stay at my place, Kitty, just as long as you need to. No strings. Really. Unless you don't pull your weight with the housekeeping!" He winked at her and opened the car door.

She was flooded with relief. She had some funds, although nothing like she should have, and a place to stay with this gentle, kind man. Could she manage to keep it all together? Would she?

Chapter 21

JENNY LOVED HER WORK. She was an administrator for a senior services non-profit organization, and managed three facilities. It was exciting to see communities embrace the programs that gave older adults an opportunity to receive supplemental services that not only enhanced their lives but also gave them ways to give something to others. The crafts program was one of the most popular, and she often dropped by the studio to see what was happening. Many of the participants already had skills they were eager to put to use, and some offered training classes at local elementary schools. Jenny longed to take one of the watercolor classes or learn how to crochet, but so far, she had been too busy (or too intimidated). *Maybe one day...*

Her week away did mean she had a lot of desk work, and lots of e-mail and phone calls to return. Thank god the headache left – now maybe she could focus on the tasks at hand rather than obsessing about her dad or what was going on between Kevin and Deena.

IT WAS two o'clock before she realized she hadn't stopped for lunch. She buzzed her assistant and asked if he could bring her a sandwich and an iced tea.

The window in her office overlooked Ocean Park Boulevard and the wide strip of green space that ran down the center of the street. Recent rain made for lots of new growth, and she could see the wet melaleuca and ficus leaves reflecting the afternoon sun. The melaleuca were messy trees, but she loved them. Their papery bark peeled and revealed inner layers in shades of gray that fascinated her. She stretched, and turned back to her desk. *Aren't melaleucas a kind of eucalyptus? They have to be, they look so similar. Transplants, then. Not a species that belonged. Something foreign and often invasive, pushing out native plants. Still, they are beautiful and they had been part of the California landscape for so long, most accepted them as classic scenery. Like palm trees. Who could say what belonged where anymore? Everything changes. Landscapes, families... nothing living stays the same for very long. Why couldn't she accept that?*

Peter knocked quietly and opened her door a crack. "Lunch Jen?"

"Yes – thanks, Peter. I think I'll take it to the break room. Want to join me for a bit and fill me in on anything special I might have missed while I was gone?"

Chapter 22

JACK DROVE BACK to the house after their stop at the credit union, and Kitty was clearly not interested in talking. She fell asleep with her head resting on the side window. He hoped she wouldn't wake up with a painful neck.

I supposed she's had enough of the pragmatics of her life for one day. Lots of intrusive questions here and there, from all and sundry, as she tried to make a new start. No wonder she's tired. I won't be pressing her for any more information just now. She may have questions for me too, questions that I may not want to answer directly, or even truthfully. It would take some time. But a big step had been taken today towards getting her on a new path. That was enough, for now. Maybe I'll set up that TV after all, in the room we cleared out. There's a cable connection in there, and I've still got all the hardware and the box to reconnect it. God knows I'm paying enough for the service every month. Maybe we could watch something that would make Kitty laugh – I love to hear her laugh.

She woke up with a start when he pulled into the driveway. "I didn't mean to sleep all the way home!" she rubbed her neck and stretched.

"No worries. Traffic was busy enough to keep me occupied! You want to finish that nap or shall we maybe see if we can figure out how to connect the TV in the room we just cleared out? Might be fun to watch a movie or something tonight."

"If I sleep any more today, I won't sleep tonight, that's for sure. Yes, let's see if we can figure out how we can get some entertainment in here tonight. That would be fun. And I'm pretty good at sorting out cables and connections – used to have to do that at work!" she laughed.

He was right. This was a good choice. "I think there are some DVDs in a box in the closet of your room. You might want to look through them and see if there is something you like while I get the equipment out of the shed."

She found the box and brought it into the living room. She also dragged a small mission-style bookcase from the guest room and placed it on the wall opposite the couch near the cable connection. The shelves were probably wide enough to hold a TV and any box or players that needed connecting. It looked good in this room – it wasn't a genuine craftsman, but close enough that it would do. She was looking through the DVDs when Jack came in with the TV.

"Hey! You should have let me help you with that, it's pretty heavy!"

"I'm stronger than I look – and I didn't lift it, I dragged it on a throw rug from the bathroom. Have you watched any of these? Some of them still have their original wrappers!"

"Lily ordered them, or Jenny brought them, somehow Lily never wanted to watch what I liked, so I just let her have at it. She was happy enough with her popcorn and movies and I was happy enough out in the garage with my trains. So no, I haven't watched many! Choose whatever you'd like!"

Jack went to the kitchen and put together a salad. Even

though they'd had a big lunch, he felt they should have something for dinner.

"So Jack, you going to watch too? I thought you had gone out to the garage, but I see you are planning to eat again. Are you really that hungry?" Kitty asked from the kitchen door, a DVD in her hand.

"Yes, I'll stay in here with you. Of course I will. I thought we should have a little something – lunch was some time ago! I'll bring some crackers and cheese." He went whistling off to the pantry for some crackers.

THE MOVIE they settled on was on old one, "Double Indemnity," and it didn't make either one of them laugh. Death and duplicity might not have been the best choice since Jack was still recovering from Lily's death, and duplicity made Kitty nervous since she obviously had not been entirely honest with Jack.

"Let's watch another one – something a little lighter, maybe? And hey, how about that glass of prosecco you promised me?"

"Sure. I'll get it – want some popcorn too? Might as well make it a real movie night."

"I love popcorn! With butter?"

"Of course! Is there any other way?!"

Kitty decided to put the DVDs in alphabetical order while Jack was busy in the kitchen. When she got to the Ms she found an unopened "Midnight in Paris." She hadn't seen it, but it was a Woody Allen and she always enjoyed those. She queued it up and waited for Jack.

He returned with a big bowl of popcorn, the bottle of prosecco and two champagne glasses. "All set. What have we got on the screen?"

"It's a Woody Allen – "Midnight in Paris" – fresh out of the box!"

"Lily ordered that one. When Jenny saw it she had a fit. She hates anything Woody Allen does – she's got a problem with his personal life. She was mad her mother even considered watching it. But I'd actually like to see it."

Prosecco was poured, and Kitty savored every sip. When Jack refilled her glass she didn't object. It's such a low alcohol wine – how could it matter, really? And I'll stick to one tomorrow, for sure. Amazing how quickly she felt the effect. She used to be able to drink a whole bottle of champagne and not feel a thing.

She started to take a sip when Jack remembered she was only supposed to have one glass. "Whoops! Sorry I poured you a second – let me take that and get you some sparkling water or a soda."

"It's okay, Jack. These are small glasses and it's only prosecco. I think I'll be okay with this much. Really."

"OK. Your call. You're the one with the blood test coming up. I'll finish the rest," and he filled his glass to the rim, emptying the bottle.

The movie suited them both, and Jack was delighted with Kitty's response, her laugh ringing out loud and clear. They each thought they'd choose different eras and places if they were able to suddenly time travel. Jack said he would pick the 1800's in America, Kitty would travel to the same time zone, but Italy would be the place, for sure.

"We would never meet in that case! And I would consider that to be very unfortunate."

"I'm so grateful for all you've done. And now I want to start pulling my own weight and making some plans for getting on with my life. I would like to stay here for a while – you're good for me. And I think I can help you with your sorting and reorganizing at least. But I want to pay room and board, no arguments about that."

"I would welcome the company and the help! But I really don't need you to pay room and board!"

"I insist. We can work that out tomorrow. But now I'm going to bed. It's late, and the wine did go to my head! It was a fun evening. Better than I've had in a long, long time. Thanks."

"It was fun. Sleep well."

"You too." Kitty patted his hand.

Jack took the dishes out to the kitchen and stood looking out the window at the back patio. He did have a good time tonight – and the touch of her hand was sweetly electrifying, energizing. Was he moving ahead too fast? *I don't care. It's the first time I've felt anything for so long. She's like a breath of fresh air; she brings new energy and purpose to my life. I know I can't push her, though. I've got to measure out my questions and my eagerness to know everything about her. She will learn to trust me...I hope.*

He took the trash out and stopped in the shed for the bottle of scotch. One drink wouldn't hurt, and he wanted to sit outside and look at the stars until his heart stopped pounding.

Chapter 23

IT HAD BEEN A LONG DAY. Jenny didn't have a long drive home, but she left right at rush hour, so it was a slow drive. Remembering all the laundry and the unpacking she still had to do made it seem even slower. She called Kevin on her cell, but he didn't pick up. Maybe he had thought to go to the store. Odd that one of the kids didn't answer, though. They should be home by now. She tried Deena's phone next, but it went straight to voicemail. Maybe she was driving. She had strict instructions not to talk on the phone when she was driving. She tried Ben. "Hi Mom. What's up?"

Leave it to Ben to get right to the point.

"Just trying to see where everybody is. Your dad didn't answer the house phone, and Deena must be driving, right?" she hoped they were on their way home.

"Ummmm I thought dad would have called you. He had to go pick Deena up at a friend's house, she, ummm, couldn't get the car to start. I went home with Lenny. Dad's supposed to pick me up here any minute. Actually I think I hear him in the driveway now. We'll be home soon."

"OK......see you there."

Jenny pulled into the garage. Kevin had obviously left in a hurry – there was something in the oven that was definitely on the burned side. She turned the oven off and opened the door. Smoke billowed out and the alarm went off. The refrigerator door stood open. She opened the back door and the kitchen window and turned on the fan. She got the kitchen stool and managed to reach the smoke alarm and hit the reset button. Thank god that worked.

She slammed the refrigerator door and took the blackened chicken out to the trash.

"Jenny, honey, what's going on? What burned? Are you okay?" Kevin shouted from the living room. She heard Deena and Ben go upstairs.

"No, Kevin, no I am NOT all right. I came home to chicken burning in the oven, the smoke alarm went off, and the refrigerator door was standing open! Are YOU all right? Why couldn't Deena call the Auto Club for a car problem – why do we even have that service if she doesn't use it!!!"

Kevin sat down at the kitchen table. "Sit down, Jen, and I'll tell you what happened. Deena is okay, but she couldn't drive. It wasn't that the car wouldn't start. Thank god I got the phone call, and she didn't try to drive home."

"Why couldn't she drive? Is she sick?" Jenny got up from her chair and started towards the stairs.

"No, don't go check on her now, Jen. Let her get cleaned up. She's really ok, she ... she just .... she's sick to her stomach. She's been drinking, Jen."

"KEVIN, no. Deena? I don't believe it! Where? When? Wasn't she doing the homecoming thing?"

"Part of the afternoon, yes. Then she decided to go over to

Carol's to do some homework. Apparently Carol's parents were not home, and the two of them decided to take that opportunity to have a few drinks. Trouble is, they were putting vodka into lemonade and couldn't tell when to stop. They both are miserable. And very, very sorry. For themselves, mostly...."

"Is she really all right? Should we take her to the doctor?"

"She's okay. Carol's cousin came home and saw the state they were in and started giving them watered down lemonade. They didn't know the difference. He hid the vodka bottle. Why they don't keep their liquor under lock and key I do not know. Doesn't Carol have a younger brother too?"

"Yes. I think he's Ben's age. Who is this cousin? I've never met him."

"He's staying with them while he earns some money. He goes to Cal Poly and they agreed to give him a room. He seems like a responsible kid. I'm glad he showed up when he did or they might have been in much worse shape. Anyway, he called me and that's why I left in such a hurry. Like you, I was worried she might need to go to ER or something."

"Mom? Are you home? I need you...." Deena sounded like a little, scared kid.

"Yes. I'm here Dee. I'll be right up."

Jenny grabbed a ginger ale and a glass of ice and went upstairs.

Should I be outraged or sympathetic? God knows my mom was BEYOND outraged when this happened to me. I don't think our relationship ever recovered. So clearly that's not the best response. But holy hell, why NOW, why TODAY??

Am I going to die?" Deena was wrapped in her bathrobe and curled up on her bed.

"No, Deena, but you'll probably feel like it for a while. It will take some time for your body to recover. And you may have a headache tomorrow. What happened? This isn't like you." *She really does look scared, poor kid.*

"I don't know. Carol just thought it would be fun. I guess she's done it before. The first drink didn't seem to do much, so we just kept going. It's a good thing Mike came home when he did. He got me into the bathroom before I threw up all over the living room. I think I passed out, mom. I don't know, I can't remember." Deena was crying. Jenny hadn't seen her do that since she was twelve.

"Hey, kiddo, you made a mistake. It was a big one, that's for sure, but I have a feeling you won't make it again any time soon. I am so glad Mike, whoever he is, came in and knew what to do for you."

"Oh, mom, I'm so so sorry. I'll never take another drink in my life. EVER!"

"That's how you feel now. And I'm glad. Remember that. The older you get, the more opportunities you'll have to test that resolution."

"I'm so thirsty but I'm afraid if I drink anything I'll throw up again."

"You're dehydrated, which is one reason why you feel so terrible. Can you sip a little ginger ale? Just a sip."

Jenny sat with Deena for an hour while she alternated giving her sips of ginger ale and water. She knew if she drank anything too fast it would all just come up again. It was the first time the two of them had spent time together for months. When Deena was younger they were together all the time, Deena like Jenny's shadow. Then Jenny had gone to work full time when Deena started high school.

I've missed so much, something I determined I would NOT do. My mother disappeared from my life when I was fourteen and I never got her back. But she was ill – I'm not ill. Deena is a good kid – but she still needs me. She won't for much longer, not in this way. And I need her.

Deena finally fell asleep. Jenny kissed her and went to find Kevin. They needed to talk. And they also needed to talk to Ben and see how this episode affected him. He was very protective of his sister, even though he was younger, and he must have been shaken. Deena was always the responsible one, almost like another parent.

Chapter 24

Kitty was up with the sun after their movie night, and restless. She turned on the coffee pot and while she waited for it to brew, she wandered out into the backyard still dressed in pajamas and flip-flops. The big pepper tree behind the storage shed caught the morning light and she could see the tiny red berries in clusters hanging from the branches. Then she noticed that behind the tree there was another building. It wasn't a shed or a garage – it looked more like a small house, with a screened porch in the front. She walked carefully over the carpet of leaves and berries to have a better look, her feet feeling every slippery berry and tiniest pebble through the thin slippers. The porch door was partially open, so she pushed it a little wider and looked inside. The screens had been disintegrating for years, and the place was full of cobwebs and dead bugs. She made her way through the mess to the front door. It stuck, but with a little push it gave way. There was a center room with a fireplace, and small rooms at the four corners. One had an old clawfoot tub in it, with a toilet and free-standing wash basin. The floor was covered with faded and cracked linoleum. But the structure itself seemed sound. No water stains anywhere, except around the plumbing fixtures, so maybe the roof was in good shape. Each room had a light fixture in the center of the ceiling, but either the bulbs were burned out or the electricity had been turned off.

———

THE CABINETS that surrounded the fireplace had been built with care, and all the drawers and doors closed perfectly. The finish had faded and there were bumps and nicks, but nothing that a nice coat of paint or perhaps sanding and staining couldn't fix.

What am I thinking! This isn't mine to fix up! It would be a great place to store what little furniture I do have, though...and maybe even a good place to live in? Temporarily. But it would take quite a bit of refurbishing, that's clear, and an investment of money, too.

The morning light streamed in on the east side, and obviously would do so again from the west when the sun moved to the other side of the building. The wide front porch would keep the central room cool, though, even when the sun was hot.

Kitty sighed deeply, realizing that for the first time in a long time, here was a project she would love to undertake. *This place has such potential. And it feels like a home place. More of a home than any other place I've known.*

She heard someone coming and moved quickly to the door, thinking if Jack found her he'd know what a snoop she could be.

"I thought I heard somebody moving around out here! What are you up to, Kitty?"

Jack handed her a cup of coffee and smiled. Kitty took the cup and tried to smile.

"Oh Jack. I'm, I'm so – sorry! I hope you don't mind. I

found this little bungalow and I got curious." She looked up at him.

"Of course I don't mind! I have nothing to hide here!" He put his hand on her shoulder. "My grandfather lived out here when he was building the house. He always called it "The Farmhouse." Couldn't figure out why, since he never actually had a farm, but that's the name he gave it. Then my dad used it when he was a teenager. I often wonder just what he got up to out here – so far from the house – but times were different then. Jenny used to play in it when she was little. But by the time her kids came along it was so dilapidated Lily didn't think it was safe for them. I personally think they would have loved it!"

"They absolutely would have! It could be a cabin in the woods or a ship on the high seas – or any number of things! I love the cabinets. Your grandfather was quite the craftsman."

"When he wanted to be, yes. Don't see a lot of that in the main house, though. I think he saved most of his talent for his clients. He was, as you say, a fine craftsman.," he sipped his coffee thoughtfully.

"Aren't you a little chilly out here? I'm about to fix some breakfast – you ready?"

"I am cold come to think of it." Kitty was grinning. *He doesn't mind! He doesn't care that I was snooping around!* "What's on the menu this morning?"

"My grandmother's coffee cake with some berries and Canadian bacon. Sound good?"

"Couldn't be better!"

They walked back to the house, and Kitty went to get dressed and put on some lotion and socks to soothe her tortured feet.

Chapter 25

Jack was anxious to settle into a routine. He did have some commitments, and for the last ten days he had let things slide. He wanted to see Kitty have a bit more independence, not only for her sake, but for his. And he needed to let people know he would have a boarder. Especially Jenny. No need upsetting her any longer than he had already.

"Looking around the old farmhouse this morning gave me an idea. What would you think about getting your things from storage and putting them in there? I could have my handyman Carlin come and fix the screens and locks on the windows and doors and make sure the plumbing and electricity work so you can use the place. It's not much, but you could call it your own little hideaway, if you liked. You probably wouldn't want to sleep out there – it's going to get pretty cold at night and there isn't any heat except what the fireplace can give. But I have a sense you would like a little more privacy than you have here, especially during the day."

"Seriously Jack? Are you sure? That's a pretty big investment for a temporary solution – who knows how long I'll be here?"

"I would consider it an investment in the property. When you decide to move on, I could probably rent it out to one of the artists from the colony. They're always looking for guest houses. So that's not an issue. Jenny keeps telling me she doesn't want me to be all alone out here, and that would give her some peace of mind too. I think it makes good sense. In the meantime, you could be my first tenant! You'd have to do the cleanup and Carlin can help with painting."

"I'm kind of speechless. Seems like a dream come true. I love the place – and the possibilities to make a great living space are amazing! But you must let me pay for any materials and share the labor cost. I insist. I've got some money, and I don't think it will take much if you have someone who actually is fast and competent!" Kitty's eyes lit up. She grabbed Jack and gave him a hug, which startled both of them. He stepped back, grinning, and turned around so she wouldn't see his red face.

"I'll just go look up Carlin's number. The sooner he can start, the better. You can leave your things in storage until we have a clean, secure place to put them."

Kitty knew there were many bungalows built in Southern California in the early part of the 20th century. She had explored the possibility of a real estate license at one point in her life and had started doing a little research about the history of the old homes in Riverside. She knew that some of them came as kits from Sears Catalog and were put together in a kind of "barn-raising" by local neighbors.

Jack remembered his dad telling him how the little farmhouse was much smaller than the ones designed for family use. His was strictly a utilitarian project, although it had elements of comfort that he borrowed from more elaborate designs. The peaked roof helped keep the rooms temperate, and the California coolers he had installed in the cabinets in one of the side rooms served as good storage for perishables. He had positioned the building favorably, too, taking into account the breezes that generally came up in the afternoon as another way to keep hot air out and cooler air moving through. The footprint for the entire building was probably less than 900 square feet. But it was clearly never intended as anything except a temporary living space until the larger building was completed. Even though he compromised on space, he had taken care to build a solid structure, and it had withstood years of neglect. Jack had made sure the roof was solid, just to protect something his dad had used and loved. But otherwise, the property had been left to itself. What he hadn't told Kitty was that his dad had, in his later years, taken to wandering out to the bungalow at night and sitting on the porch. He never talked about any particular memories, but he seemed drawn to the place, and had a cushioned rocker placed so he could look out at the pepper tree. If Jack's mother couldn't find him in the main house, she knew exactly where he would be. Some nights he sat out there until well past midnight, only coming in when Jack's mom insisted.

After breakfast, Kitty went back outside to look at the place again. She leaned against the rough bark of the huge pepper tree and tried to imagine living in a space that she could shape. She had never had that opportunity before. And even though this little place wouldn't technically belong to her, she thought that Jack would probably give her a free hand to pull it together any way she wanted. *Maybe the bathtub will be usable! Imagine a nice long bath in that deep tub. Better than a jacuzzi!*

She went to inspect the condition of the bathroom. Rust stains – but maybe if they figured out how to refinish the tub and washstand? She wished she had her computer so she could start doing some internet searching – but that was either in storage or gone. There was information on it that Gray would want to erase, she was pretty sure of that. Damn. She had bought that computer with her own money. Unless maybe he hadn't thought of that? Time would tell. He probably had not been the one to clean out the apartment, he would have hired that out. Maybe, just maybe, it would be in the storage locker.

Kitty went back to the house, hoping that Jack would let her at least begin to clear out the cobwebs and sweep the floors. It wouldn't be much, but it would be so good to see the place get some loving attention.

Jack hadn't been able to reach the handyman, so they continued working on clearing out the big house. There was still a large family room and two bedrooms that hadn't been touched. There was much to be done. Kitty decided to hold off on asking about sweeping out the cottage and sent Jack for boxes. Then she started to pick through cupboards and closets to see what could be useful and what needed to go. Now that she might have another space for herself, she kept that in her mind too. She had already decided that much of what she would find in her own storage should probably go. There was nothing there, really, that she valued – and too much of it would just remind her of her much-regretted history with Gray. Time to make a new start. On so many levels.

Chapter 26

JACK COULD SEE a few remaining summer wildflower blooms along the roadside. Wild radish and mustard flourish in Southern California. He knew that both were considered invasive plants, killing off the native species. They were beautiful, though, when in full flower. Sometimes wildflowers covered the San Jacinto hills, if the rains had been plentiful. Native poppy, lupine and California Lilac had not, so far, been pushed out. Maybe the vintners moving into the Temecula area would do as their Northern California counterparts and realize that mustard could be a very beneficial part of the feeding of the soil and the vines. He and Lily had made a trip to Sonoma a few years before her death, and they were there just when the mustard was literally carpeting the vineyards with bright yellow flowers. He had pictures somewhere – he'd have to show Kitty.

There was so much he wanted to share with her, and he could sense she was feeling more comfortable with him – but she also had a wariness that made him cautious. He didn't want her running off, as she could do so easily. Especially now that she had access to some money.

Life changes are not to be taken lightly. He wanted to start this new adventure, but he realized that at his age it could be a challenge beyond his time and energy. So far, he had felt nothing but energized, but he also knew he had to go cautiously and not get too ambitious with his planning. The refurbishing of the old farmhouse was one thing, and the weeding out of Lily's collections another. Those two were enough for the coming weeks. Then maybe, if things worked out, they could take a break and get away for a bit. Go on a road trip, or maybe take a little cruise? *Nothing like anticipation to give an old man a boost! And I'm anticipating just getting back to the house and packing boxes. Happy. I'm happy.*

THE FAMILY ROOM proved to be a bigger challenge than Kitty thought. There was a door that opened onto a covered porch, so she started by moving some of the boxes and smaller pieces of furniture out there. It was hot, heavy work. And dusty. She wasn't even going to start opening boxes until she made some space and order out of the room. And she couldn't move the big pieces on her own, she'd have to wait for Jack. After an hour of pushing, lifting, and shifting things around, she needed a break. Where was Jack, anyway? How far did he have to go for those boxes?

She went to the kitchen and poured herself some water. The kitchen clock said 11:12 and she was already hungry for lunch. She cut herself a piece of the coffee cake they'd had for breakfast and carried it out to the backyard. If this were her home, she could make some lunch, put on some music, and work to her own pace. But this was not her home. She needed to earn her keep and pay her own way as much as possible.

She decided to take another look at the farmhouse. If she

really could rent it, then she might consider it hers, at least for a time. It felt like it was meant to be hers. Something about the way it smelled – old and musty – reminded her of her grandmother's house. Everything in that house had been in the same place for years. And much of it had been undisturbed for years, too. She could remember looking for something in the linen closet and discovering tablecloths wrapped in tissue paper that had turned brown and crisp. Even the silverware in the drawers in the kitchen seemed to be annoyed if you disturbed it. Everything was settled in, solidly. Rooted, almost. At least that's how she had felt as a kid. Nothing changed at grandma's. Frozen in time. The china dog and cat on the mantel always in the same place, the bowl of lemon drops on the coffee table melted together with a fine layer of dust. Grandma's house. Familiar, constant, but still, it wasn't hers.

She heard the truck pull into the driveway and went to help Jack unload boxes.

Chapter 27

CARLIN FINALLY RETURNED Jack's call. He would have to start work soon, and finish soon, because he had a big job in Riverside beginning in two weeks. That suited Jack and Kitty perfectly. He agreed to come and do some assessment that afternoon. He liked to have all the materials needed for the whole job on hand before he started. He hated interrupting his day to go out just to get another can of paint.

"Carlin sounds a lot like you, Jack! Everything in order, everything available as you need it," she smiled.

"That's probably why I like his work. He's fast, and his work is solid. I like that he plans ahead."

Jack and Kitty worked in the family room for another hour, and then Jack decided it was time for lunch. They made some burritos out of the left-over chicken, beans and rice, and took some iced tea out to the table on the back patio.

"I haven't made any dinner plans. Would you like to go out tonight? Or shall we defrost something? We still have salad makings."

"Why don't you let me cook something tonight. Just to prove I can! Do you like baked potatoes? I know you bought some Russets when we went shopping. There's cheese and some ham in the refrigerator – I could do twice-baked – if you like. That and a salad would do me fine. Then let's watch another movie. I'd like that."

"Sounds great."

Carlin spent over an hour walking through the old farmhouse, measuring and evaluating. "You want to keep this old linoleum in the bathroom and kitchen?"

"What kitchen?" Kitty hadn't seen any kitchen. Just four tiny rooms off the one large living space.

"That back room was used as a kitchen. There's a sink and a drainboard that's underneath those planks, and although the plumbing is gone, there's a hole in the floor where the drainpipe went. I'll need to go underneath the house to see what's going on with the pipes. I think they will all have to be replaced – too old to stand any water pressure, really, and you'll want copper in there now anyway."

"Maybe we should forget about restoring any kind of kitchen. If there is a bathroom out here, wouldn't that be enough?" Kitty looked at Jack. That sounded like a much bigger job than they had anticipated. New wiring would be needed too. That wasn't going to be cheap.

"I think if we're going to do it with a view towards eventually renting it out, it's going to need a kitchen. Since you will be replacing the bathroom plumbing, will doing what's needed for the kitchen add much more cost?" Jack looked at Carlin.

"No – the rooms are so close together it really won't cost much to hook up water and a drain. In fact, the water pipes are all in that wall between them. If we replace the wiring, we can put in a tank-less water heater on that outside wall for your hot water, too. Don't know what your grandpa did for hot water – he must have heated it over the fire!"

"What's under the linoleum flooring in those rooms?"

"Well that's the funny thing. You'd think it would just be some kind of sub-flooring, but it looks like he laid the same wood floor that he had in the living area. So we could lift that linoleum, sand and refinish all the floors and maybe put some tile in front of the kitchen sink and around the toilet and tub in the bathroom. I've got some nice ceramic Spanish tile left over from another job that I think would look great. I can give you a great price on that!"

Kitty excused herself and went back into the house. This was a conversation that Jack and Carlin should have. The project really needed to be something Jack could afford, and her opinions about any of it should be kept to herself. If it was his decision to make, not hers.

THEY HAD MADE enough progress in the family room that she could start organizing the boxes by contents. What she had moved out to the patio was a muddle of clothing, some of it never worn and still with price tags, as well as knick-knacks, dishes, games, puzzles, toys, books. Much of it was vintage. She knew, if it were marketed properly, it would sell. Maybe that would help pay for the repairs on the little home place. She liked calling it that, even if it was just in her own head.

She decided to do a rough inventory as she repacked the boxes, so that if Jack or his daughter needed to find something at least they would know where to start looking. She was pretty sure none of this could be sold or given away without a review by one or the other.

Jack had been talking with Carlin for some time. When he came back to find Kitty, he was amazed at what she had accomplished. Most of the boxes he bought had been assembled and filled and labeled. She had stacked them against one wall and was sorting what was left in the boxes on the patio.

"Hey! You hire some extra help in here I don't know about?!"

"No! It's not as good as it looks. I've just done a rough sort. I thought you and your daughter would want to look through all of this and see if there is anything you want to keep. And I thought if books were in one box and knick-knacks in another, it might be easier. There's so much clothing, Jack! And much of it is new!"

"I know. My wife had these episodes where she would buy everything under the sun. God knows what she planned to do with it all. I couldn't keep up with it, as you can see. When she was like that, getting through the day was all I could manage. She'd go days without sleep and I'd hear her rummaging around in here with all this stuff."

Remembering the kind of chaos his wife had created – had needed – took the wind out of him. He sat down heavily on one of the couches.

"You okay Jack?"

"I'm all right. Just realizing how I have lived for a long, long time. And how different my life could have been. It's just stunned me. I probably would never would have gotten through all this without you, Kitty."

"You were already making a start when I got here! Your office, your room, the kitchen...?"

"True – but you have no idea how much energy that took, and how I had to push myself. With you here to help it seems like a different task, easier, one I'm eager to do. I want my life back." He took a deep breath, and she could see he was fighting back tears.

Kitty could see it was time to change the subject, get him thinking about the future, not the past.

"Let's not eat here tonight, Jack. Let's get cleaned up and go out for dinner. My treat. Can we leave those boxes out on the patio?"

"If somebody takes them, that's just less we have to sort! Yes. Leave them. Let's do it. Let's go out!"

Chapter 28

Kitty took a quick shower and ran a brush through her hair. It was still warm, so her skirt and gauzy blouse would be fine. Not much to choose from, in any case.

Jack hadn't appeared yet. She turned on the TV and flipped through the cable options. There was a music station, and she selected "Swing with Big Bands." There was a time she loved to dance. Did Jack?

"Hey – that's West Coast Swing! You know how to do that?"

"Of course I do! I used to dance all the time when I was younger. I love swing."

He grabbed her hand, and they did a few steps and a tuck and turn. Kitty laughed and dropped onto the couch. "I'm a little out of practice though! You're good, Jack!"

"I loved dancing when I was younger. Lily didn't like it much, so it was something I had to leave behind. We should do a little practice and then I'll take you to one of the swing events here. There's a group that moves from venue to venue – wherever they can get cheap drinks and music! Would you like that?"

"Yes! But I think I'll have to get some better shoes or I'll be falling all over the place. These aren't really made for dancing!" and she stuck out her sandaled foot.

"Bring your shawl, Kitty. It can be chilly inside the place I have in mind."

THEY WENT to a quiet little Italian restaurant. Kitty told him about some of the circumstances that brought her to the shelter. She knew she'd have to be honest; if he ever found a piece of her story didn't ring true, that could be the end. She chose her words carefully.

Jack was a sympathetic listener. He could see she wasn't telling him the whole story, but she also was trying hard to tell him the real one. Someday she would trust him enough to tell him everything. He could wait. This was enough for now. Could it be more than just ghosts chasing her?

"Are you feeling like some dessert, Kitty?"

"You haven't said anything about what I've told you. Are you shocked? Do you want me to leave?"

"I'm not shocked – I'm too old to be shocked! And no, I do not want you to leave. I want you to stay for as long as you are comfortable here. Really. I do. Besides, now that you've got me thinking about fixing up the Farmhouse, you are committed! Can't do it without you."

She smiled. "In that case, I'd like some dessert. You choose."

They made it an early night, remembering that Kitty had to do another blood test in the morning.

Chapter 29

Jenny and Kevin took their coffee cups out to the patio. Neither one wanted any wine tonight, not after today's experience with Deena. Ben came out after he finished stacking the dinner dishes.

"No video games tonight, Ben?" asked Kevin.

"Naw – I think I'll sit here with you guys for a while. Is Deena okay? Lots of noise on twitter about what happened this afternoon at Carol's."

"What are they saying?" Jenny put her cup down and looked at Ben.

"That Deena was really drunk, and that Carol thought it was funny."

"What do you think?"

"I think it was stupid to go over there in the first place. Carol isn't really a good friend, and if you want to know what I think, I think the only reason Deena went was because she thought she might see Mike. I think she really likes him."

"Interesting. I saw the two of them the other day at the supermarket. He was buying beer." Kevin couldn't look at Jenny.

"What?! You saw her buying <u>beer</u> and you didn't tell me any of this? Was this why you two had a fight last night?"

"We didn't really have a fight – she got mad because she said I didn't trust her. She told me the beer was for Mike, and that she wouldn't touch it! And I believed her, I still do. Whatever happened today was something else. You need to talk to her, Jenny."

"No, YOU need to talk to her! I've been as patient and supportive as I can. Right now I'm angry. She's asleep, anyway, nobody needs to talk to her now."

"Is she okay, mom?" Ben looked worried.

Deena was standing at the top of the stairs. "I'm okay, Ben. And you're right mom, asleep or awake, nobody needs to talk to me. Not now, not ever!" Deena was standing at the top of the stairs. She turned around and went back to her bedroom, slamming the door.

"Well, at least she's feeling well enough to be mad. You satisfied, Jenny?" he tossed Ben his sweatshirt.

"Isn't it time for you to go to bed? You have school tomorrow. And pick up your clean clothes from the laundry room so you've got something to wear."

Jenny looked at Kevin. "I'm going to bed too. I've got work tomorrow. You can sleep in the den."

"That's just fine with me. Then nobody has to talk to anybody, like Deena said."

"OHHHH you always take her side!"

"Nobody's on anybody's side, here Jen. You need to get some rest. I'll see you in the morning."

JENNY COULDN'T SLEEP. She finally got up at 3 a.m. and took some aspirin and an allergy pill that she knew would knock her out. When the alarm went off Kevin was already up and downstairs. She turned it off and went back to sleep.

Kevin made breakfast for himself and the kids. He knew Jenny would only want coffee. Ben came down fully dressed, hair combed. Not a usual look for him that early in the day.

"Hey, Dad. Everything okay this morning? How's Deena?"

"Everything's okay, Ben. Everything will be fine. Your mother is still asleep and so is Deena. I imagine they both may have headaches when they do get up. Not for the same reason, but still..." he chuckled. "Eat your breakfast – I'll take you to school today."

Ben smiled, relieved that his dad had things under control. Kevin put a plate of pancakes and bacon in the oven to keep warm and left a note on the kitchen table to say he was taking Ben to school. "Grab a jacket – it's chilly this morning."

Ben found a jacket in the family room and picked up his backpack. "I'll have time to do a few laps before school if we leave now – for once!"

Chapter 30

DEENA DID WAKE up with a headache. She took a long, hot shower, pulled on her sweats and went downstairs. The house seemed empty, and she was glad. She poured herself a glass of orange juice and swallowed a couple of aspirin. *So Dad took Ben to school – he'll be happy about that. I always get him there just before the bell and he doesn't have time to run laps.*

The idea of food was not appealing – in fact she was regretting the orange juice. Maybe some tea would be a good idea. She turned on the kettle and waited for the water to boil. Her phone wasn't sitting in the charger – it must still be in her purse upstairs. Or was her purse upstairs? She couldn't remember. She went to look for it just as Jenny was coming downstairs. They froze – mother one step up, daughter one step down – and looked at each other. Jenny knew it was her move to fix this, and she wanted to try, but all she could manage was a clipped "How are you feeling?"

Deena dropped her head and said. "Lousy. My head is killing me."

"I'm not surprised. Did you take some aspirin?"

"Yes. With my orange juice. I'm not sure that was a good idea."

"Probably not. How about some tea?"

"I put the kettle on. I was just going to get my phone."

"Leave the phone for now. Let's have some tea." Jenny put her hand on Deena's shoulder, trying to be the comforting mom.

Deena turned and went back downstairs, knowing that if she crossed her mother now, things could get much worse.

"I assume you don't feel up to going to school?"

"Hardly. Dad took Ben."

"Good. I think chamomile tea might be best for your stomach – but what do you feel like?"

"I hate chamomile. I'll just have regular tea. Why does the kitchen smell like burned meat? That's not helping."

"Your dad left a chicken in the oven when he went to get you. By the time I got home the kitchen was full of smoke."

"I suppose that's my fault too."

"Well, I guess it's at least partly your fault! I want to know what happened yesterday, Deena. Really. I could believe it of Carol, but not you."

"Can I just go back upstairs? I think I'm going to throw up again. Can we talk about this later?"

"You and your dad – always pushing me away! Go. Just go. I have to go to work anyway. But we WILL talk about this, Deena. This is not something we can pretend didn't happen. I'm not your dad!"

"Believe me, mom, I *know* you are not dad!"

The teakettle whistled, Deena covered her ears and ran upstairs. Jenny turned off the stove, grabbed her purse, and slammed out the back door.

Kevin drove up as she was getting into her car. "How's Deena?"

"Deena is not feeling that great this morning, no surprise. She's gone back upstairs. When her stomach settles get her to help you clean up the mess in the kitchen. It's as much her fault as yours and you have to get that burned grease smell out of there. Don't try to go get her car. In fact, confiscate her keys until we've had a discussion about all of this. I should be home around six."

She didn't wait for his response.

Chapter 31

THE CLINIC SCHEDULED Kitty for the first appointment of the day, so they were in and out pretty quickly.

"How were the test results?" Jack was anxious, he'd been pacing outside the clinic, all his old anxiety about things medical flooding through him.

"I'm okay, Jack! They took another test just to be sure, and they'll call with those results. You don't look so good – are you okay?"

Jack's shoulders straightened. "I'm okay too."

Kitty raised an eyebrow as she looked at him. "Hmmm. Well, let me take you for some breakfast. You look like you could use it."

"No way are you paying. Save your money for now. I've got it covered. Besides, it's early enough that we can get a two-for-one at the Snowbird."

———

CARLIN HAD ALREADY UNLOADED his truck and stacked the materials he would need on the patio of the Farmhouse. But before he started on anything, he wanted to check out the pipes under the house. He wouldn't attempt the plumbing or electrical – that wasn't his thing – but he had a friend who was recently retired and loved to work on these old places. *Jack may not be ready to pay what this is going to cost. I'm itching to get started on it, though. I love these old places too. At least I can repair windows and doors, and make sure the roof is sound. Doesn't look like any water damage from rain, but you never know. And I need to get somebody out here to check that fireplace and make sure there are no cracks in the flue – or any bird's nests.*

When Jack and Kitty returned, they brewed a pot of coffee and took it out to the back patio along with coffee cake. "I'll go find Carlin and make him take a break. I have a feeling he's already been here for at least three hours – maybe more!"

But before he got very far, he could see Carlin coming their way. He was brushing cobwebs out of his hair and dirt off his jeans as he walked. He seemed full of energy, though, and greeted them with a broad grin.

"Well, looks like you are going to have to replace all the plumbing as well as all the electrical. Those pipes are shot, and if you made that electrical system live you'd burn the place down in a week. So – that's going to raise your costs. You still game?"

Jack handed him a cup of coffee and a piece of coffee cake wrapped in a napkin.

"I had a feeling you were going to tell me that. But you know, I don't think I want to back off this project. I think it's wise to put money in this place. My grandfather and my dad did, and it paid off for them. Property improvements, especially if you already own the property outright, seems like a good idea to me. Not much else you can invest in these days that brings that kind of return."

"Then I'll call my guys and get them to cost it out. The good thing is the place is small, but the bad thing is there isn't any of the plumbing or electric that can be salvaged. It's all going to have to go. And we need to get a fireplace inspection. We can leave that until the rest is done, though. When I'm up on the roof I'll make sure the flue is clear. You'll need a new spark arrester up there." He had already wolfed down the coffee cake and drained his cup.

"Well, I'm back to work. I'll be around here until four or five. Going to work on those double-hung windows – and if I have time I want to tear out all those old screens on the patio. You can decide later if you want to replace them, but right now they aren't doing any good anyway."

"You want to stop for lunch at some point? We've got plenty here."

"Nope – I've got a sandwich in the truck, and I don't usually eat much while I'm working anyway. Slows me down. You can run me out some water if you think of it. Otherwise, I'll just get some from the hose." He was gone before they could answer.

Kitty looked at Jack and laughed. "Wow. He's really motivated!"

"That's Carlin. I do think this job is going to take longer than we thought, though. You still going to be comfortable in the house?"

"Of course! I do have one favor to ask. Sometime soon I'd like to go to that storage place in Perris and see what I've got. If I'm lucky, my computer will be there. I've got an account that makes it easy to sell things online, and maybe I could use it to help you move some of this stuff out, and make you a little money. You'd be surprised how many people are looking for deals and collectibles online."

"I don't really care about making any money, but if that pleases you, let's do it. We can go tomorrow."

"In the meantime, I'd like to do some laundry – including yours! And maybe a little ironing? Show me the ropes, and I'll get started."

"You sure you want to do MY laundry too? I'm a big boy, you know."

"Let me, Jack. Let me do something to earn my keep besides the sorting and organizing. I want to."

"All right. I'll help Carlin while you're busy in the house."

Chapter 32

Deena was on her bed when her dad came upstairs. "How are you feeling, Dee?"

"Pretty crappy. I threw up again. Including the aspirin I took – I could see it."

"Ugh. Well I brought you some tea and toast, and some Tylenol. Eat first, and then take it. It won't be so hard on your stomach and might help that head of yours. I'm going back downstairs and I don't want YOU to come down until you feel better. Got it?" he patted her hand.

"Thanks, Dad. You're the best. I think I might be able to sleep if I can get the edge off this headache."

"Good. I'll see you later."

<hr>

The kitchen was a mess. Greasy smoke stains covered the wall over the stove, and the plate he'd left in the oven on warm only added to the smell. He went to his computer to find out how best to clean up the mess.

He was going to need some supplies to tackle the kitchen.

He left a note for Deena on the table in case she came down, and went to the store. Might as well stop and pick up some lunch while he was out, too. She'd probably sleep for at least an hour or so.

THE TOAST and Tylenol went down and stayed down. The headache was waning. Deena heard her dad leave. She went downstairs and found his note – he wouldn't be back for at least an hour. That would give her time to pack and get out. She didn't care where she went, she only knew she didn't want to be there to talk to anybody. Not now. Not yet.

She threw some things in a canvas bag, grabbed her purse and keys. I should leave a note – they'll be frantic. But I don't want to see any of them, not today.

She turned her dad's note over and scribbled "I'll be gone for a few days. Don't worry about me. I'll go to Grampa's. I know he'll let me stay, and maybe I can think there. I've driven there before, so don't worry. I know how to get there. Deena."

It wasn't a long walk to Carol's house to pick up her car, only a mile or so.

Just to be sure she did know how to get there, she set her phone for driving directions to his address. She remembered what freeway to get on first, but after that it was a bit hazy. It would take her more than two hours, that much she did remember. There was bottled water in her car, and she had a little cash if she wanted to get something to eat before she got there.

She was on the freeway by the time her dad came home. He spent the day cleaning the kitchen and waiting for Jenny. No use calling her at work, it wasn't news he wanted to tell her over the phone. And Deena would be fine. She was a good driver, and maybe this would be what she needed, to be the one leaving for a change. Her mother had certainly done it enough.

AFTER ABOUT AN HOUR of freeway driving through towns full of tracts of new homes, the road began to follow miles of railroad tracks with deteriorating box cars, abandoned engines, and nothing but dirt and clumps of scrub grass. There were new industrial centers springing up here and there, and huge shopping malls, but most of it was like looking behind the scenes at an amusement park--great appearance out front, nothing to see but machinery behind. *God, this is awful. I hadn't realized the air was so bad and how dirty and dry everything is. Guess I've always been on my cell or reading when I've come with mom and dad.*

When the San Bernardino mountains gave way to the San Jacintos, it was a very different scene. Sometimes there was snow on the highest peaks, contrasting with the dry heat of the foothills. It had rained recently, and there was a light shimmer of new green growth between giant boulders and oak trees. Wildflowers covered the side of a hill. Deena's mood lightened like a curtain lifting as she drove past a swath of bright orange poppies. *At least Grampa won't ask me a lot of questions. He never seems to be interested in me or my life. The only person he ever paid much attention to was Grandma Lily. But he'll let me stay I think. I hope.*

She stopped at a fast-food stand and ordered a taco and a coke. She was hungry, and Mexican food sounded like something she could tolerate, for some reason. She decided to call her grandfather and let him know she was on her way. He didn't pick up, so she left a message. It was eleven thirty, she should be there by one. If he wasn't home, she could wait.

WHEN JENNY CAME HOME from work that night and Kevin showed her the note, all she could say was "Well leave it to Deena to run away from home and then tell us where she's going – but honestly, Kevin, how did you let this happen? Why didn't you take her keys before you left the house? Didn't you THINK that she might pull something like this? No, don't answer, you never DO think." She poured herself a glass of wine and went upstairs to change.

"Your dad called and left a message – she got there around 2," he called after her.

In case you're interested whether she got there safely. "And I'm going to pick up Ben!"

JENNY WENT into Deena's room and looked around. As usual, she was amazed at how tidy it was. The bed was made, and the clothes she'd left on the floor last night were in the hamper. Her backpack was gone. Maybe she'd left it in her car.

There was something forlorn about the space – as if it were inhabited by a stranger, and not by the kid Deena had been. The clutter of stuffed animals and doll house furniture was gone. It made Jenny sad to think she had somehow missed that transition. When did it happen, exactly? Was it the year she was twelve, or thirteen? Something had changed her. The sunny disposition gave way to a serious purpose – purpose in her studies, and commitment to the causes she believed in.

Jenny had been that way once, herself. She was going to save the whales, feed the homeless, educate the masses. I suppose what I do now is like that. I work to give seniors purpose and meaning, some happiness and independence, and a balanced meal at least once a day. But how did I lose track of my own kid? I don't know how to do this gig. I was lost as a teenager, at least from my mom. She just disappeared into her own world of paranoia and mania. And when the cycle changed, her depression enveloped the whole house, occupied all of dad's energy. Who knows what Deena will encounter down there with him now, especially with a stranger in the house. I should drop everything and just go bring her home. Shouldn't I?

She closed the door and went to change out of her work clothes. Another glass of wine was calling her. She'd talk Deena's situation over with Kevin – and maybe Ben, too. Ben was old enough to see what was going on and he often had something insightful to say when she and Kevin were at a loss. *God, was _he_ growing up too soon too?*

Chapter 33

KITTY HEARD the phone ring and then go to voice mail. She also heard Deena's message "Hi Grampa – It's Deena. I'm on my way to visit. Hope you'll let me stay a couple of days. I haven't been feeling too well and I thought getting out of town for a bit might do me good. I won't be any trouble, I promise. See you soon! Love you!"

Kitty put down the iron and went to find Jack.

"Really? She called just now? I wonder what happened. No doubt she and her mother have been at it again. Jenny just can't seem to give that girl any credit or any space. That relationship has been rocky for too long. Well, we certainly have room here. She can sleep in the living room now that we've cleared things out of there. The couch has a pull-out bed, and now there's a tv in there so she'll have some entertainment if she wants it."

Kitty looked worried. "But how do we explain ME?"

"I told Jenny you were an old friend of Lily's who needed a place to stay for a bit. Remember? I don't see any reason to change that little fiction, do you? We'll be fine. Let's see what the kid has to say when she gets here."

"If you're sure. I could go to a motel. I do have some money."

"Don't be silly. Stay. You can help me entertain her if that's what she needs. She's a good kid, really. Smart. Gets good grades, stays out of trouble – usually! Let's see how it goes."

"Okay – I've made some lunch. You coming? Looks like Carlin is taking a break."

She nodded towards Carlin who was sitting on a rock, eating his sandwich.

Carlin picked up his lunchbox and headed toward his truck. "Go on, Jack – I'm going to run on over to the hardware store. I don't want you messing around here while I'm gone! Go have your lunch."

KITTY HAD MADE a salad and a cheese plate with crackers and fruit. She poured them each a glass of iced tea.

"This is great. I haven't had anyone make lunch for me in a very long time. Thanks."

"It isn't fancy, that's for sure."

"I think I'll put that skirt steak we bought into a marinade for tonight. I'll Barbeque it. Deena always liked that. Maybe you could do another salad and throw some potatoes in to bake around 4:30"

"Yes, Remember I was going to make twice baked potatoes tonight anyway?!"

"Even better!"

They finished lunch in silence, each of them thinking about how this new guest would fit into what was becoming a comfortable routine. Kitty thought about her own daughter, remembered the tension and distance between them. She recognized long ago that her daughter craved a stability she wasn't able to give her, and that her drinking and relationships with men had made everything worse. Lots of regret, there, and heartache. Allison was her only child, and she had lost her long ago.

"You look so sad, Kitty. You okay?"

"Oh – I was just thinking about my own daughter, Allison. And it made me sad. I'm okay."

"Where is she, do you know?"

"I heard from her father last year – she's living in San Bernardino, now. He said her marriage is in trouble. I'm not surprised. She has a very strong personality."

"Is that a kind way of saying she's stubborn and demanding?" He winked.

"Well, yes. It is. But then I can be that way too. I should have had more patience with her when she was growing up, but I was caught up in my own drama."

"It's never too late. Maybe someday, when you feel up to it, you can look her up and see how she's doing."

"No. I think not. I would just mess everything up again." She picked up their empty plates and put them in the dishwasher, wiping a tear with the back of her hand. "You go on back and help Carlin. Maybe I'll see if Deena could use that other small room? She might appreciate more privacy than the living room. Is that okay?"

"Sure, if you want to go to the trouble. Have at it!"

Kitty smiled. "You'll probably hear her car when she arrives. I'll let you come greet her. She won't want to be surprised by a strange woman in the house."

Chapter 34

THE OTHER SMALL bedroom faced the backyard and had a large window with a sliding door onto another small patio. Kitty opened the closet and found that it was almost empty. Good. She could put the boxes in there and pulled the storage bins outside. They had secure lids and would be protected from the weather and any bugs. She found some twin sheets in the linen closet and decided to wash the blanket and quilt folded at the foot of the bed. They were dusty, but lightweight, so it wouldn't take long. She ran a dust mop over the wood floor, and then did it again, this time with a damp mop. So much dust! Fortunately there were no knick-knacks on the dresser, so all it took was a good wipe down and polish. The mirror was harder – it was old, so old that the glass gave a slightly distorted reflection. Or maybe that was the way she looked, now? A morphing Kitty? *Ridiculous.*

She picked some wildflowers from the front yard and put them in a mason jar she found in the kitchen. They, on the other hand, looked perfect on the dresser in front of the mirror. When she put the clean blanket and quilt back on the bed, she saw that the wildflower colors were reflected in the pattern of the quilt. Such an unusual flower – bright orange with a yellow border, and a dark center. She had never seen anything like it before, but then wildflowers had not been in her world before – she would have labeled them weeds, before now. Before Jack.

She heard a car drive up, and flew out the sliding door, dust cloth in hand, towards Jack. He was already on his way, heading around the house to the front. She decided to keep going and see how far Carlin had gotten with his repairs. *Jack can settle her in and give her a heads-up about "Lily's old friend."*

Deena saw her grampa coming around the house and waited for him to get to her. She realized she wasn't as recovered as she had thought – and the taco and coke hadn't settled well. Her headache was back, too.

"Hey, kiddo! This is a surprise! Didn't expect to see you today! How're you doing?"

She opened the car door and stood up, shaking her head. And burst into tears. "Deena! Oh my darling girl!" He put his arms around her.

It was like a dam had burst. She couldn't stop crying. He just held her, and when the sobs finally turned to deep breaths, he stepped back, still holding onto her arms, to look at her. "Let's go inside where you can lie down, and we can talk, if you want. Is that your bag on the backseat?"

She nodded. He grabbed the bag and guided her through the front door and into the living room.

"Why don't you sit here – or lie down if you want – and I'll get us some iced tea. Feel you could handle that?"

"Yeah – I can try. My stomach is a little off – and I have a headache."

"Maybe some Tylenol then with that tea? That shouldn't upset your stomach. Want to try it?"

"Anything. Anything not to feel this way!"

He winked at her. "That's my girl."

She hadn't ever heard so many terms of endearment from him – at least not since she was very little. It almost made her start crying again, and then she realized that would make her headache even worse. She took her purse and went into the master bedroom to the bathroom. It was the only one that was accessible, in her experience. Her grandma had stuffed every other room with boxes and boxes of junk.

Her mass of long black hair had come out of the loose pony tail she'd put in this morning. She brushed it and pulled it back as tight as she could. *I look terrible. No color in my face and dark circles under my eyes. I look like an old woman! I look like Grandma!*

She used the toilet and washed her face and hands. *Grampa must have thought I was dying.* She pinched her cheeks and put on some lip gloss. That was better, but she still had those dark circles – and her eyes were bloodshot, too.

She went back out and sat on the couch. She realized the room was completely different – no junky knick knacks, lace cushions, side tables or boxes of stuff. And the T.V. was hooked up in here; that was new. *There was a hard and fast rule about that one.* She remembered her mother trying to persuade her Grampa to put one in so he could watch DVDs. *What could have changed his mind about that?*

Jack came into the living room with a tray with crackers, iced tea, and a bottle of Tylenol.

"It might be best if you could eat one or two of these crackers before you take the pills. You want to try?"

He looked so concerned. She brightened up a bit and smiled. "Sure. I'll try. I can't feel any worse, that's for sure."

He patted her hand. "So, you want to talk? Or do you just need some space until you feel a little steadier?"

"How about you talk – tell me what's happened in here. It doesn't look like the same place! I'll talk later."

"I'm clearing things out, you know, trying to make a new start. At my age! But, well, I guess it's time I took control of some things around here. So, we – uh I – started in this room. Even moved the TV in! Your mom will be happy to see that. Actually watched a couple of the movies she sent down."

"We? Did you say 'we'?"

Jack cleared his throat and took a sip of his tea. "Yes, I did. I don't know if your mother told you, but I've got an old friend of your Grandma's staying here. She ran into some difficulties and needed a place to stay, so I offered the guest room to her in exchange for some help with the clearing out. She's very nice, you'll like her!"

"No – mom didn't tell me. She doesn't tell me much of anything, anyway. Should I not have come? Won't I just be in the way?"

"You will NOT be in the way. I'm glad you came. I'm glad you will be the first to meet Kitty. There's something about her that is special, I think. What do you mean your mother never tells you anything? Is there something going on I don't know about?"

Deena did not say, *well yes there is a lot going on that you don't know about because you never seem to have much interest,* but since he had been so sweet just now, she didn't have the heart. She ate two crackers before she responded.

"I don't know. Mom has a big life outside of the family. She works all the time, and travels a lot, and we seem to be like an inconvenience, well, mostly me. Sorry, I guess the headache is making me say things I wouldn't usually say," she picked up the pill bottle and read the dosage label.

"You can read that little tiny print?" Jack laughed. "You can take two. I memorized it so I wouldn't have to get out the magnifying glass! And Deena, don't worry about telling me what's going on. I have some experience with mother-daughter problems, although I was never much good at solving any of them. But your grandma was a special case, so things weren't exactly normal for her or your mom."

"I know. But everything I do seems to irritate my mom. And last night I really blew it, big time," she started to tear up again.

"Do you want to talk about it now?"

"I'd really like to lie down. I'm just so tired."

"You go ahead and lie down on my bed and rest as long as you like. I'm doing some work out back, but you can come to the door and call me if you need anything." He gave her a hug and picked up her bag to carry it to his room.

"Thanks, Grampa. We will talk later, I promise."

He turned the phone's ringer off, and he muted the answering machine. Then he called Kevin to let him know Deena had arrived. No answer, so he left a message.

KITTY WAS LOOKING around the farmhouse, trying to stay out of Carlin's way. She saw Jack coming their way, so she went to meet him.

"How's it going?" she asked.

"She's really upset about something – and she had a headache and wanted to lie down, so I told her to use my room. That way we won't disturb her while we're getting dinner. I hope she will sleep. Poor kid really looks like she's been through it."

"I cleaned up the other bedroom. I hope you don't mind. I put the boxes in the closet and moved the storage bins out to the patio. It thought she might like more privacy than the living room couch."

"I think you're right. She used to stay in that room when she was little, she'll probably like it."

"I need to go back and give that bathroom a cleaning, though. It looked pretty neglected."

"Don't fuss, Kitty. You've done enough already."

"No, I won't fuss, but I will clean!" she smiled and walked back to the house.

It was important she make a good impression on his grand-daughter. Why, she couldn't say – she only knew she was certainly, absolutely, going to try.

Chapter 35

DEENA SLEPT for most of the afternoon. When she woke up, she tried to call Mike on her cell, but found it needed charging. And the only charger she had was the one in the car. *Shit.* She went to the kitchen for a glass of water and saw her Grampa on the patio fussing with the Barbeque. Good, dinner would be soon. The smell of potatoes baking filled the kitchen. She picked up an apple from the bowl of fruit on the kitchen table and went outside.

"Anything I can do to help?"

"Hey! How are you feeling? You had a pretty good sleep, I think. How's the headache?"

"I'm much better, thanks. And I'm getting hungry! What's for dinner? Where's your houseguest?"

"I think she's taking a shower. She'll be out soon. Dinner will be in about a half-hour. We're having the marinated flank steak you always liked. If you'd want to move your stuff into the little guest room and freshen up, it's all ready for you. Kitty cleaned it up this afternoon."

"She cleaned it up in an <u>afternoon</u>? She must be a miracle worker! That place was packed with stuff the last time we were here!"

"I had already started to get rid of things—and there are still boxes and storage containers full of the "stuff" as you call it. But the room is cleared out and the bathroom and the bed are clean and ready for you. By the way, I let your folks know you arrived here safely. Didn't want them to worry."

"Oh. Okay. Good."

DEENA WAS amazed when she saw what Kitty had done. The room was perfect, just the way she liked things. No clutter, no fuss, except for a bunch of wildflowers on the dresser. *What did Grandma call them? Indian Blankets? Yes. I'm sure that was it. How lovely. If only Grandma had been able to keep things like this, she might have had more visits from us. The chaos drove Mom crazy, though, and Grandma drove her crazy too. Well, Grandma was kind of crazy.*

She had time for a shower before dinner. She had packed a pair of jeans and a couple of shirts; the sweats she'd slept in today were the sweats she'd slept in last night, and she needed a change. She opened the top dresser drawer to see if there was space to unpack the few things she had brought. It was empty. She opened the other drawers and found every one of them crammed with photos and other mementoes from her grandmother's life. *Thank goodness Grampa didn't get rid of these! Looks like all of mom's childhood pictures are in here – and baby pictures of Ben and me. This stuff needs organizing. Maybe Grampa would let me tackle it.*

She pulled out a picture of her grandmother and stuck it into the mirror frame. It had been taken when she was about Deena's age, probably not too long before she married her

Grampa. She was holding a kitten up to her cheek and smiling at the camera. *I do look like Grandma. Same dark hair, same dark eyes.*

By the time Deena finished showering and fussing with her hair, the steak was on the grill. Kitty had set the patio table and brought out the potatoes, a slab of butter, and a big salad with Jack's tomato dressing. There was a stack of tortillas wrapped in foil, warming on the grill.

"Anything else we need out here? Oh – salt and pepper!" Kitty went back to the kitchen just as Deena came out her patio door.

"Hey, Grampa. Can I help?"

"No, kiddo, just sit down and make yourself comfortable. There's some iced tea on the table if you want some. The steak is just about done."

Kitty came out with the salt and pepper and Jack said "Ah – here's Kitty! So Kitty, this is my granddaughter Deena, and Deena, meet Kitty!"

"Pleased to meet you," Deena said, and stood up.

"And I'm happy to meet you! Please, sit down! I'm not used to this kind of formality!" she laughed and put the salt and pepper down.

Deena noticed there was no alcohol on the table. That was unusual. Since she could remember, Grampa always had a drink or two before dinner and wine with dinner. Had he given it up? Maybe she'd find out later. Not that she wanted anything! No, she'd had quite enough of that yesterday. *Why did people drink, anyway?*

Kitty was a good conversationalist when she wanted to be, and she was able to draw Deena out with just a few questions. Deena found it easy to talk to the two of them – in fact they were so easy to be with she even dared to risk a few words like 'shit' and 'damn' – something her mother would NEVER have allowed. They didn't seem to notice.

But when Deena tried to ask Kitty something about her past, and her friendship with Lily, Kitty managed to refocus the conversation on Jack, or the dinner, or Jack.

"Your Grampa is fixing up the old farmhouse, did he tell you?"

"No, really? How cool is that! I would have loved to explore that old place, but mom would never let us go near it. She was afraid of spiders or lead paint or something – I don't remember. But it always intrigued me. Why are you fixing it up now, Grampa?"

"I think it's a good investment. I know your mom worries about me living out here alone, and Kitty may need a place to stay for a while. I'd like her to have her own space, and she'd like that too. Then when she leaves, whenever that may be, I could rent it to a student or one of the artists from the colony. Give me some company that's not too close, and a little income."

"Can I see it? Before it gets too dark?"

"Sure you can! Kitty why don't you take her out there and I'll get these dishes into the kitchen. I'll make us some coffee, too. Deena – you want coffee?"

"No thanks – but I will take some tea if that's okay."

"Tea for me too, Jack."

The farmhouse looked smaller than Deena remembered. And with the porch screens gone, it had an open and vulnerable look. "It's a cute little place, isn't it? What needs to be done to make it livable?"

"Surprisingly little. Your Grampa's friend Carlin has just finished up the plumbing under the house, and he'll install a tankless water heater tomorrow. He told me that the electrical work isn't as bad as he originally thought. Your great grandfather had started to replace it not too long before he died, and it's in pretty good shape. He figures that will take another day or so. So maybe by next weekend we can start with the floors and then paint. Oh, and some of the windows need repair, but the glass is all intact. And they all need screens."

"Will he replace the screening on the porch?"

"No, I don't think so. It seems more inviting without it, more open. What do you think?"

"I think that's right. I love the bones of this place. I can see it with a few window boxes filled with geraniums – a rocker on the porch with a pillow and a cat!"

"Me too. There's something about the ambience – the vibe – that's just so ---so ---right! Let's poke around inside and you tell me what you feel, how you might see it coming together."

Deena was surprised that an adult would ask for her opinion about anything. And pleased. Kitty was openly friendly and genuinely interested in her opinion. She was happy, almost light-hearted. She hadn't felt this good in the company of adults for a long time. It was like she was one of them.

Chapter 36

KEVIN PUT a frozen lasagna in the oven before he went to pick up Ben. The casserole still wasn't heated through when they got back, so he put out some bread sticks and flavored olive oil. He poured Ben a glass of milk and opened a bottle of chianti.

Jenny held her glass out, and asked "Ben, are you up to talking a little bit about what's going on with your sister? Her behavior last night is mystifying to me. She's just not that kind of kid."

"She's not a kid anymore, mom. She's eighteen."

"You know what I mean. What's going on with her? And who is this Mike guy that lives at Carol's?"

Kevin checked on the lasagna. "You'd know if you were ever around here to talk to her, Jenny. Mike is Carol's cousin. He goes to Cal Poly and is on break this semester earning some money for tuition."

"Don't attack me, Kevin. I don't want a fight about this. I really want to talk."

"Alright, but that means you have to stick around and listen." Kevin was obviously still angry about their last conversation.

"I know. I'm sorry about this morning. Ben?"

"Well, Carol really isn't a big friend of Deena's, you know that, right?"

"I guess so." Jenny took a sip of her wine.

"But Mike, well Deena really likes him. I don't know if it's anything more than friends, but they spend a lot of time talking. He's helping with the engineering on the float, and he's a nice guy, mom. When he graduates from CalPoly he's going to graduate school and eventually he wants to build bridges and stuff. He's cool.

"So yesterday Carol asked Deena if she could run her home early. She said she had a lot of homework and needed to get started. Dee agreed, and they went off. When she didn't come back to pick me up, I asked Lenny's dad for a ride to their place. Figured somebody could pick me up there. That's all I know about what happened. Really."

"I just don't get why she let things get so out of control. It makes no sense. She's such a sensible kid."

"She hasn't been that happy lately, mom. Haven't you noticed? Kids at school are talking, though. Everybody was asking about her today. Why she wasn't there. They knew, of course. Carol talks. <u>She</u> wasn't too sick to be there – this kind of thing has happened with her before, and she kind of bragged about getting Deena drunk. She seems to think she'll get a medal or something. But none of Deena's friends were buying it. Carol's a drip and everybody knows it."

Kevin and Jenny looked at each other. They had the same reaction to Carol's parents.

"Mike's good, though. He was there again this afternoon to help on the float. He asked if Deena was okay. I told him she was, but that she didn't come to school today. He seemed worried about her."

Kevin got up to fix some coffee. "It's a good thing he came

home when he did. I think his intervention with watery lemonade made all the difference. Those girls could have been a lot sicker."

Jenny poured herself another glass of wine. That made four, and she knew she was on the edge of slurring. Given the topic, she decided not to drink it. She got up to clear the table and poured the wine down the drain.

"Hey! That's good chianti! I could have had it if you didn't like it!" Kevin looked mystified. Pouring wine away was not like Jenny.

"Oh – sorry. I just thought I'd had enough. Especially given what we're talking about."

"Good for you, mom. I'm glad you did that." Ben headed for the back yard. "I'm gonna shoot some hoops."

Jenny looked at Ben. Was he watching how much she drank? "Yeah. Good for me. It's important to know your limits. In a lot of ways, and for a lot of good reasons."

Jenny and Kevin sat at the kitchen table for a long time after Ben had gone to bed.

"I feel like I'm the cause of all of Deena's problems, Kevin. Ben seems to think so too."

"You've had your own drama to deal with lately, Jen. Your mom's death was not that long ago, and processing that is hard enough. I feel like it has also brought up all the old problems you had with her and your dad. It's going to take some time. You are right that this little blip for Deena is out of character. She is a good kid, and she does have a grip on reality. Her slip-up is pretty normal, and she isn't entirely to blame, either."

"I should have handled it differently. I wish we had talked

before she left this morning. I was so angry. I just don't know how to cope with it all."

"It will do her good to be with your dad for a while, get some space. We know she's safe, and we know he will take care of her."

"But what about this Kitty person who is staying there? That's got to have an impact. She's got some troubles of her own, apparently. Who knows how my dad will sort <u>that</u> out. In my experience he supports the neediest, not the most deserving – he could leave Deena to fend for herself."

"I think we can trust Deena to leave if she's uncomfortable. Let's wait and see. She'll probably call tomorrow. Then we'll know more about what she wants to do. You are right, you know. She is good at making thoughtful decisions... most of the time. I'm going up. You coming?"

"I want to load the dishwasher and then I'll be there."

Kevin climbed the stairs. Something had shifted between them. He felt like Jenny had softened a bit, maybe was a bit more open. Owning that she had some responsibility for what happened could not be easy for her, he knew that. She'd been tied so tight for so long. He was hopeful, and a little wary. Change can be hard, even if it's for the better.

Jenny decided to do another load of laundry after she finished with the dishes. Deena's clothes from yesterday were on the top of the hamper. She put them in the washer and suddenly began to weep. Tears streamed down her face as she added detergent and turned on the machine. *I don't do this. I don't cry – I usually can't cry, even if I want to.* But the deep sadness she was feeling had broken open, and there was no other way to let it go, she had no choice but to let the tears flow, and to feel.

Chapter 37

DEENA AND KITTY walked through each room of the farmhouse, both thinking exactly what they would do to make it theirs; to make it a comfortable and serene space. "I'd love to have a place like this for my own. I can just see one room for books and study space, a bedroom with a loft bed, and a comfy couch by the fire. Is there going to be a sink in that room in with the counter? It looks like there is plumbing there."

"Yes. It will be a tiny kitchenette, I think. Maybe a kind of retro free-standing cabinet with an old-fashioned sink."

"Oh – and a pie safe for dishes and stuff?"

Kitty was surprised Deena would know what a pie safe was. "You know about pie safes?"

"I watch a lot of D.I.Y., and they are always refinishing an old pie safe and using it for storage. I love the look."

"So do I! Those mesh cupboards you can see through on the top – I can see those with dishes and cups inside. Maybe even some Fiesta ware? In different colors?"

"YES!" Deena's eyes were shining.

"We'd better start back. The light is fading. But can you imagine sitting out on the porch in the evening with a cup of tea? So peaceful. And so pretty with the curtain of leaves from the pepper tree and the maples. So snug."

They both sighed, then looked at each other and laughed. Jack could hear them chattering away as they came back towards the house, like two teenagers. He smiled as he set out the coffee and tea. It was good to know they were comfortable with each other. That was important. Kitty needed to feel comfortable with his family.

"Grampa, the farmhouse is going to be so great! It already IS great! Are you going to be able to use the fireplace? That would make it absolutely perfect!"

"I think so, but I'm going to have it inspected. I'm thinking it might be wise to put an insert in there – you know, something like a Ben Franklin stove that would provide heat for the place when it turns cold. And that would make it even safer."

"Really? That would be amazing! Can I help with cleanup or anything tomorrow? I'd love to."

"I don't think Carlin is quite ready for us to get in his way. But if you're here this weekend, maybe we can get started on the floors, or do some painting. Are you planning to stay that long?"

"I'll have to check with mom. But I'm pretty sure she'll be glad to have me out of her hair for a few days. And to tell you the truth, I need some space too. I'll call her tomorrow. My cell is out of juice – you don't happen to have any cell chargers here that might work, do you?"

"I doubt it. My cell phone is so old I doubt my charger would work. Maybe we can get something tomorrow. We are going to run an errand in the morning, so I'm sure we'll find somewhere that will carry what you need. You can come with us if you like."

"I think I'll pass. I've got some reading to do so I'm not too far behind when I get back to school. But I'll give you the model number of my phone if you don't mind picking up a charger? I can pay for it. When I get back home, that is."

"No need to pay for it! I'm sure it won't cost that much."

"I did bring my computer. Do you have an internet connection?"

"Gosh – I don't know. I have a cable connection but I'm not sure about a connection to the internet."

Kitty said, "Yes, he has a connection to the internet. I checked when I hooked up the TV and the DVD player. I think we can figure out how to get you connected. I don't have my computer with me, or I would have done that already."

Jack had a fire going in the fire pit. They sat in the mild desert evening and watched the stars come out, each of them lost in their own thoughts. Conversation wasn't necessary. Sitting together in comfortable silence was enough.

Deena was filling up a hollow space inside herself. She looked at her Grampa. She had never seen him so happy, so relaxed. It was good to be with people who were easy with each other, and who were obviously content in each other's company. That had been missing from her life for a long time.

Kitty stretched and yawned. "I'm going to bed. Sorry, but this has been a busy day and I'm really tired. I'm glad you came, Deena. I hope your room is comfortable! I'll see you both in the morning."

"Good night. I'm sure I'll be fine. All I really need is a bed and a pillow. I'm pretty whacked myself."

"'Nite Kitty." Jack poked at the fire. "Stay for a bit, Deena, so we can talk a little. Or are you too tired?"

"No. I'd like that."

Deena gave him all the details she could remember of her afternoon at Carol's, and of her evening at home. She didn't want to burden him with her complicated relationship with her mom, but she did tell him about how lonely she had been. And she told him how disapproving her mother was most of the time, and something about how that made her feel. He didn't talk much, just listened.

One of the logs burned through and fell apart with a whisper and a fountain of sparks, the breeze pushing them up into the night sky. "Beautiful – and sometimes dangerous. Right, Deena?

"Reminds me of a time when your mom was about your age, and we sat out here watching the fire. We were having a conversation about the same kind of circumstance that caught you up. Your Grandma was always hard on her. Seemed like once Jenny became a teenager and started having opinions of her own, Grandma couldn't figure out a way to be with her. They fought a lot. And I admit, I generally asked your mom to just understand that her mother wasn't well, wasn't really normal. That's a lot to ask of a kid, year after year. And it may be why she is having trouble relating to you. What do you think?"

"I guess it could be. But I'm not her, and she's not Grandma. Why doesn't she realize that? Why should we have to repeat that crazy drama?"

"Can't pretend I understand these things, Dee. But maybe it's something to think about. I do know your mom loves you very much, and so does your dad."

"I suppose. But right now, I'm not feeling it. At least not from mom."

Jack stood up and covered the smoldering ashes, pulling a spark screen over the pit.

"We can't figure everything out tonight, that's for sure. Why don't you go to bed and maybe I'll see you at breakfast. We'll want to get an early start tomorrow, so if you aren't up by the time we leave, you can find what you like to eat. There's fruit and yogurt, and eggs. You know where to find the bread and how to use the toaster!"

"I'll be fine. I'll probably be up. 'Nite Grampa." She gave him a hug.

He looked after her. Suddenly he had such a strong memory of Lily it knocked the breath out of him. Deena was so like her, in appearance anyway. *Dear God, please let that be where the likeness ends. Don't let her ever be tortured by the same demons.* Jack wasn't a religious man, but his prayer was real. No one should have to suffer the way Lily had suffered.

Chapter 38

DEENA PULLED BACK the covers on the bed and noticed that the pillowcase had been ironed. Something about that made her sad. Her mother would have loved it. She was always apologizing for the way her Grandma kept house--or didn't keep house. She would love to see this transformation. Too tired to give it more thought, she stretched out and pulled the covers up. A long time ago she had slept in this room; when her Grandma was happy. Her mom was smiling when she tucked Deena in. Thinking about that made her sad, too. She drifted off, and when she woke in the morning, her pillow was wet with tears.

Jack and Kitty had already left for the storage locker when Deena came into the kitchen. She found a note telling her they should be back not too long after lunch. Grampa's coffee cake was on the table, and there was coffee in the pot. She took an orange out to the patio. There were birds in the birdbath, bees and hummers in the bottle brush. Carlin was already at work on the farmhouse. It was a peaceful morning, and one with no pressure on her to do a thing. She stretched, yawned, and went inside for the rest of her breakfast.

The note said that she could connect to the internet in the living room, and left directions. They didn't have a wireless connection, but there was no reason Deena couldn't work at the desk. If that's what she chose to do. Right now she was more in the mood for checking out the farm house. Maybe she would take Carlin some of the coffee cake and do just that. She remembered him from the time she came to visit and he was helping with the set-up in the garage for Grampa's trains. She wondered if he would remember her.

THE DRIVE to Perris took Jack and Kitty longer than they planned. Traffic was heavier than Jack remembered, but Kitty reminded him that they had left in the middle of the morning rush hour. They found the storage facility easily, and Kitty went to the office to get directions to the space with her things. The clerk at the desk directed her to a first-floor cubicle at the back of the building. "You picking up or are you gonna leave your stuff here?"

"I'm not sure. I'll let you know before I leave." She couldn't tell him she had no idea what was in the unit.

"If there are any problems, you let me know."

"Sure." She got back into the truck and they drove to the back of the lot.

"You want some privacy while you do this, Kitty? I can run pick up that charger we need while you're sorting through stuff."

"I think I'd rather you stayed with me if you don't mind. I'm feeling a bit shaky."

"Of course. Here, let me see if I can get that key to work." Kitty had been struggling with the lock. "Boy, it's stiff!" It finally turned, and they were able to open the heavy door.

It was a small unit, and by no means full. There were several boxes, a large cardboard wardrobe, and that was it. No furniture. The boxes were labeled with the name of the storage place. "Gray must have hired this place to clean out the apartment. I'm surprised he didn't do it on the cheap. He really <u>was</u> in a hurry."

"There's not much here, Kitty. It would all fit into the truck if you want to take it now. What do you think?"

"That makes sense, I guess. I'll ask if there's someone who can help us load." She walked back to the office while Jack started loading. By the time she came back, he had most of it loaded.

"Wow. That was quick! He's sending someone now. At least he can help with the wardrobe – that looks pretty hard to maneuver."

"None of it was very heavy. And I always have that little dolly in the back, which makes a big difference." He had left just enough space for the wardrobe to fit. "We'll have to put the wardrobe on its side – no way to stand it up or lay it flat."

"I couldn't care less about messing up the clothes. I just want to get out of here. Something about this whole place gives me the creeps."

"I understand. Sure you even want to take this stuff? We could just leave it here and you could walk away from all of it."

"No, I need to see if there is anything of value. And I'm hoping the files I had are in one of those boxes. There is information I want to have, want to keep."

"Of course."

Kitty had to admit it was tempting to walk away--just leave the past behind, and walk away into a new life, with new people, a fresh start.

DEENA FIGURED out how to get to the internet and sent Mike an e-mail to let him know she was okay. Then she wrote to her mom. She apologized for making her worry and told her she was enjoying her time with her Grampa and Kitty. Monday was a school holiday, so she asked if she could stay over the weekend and drive home Monday afternoon. It was only a few minutes until she heard from both of them. Her mom said it was fine for her to stay, but she wanted her home before dark on Monday. Mike was glad to hear from her, said he missed her, and asked if he could drive down on the weekend if she would still be there. She told him she'd have to check with her Grampa, but it was okay as far as she was concerned. She was surprised he wanted to come. Their relationship wasn't that intense, they were just friends. Weren't they? She smiled. *Maybe – maybe not.*

The reading she had to do would take her a couple of hours, at least. History had never been her favorite subject, but this year had been different. The supplemental reading was proving to be especially interesting. She wondered what her Grampa would think if he knew she was reading SAVING CAPITALISM by Robert Reich. He'd probably call her a communist. Last time she heard him talk politics he was ranting on about William F. Buckley. She knew about Buckley, too. She had read articles from THE NATIONAL REVIEW and seen some clips of his T.V. shows. Her AP class this year was studying democracy, and her term paper was supposed to be about whether that ideology actually worked. So far, she was not convinced. Politics and money had way too much sway over the process. Madison Avenue ran the world. Mike was the one who pointed that out, and she felt he was absolutely right.

Chapter 39

JENNIE HAD a frantic day at work. One of the facilities had a plumbing emergency and her office had to close it down. They found transport to another facility for seniors who were there for the day, and organized lunch to be brought in for them. Easier than it sounds – many of the people who used their services were on special diets because of diabetes or food allergies. But they finally managed to take care of everyone and would provide transport home as needed. Care givers were notified and told that the facility would be closed until Monday in order to make sure the facility was safe and the kitchen fully operable. She would have to make sure to get a cleaning crew in over the weekend, another cost, another problem to solve. And one of the staff would have to be there while they were cleaning to make sure everything was done properly. Fortunately, Peter was available, and she could trust him.

"Go home, Jenny. You look exhausted. I'll take care of finding a cleaning service, and when Monday morning comes everything will be better than before. Trust me. It's six-thirty. You've had a long day."

"So have you! But I will go and leave the weekend to you. Call me if you run into any snags."

———

Kevin and Ben had dinner on the table when she got home. The pasta primavera smelled amazing – just the right amount of garlic, olive oil, fresh tomatoes, and grated parmesan cheese. That was Kevin's contribution, for sure. And Ben had chopped romaine, cucumber, and red onion for the salad she adored – with lots of Greek olives. A glass of chianti had already been poured, and bread sticks stood up smartly in a narrow glass.

"This is amazing! Thanks, guys! Here's to the chefs!"

"Peter called about an hour ago and told me you'd had a particularly rough day. I think he wanted to make sure you had a chance to relax tonight. Did you hear from Deena?"

"Yes, she sent me a text. I told her she could stay with Dad until Monday, but I wanted her home before dark. She sounded good. She's enjoying getting to know Kitty, whatever that may mean."

"Carol's mom called to see how Deena was doing. She apologized and wanted to know if there was anything she could do. Apparently this isn't the first time Carol has done this afternoon cocktail hour."

"Why in heaven's name don't they keep the liquor locked up, then? I'm not going to be able to talk to her until I've had some time to process all of it."

"That's exactly what I told her. Anyway, let's just have a nice dinner with Ben tonight. He's had a rough couple of days too."

"I'm okay, Dad. Just really glad Dee is okay. This will probably all blow over by next week. There was no more tweeting about it this afternoon, anyway. It's not that big of a deal."

After dinner Kevin and Jenny carried a glass of wine out to the back garden. The moon was up, big and orange, as they sometimes are in the fall. Jenny reached for Kevin's hand – "We've really been putting you through it, haven't we?"

"Now that you mention it. But we are in it together, and that's what I care about. I hope we can all slow down a bit and recover. I think your mom's death has been hard on the rest of us, too. Sometimes it takes a while to realize that."

"I know. And I'm not sure going on retreat was the best idea for me, either. Especially since we never had time to process the idea as a family, even though it was six months ago. I'm sorry, now, that I left."

"Well, you're here now. And that's what matters." He pulled her close and gave her a kiss.

"Let's go up to bed, Kevin. I'm tired. Let's have one of our early nights," and she kissed him back.

They hadn't made love for a long time; at least not like they did that night. It was getting to know each other again from a different place, from a different perspective. Kevin was a good lover. He was gentle and patient, and she found herself responding with the kind of passion she thought had left their marriage long ago. Or was it that she had left? Jenny realized how much of herself she had locked away when her mother died. Or was it even before that? Trust took courage, and she needed to trust before she could love. Tonight she felt safe, protected. And yes, courageous.

They fell asleep in each other's arms.

Chapter 40

THE DRIVE back from the storage unit was complicated by a few lane closures and was taking longer than they expected.

Kitty sighed and looked at Jack. "Thanks so much for being willing to bring all this stuff back to your house. I hope we can put it somewhere out of the way until I can go through it."

"I thought about that. Lily's car is in the garage. We can move that out to the driveway. Your things should fit easily in the space. And, I always keep the garage locked, so it should be secure."

"How am I ever going to repay you, Jack? I'm so much in your debt already. And you have other problems. Deena has real concerns about her mom and dad. Isn't that something that should take precedent over me and my problems?"

"Kitty – I have rarely been as happy as I've been since you've been staying with me. You're good company. And you have been more than helpful with all the sorting and cleaning! Please, let's not talk about repayment. I am grateful you're here. And I think Deena may have opened up to you more than she has to me. Even though she doesn't really know you well, she trusts you. That's good for her, too."

Kitty smiled "She's a great kid, Jack. And she seems to know quite a bit about what's trending with people interested in mid-century items. After I unpack a few boxes and find my computer, I'm hoping I can set up something on the internet to market some of that stuff. You'd be surprised how much money people are willing to spend. That way I can contribute more than just sorting and cleaning."

"Good plan. Now, what shall we fix for dinner? Unless the kid surprises us and has already made a plan! I suppose we'll just have to wait and see."

DEENA CLOSED her book and stretched. Should she be worried? It seemed like they should have been home by now.

She wandered out to the kitchen and thought about starting dinner. Should I do that? Would Grampa mind? He's fussy about the kitchen, and I know I can be a messy cook. But, if I'm careful, it might be a nice surprise for them.

The refrigerator had a big selection of fresh vegetables, some cheddar cheese, and a package of ground turkey. Maybe she could make that rice casserole with the turkey, chopped peppers and onion, tomato sauce and garlic. That was easy, and filling. She found the tomato sauce and a can of black olives in the pantry. The turkey was just beginning to brown, and she was chopping vegetables when Jack and Kitty walked in.

"Smells great! What're we having?" Jack picked up the empty meat container and put it in the trash.

"I hope you don't mind – I thought I'd make a casserole that mom used to make for us. It will be about another hour before it's ready. I think she called it Texas Hash."

"Oh my god – I remember that! Your grandmother found that recipe in one of her magazines when your mom was a teenager. We used to eat it all the time. As I recall it had a can of tomatoes in it as well as the sauce? Right? Let me see if I have some."

"Come on, Jack, leave the kid alone and let her cook! She looks like she knows exactly what she's doing! We can start unloading the truck." Kitty pulled Jack's shirt sleeve and he followed her out to the truck. "Well, ok, but Deena if you need any help just let me know!"

"Don't worry, Grampa. I'll be fine. I've made this before. It isn't that hard!"

She set the oven to 350 and pulled out a casserole dish. Should she grease it? Well, a bit of butter never hurt. And Grampa was right about the tomatoes – one can of tomato sauce wouldn't be enough liquid to cook the rice.

The onions, garlic, and green pepper went into the frying pan along with the meat. She remembered the onions just needed to be translucent, not browned, before everything went into the casserole and into the oven. She grated the cheese and when that was done, measured out and rinsed the rice. Onion and garlic skins, green pepper seeds and bits of cheese were all over the counter. She'd dropped some rice on the floor. Oh well, she'd clean that up when she was done. Hopefully no one would come back in until she had a chance to do that. Was there supposed to be a lid on the casserole? She thought so – but couldn't find one that fit. She covered the dish with foil and popped it into the oven.

Jack came in just as she was setting the timer. Her back was to him, and he had another image of Lily in the kitchen, surrounded by the same kind of mess. His heart was pounding. He took a deep breath and said, "How's it going?"

"Good! Just got the timer set. Dinner in one hour!" She picked up a sponge and wiped down the counter. "Where's your broom?"

"I'll get it for you." He brought her a dustpan and brush from the back porch.

"There! All clean and tidy! I'll put these back on the porch and go get cleaned up myself."

Jack waited until she had gone to her room before he rinsed down the sink and ran the garbage disposal. Then he got the brush from the porch and swept up several grains of rice she had missed. *Yep, just like her Grandma!*

Chapter 41

Jack's train collection and track took up one side of the garage. Kitty's boxes just barely fit into the other side where Lily's car had been. She decided to open the big wardrobe box first to see what she might want to keep. The rest could go out with the other things Jack was getting rid of. She pulled out some basics – slacks, a few blouses, and a leather jacket. Her underwear and sweaters would be in one of the other boxes. The rest was all cocktail dresses. Most had been chosen by Gray to fit her out in what he considered up-scale quality to go along with his Armani pin stripes and Ferragamo shoes. *God, what a snob he was when it came to clothes. But this all looks so cheap, no matter how much he paid for it.*

She left the beaded, gold lamé and sequined finery in a plastic garment bag.

She hung the garment bag on a hook and started breaking down the box. Something therapeutic about tearing things apart. A gesture towards finality. Like throwing love letters into a fire. God knows there was no love in that relationship. It was convenient, and she liked the lifestyle or at least she thought she did. How long had they been together? Five years? She couldn't remember.

She wondered if he had taken the computer he stored in her apartment. It had information about his liquid assets and tax returns. She had suspected for some time he had been siphoning money out of the business and into his own pockets. Had his wife found out? She may have finally had enough of his neglect and pulled the plug on his free-wheeling lifestyle. The business was hers, after all, at least the biggest share of it. *Oh god what if he had stored some of his drugs there too! Would she come across those in one of her boxes? She remembered a briefcase he carried and often left at the back of a closet. No good thinking about any of that now. Nothing to do about it until I see if it's actually here. Surely, he wouldn't have left it or his computer. Too incriminating.*

"The kid has dinner in the oven, should be ready soon. Wow – you've been working! I'll bring the recycle bin over and we can see how much of that cardboard will fit."

"Great. I think I'll go in and shower, I'm pretty sweaty." She picked up the clothes she was keeping and went into the house, trying to shake off the anxiety that had settled on her like dust.

The pieces from the cardboard wardrobe filled the recycle bin to overflowing. But the trash would be picked up tomorrow. Jack looked at the plastic garment bag hanging on the garage wall. It glittered in the late afternoon sun like a pirate's treasure. What kind of life required those fancy clothes? There was still so much about Kitty he didn't know. Especially her recent past. He wondered what else he might learn as those boxes revealed their contents. Or would she let him help with that? Maybe not. He had plenty to do anyway. With Deena here for the weekend, he needed to focus on her.

Texas Hash lived up to its usual level of comfort food, both tasty and filling. Jack and Kitty had two helpings, and Deena had three.

Jack stacked their dirty plates and took them to the sink. "Hey, how about walking over to the Springs tonight? I think there's usually music on Thursday nights."

"Oh yes please! I haven't been there for ages! Has Grampa taken you there yet Kitty?"

"No – what is 'The Springs', anyway? A bar?"

"No – it's just an outdoor park kind of – where people gather to eat, or sing, or let the kids run around. It's a lot of fun. Some artist did this crazy sculpture made of springs and then put a water pump in so it sounds like running water and rain, too. It's so cool! Please say you want to go!"

"Just let me grab a jacket. Should we take some coffee or something?"

"No, there's always a food truck of some kind with snacks and coffee. We'll be fine. Deena, you grab a jacket too. You did bring one?"

"No – it was hot when I left and I didn't think...."

Kitty said "There's one in the closet in my room. I think it may have been your mom's. I'll get it."

Chapter 42

THE WALK only took fifteen minutes, and by the time they got there the sun was just slipping down behind the mountains. "Damn. I should have thought to bring a flashlight! We'll have to be careful when we go home. No streetlights out this way, that's for sure." Jack guided Kitty and Deena to a table with benches. "You girls want some coffee?"

Kitty asked for decaf, and Deena asked for a churro. She smelled them before she even saw the taco truck. The long, fried sticks of pastry covered with cinnamon and sugar were a favorite.

The music hadn't started yet, but a couple of people with guitars moved towards the fire pit. Deena found herself hoping they would play some of the folk music her parents loved.

As Jack was coming back to the table with the coffees and Deena's churro, his friend Steve came up. "Hey there! Good to see you! Would you like me to make those coffees more 'authentic'? I've got a little something here I would be happy to share." He winked at Kitty and Deena.

"Ladies – this is my friend Steve – Deena you probably remember him. Steve, this is Kitty, Lily's old friend."

"She doesn't look old to me! Hi, there. Good to meet you. Seriously, you want a little tequila in that coffee?"

"Not for me, thanks. Not tonight," Kitty smiled at Steve.

"Me either. But thanks." Jack put his hand over his coffee cup.

"Suit yourself. Maybe we can help them get that fire started, Jack. Doesn't look like they're having much luck."

"Sure." Jack set his coffee down and they walked over to the fire pit.

"That will never burn! Well, and if it does, it's going to smoke us out." He started rearranging the logs. Steve handed him some kindling.

"So...Jack. Some guy came into the Snowbird this morning and passed a picture around, asking if anybody had seen this woman. Said he was a private detective and that her family was looking for her. Looked a lot like your Kitty, there. Said her name was Catherine. You know the whole story here, Jack? Should I be worried about you?"

The fire finally caught. Jack stood up and looked at Steve. "Did anybody recognize the picture?"

"Naw. The picture was one of those professional shots. She was all dolled up. But now that I see Kitty – and Kitty is a nick-name for Catherine – could it be possible?"

"Maybe. But I doubt it. Kitty doesn't have any family, as far as I know. That's why she's here with me. If she had family, she'd be with them. I don't think there's any need to worry, Steve. But thanks for the heads-up anyway. I appreciate your concern."

"Okay – if you say so. Just wanted you to know. So Deena visiting for a while? Is Jenny here too?"

"Just Deena. She drove down – needed a few days away, I guess. I'm glad to have her. Seems like I'm running a boarding house for women! I'd better get back – don't want to leave those two on their own!" He gave Steve's shoulder a quick squeeze and walked back to the table.

After an hour of eclectic guitar music, some better than others, Jack decided it was time to head home. Kitty and Deena agreed – they were both getting cold. The firelight was enough to make their way to the street, but after that it was dark under the trees. And there were peppercorns under foot everywhere, making the going a bit treacherous. Suddenly, Kitty slipped, grabbed Deena's arm, and they both went down. Kitty scrambled up immediately. Jack tried to pull Deena up, but she cried out in pain. "My knee, I twisted my knee! I don't think I can walk!" Tears welled up and she bit her lip, trying not to cry.

"I'll go get some help. Kitty, you stay here with her."

Jack ran back to the fire and found Steve. "Bring your truck around – we need to get Deena home, she's fallen."

"Should we call the paramedics?"

"No, I don't think so. But I can't tell anything out here. Let's just get her home."

Deena was sitting up when they got back, but there was no way she was going to be able to stand and walk. The two men lifted her into the back of the pickup, and Kitty climbed in to help brace her.

When they got her home, Steve carried her into the living room and put her on the couch. Her knee was already swelling, stretching the fabric of her jeans. "You'll need to get out of those jeans before there's any more swelling. Kitty – come help her. Jack and I will get some ice."

Jack followed him into the kitchen. He was almost as pale as Deena, and his hands were shaking as he pulled the ice out of the freezer. "She'll be okay, Jack. She's young, she's tough, and it's probably just a twisted knee. Won't be able to tell anything until the swelling goes down a bit. You got any ibuprofen? That will help with the pain and the swelling."

"In my bathroom."

Kitty helped Deena wiggle out of her jeans, trying not to move the injured knee. Then she covered her with the afghan from the back of the couch. "I'm so cold, Kitty."

"I know, kid. I'll get you something warm to drink. Hang on, you'll feel better soon."

"Do you think I broke anything?"

"Let's see – your leg is out straight. Can you bend it? Just a little?"

"Yeah – but it hurts like hell."

"I think if you can bend it, it's probably not broken. I bet your Grampa will have it checked out to be sure." Kitty went to make some tea.

Steve came back with ice and ibuprofen, and Jack called the paramedics.

"You okay, Jack? You don't look too good. Want some water?" Kitty asked.

"I feel a bit lightheaded. Maybe I should sit down." But before he could lower himself into a chair, he collapsed.

Kitty screamed. Jack's eyes fluttered open, and he said "I'm okay, I'm okay. I think I just fainted."

Chapter 43

KITTY WAS SOBBING as if her heart would break. She took Jack's hand in both of hers and laid her head on his chest.

"Grampa?!" Deena called out. "What happened?"

"It's okay, Dee. I'm okay. The paramedics are on the way. Just stay calm."

"Kitty, weren't you making some tea for Deena? I'd like some too. Help me up, so I'm not lying on the floor when they get here."

She pulled a chair over close and helped Jack get his knees under him and then up into the chair. "I feel like a bloody fool." His color had returned, and his pulse was strong and steady.

"Nobody would call you a bloody fool, Jack. Let me get that tea."

The paramedics had two people to check out instead of one. Deena probably had not broken anything, but they suggested she see a doctor the next day to be sure. In any case, the swelling would have to go down before x-rays could be taken. And that meant ice, rest, compression, and elevation. They wrapped her knee and told her to stay off that leg until a doctor had given her the all clear.

"How am I going to get to the bathroom?" she whispered.

"Crutches – we have some in the ambulance. We'll show you how to use them before we leave."

Jack's vitals all were good, although his blood pressure was a little low. He found that surprising since he had been dealing with an emergency. "Seems like it should be higher than normal, not lower." They suggested he check with his doctor the next day, too.

Deena called Kitty over and asked her to bring her some loose pants or shorts to wear. If the paramedics were going to teach her how to use crutches, she didn't want them to see her in her underwear.

"Sure, kid. I'll find something."

She came back with sweats that were easy to pull on. "Jack you and Steve should make yourselves scarce while I help Deena."

"Come on Jack. Let's go sit on the patio. Bring that tea with you."

STEVE PULLED a jacket off the hook by the door, and made Jack put it on. "Want me to light a fire for you?"

"You know what? Let's go sit in my study and light a fire in there. I think it's just too cold out here right now. For me, anyway."

DEENA LEARNED QUICKLY how to navigate on crutches, and as soon as the paramedics left, made a quick retreat to her bathroom. When she came back out to the living room Kitty had turned on the TV. "Want to watch something? There are a lot of DVDs here – some haven't even been opened. Might take your mind off the pain for a bit?"

"Maybe one of Grandma's favorites – just because I did that with her when I'd come down here. I'm pretty sure there's Sleeping Beauty. Or is that too lame?"

"Sleeping Beauty it is. My daughter loved that one too."

"You have a daughter?"

"Yes – but I haven't seen her in a long time."

"I'm sorry. Will watching the movie make you sad?"

"No. I think it will make me happy, actually. Here's the remote. You can fast forward through the previews if you want. I'm going to make some popcorn. Go ahead and start it when you want. I think I can remember the plot!"

She went to check on Jack before starting the popcorn and found him with Steve in his study. "You two look pretty comfortable! Deena and I are watching a movie. Do you want some popcorn?"

"Not for me. I'm heading out. It's been a big day and a big evening! Thanks, though. See you soon, Jack. Don't forget to check in with your doctor tomorrow."

"I won't. Thanks so much Steve. I'll call you." He smiled at Kitty.

"I think I'll head to bed. I'm exhausted. Deena doing okay?"

"She's fine. They gave her a pair of crutches to use and she's comfortable enough. I'll keep an eye on her, don't worry. You get some rest."

"OK – good night, Kitty."

"Jack – I'm so sorry. I feel like all of this is my fault. I'm the one who grabbed Deena and made her fall. None of this would have happened if it hadn't been for me."

"Accidents happen! Who knows – that slip and fall could have happened even if you hadn't been there! I feel stupid for not bringing a flashlight. I know better. But that kind of thinking is only going to make all of us crazy. Go watch your movie and forget about blame. OK?"

"I'll try. You get some sleep. I'll get the coffee maker ready tonight, like you always do."

When Kitty went back to the living room with popcorn, Deena had fallen asleep. She turned off the TV, locked the front door, leaving a light on in the hallway. Her bedroom was close enough to hear if Deena called out.

Too tired even to brush her teeth, she pulled off her clothes and crawled under the covers. What if Jack had really been ill, what would she have done? What could she do? Where would she go? A loop of worry started an infinity pattern in her head. But exhaustion won out, and she fell asleep.

Jack had a similar loop of his own, only his included the nagging information Steve had brought him at the food truck. Why would a private investigator be snooping around looking for Kitty? What was she hiding? He had to know more. His confidence in himself had been badly shaken tonight. Eventually, he slept. His dreams were full of puzzles he couldn't solve and things he was looking for but could not find.

Chapter 44

THE TRUCK WAS TOO hard for Deena to manage with crutches, so Jack decided to use Lily's car when they went to see the doctor the next morning. She could slide into the back seat and keep her leg elevated.

"Jack, why don't you let me drive? I think it might be best until you've been checked out, don't you?" Kitty asked.

"I'm sure I'm okay, but maybe you're right. Good plan." He handed her the keys.

The swelling was still too severe to get a good x-ray on Deena's knee, but the doctor assured them her ability to bend it meant there was probably no fracture. It would take a few more days of rest and ice before they could be sure. He gave her some gentle range of motion exercises to do and told her to stay off that leg until he could make a more definitive diagnosis. "Come back on Monday. By then the swelling should be down enough to see what we are dealing with. I'll give you a knee brace that may help support and protect the joint. If it becomes uncomfortable you don't have to use it. But ice, rest, elevation are still important. Hope you've got some good reading or TV lined up for the weekend!"

Deena smiled. "I'll be fine."

JACK HAD A BLOOD TEST, and an EKG. The tests did not reveal anything alarming, but the doctor was concerned that his blood pressure was high. "You still taking the medication I gave you to get that blood pressure down?"

"I thought the reason I fainted was because it was too low! And yes, I am taking it."

"Well, even so, it's high now. You've been through a lot over the last year. And I'm sure Deena's fall was pretty alarming. That could be a cause, also. Let's monitor your pressure over the next couple of weeks and see if we need to change your meds. I also want you to start taking B12. I've got some samples here I'll give you. And make sure you are drinking enough water. That can be a cause of fainting – dehydration is serious once we're over a certain age. And it's been hot lately."

"I've got a BP cuff at home I can dig out."

"Use that every other day for a week, once a day, and call the office with your readings. Then we'll see what's next. If you get anything higher than what we've measured today, come on in and see me."

DEENA WAS by herself in the waiting room when Jack came out. "Where's Kitty?"

"She said she had an errand to run. She'll be right back."

Jack sat down and asked Deena what the doctor said. 'Looks like I'll be here a little longer than I'd planned – he wants me back on Monday for an x-ray. The knee is still too swollen, but he doesn't think it's broken. We'll be able to tell on Monday for sure. In the meantime, you're stuck with me."

"I'm glad he thinks it's not broken. We'll have to get out the Monopoly! Or maybe watch all those movies we've got. I'm happy to have you here, kid. Really. We had better call your mom when we get back and let her know what's going on. Wouldn't be surprised if she came and got you, but I hope she'll wait until we know more on Monday before she does that."

"I know. I hope she will too. I'm enjoying a little break, and I would bet she is too." She put her hand on his arm, and said, "Umm -- Grampa I think a friend of mine is planning to come down on Sunday to see me. I hope you don't mind."

"No! Of course not! Somebody special?"

"Just a friend. But it is a guy. He goes to Cal Poly, and is taking a semester off to work in L.A. I think you'll like him. He's studying architectural engineering."

"I'll look forward to meeting him!" He patted her hand. "Wonder what this errand of Kitty's is? How long has she been gone?"

Jack got up and looked out the window into the parking lot. "She left when I came out, so it hasn't been long, Grampa. Are you worried? You look worried. How are YOU by the way? What did the doctor say?"

"I'm fine. Just have to monitor my blood pressure for a while and see if he needs to change my medication. Gotta drink more water, too! And take these B12 vitamins. Seems strange, but I'll do what he says! Never thought vitamins really did anything."

He started to pace, looking out the window every few seconds. When he saw the car pull into the lot, he breathed a sigh of relief. "See? I told you she wouldn't be long! Don't you trust her, Grampa?"

"Of course I do! Just a little nervous, I guess." Did he trust her? Really?

"Come on, let's go out there so she doesn't have to come in."

Deena pulled herself up on her crutches with his help, and they went to meet Kitty.

"You can let me drive. I'm fine. Where did you go?"

"Don't like my driving, huh? Or is it you don't like a woman driving you around?!" she winked at him.

"No no it's not that. Just don't like to put you out..."

"Well you ARE putting me out of the driver's seat! But okay, I don't want to rob you of your masculinity!" and she smiled at Deena. "I went to get the results of my lab work, remember?"

"I'd forgotten about that. Of course. Everything okay?"

"Yes – my numbers are good. She thinks I may have been dehydrated, which put my kidney function out of whack. More fluids, I guess. And limited alcohol, sadly.... How about you?" Kitty had told him enough. He didn't need to know all the details. At least not yet.

"I'm fine. I need to monitor my pressure for the next two weeks and drink more water. We'll be floating! Let's go get some lunch. I'm hungry."

They were early for lunch, and the Snowbird was almost deserted. Finding a place for Deena to sit so she could elevate her leg wasn't a problem.

Jack had forgotten that this was the place where an investigator was asking about Kitty, but it was too late to go anywhere else now. And was it likely the P.I. would come around again if no one was able to help the first time? He hoped not.

"I should call mom and let her know what's happened. She

won't be happy about me having to stay past Monday." Deena looked worried.

"If she wants you home, they can come and get you. But I don't see any reason you can't stay here. We'll keep you entertained. Let's see what she says." Jack patted her hand.

"Did you pick up a charger for my phone? I'd like to be able to text my friends."

"It's in the glove compartment of the truck. I forgot to bring it in yesterday. We'll hook you up the minute we get home."

Jack and Kitty ordered hamburgers, Deena chose an Asian Chicken salad with mandarin oranges and green onion. Kitty excused herself to use the restroom just as a man walked in and spoke to the waitress. He showed her a picture and she shook her head. Then he approached Jack and Deena.

"I have a client looking for a relative who went missing over the last week." He showed them his ID. "Her name is Catherine Somers." He pulled out a picture.

Jack took it and held it so Deena couldn't see it. "No, I don't recognize her. Sorry." He handed the picture back, turned face down. "And this young lady doesn't live here, she's just visiting from Los Angeles. This is the first time she's been out of the house since she got here."

Deena bent down to retrieve one of her crutches that had slipped to the floor.

"I'll leave my card. If you do see her, or anyone resembling her, please give me a call. She has her family pretty worried."

"Will do. Hope you find her!" Jack slipped the card into his pocket.

Kitty came out of the restroom just as the door was closing behind the investigator.

"What's up? You look like you've seen a ghost!" she slipped into the booth beside him.

"Nothing. Just some guy looking for a missing person."

"Oh. Is it a kid?"

"No, it's a woman. I told him I hadn't seen her."

The waitress brought the burgers and salad. Jack noticed that she looked at Kitty as she put her plate down. A flicker of confusion passed over her face, and then she looked at Jack, raising an eyebrow.

Jack ignored the raised eyebrow and picked up his burger. "Where's Jess today?"

"Her mom's sick. She'll be gone for a few days."

"That's too bad. If you talk to her, tell her I'm thinking about her."

"Will do."

So it really was Kitty this guy was tracking. It wouldn't be too long before he found someone who had seen her with him in the grocery store or the clinic, and they would track her down. He had to get more information about what was really going on.

Chapter 45

DEENA'S TEXT came through to Jenny's phone as she was getting ready to go out with Kevin for the evening. Ben was going camping with a friend, so they were taking the opportunity to have a real date.

Hi mom. Letting you know that I had a little accident and managed to sprain my knee. I'm ok, don't worry, but the doctor says I won't be able to drive for several days. Need to get an x-ray on Monday after the swelling goes down. Grampa and Kitty are taking good care of me. Call you later. Love you, Deena

Jenny was not one to wait for a call later. She picked up the phone and punched in Deena's number. It went to voicemail. Then she called her Dad. He picked up and before he could even say hello, Jenny was shouting "What happened? Is Deena okay? What does she mean she 'had a little accident?' What's going on?"

"Hey hey – she's okay, really! She's fine. We were walking home from the Springs last night after dark, and she slipped and twisted her knee. She saw a doctor today and he checked her out. They can't get an x-ray until the swelling has gone down, so we'll take her in again on Monday. We are taking good care of her, Jen. How are you?"

"I was pretty good until I got Deena's message. Let me talk to her."

"Sure. Hold on. She's watching a movie with Kitty. I'll take the phone to her."

He handed the phone to Deena. "It's your mom." Deena grimaced.

"Hi mom."

"So are you really okay? I think we should come get you and have you checked out here at home. Dad and I can be there in a couple of hours."

"No, really, don't rush down here. I'm fine. The swelling is going down, and I'm doing everything I'm supposed to do, which isn't much. Rest, ice, and elevation is what the doctor said. And that's all that can be done right now. I'm having a good time with Grampa and Kitty. I'll be fine until I can drive home next week."

"How are you watching a movie? I thought Grampa had put the TV in the storage shed along with the DVD player."

"Oh, everything is different here now, mom. Things have been cleaned out and furniture has been rearranged – it's great. You're going to love it. The TV is in the living room so we all can watch it. Kitty has been helping Grampa sort things out and move things around. She's great at organizing."

"Really. Well I guess I'll see for myself when I get down there. You sure you're okay? Because Dad and I can come down right away. Ben's going camping with Lenny's family, so we could stay over and bring you home in the morning."

"No! Don't do that! I think Mike is going to come visit tomorrow or Sunday, so he can see for himself that I'm okay and report back if you want."

"I'm not sure I trust MIKE to report back!"

"He's a good guy, mom. If it weren't for him I'd have been much sicker the other night. Once you have a chance to meet him, you'll see."

"Let me talk to Grampa again. I'll talk to you in the morning. Keep that ice going!"

"I will. 'Bye mom."

She handed the phone to Jack.

"We're all fine, here, Jenny. Don't fuss. Deena's a big girl now, and she's following doctor's orders. Since I know you're wondering, she's eating well and we are keeping her comfortable."

"If you're sure. But please call me if she wants to come home and we'll work something out. Next week is dicey for me. I've got a crisis at work to deal with, so it might be hard to leave. We could come this weekend, though."

"All the more reason to leave her with us. We aren't going anywhere next week, and we'd love to have her stay until she can drive. If she really wants to come home, her friend could drive her this weekend and you could come collect the car when it's convenient."

"That's true. I'll call tomorrow and see how things are going. Kevin and I are going to get something to eat, but I'll have my cell with me."

"Enjoy your evening out. We'll talk tomorrow."

Kevin heard her end of the phone call and asked what the comment about Mike meant.

"Apparently he's going down there to visit her this weekend."

"And how is she? She in a lot of pain?"

"No. But she has to keep her weight off of that leg until they can x-ray it on Monday."

"I take it she doesn't want us to pick her up."

"No, she's having a very good time, in spite of a twisted knee. Seems hard to believe. She says the place looks very different. Kitty has been helping Dad sort through stuff and rearrange furniture. Interesting he'd take HER help, but didn't want us to give him a hand."

"Yeah – that is interesting. She must be more persuasive – and maybe she feels she owes it to him since he is letting her stay there. I'm curious about what her 'problem' is, aren't you?"

"Of course I am! If I didn't have so much going on at work I'd go down there and see for myself. But I've got a facility off-line, and a report to write for the Board of Directors meeting on Friday."

"I'd go, but I think Ben needs one of us to be available next week. So we will have to trust Deena and wait and see. Hard, I know."

Jenny picked up her purse and sweater. "Let's go eat. I'm starving, and I need a drink. And I feel guilty about that, especially given what happened to Deena."

"Hey – YOU didn't force Deena to drink too much. Let's just go have a nice dinner and relax a bit. You do deserve that!"

Chapter 46

THEY DECIDED to drive up the coast to a restaurant on the beach. It was crowded, so they settled in at the bar to wait for a table. "You really trust this Mike guy who's driving down to see Deena?"

"He seems like a nice kid, Jen. He did the best thing, in my opinion, to keep Deena safe. He called today to see if we had heard from her. And in every other instance, Deena has been like a rock. Everybody can make mistakes, and it's about time she made a few."

"I hate that she's there with that Kitty person. We know nothing about her – don't even know her last name! I never heard mom talk about anybody named Kitty. I keep wondering if she's a sneaky con-artist who plays on widowers. They do exist, you know."

Kevin laughed. "Your dad is hardly likely to be taken in by somebody like that. You don't really think that's possible, do you?"

"I don't know. He married mom, and that wasn't exactly a good choice in the end, was it? She was pretty, but also unstable. Bipolar into the bargain. And almost a certifiable hoarder. I don't know how he did it for all those years."

"If he hadn't made that choice, I wouldn't have you and the kids. I'm not going to say I think it was a bad bargain. And I don't think he would, either. They had some good years, as well as a lot of tough ones. I think he was as happy as he could have been."

"I always felt if I'd had the chance for even a little while, I could have made him happy too. But he was always pushing me away. We were close when I was little, but when I started high school mom really started acting weird. It was like she was jealous of me – her own daughter! Things went south after that." She sighed. "You know that whole story, anyway. No need to retell that one."

"No. No need. Our table is ready – let's go eat. I asked for a corner booth by the window. Should be nice to watch the sun go down."

They settled in and ordered the sampler platter of shrimp, mussels, crab, and calamari. Ben ordered an expensive bottle of champagne. The ocean went from sky blue to navy, and then it was so dark all they could see was white foam as the waves broke over the rocks on the shore, until the moon came up and made a ribbon of light on the water.

"Dad used to love this place. He and mom came here all the time. I wonder if he misses the ocean?"

"Maybe. But he seems happy where he is. And it really isn't THAT far from the coast if he's willing to drive. Laguna Beach is what, an hour away?"

"No – it's more like two hours. I think if he drove that far he'd want to stay overnight somewhere. When they lived in the Valley the beach was never more than twenty minutes away – well, half an hour."

"Are you still hungry? Want to order something more? Dessert?" Kevin motioned the waiter over.

"I'd like a glass of chardonnay too."

They lingered over dessert and coffee. Jen watched the moon on the water, and Kevin watched Jen. She prided herself on keeping calm and cool, but he could tell she was full of a deep sadness. She would have to unpack all that emotion on her own terms, and in her own time.

Chapter 47

CARLIN HAD LEFT EARLY, and by the time they thought of going out to check on his progress, it was too dark to see much. It would all still be there in the morning, in any case. Dinner was next. Jack threw together some vegetarian chili. Kitty grated the cheese, and Deena sat at the kitchen table and chopped some red onion.

"Mom says eating in front of the TV makes you fat." Deena said, putting more cheese into her bowl of chili. "Do you think that's true?"

"I think eating too much makes you fat. If you let your body tell you when you've had enough, you aren't going to do that." Kitty reached for more chips. "And right now my stomach is telling me I need more of these....."

Jack laughed. "What are we watching tonight?" He had already set up three tv tables in the living room and was filling his own bowl from the steaming pot on the stove. "Let me carry that for you Deena."

"You'll have to! No way can I walk and carry. Stand and fill up my bowl, but not walk and carry."

"We are going to watch 'An Affair to Remember' with Cary

Grant and Deborah Kerr, and you, Jack, are going to watch it with us!"

"If I must. You ladies have obviously made up your minds. Is that the one where they meet on board ship?"

"Yes. But Deena hasn't seen it yet, so don't say any more about it."

They made Deena comfortable on one end of the couch. Kitty sat on the other end, and Jack pulled up a chair next to Kitty.

The credits rolled, and Jack remembered that this was a movie about fidelity and faith, trust, and choices. Was he making the right choice keeping Kitty here, keeping her whereabouts a secret? Should he contact the investigator or let her tell him what was going on? Until today he hadn't given much thought to possible circumstances. And she hadn't given him any reason to distrust her; but neither had she given him much information about her circumstances. He was beginning to think he was entitled to a bigger window into her life. Maybe after Deena went to bed, they could have a nightcap on the patio and he could get her to tell him more. He wanted desperately to believe that she was someone who had come into his life for good. And he wanted desperately to trust her. His life had started to take on color for the first time in a long time. He looked forward to working on the farmhouse and making it a home for her if that's what she wanted. And he looked forward to making her a part of his life.

On the screen, Cary Grant was greeted at the dock by the press, and Deborah Kerr was making her way to her boyfriend who was waiting for her. Were they destined to meet again – have a life together? Or would this be the beginning of the end? Deena looked worried. Kitty looked sad.

Jack picked up the dishes and carried them to the kitchen,

returning with a bowl of fruit and a bar of chocolate. "Shall I make popcorn?"

"Not for me – my stomach is telling me all it wants is some of this chocolate." Kitty reached for it.

"Not for me either. My stomach just wants one of those oranges AND some chocolate. Thanks, though, Grampa."

Jack sat through the rest of the movie, watching it with half of his mind on how to get Kitty to reveal more of her story. Was she keeping secrets to protect him or to protect herself? It made a difference. Did she know which it was? Maybe both were true. But he knew he couldn't rest until he had the whole picture. The pieces she had given him weren't enough. And her own admission that she had run away from things in the past made him uneasy. He knew about background checks, but that seemed a dirty trick if he was wanting to build a solid relationship. He would give her more time, but he did need to let her know someone from her past was looking for her. That was only fair.

"I HATE it that she had to wind up crippled! Why did they have to put that in? Was the author trying to punish her for being unfaithful to her first boyfriend? I don't get it." Deena crumpled up the napkin she'd used to dry her eyes and blow her nose.

"I think we have to remember that movie was made in the 1950's and people were still pretty conflicted about loyalty and one-true-love stuff." Kitty was crumpling her own napkin. "Morality was a little different, at least as they showed it in the movies. Black and white, right and wrong, were absolutes. In a way, I think this movie pulled some people into a more compassionate space."

Deena struggled up off the couch. "Anyway, I'm tired. Thanks for everything Grampa – and Kitty. I'll see you in the morning."

"You need any help getting ready for bed, kid?" Kitty asked.

"No – I'm just going to brush my teeth and pull on my pj's. See you in the morning."

Chapter 48

KITTY WENT OUT to the kitchen and loaded the dishwasher. Jack went to get a bottle of wine from the refrigerator in the garage. When he came back in, he showed Kitty the label. "Want to have a glass out on the patio?"

"Yes I do. Let me get a sweater or something, it's probably cooling off. I'll see you out there. You going to light a fire?"

"Of course!" He put the wine on a tray with glasses, the corkscrew, and a bowl of roasted almonds.

By the time Kitty joined him, the fire had caught and he had poured the wine. She looked so pretty – she'd brushed her hair and put on some lipstick – and her shawl did bring out the incredible blue of her eyes. She was a different person from the one he had picked up by the side of the road just a short time ago.

"This will probably go straight to my head, it's been so many days since I've had anything!"

"I'll keep an eye on you and make sure you don't lose that pretty head."

"You do remember that in the past I have made rather a mess of my life with alcohol."

"A lot of people do that. But sometimes, people can still enjoy a glass or two and not mess up anything. It is a matter of temperance, for some, not abstinence. And I know that from my own experience."

"Oh?"

"My life has often overwhelmed me. And alcohol seemed to give me a little break from the turmoil. But too much, too many times, made things so much worse. I learned to manage, balance, and so far that's worked for me. You know, you can have a slice of cake, but you don't have to eat the whole thing. Like you were saying before dinner, listen to your body. For me, that works."

"I've always been around people who encouraged me to eat 'the whole cake,' and sometimes order another one! It's hard when your friends and companions are taking it to the next level, to stay behind."

"Then maybe you just need new friends and companions."

"Maybe. Probably." The fire popped, made a bright flame, then settled. "Are you my friend, Jack?"

"I hope so. I do care about you, Kitty. And I hope we can be completely honest with one another." He poked at the fire, rearranging the logs. "I want to hear more about what brought you to this place in your life. And, because I need to be completely honest with you, I need to let you know that the guy in the restaurant was looking for you."

"Ah. I thought something was shifting. Why did he say he was looking for me?"

"He said your family was worried about you."

"Well, that's not true. The only family I have is my daughter, and she's been out of the picture for so long there is no way it could be her. She stays in touch with her father, and her father certainly doesn't stay in touch with me."

"So who, then, could be looking for you?"

"Probably that guy I used to work for, Gray. It's not a story I am up to telling tonight, Jack. But I admit that it was not a good relationship, not an honest one. He was never really interested in who I was, what I thought, what I wanted. It was a matter of what I could do for him, and on my side – what he could do for me. I am certainly not proud of being drawn into the relationship for either of those reasons."

"We'll let it go for now, then. But I hope you will feel comfortable enough to tell me something about it soon."

"Yes. Soon. I will tell you the whole, sordid story. Soon."

They watched the fire, sipping their wine, one of them full of questions, the other full of misgivings.

Deena's window was open to let in the cool evening air. Their voices carried with the smoke of the fire. She heard enough of the conversation to understand Kitty was not who her Grampa had led her mother to believe. Another piece of the puzzle, perhaps, but it didn't make the picture any clearer. Yet he seemed to trust her – or did he? Those moments in the doctor's office waiting for her to return had obviously worried him, and his sigh of relief when she got back seemed to confirm that.

Deena was usually a pretty good judge of people, but Kitty confused her. She was so likable, so helpful, and obviously not afraid of hard work. It wasn't really her problem; her Grampa could take care of himself and it sounded like he was pressing Kitty for more details about her past. That was a good thing. People who care about each other shouldn't have secrets, at least not important secrets.

THE FIRE WAS BARELY PERCEPTIBLE – Jack put on another log and made sure it caught. He sighed, and said, "I don't mean to press you for more information than you are ready to share, but may I ask just a few questions? I don't need any sordid, as you say, details. Just a few basics. OK?"

"I'll try."

"Gray? That's who is looking for you?"

"Probably. He may be looking for information he used to keep in the apartment that could implicate him in some questionable business practices. I didn't ask too many questions because I wasn't directly involved and I didn't want to know. He's the Gray Carmichael you see on billboards all over Riverside – owns a string of automobile showrooms."

"What was your job?"

"I guess you really <u>do</u> need to talk about this tonight. Okay – but may I have another glass of wine?" Jack filled her glass.

"He called me his personal assistant. Those duties mainly turned out to be social, and very personal, as it happened. I had started out as a bookkeeper, but that didn't last long. He was an opportunist, and so was I, I guess. I'm not proud of what I did. He set me up in a very nice apartment and made sure I always had a new car to drive. I had made such a mess of my life I was grateful for his attentions. I was always available on a moment's notice for "business" weekends with some of his cronies and clients. He made sure I had a line of credit for clothes and paid me a salary that was enough to feed me and pay for incidentals. I was still listed on the books as an employee, but I never went to the office."

"So, he isn't married?"

"Oh yes, he is married! But it's not the kind of marriage most people have. She's older than he is by about fifteen years. Her father owned the business before Gray came into the picture. Gray started in sales, and he was very good at that. Went right to the top. Eventually he married the boss' daughter and inherited a sizable share of the business. There are some strings to the inheritance, however. She gets everything if they divorce. As it is, she owns more than half the stock in the company. The marriage is for show. She's not interested in the business at all. And, until recently, she never cared what Gray got up to. She knew he was unfaithful. I wasn't his first."

"Something must have changed, though, if he fired you and left you in a homeless shelter!"

"Oddly enough, I don't care. Whatever brought me here, it was worth it." Her voice was tentative, soft, barely a whisper.

Jack poured a little more wine into her glass and refilled his own. The fire was almost out. He got up to add another log, and when he looked back at Kitty her face was wet with tears. "Yes. You are here, now. Don't cry, Kitty – we'll figure this out. There's a lot of life ahead for both of us." He squatted down in front of her and took her face in his hands. "Let's build it together."

"I feel like I've been spoiled, though, Jack. I'm not good enough for you. You have a family, responsibilities to them, and a lifetime of integrity behind you. All I have is a string of failed relationships and involvements that shame me, now."

"Everybody has a past. And not everything in my past is as blameless as it may look to you. But I don't want to live in that past anymore. And I hope you don't want to live in yours, either." He kissed her on the forehead and stood up.

"There are still some things to sort out, obviously, if Gray is searching for you. And I think – I hope -- we can face whatever that is together. You are not alone unless you want to be."

The fire popped, hissed, and sent a shower of sparks upward. "See? That's a sign – things are going to be ok. Let's finish this wine and see what tomorrow brings. I don't think we need to do anything about Gray until Deena has gone home. No need to complicate things. Maybe we can make a little headway with the farmhouse, see if Carlin wants some help."

"Actually, I think I've had enough wine. For the first time in my life! I'll sit here with you while you finish yours."

Chapter 49

CARLIN ARRIVED EARLY the next morning. Jack heard the truck going through to the farmhouse and pulled on some jeans and a sweatshirt. He was eager to see how the restoration was going. The coffee maker had just finished brewing, so he poured a cup and went out through the kitchen. The air was chilly, so cold that the coffee made a cloud of steam as he sipped it. Fall was on the way.

"Hey Jack! Where were you yesterday? I thought you'd be checking up on me!"

"We had some errands to run. Deena had a fall Friday night and we had to take her to the doctor – she did a number on her knee, poor kid. She's okay, but hobbling around on crutches for awhile. So, fill me in – bring me up to date with our project!"

"The plumbing and electrical work are finished. Went quicker than we thought. I was going to fix the double-hung windows – but wanted to ask you if you would rather replace them with new ones instead. Won't look quite the same, but they will give the place better protection from the weather."

"Since none of the glass is broken, let's just repair the old ones. I like the original look, and I know those new ones just won't be the same."

"Okay, you got it! I have to hand it to your grandfather; he really was a good craftsman."

"When he wanted to be. I wish he'd taken the same kind of care with detail in the big house. Kitty and I thought we might give you some help here today if you'll let us. Maybe just start cleaning up a bit? Deena can sit and watch if she wants. She's so excited about this place."

"You can help me with the windows – really need two people to do that, anyway. I was going to ask Charlie to come over, but if you're up for it, that's great. As long as the girls stay out of our way, they can do whatever they like."

Deena and Kitty were just finishing breakfast when Jack returned. He picked up an orange and started to peel it. "Carlin says you girls can come out and look around – see if you want to start some cleanup. Deena you can't do much, but you can supervise if you'd like."

"I want to see what's happened so far. Probably best for me to come back to the house though, and continue with the rest-ice-elevation thing. I think the swelling has gone down quite a bit, and I'd like to make sure that continues."

"Why don't you wait until this afternoon, then. Kitty and I will go. I'm going to work with Carlin on the windows. Maybe after lunch I can drive you out there so you won't have to crutch it. The ground is pretty uneven."

Kitty was already dressed in jeans and a t-shirt and had a bucket of cleaning supplies organized. She handed Jack the broom and said, "I'm ready when you are!"

"Let me finish this orange and have another cup of coffee. You go ahead – I'll bring the broom when I come."

"Oh, I can carry it!" She took it back from him. "See you in a bit."

Jack sat down at the table with Deena and picked up a bagel. "Don't you want to toast that Grampa?"

"No – I'll just put a little cream cheese and jam on it and be good to go. Need to have something in my stomach when I take my blood pressure meds. How are you feeling? Is the pain going away as well as the swelling?"

"Yes, thank god. I've been doing a few of those exercises the doctor suggested, and I think that's helping too." She stretched out her leg and bent her knee three times. "See?"

"Excellent! Keep that up and you'll be running around here good as new!"

"So, Grampa, I heard you and Kitty out on the patio last night before I went to sleep. I only caught a few things she said, but it sounded to me like she isn't who you told us she was. She never knew Grandma at all, did she?"

Jack looked at her thoughtfully. "Wow. You heard quite a bit I guess. No, she's not who I said she was. And I don't like to lie, but it seemed harmless, when I first said it. She was someone in trouble, and I wanted to help. It has been a long time since I could look outside of myself and see someone else's pain. And although I still have plenty of questions about how she got into the situation she's in, I want to help her. I knew your mother wouldn't approve. She had so much grief over your Grandma's death – and I can't fix that for her. She puts some of her pain on me, telling me how worried she is, how I shouldn't be alone out here. Maybe this is one way I can at least put some of those worries to rest, too. If Kitty decides to rent the farmhouse, I won't be all alone out here. And she's good company, we work well together."

"Are you in love with her Grampa?"

"Whoa -- I'm still not really sure who she is. I need a lot more time to figure out the answer to that question! I've come to care about her, and I think she cares about me. But that's about all I know right now. I want to be sensible. Too many people rush into relationships without taking some time to be sure."

"Did that happen with you and Grandma?"

"That's a long, long time ago – and a long, long story. We were both so young. And infatuation can be a powerful drug. I don't regret marrying her. Our life together wasn't always easy, as I'm sure you remember. But it was a good life. And we did truly love each other. Maybe, in part, because things weren't easy. She was ill a good deal of the time, one way or another."

"I think mom still has a lot of work to do figuring out the relationship she had-- or didn't have --with Grandma. She doesn't talk about it much, but sometimes something will slip out and I can tell she's still confused, not really at peace, even though Grandma is gone."

"That probably makes it even harder. Can't fix a relation-ship that doesn't exist anymore – but maybe she will come to some understanding one day. I hope so."

Jack poured himself a glass of water and took his medica-tion. "I hope you can give me some time to sort this out before you tell your mom what you've learned about Kitty. I don't ask that you lie for me, but just maybe don't volunteer any informa-tion she doesn't have. Is that fair for me to ask?"

"Of course. And I don't want to cause mom any more worry than I have already over the last few days."

Deena pulled herself up from the table and went into the living room. She settled herself on the couch with her phone and her book. She had a text message from Mike.

How are you doing? Still think it's okay for me to come down for a visit tomorrow? I could be there around noon.

She texted back with a big thumbs up, and the address. It would be nice to have Mike here. She wanted to introduce him to Grampa and Kitty. There was something about letting them meet him first, before her mom, that gave her a little frisson of satisfaction. There was nothing to hide, no relationship beyond friendship, but it felt like something separate, something grown-up about her own choices and how her life might be from now on. People needed to learn how to make good choices, even when they were as old as her Grampa. He knew that, and she felt pretty sure he wouldn't make a decision that would be foolish or hurtful to any of them. And yet, there was a little bit of uncertainty lurking in the corners of her mind. What was it she'd heard? Oh yeah – there's no fool like an old fool – but her Grampa surely wasn't one of those.

Chapter 50

"Where can I start in here, Carlin?" Kitty wanted to make sure she wasn't in his way.

"We'll be working in the living area today, and if we have time we'll move to the bedrooms. So you can tackle the kitchen area. Lots of spider webs and dust in there. The bathroom tile is still setting. The sink, toilet, and tub are a dead loss. I just put those in my truck for a trip to the dump. So you'll need to think about what you want in there. Might have something from another job where they were upgrading. Is Jack coming out soon?"

"He'll be on his way in a minute. He was just finishing breakfast when I left."

There wasn't much beyond sweeping and removing cobwebs that could be done in the kitchen. They needed to decide on a countertop and sink. She thought a cabinet of some kind might work, with a drop-in sink. There wasn't a lot of space. But cooking for one didn't require a lot of space. And the top of the built-in drawers on the other side of the room would provide a place for electric appliances.

The work was satisfying. She felt as if she were cleaning up her life as well as a living space. Would that space be hers to use? That remained to be seen. There was still so much Jack didn't know about the mess she'd left behind. Whether or not he could be accepting of all of that would be a question for another day. But for this day, she was feeling good about the work she was doing, good about seeing what could be made of an abandoned building, making it something useful and beautiful again. Could she do that with herself? Or was she too old to change direction, change old habits? That would unfold day by day, minute by minute.

She stepped out onto the porch where Jack was helping Carlin with one of the windows. He smiled at her. "You've got cobwebs in your hair! You look like something out of a fairytale!"

"The wicked witch?"

"No, more like the fairy godmother!"

"I'm going up to the house for some lunch. I'll see if Deena's hungry. Do you want me to fix you something?"

"Sure. Anything you can find. I'm going to need to do another shopping this afternoon – especially if we are having company tomorrow."

"Anything I can get you, Carlin?"

"Nah. I'm good."

The weather was cooler than it had been, but still simmered with the residue of summer heat. The pepper berries gave off a sharp smell, barely there, but enough to mark their presence. Kitty walked through a swarm of tiny gnats, batting them away and moving as fast as she could without slipping. By the time she reached the house she had accumulated not only cobwebs, but a few gnats and leaves in her hair. It was a very different collection from the one she had brought out of storage yesterday, which was waiting for her attention in the garage.

"Hey Kid! You hungry? I'm fixing some lunch," said Kitty, washing her hands at the kitchen sink.

Deena came out to the kitchen and smiled. "You building a nest in your hair?"

"Your Grampa told me it was full of cobwebs! Guess I'd better set it straight. Be right back. Can't wait to show you the progress on the farmhouse!"

"Can't wait to see it!"

———

CARLIN AND JACK finished the windows in the living area and decided to break for lunch. It had taken them all morning to do just two, but now that room was done. "You planning to paint in here? I've got a couple of guys finishing up on another project, and I could send them over. They're fast – and careful. If you're not picky about colors, we could use what's left from the other job. Most of it's pretty neutral."

"I'm not picky – but Kitty might be. Let's ask her."

"You got something going on there, Jack?"

"Naw – nothing like that. I barely know her. Just trying to help out a friend. But, if she's going to rent the place for a while, might as well let her be happy with the color of the paint. What did you find out about the fireplace?"

"The chimney is solid. Needs to be swept out, but that's easy enough. Like I said, I'd get an insert to make the heat more efficient. The hardware store downtown has a few marked down. You should look in there, might get a good deal. We could slip one of those in there and you wouldn't have to worry about chimney fires or cracks in the bricks. Could even run a gas line for gas logs, if you ever wanted to do that."

"I'll think about it. But no gas line. I love a real wood fire."

"They may not be allowing them much longer – for new homes, anyway. Sad. I love a good wood fire too."

"I've got to do some shopping this afternoon. I'll look at what they've got. Can you manage out here on your own?"

"I think I'm going to call Charlie to help me. You're help was great, but Charley is fast – he does this stuff all the time. No offense."

Jack laughed. "Let me know if you need anything at the hardware store. I'll check with you before I leave."

"Okay."

Carlin walked to his truck and Jack went back to the house for lunch.

Chapter 51

DEENA FINISHED HER READING, checked her e-mail and text messages. She felt hot and sticky and wanted to clean up before dinner. She dragged a plastic stool from the pantry into the bathroom so she could sit on it in the shower. Planning every move carefully, she managed to get clean and even washed her hair. But by the time she was finished, she was exhausted. Thankfully she had thrown clean underwear, shorts, and a few tank tops into her overnight bag. She sat on the bed, her head wrapped in a towel, and managed to get herself dressed. Her knee was throbbing. Kitty knocked on the door. "You okay in there? I thought I heard furniture moving around!"

"Come in! I'm fine, just wore myself out taking a shower."

"Can I help with anything?"

"Maybe some ice for my knee. It's really starting to hurt again."

"Sure. You want to stay in here or come out to the living room?"

"I'll stay here and rest a bit, maybe try to do something with my hair."

Kitty brought her an ice pack and a glass of water. "You might want to take some more ibuprofen."

"Yeah – I will. Thanks."

Deena leaned back against the pillows, and was almost immediately asleep. When Kitty checked on her half an hour later the ice pack was on the floor. She pulled a blanket over Deena, picked up the ice pack, and closed the door as quietly as she could. *Poor kid. She's been through a lot over the last few days. No wonder she's exhausted.*

JACK HAD RETURNED from the market and was putting away the groceries. Kitty came out to the kitchen stretching and yawning, her hair still damp from a shower. "Good grief, Jack, you buy out the store?"

"We'll be feeding company tomorrow, and I wanted to be sure I didn't have to shop again next week."

"Looks like enough for a month!"

"I like to be prepared."

"So I see! Can I help?"

"No, I'm pretty fussy about what goes where."

"Can I at least help start dinner?"

"Where's Deena?"

"She's taking a nap. Wore herself out taking a shower."

"You can wash the lettuce and whatever you want to put in a salad if you like. Get that started. I'm going to barbeque some chicken and make potato salad. Sound good to you?"

"Sure!"

Dinner was almost ready when Deena emerged from her nap.

She'd braided her hair, and she looked about twelve. Jack smiled. "Feeling better?"

"Yes, thanks. And I'm hungry!"

"Good, because dinner is almost ready. You sit here and put that leg up. I'm going to bring in the chicken."

There is nothing like good food to encourage conversation. But even if all that's talked about is what's on the table, it can spark memories of other meals, other family gatherings. Deena remembered the many times her family sat around this table with her Grampa and Grandma. Often the meal was silent, strained, or fraught with her mother trying to contain and direct conversation away from the incoherent and rambling monologue of her Grandma. She was grateful that this meal-time conversation was as comforting as the food, and as delicious. They talked about the farmhouse and the progress being made. Ideas for decorating and furnishing called for paper and pencil. Deena sketched and took notes, between bites of potato salad and chicken. Kitty asked about Mike, and Deena happily described her friend, making sure to emphasize that he was truly "only" a friend. There was no mistaking the sparkle in her eyes when she talked about him, though. Jack looked at Kitty and smiled, she winked back.

Deena picked at what was left of the salad as Jack and Kitty cleared the dishes and loaded the dishwasher. "Shall we watch another movie tonight? I was thinking we might see if there's another old film noir movie. I think mom sent a collection to you, Grampa, didn't she?"

"Yes – she did. And I'm ashamed to say I never even took it out of the box. It's in there with the others. Which movie are you looking for?"

"LAURA with Gene Tierney. I watched it with mom once,

and I love the music. And all the retro furniture and clothes. It's a good story."

"Is that the one with Clifton Webb in the bathtub in the opening scene?" Kitty asked.

"I think so. I'll go see if I can find it."

Jack remembered that movie. It was a murder mystery with Dana Andrews falling in love with the suspected killer. The pieces of that puzzle didn't fall into place until it seemed all hope was lost. He wondered if it really was a good choice. "How about something a little more fun? That's a murder mystery."

"Oh don't be so silly, Jack! Those film noir movies ARE fun to watch! Scowling detectives, rainy Los Angeles, old cars and everybody wearing hats!"

"If you're sure...."

Deena called out from the living room "It's here! I'll cue it up! Can somebody make popcorn?"

Jack looked at Kitty. "She can eat popcorn after all that dinner she put away?!"

Chapter 52

A CAR PULLED into the driveway just as they were settling in front of the T.V. Jack got up and turned on the porch light. Kitty made a very quick exit to her bedroom, whispering to Deena "Gotta use the restroom. Go ahead and start the movie without me."

Deena looked at her and saw fear on her face. Jack went out the front door, closing it behind him. She suddenly felt cold, a nudge of fear in the pit of her stomach. She could hear two voices in the driveway, one of them her Grampa's, but she couldn't make out what they were saying. She pulled herself up and made her way to the window. It was dark in the living room, so they couldn't see her, she hoped. The voices got louder, and it sounded as if they were having an argument. The moon suddenly broke out from behind a cloud, and she saw a tall man in a business suit. He grabbed her Grampa's arm then shoved him away. Jack stumbled back a few steps, then regained his balance. "Look, I don't know who you are, and I don't have any idea what you hope to gain by pushing me around, but I can assure you Catherine does not want to see you."

Deena saw Kitty come down the driveway from the back of the house. She walked up to the man in the business suit and said "He's right, Gray. I don't want to see you, but yet here you are. Why?"

"You don't have to talk to him, Kitty. Go back in the house."

"It's all right, Jack. I can handle him. You go back in the house. I'll only be a minute."

"I don't want to leave you alone with him – I think he's drunk."

"Probably. He usually is about this time of night."

Then Deena saw someone get out of the car. "Come on, Gray. You've found her, you know where she is. Let's go. That's all you said you wanted."

"Oh, no, Frank. I want much more than that! She owes me plenty and she knows it. Right, Miss Kitty?" he grabbed at her, but she moved away and he slipped on the gravel and fell. George helped him up and pushed him towards the car. "I'll be back, Kitty. And next time I'll make sure I get what I want!" Gray yelled over his shoulder.

Frank shoved him into the back seat, got into the driver's seat and backed the car out of the driveway.

Deena had her phone in her hand and snapped a picture of the car as they drove off, hoping she had enough focus to be able to read the license plate.

Jack put his arm around Kitty and led her back to the house. He made sure the door was locked and the deadbolt thrown, then looked at Deena. "Everything's okay, kid. That was a guy who has been giving Kitty some trouble, but we'll get it sorted. He won't be back, not tonight. Why don't you go ahead and watch the movie. I'm going to take Kitty out back so we can talk without disturbing you."

Kitty's face was drained of color, and her Grampa looked

shaken. Deena was worried, and she was scared. "Are you guys really okay? You don't look it."

"Yes. We are. Nothing for you to worry about. He will have passed out by now. He was drunk, and he was high on something. Sorry you had to see all of that. Are you okay?" Kitty put her hand on Deena's shoulder.

"I'm scared. I haven't seen anything like that before – except in the movies."

"Then you are one lucky kid. Something like that happened in my neighborhood every other night when I was a kid."

"How awful for you."

"Well, I'm a survivor. And really, I know this guy. He won't be back. Can't imagine what he thought he wanted from me. He's the one who threw me out. He was off his head with drugs or drink. Let's just watch the movie, kid. He won't be back. Not tonight. Hopefully not ever."

"We are getting you an attorney in the morning. You may need to file a restraining order against this guy. I've got a friend who can advise us." Jack sat down and rubbed his face.

"It isn't your problem, Jack. I need to handle this."

"I know, but sometimes people need help. And I think that this is one of those times. Seriously, Kitty. I insist."

They watched the movie, but before it was over Deena said she was tired, and went to bed. Kitty and Jack sat in front of the TV, neither of them really concentrating on the screen. They wanted to be sure Deena had settled for the night before they went outside to talk.

Jack was used to family drama, but never anything like this. He excused himself, saying he wanted to get the fire going outside. When she went out to join him, he was setting out two glasses of scotch. "I think we might need this tonight."

Kitty couldn't have agreed more.

DEENA HEARD Jack and Kitty talking on the patio, their voices sometimes argumentative. She tried to focus on Mike's visit, and finally drifted off, her dreams surreal and menacing.

"So you think there might be something in those boxes we picked up that Gray wants to recover?"

"I don't know – but I can't think of any other reason he would be so intent on tracking me down. I did know, but not directly, about some of his business deals that were less than straightforward. He kept two sets of tax records, for instance, but if he was worried about anything he was keeping in the apartment, he could have retrieved it before he had it cleared out."

"Maybe he didn't have anywhere to store whatever it was he's looking for now."

"Maybe – but knowing how his mind works, he wouldn't have any trouble finding someplace a lot closer and easier to get to. I'll have to start going through the boxes and see what's there. But not until Deena leaves. I don't want her worried about any of this, or your family dragged into it. Or you, Jack. I should just have it all moved to another storage area away from here, someplace Gray can't find. I've got the money to do that."

They watched the fire and sipped their drinks, both too tired to do much thinking.

"Kitty, I hope you know I will do whatever I can to help you through this. Whatever brought you this misery is behind you – there's a better future ahead." Jack picked up their empty glasses and walked back to the house.

Kitty sat by the fire, watching the dying embers. Jack was right. She could walk into a new future. But he didn't know how many things could pull her back. He didn't know how close she had been to the edge of colluding with Gray's fraud and deception. It might be true that she would be implicated in any number of the schemes Gray had perpetrated to manipulate funds and line his own pockets. He could drag her down with him. Or worse.

The scotch had given her a bit of a buzz. Now she really wanted another drink. She'd have to content herself with water and another valium – she had one or two left. She could think about this mess in the morning. Every time she had an opportunity to make a better life something seemed to knock her off track. Jack was trying hard to help her move in the right direction, but was she able to really believe that was possible? She needed him to stay strong. He looked so tired tonight – how had all this drama affected his blood pressure? And Deena – she was scared. Tomorrow had to be free of any dark drama so they could all think and regain their balance. *I'm good at putting on a bit of a show. I'll get them thinking about the remodel. And Deena has Mike coming. That should take her mind off my problems.* She went into the kitchen for a glass of water and then to the guest room to try and find sleep.

Jack's dreams were full of frustration and loss. He woke after only a few hours and knew that if he didn't make a plan to get Kitty some protection, he wouldn't be able to sleep again that night. He did have a connection with an attorney who specialized in women's rights, one who had run the Women's Center at the University where he taught Anthropology. One of his colleagues, George, was her husband. He wondered if she was still practicing law. She was quite a bit younger than her husband, so it was entirely possible that she was still working even though George had retired. He went to his desk and pulled out an old campus directory. He thought he could try her office number and even though it was the middle of the night, if there was a voice mail that belonged to her, he could leave a message. And then maybe he could get back to sleep, knowing he had at least acted to get some legal advice. The message on her voicemail confirmed it was still her number, so he left a message asking she call him as soon as it was convenient. He sat at the desk, his head in his hands. *Maybe I should get Steve involved. He's retired from the police force. He might have some connections that could tease out more information about Gray..* He took a deep breath, went to the bathroom and took a couple of Tylenol along with an antihistamine. That usually helped him get to sleep when he couldn't turn his brain off.

He could talk to Kitty in the morning about next steps. But he'd need a clear head.

Chapter 53

MIKE WASHED his car and filled the gas tank. He called Kevin and asked if there was anything he could take to Deena.

"Jenny—anything you want to send to Deena? Mike can swing by and pick it up if you do."

"No, I don't think so. She hasn't asked for anything. But ask him to call when he gets back and let us know how she's doing."

"Just give us a call when you get back, Mike. And thanks for asking. Have a safe trip. I'm sure Deena will appreciate your visit."

"Poor kid. I'm happy to do what I can to cheer her up. And I will call you as soon as I get back."

He was supposed to be there at noon, and it was only 9:30. He'd have plenty of time. He sent a text to Deena to let her know he was on the way. She sent back a smiling emoji.

He'd made this trip, or half of it, often. Cal Poly Pomona was only about an hour away from where Deena was. He liked the stretch of railroad tracks, something most people didn't really get. So many different cars. Old engines, and caboose cars, those were his favorites. Although some of the logos on box cars had a certain appeal also. The art of transporting goods and people had changed so much over the last fifty years. He was glad there was an effort to restore some of the old stations and even some of the trains themselves. He'd like to take Deena to the one in Fullerton. There were two beautiful buildings there – built in the twenties and thirties. She'd appreciate that look back to an era when train travel was the thing to do. He had a feeling she would understand taking time to get some-place, of actually watching the landscape rather than flying over it.

EVEN THOUGH MIKE was used to the drive – the University was just off the 10 near Pomona -- he knew it was smart to use his GPS to find the best route since there always seemed to be construction happening on one south-bound freeway or another. He was wise to do that, because it turned out the quickest route was via the 210 to Beaumont and then dropping down to Hemet on the 10. More miles, less traffic. And a better view of the mountains from the freeway that skimmed along the foothills. So going north before going south would work best once again.

He thought about picking up some flowers and chocolate before he left but decided it would be smarter to wait until he was closer to his destination. His air conditioning worked well, but not enough to keep flowers and chocolate from wilting.

He turned on an audio book and headed for the 405 north. He knew this part of the journey was the worst, and just resigned himself to stop and go traffic until he hit the freeway.

His route would take him past some new developments springing up along the 210. It always interested him the way business "parks" were kept separate from residential housing, requiring everyone who still went to an office to be part of the commuter crowd. Wouldn't it be more sensible to have business actually integrated into the community and make the "parks" real green space for everyone? His dream was to be able to build something that would provide living space and working space in the same development. Shops with apartments on the second story, homes built around green space with community gardens and playgrounds, and business buildings that had childcare and maybe even schools right on site. He knew it was a big dream. And it would take some visionary to make it happen; some financier with a heart for the planet and the quality of life for everyone. But it was all within reach, if only people could see it, claim it, do it. He was getting ready. Deena had been so excited about his ideas. He was surprised that she could see what he saw, even extrapolate, and take it to another level. She talked about native plants, and waste management that improved the land. Good head on her shoulders. And what pretty shoulders....

He didn't want to get too far down that road. She was quite a bit younger, and she still had a lot of years before she was ready to make any romantic choices. He didn't think she'd even dated much so far. But she was a very special girl. Did she ever think of him as anything more than a friend or kind of big brother? He wondered.

He was already half an hour into the audio book and realized he hadn't really listened to any of it. He turned it off and drove in silence.

Chapter 54

KITTY WAS UP EARLY MAKING coffee. When Jack came out to the kitchen she handed him a cup. "You sleep okay? I thought I heard someone talking on the phone in the middle of the night."

"Yes – finally. Had some thoughts I needed to follow through on before I could settle down. I left a message for someone last night who might be able to give us some help and get you some protection from Gray."

"Oh Jack, you don't need to get involved any more than you already have! I don't want you to worry about me. Really."

"It's too late for that, Kitty. I am worried. I've contacted an attorney. We can trust her completely. She's had her share of problems in the past, and she is discreet and wise. Really. We were friends when I was working at the University. Her husband was a colleague, and she ran the Women's Center. She will call as soon as she can. And I've had another idea. My friend Steve, the one you met at Colony Springs, is a retired detective. He may have some connections that can shed some light on what's going on with Gray so we know how to make sure you are protected from whatever he may be involved in."

"Maybe that's a good idea. Something must have triggered him to pack up the apartment and dump me in a homeless shelter. But I'm worried that whatever turns up is going to implicate me. Gray has always been good at blaming other people for what he's done and getting away with it. I may turn out to be one of his scapegoats."

"That's why we need an attorney. Don't worry. Doing something to get more information will only give you more power, make you less vulnerable. You'll have to trust me." He opened the refrigerator and looked in. "Now, what would you like for breakfast? We have to eat. Omelet and sausage sound good?"

"My stomach's in a knot. I'll just stick to toast and coffee."

"OK – suit yourself."

WHEN DEENA WOKE up she could hear Kitty in the kitchen. She went to ask if she could look for a t-shirt in the guest room where her mother usually slept. Sometimes her mom left a change of clothes, or her Grandma would have bought something she thought Jenny might wear.

"Of course! And if you see anything in there of mine you'd like to borrow, feel free. Getting dressed up, kid?"

"No – just wanted something that didn't look quite so scruffy, if you know what I mean. And I have to figure out something to do with this hair! It's a mess. I'm not fussy, but I don't like to look funky, either."

"I could do a French braid for you. In one of my past lives, I was a hairdresser, and I'm not too bad at it."

"Really? That would be great! I can't ever manage to make one that looks like anything."

"Go see what you can find to wear and come back out here for some coffee and breakfast. We'll see what we can do!"

The guest room was very different from what Deena was used to. It was tidy, no boxes stacked against the walls. She looked in the dresser and found a peasant blouse. She remembered her mom wearing it once, and then saying it wasn't her style. But Deena thought it would be great with her jean shorts. It looked comfortable, too, with a drawstring neck and loose sleeves. The front had a panel of embroidered, brightly colored birds, fruit and flowers from the neckline to the hem. She pulled it on over her tank top and went back to the kitchen for breakfast.

"How's the knee this morning? It doesn't look quite as swollen. Still pretty painful?"

"It's okay – hurts when I try to turn over in bed. I'm hoping the swelling will have gone down enough for them to x-ray it tomorrow. I probably should ice it more today. I didn't really do a lot of that yesterday."

"Your grandad picked up some cold packs when he went shopping yesterday. Should be a lot easier to manage. Want one now?"

"Oh yes, please."

Jack came in from the patio, coffee cup in hand. "Carlin wants to keep at it today – and he's brought Charlie. They will get those windows done in no time. Charlie's going to clean the chimney too. We'll need to get that out of the way before we paint, that's for sure."

"It's amazing to me that you have all these handymen ready on a moment's notice! In San Bernardino we'd have to wait weeks between visits, and nobody does more than one specific task."

Kitty scooped scrambled eggs onto a plate and handed it to Deena. "You want sourdough or wheat toast?"

"Sourdough, please. Thanks."

"These guys have been part of the landscape so long they've learned just about every building trade there is. Very adept, and very flexible. Comes from finding out what you like to do and just doing it, I think. They are never out of work, that's for sure."

Deena wondered if she would find that kind of passion and drive. She knew she wanted to go to college, keep learning, but she had no idea what her focus would be. How did Mike decide what he wanted? He seemed so sure about his direction.

Kitty cleared the table and put the dishes in the dishwasher. "OK Jack, you go supervise out at the farmhouse. I'm going to help Deena do her hair. Mike will be here around noon, right? Have you thought about lunch or should I do that?"

"I thought we could grill some burgers and hot dogs. And we've got some tortilla chips and coleslaw. Does Mike drink beer? I've got a couple of bottles from one of our micro-brewers out in the garage refrigerator."

"Yes, he does! Thanks for thinking of that Grampa!"

"We've got lemonade and iced tea also, so I think we're all set. You girls have fun playing beauty parlor!" He winked at them and went out, the screen door banging shut behind him.

Deena's mom did not have a gentle touch when it came to dealing with Deena's hair. She yanked and pulled through tangles, while Deena gritted her teeth and tears came to her eyes. When she was little, her dad would often rescue her and take his time, carefully combing through snarls and tangles, bottom to top. It took longer, but he had patience, and though Deena would get squirmy sitting so long, she realized she was in much better hands. She took over the task herself as soon as she could.

Kitty had a professional touch, which meant she would be

as fast and firm as she could, but always asked if her client was comfortable. When Deena winced at the first pass of the brush, she realized she'd have to be especially careful. "Did you use a conditioner yesterday?"

"No, my knee was throbbing, and I just wanted to get it clean. I didn't see any conditioner in the bathroom, anyway."

"I've got some. Let's just work a bit into your hair and get it a little damp. I think that will help."

Deena relaxed as Kitty worked the conditioner through her hair, gently pulling the tangles apart before she tried to use a comb or brush. "You've got enough hair on this head for three people!"

"I know – if I go to a hairdresser they always want to thin it. I won't let them, though. It's terrible to work with when it's all different layers. Something's always sticking out."

"You're right not to let them do that. Makes it easier for them, but harder for you! When you braided it yesterday had you really combed through it?"

"As best I could. I'm afraid when it dried and I slept on it everything just got worse!"

"Well, no matter. When I'm through here you'll have a braid that should last for a couple of days at least."

Chapter 55

THE FARMHOUSE WAS TAKING shape faster than Jack thought possible. Carlin liked to see a job done well, but he also wanted to work efficiently and get on to the next one. The fact that Jack had helped him through some difficult times also was a motivator. He spent a couple of years pretty close to the edge of himself after he lost his son, and Jack was always there when grief threatened to overwhelm him. His own wife hadn't been dealing with it well, and spent a year on one drug or another trying to get through her pain. Carlin wouldn't take drugs. He wanted to feel, not to numb the pain. Seemed like disrespect, to him. He met his grief head-on, and when he was flooded Jack would be there and somehow get him talking and get him through to the other side. Sometimes they just sat together in silence, watching the fire turn wood to ash. Nothing lasted, but nothing disappeared completely, either. Maybe a different form, a different manifestation.

Eventually Carlin was able to take comfort from his work, and his wife found solace in volunteer work at the VA. They would never recover from their loss. They were different people, in different circumstances. Losing a child left a blank space. Where there had been three, now there were two. Memories filled some of the void, but there could never be enough, not now.

"I can't believe you've finished all the windows!" Jack handed Carlin a cup of coffee.

"We were lucky. Your Dad replaced the sash cords on the ones in the back, and we just tightened them up a bit. I found some hardware that looks like it's from the 20's, so you can lock them, too."

"I wonder what he was planning for this place? He never told me he was doing anything to restore it. If I'd realized how much was already done, I might have finished the job a long time ago. This would have made a good studio for Lily. She could have had her collections out here and organized them like she always said she wanted."

"Come on, Jack, do you think she really would have undertaken a project like that? Our Lily? I know she loved to collect that stuff, but I don't remember her as much of an organizer!"

Jack looked at his feet and chuckled. "I know. I know. It was a fantasy of mine that someday she might take an interest in taking control of all the stuff in her life. Pretty unrealistic, I guess."

"Unrealistic? I'd say it was a pretty big fantasy you had going on there in that head! I loved Lily too, but not for her ability to order her world! Looks like her friend Kitty is pretty good at it though. She worked like crazy out here the other day. I couldn't believe what she accomplished. Very systematic, too. I admire that."

"She's been a great help, that's for sure. She's a good person. And you're certainly right about her being a hard worker. You'll have to come see what she's done in the house. You won't recognize it."

"Really? You getting a little more than fond of her there, Jack?"

"Lily's only been gone six months, Carlin. I'm not ready for anything more than a helping hand at this point. And I'm glad I've been able to help her out, too. She was stuck in a tough place. Still is. I don't know all of it, but for now I'm just glad she's here. She's good company. Gets me thinking about something other than myself. She's a breath of fresh air, in spite of her problems."

"I saw you haul in a load of stuff yesterday. That all hers? What's she going to do with it?"

"For now, she's just storing it in the garage until she can go through it and decide what to keep. There's no rush. She's certainly earning her keep."

"I can see that. Just be careful, Jack. If you don't know that much about her, you could be getting into some deep water. Moving all her stuff here seems like a pretty big thing. And how're you going to work on your trains with all that stuff in the garage? Aren't you and Steve still working on that miniature railroad?"

"That's on hold for a while. Just until Kitty gets situated. Steve's got plenty to do in his own shop. And if I'm in the mood I can go over there and work. For now, my focus is on getting this property in order for the first time in years. And helping Kitty sort out her situation, too."

"I hope you get the details on that situation pretty soon. As I say, you don't want to get in too deep – especially if you don't have all the information or the whole story. I'm just sayin'. It's advice you'd give me, if I were in your shoes. You know it is."

"Yeah – and thanks for the input. Really. So -- what's on for today? Did you find out if the chimney is sound?"

"It's in pretty good shape. But if I were you I'd get one of those inserts like I told you about. Did you check them out when you were in town?"

Jack smiled. "Yes. In fact, I bought one. There was a little Ben Franklin on sale. I'm just hoping it will fit because I never thought I'd buy something like that on impulse. It's in the truck."

"You get the stove pipe and everything?"

"Yes. You can check it all later today. I'll drive the truck back here and you and I can unload it. Is Charlie coming today?"

"I can call him. He's the expert when it comes to fire safety and chimneys. We should have him look it over before it goes in. All those years he spent as a building inspector have come in handy for me many times!"

"Should we have pulled a permit for this work we've been doing? Did he say anything about that?"

"Naw – we're just doing repairs. Even the plumbing was already in, just had to do a little rerouting. Only thing I was concerned about was the old electrics, but that's been taken care of too. You're good.

"Today I'll run the sander over the floors. Then you can decide how you want to finish them. Might just need a good sealer and some wax. You going to do the painting, or do you want me to call my guy?"

"I'll talk that over with Kitty. She seemed eager to be involved in that – at least with choosing the colors. If I'm going to make this into a rental, I think she can help me figure out how to make it really appealing. Deena's got some good ideas, too. Can I help with the sanding?"

"You got a respirator? I've only got one. This machine is pretty good at vacuuming as it goes, but with something this old you'd want to make sure you were protected."

"No, I don't have one. I guess you're on your own for this one."

"It won't take long, place is so small. I'll let you know when I'm done and it's safe to breathe out here!"

"Okay then – come on up to the house for lunch if you like. Deena's got a friend coming and I'm going to grill some burgers and dogs."

"We'll see how this goes."

Chapter 56

IF KEVIN and Jenny made an early start, they might have a good chance at a parking spot, and maybe even a picnic table. It was the first time both kids had been out of the house for the weekend. Jenny wasn't obsessing over work or her mother's death, and Kevin was enjoying the fact that Jenny was more relaxed and happier than she had been in a long, long time. He often felt helpless when she started the obsessive, anxious pattern that surfaced when she was overwhelmed. She'd be withdrawn, and then angry. The kids knew how to protect themselves when that happened-- they kept busy and out of her way-- but Kevin was there to draw her fire, trying to engage her, distract her or soothe. Her retreat was supposed to give her time to reflect, to heal; but she came back more tightly wound than when she left. What happened while she was there? She didn't want to talk about it, but obviously her sessions with her advisor had not been helpful. She came back wound into an even tighter circle. And Deena's escapade didn't help. But at least for this moment, this day, they were enjoying time together.

There was still a mist over the ocean, but that would burn

off before too long. They found a table under a tree and Jenny spread the tablecloth they always took on picnics. It had belonged to her grandmother and was so threadbare you could almost see through it. But the pattern was, amazingly, still clear – a bright yellow border framed a checkerboard pattern of blue and white.

Kevin opened the picnic basket and took out the vintage plates and knives and forks. He opened a jar of watermelon pickles. Jenny broke off a piece of bread from the long loaf fresh from the bakery and spread it with sweet butter. There was cold chicken, hard boiled eggs, and potato salad.

"I almost forgot! I've got a cooler in the car with our drinks – I'll be right back."

Kevin jogged back to the car, and Jenny watched him go. How was it he still ran like the young guy she had married twenty years ago? From the rear, he still looked about nineteen, with that bouncy run, up on his toes. She knew she couldn't do that. She hadn't felt light enough to do anything but slog through her responsibilities and then fall into bed at night, especially since her mother died. Peeling back the layers of her grief on retreat had been hard work, she had felt unprepared for what she discovered. Maybe she should see a counselor here, keep working on those issues. She sighed and shook off the gloom that threatened to destroy her mood.

Kevin came back with the cooler and a thermos "I remembered to bring orange juice and champagne! And coffee!"

"You are remarkable. I've always known it, and now I see it!" Jenny pulled out two champagne glasses from the basket. "And I remembered these!"

They sat side by side as the mist lifted, sipping champagne and watching the waves. Life was good, in this moment, and all was well.

Chapter 57

"So, Grandpa, what do you think?" Deena turned her head so he could see what Kitty had done with her hair.

"Wow, kid, that's spectacular! Did you do that yourself?"

"Nope. Kitty did it! Isn't she great?" Deena was beaming. "Mom could never do that! Not that she ever really wanted to. I love it!"

"Well, your mother does have other talents, though, Dee."

"Right. You're right. I didn't mean..."

"No, no – it's fine. You look wonderful! How's the knee this morning?"

"Better, I think. But it still wakes me up at night when I turn over. I'll be glad when they take another look tomorrow. The swelling is down quite a bit. I'm so tired of the crutches!"

"I can imagine. What are you going to do now until your friend gets here? We can't do anything out at the farmhouse today. Carlin is sanding the floors, and it's a messy business."

"I've got some reading to do. Guess I'll prop myself up in the living room and get on with it."

"Where's Kitty? I didn't see her out back."

"She's in the garage, looking through some of the boxes you

brought back yesterday. She said she was hoping her computer might be in there somewhere."

"Oh. Hope she finds it! I'm going in to take a shower and then I'll start doing some prep for lunch. Your friend does eat meat, doesn't he?"

"Why does everyone always ask that question?! If someone doesn't eat meat, they will just eat whatever else is available. Most vegetarians I know are fine with that."

"Young people seem to have all kinds of dietary restrictions these days. I just want to be sure the guy doesn't go hungry, that's all."

"Yes, he eats meat. In fact, he tells me he is quite a good cook himself. He loves to barbeque. I haven't had the chance to test that claim yet, though."

"Maybe I should run over to the corn stand. Fresh corn on the grill is pretty good. Would you like that?"

"I'd love it! But don't go to so much trouble, Grampa. Mike's easy. I don't want you to fuss."

"Actually, I just wanted a good excuse to run over there anyway. If they have some nice ripe tomatoes those would be great on the burgers. I'll see if Kitty wants anything special." He grabbed a couple of grocery bags and went out the back door.

KITTY FOUND what she was looking for in the third box she opened. When she opened the first box, she didn't recognize anything that belonged to her. She hadn't realized there was so much of Gray's stuff in the apartment. Where had he kept all of it? She couldn't remember seeing any of it before. One of the boxes contained files and a locked bank bag, along with several small empty jewelry boxes.

The second box had some of Gray's clothes and toiletries, all smelling faintly of his expensive cologne. What was it? Straight to Heaven? Yes – that was it. More like Straight to Hell, as far as Kitty was concerned. She felt nauseated by the memories that scent brought back.

She moved the two boxes off to the side thought they might have been the reason he came by last night. Had he wanted to retrieve them but was so drunk he forgot? She pushed them into a corner, thinking at some point she could drop them off at one of his showrooms to get rid of them. Or she could just take them to the dump. Serve him right. He dumped her. She could dump his stuff with no regret at all.

The third box had her computer and the contents of her desk drawers. Her personal phone and charger and the computer cords were all there.

She opened the rest of the boxes to scan what they contained. No need to unpack them, and no place to put anything, yet.

She jumped when Jack came around the corner of the garage. "Didn't mean to frighten you, Kitty! I'm off to pick up a few things for lunch at the corn stand. Anything you might fancy in the way of fresh vegetables? Or fruit?"

She took a deep breath and thought for a moment. "How about some ripe peaches? Maybe I could make a cobbler! I think I could manage that."

"Okay, if they have any, I'll bring some back. See you in a bit. You need any help moving those things around? I could do that before I go."

"No, I'm fine. I'll just keep poking around. I want to find some of my clothes. But thanks."

She opened another box. "Ah. Here's my underwear!"

Jack blushed. "Ummm I'll just be going, then."

Kitty laughed. "Okay – see you soon."

She smiled and waved as he pulled out of the driveway.

Jack's face still felt hot, even after he put the window down and turned on the air. He couldn't remember when he'd felt so embarrassed. Or excited, either. He'd been attracted to her from the beginning, even when she was hot and dirty and still hung over. Something about her bearing, her voice, had captivated him. Well, caught his attention, anyway. He knew how vulnerable he was. Recent widower, lonely, looking for new purpose and connection. He was old enough to know he needed to slow down. But he was also old enough to know that he wanted to make the most of what his life was now. Each day he wanted to feel this excitement, this thrill of possibility and joy. Each day he wanted someone to share his breakfast table, sit with him in the evening with a glass of wine or scotch. Share his projects, share his bed. There. He'd admitted it to himself. He wanted Kitty in his bed. Very much. But maybe not immediately. No, not right away. He still needed time to be sure this was a good choice, a right choice, for him. And he'd have to see how Kitty felt about him. He knew she enjoyed his company, but that was about it, and she was grateful for the help he had given her. But that wasn't enough. There would need to be more.

Chapter 58

JACK WAS JUST PULLING into the driveway from his trip to the vegetable stand when a car pulled up in front of the house, and for a moment he was afraid that Gray might have returned to have another go at Kitty. Relief washed over him when he saw a young man get out of the car. "Hi there! You must be Mike?"

"Yessir! That's me! Here to visit the sick! Can I help you with those bags?"

"No thanks – looks like you've got your own load to carry! I'm Jack, Deena's Grampa."

"Nice to meet you. I've heard a lot about you from Dee. So sorry to hear about your wife. It hit Dee's family pretty hard. I can't even imagine how it must be for you."

"Thanks. Taking longer than I thought it would, that's for sure. Deena's visit has done a lot to remind me that the world still has a lot to offer."

Mike reached into the car for the beer. "Hope you like dark beer – this is from a local microbrewery and I thought you might appreciate it. Don't know why, really!" He laughed.

"I know the guy who owns that brewery! I'll really enjoy that! Thanks so much. Come on in – we'll give it a try!"

Mike grabbed a bunch of flowers and a little stuffed owl he had bought on impulse for Deena, and followed Jack to the house. He was surprised to see how young Jack looked – and how fit. He'd expected an old man.

Deena was on the couch in the living room, ice pack on her knee. She heard the car pull up and her heart did a little flip.

And then there he was. Mike. Tall and tan, head full of dark curls. He ran his hand through his hair, and then handed her the flowers, the owl tucked into the middle of the bunch.

"Shastas! I love these – how did you know? And Pooh's Owl! Oh Mike, thank you!"

Kitty came out from the kitchen, drying her hands on her apron. "Here, Deena, let me put those in water for you. Aren't they lovely? You called them 'shastas'?"

"Yes. Shasta Daisies. Grandma loved them too. Oh – Mike, this is Kitty. She's staying with Grampa for a while. She's an old friend of my Grandma's. Kitty, this is Mike!"

"Nice to meet you – excuse me while I find something to put these in." She smiled, handed the stuffed owl to Mike and said, "So an owl reading a book!"

Mike looked at Deena. "What do you mean, 'Pooh's Owl?' You know this guy already?!"

"'Course I do! It's the owl from Winne the Pooh, don't you recognize him?"

"Oh yeah – now that you mention it, I do! Wow – is that still popular?"

"It will NEVER go out of date as far as I'm concerned!"

"I just thought it reminded me of someone who had their nose in a book all the time..." he winked.

She laughed. "Ah – I get it! Well sit down. Tell me how things are going at home. I assume you've talked to my parents."

Jack followed Kitty into the kitchen. "I'm going to check on the coals – and crack one of these beers. Come on out and join me when you've had a chance to chat a bit."

Mike sat down on the end of the couch. "Is that cold pack still working? Can I get you more ice or something?"

"No. I'm fine. Just tell me how everyone is at home. Am I on Mom and Dad's bad list again?"

"You're on the list of concern, more than the list of bad, I think. They're worried about your knee. How is it, by the way?"

"It's much better. The swelling is almost gone – but it still hurts if I put any pressure on it. I'll be glad when they take x-rays and I can know exactly what's going on in there."

"That's scheduled for tomorrow, right?"

"Yes. Early, thank goodness. I want to be able to get around on my own steam. These crutches are giving my arms a real workout."

"Your grampa seems to be enjoying your stay, although I know he feels bad about your fall. How'd it happen, anyway?"

"Oh we went to hear some music at this really amazing place called Colony Arts Springs – it's not far – we walked over. There's a big firepit, and some tables and benches – food trucks come around when there's something going on – it's fun! But it was dark by the time we left, and we didn't have a flashlight, or a cell phone. Kitty slipped on some pepper berries and fell on top of me! We must have looked like a comedy routine."

"Wow. How did they get you home?"

"This friend of Grampa's took us in his truck. It was a painful ride. Then they called 911 when they got me here. The paramedics had to treat two of us, in the end. Grampa had a dizzy spell and passed out. Too much excitement, I guess. He's fine now though. I guess his blood pressure dropped, or something."

"Does your mom know about that?"

"No, and I don't think Grampa wants her to. He checked

with his doctor, and they're monitoring his pressure. It seems okay now. Mom worries too much. About everything." Deena frowned.

"She cares about you, Dee. Of course."

"She sure has a funny way of showing it. Most of the time I feel like an unnecessary annoyance."

"That's sad."

"I don't want to talk about it now. Let's go check on Grampa and the Barbeque process. I'm starving."

Mike handed her the crutches and followed her out to the kitchen. Kitty was putting the relish tray together. She had neat rows of lettuce, tomatoes, onion, and cheese slices. "Think anybody will want sliced pickles on their burger?"

"That would be a yes for me." Mike raised his hand, laughing.

"Me too – if they're those kosher dills!"

"Well, they are. You guys going to check what's happening outside? Let me know when to bring things out. Mike, maybe you can help carry?"

"Sure. Anything else we can do?"

"Tablecloth and plates are on the sideboard. You guys can set the table. Dee, show him where the knives and forks are. And don't forget the napkins!"

"We are on it, Kitty."

They got themselves out the back door, Mike's hands full of tableware, and Deena's busy manipulating her crutches. Jack rushed over to help.

"We're okay, Grampa! Just came to see when Kitty can bring out the burgers and hot dogs. Coals ready yet?"

"Just about. Maybe five more minutes. Here, Deena, sit at the end of the picnic bench and I'll pull a chair up so you can put your leg up."

Mike spread out the tablecloth, and left the plates stacked, so Jack could pick them up when the burgers were ready.

———

"Looks like you have some experience with this whole process!"

Deena laughed. "Mike says he loves to cook. However, I have no proof of that yet."

"Anything I can do to help with the grill, Mr. .... Ummm" he realized he didn't know Jack's last name.

"You can call me Jack, Mike. No, I think things are all under control. I'll just go in and help Kitty carry. You stay here and provide some entertainment for Deena."

Chapter 59

"Your grampa is quite a guy. And this is a nice piece of property. How far back does it go, anyway?"

"I'm not sure how much of it is his, but it goes back far enough that there's another little bungalow in the back. That sound you hear is the floor being sanded out there. My great grandfather put up a kind of craftsman style house to live in while he was constructing the ranch house. It's so cool. I hope we can get out there to see it later. You'd love it. Kitty and I have great plans for the décor. I think she may wind up living there. She has an incredible eye for decorating."

"What's the story with her? She seems pretty comfortable here – but I think your mom said she's only been here for a little while? Was she a friend of your grandmother's?"

"Well – if you can keep a secret, I'll tell you something about her." Mike nodded.

"She wasn't a friend of my grandmother's. That was a fiction my Grampa made up to keep the gossip down around here. It's a small community, and people would talk. Especially since my Grandma Lily has only been gone for six months. From what I can understand, Kitty was in trouble somehow and Grampa took her in. She's been working around the house to kind of earn her keep –but I think he's growing very fond of her. There were some weird guys who came by last night, one of them was drunk, and they wanted something from Kitty. Grampa finally got them to leave, but not before they'd had a big fight. It was terrible. And kinda scary."

"Oh my god! You mean he knows nothing about her history or these guys and he's letting her stay here?" Mike looked worried. "I think you should let me take you home after we have lunch. Your knee can be looked at by your own doctor, at home."

"No, Mike, please. Let me stay. I really like her and Grampa doesn't think they'll come back. If they do, he'll call the police."

"Maybe I should stick around, just in case. I mean, I can see Jack's pretty fit, but he's got some health problems and who knows what could happen. I'm off work until Tuesday, so it wouldn't be a problem."

"Really? Could you? I'd like that. I'm sure they wouldn't mind."

"Okay. That's settled then. Think I'll grab one of those beers – you want something?"

"Just water. Or if there's lemonade, that'd be good."

The weather was kinder that day than it had been for some time. Warm, but not the kind of relentless, brutal heat that sometimes smothered the desert. There was a bit of a breeze, and there was the faint scent of citrus blossoms from a neighboring orchard.

Jack did a great job with the burgers, knowing just when to take them off the grill so they were still juicy, and just rare enough. The conversation, steered mainly by Deena who didn't want to talk about any of the drama of the previous night, centered on Mike's plans for a sustainable community that housed services and schools, as well as residential space. Kitty proved to be a good listener and asked some questions about recycling and waste management. Jack was impressed by Mike's knowledge of the latest research and his commitment to do more than simply make money. As an archeologist Jack had a lot of opinions about what modern society was doing to the earth. He had studied ancient civilizations and been particularly interested in how quotidian tasks were accomplished. More interested in those than any big monuments or structures. Comfort in the day to day was what made life worth living for most people. That, and the ability to do something creative.

If, of course, you had someone to love. He looked at Mike and Deena – so young, so full of life -- and envied them. They looked forward to a future full of building, planning, making something sustainable. Whether there was more to their relationship than just friendship wasn't apparent. Yet. But whatever happened he could see that they were in full agreement about what needed to happen to protect the earth. It made him feel that his future was in good hands, even if there wasn't a whole lot of it left.

Kitty thought it was time for the peach cobbler she made and went to get it. Jack followed her to the kitchen to make a pot of coffee.

"You know, if I didn't know those two were almost complete strangers, I would think they were an old married couple!" Mike whispered.

"It does seem a little weird, doesn't it? They are awfully comfortable together."

DEENA ASKED Mike for more lemonade and said, "Hey, how would you like to go see Colony Springs when we finish here?"

"What's to see there?"

"It's a little artists' community. I think you'd like it. I do. And we don't have to walk around – you can pretty much see whatever there is to see from the car."

"Sure! Let's do it!"

THE COBBLER WAS A HIT. Kitty smiled when they all asked for seconds. She had surprised herself most of all with its success.

"WE WANT to check out Colony Springs. OK with you, Grampa?"

"Sounds great. Back for dinner? Or will Mike need to get back before then?"

"Would it be alright if he stayed over, Grampa? He could sleep on the couch. He wants to stick around until we find out what's going on with my knee. Then if I'm okay to travel, he'll take me home. Mom and Dad can figure out how to get my car. I know Mom wants to come visit."

Kitty looked up from stacking the dishwasher. Jack looked at her and winked. "Fine with me. See you two later, then."

Kitty waved them off. *Oh great, a visit from the daughter soon? Sounds like she'll be pretty hard to please.*

"Jack, I think I'll go do some more sorting in the garage. I've already got a box full of things to get rid of. You need any more help with cleanup?"

"No, we're fine here. I'm going to take some of your cobbler out to Carlin and see how he's doing. Haven't heard any activity there for a while."

Jack found Carlin loading up his sanding equipment. "Hey – want some peach cobbler? It's not bad. Kitty made it."

"Sure – I can always go for cobbler. So, not only is she something of a looker, but she can also cook? Oh dear, Billy Boy Billy Boy..."

"It's not cherry pie we are talking about here, Carlin. And as I told you, there's nothing there. Yet."

"Aha! So you do have your eye on her! I knew it. Well, better do a background check before you get in too deep, my friend. Never hurts. Those of us who have been around awhile may not be what we seem – or even who we seem!"

"Speaking from experience there?"

"Yep. Speaking from experience and a few entanglements that proved harder to get out of than I would have thought. So go carefully." Carlin was talking with a mouth full of cobbler. "Tell me what you think of the floors.

"Can't believe you are done!

"When should we refinish?"

"I'm gonna do that this afternoon. Can't leave that porous wood exposed for very long."

"Oh? I thought you were leaving the finish up to me!"

"Well if you're gonna rent this place, you'll want something that will stand up to some pretty heavy wear. So I think your best bet is to put a polyurethane finish on it."

"Guess you're the boss, then! Sounds fine to me."

"Have you thought about putting some tile in the fireplace to put an insert in there? Probably would look a lot better. Safer, too. Could make a little edging to set it off."

"I think that's wise. Go ahead and do it. You still got some tile you can use for that?"

"I've got some Mexican tile that I think will work. Pretty design, too, blue, yellow and white."

"Perfect!"

Carlin looked pleased. "So, you got a shop vac we can use? That will help to get the dust out of here so I can lay down the finish on this wood."

"Sure – I'll bring it out."

Chapter 60

THE STORAGE BOXES were proving to be full of surprises. Not only were there the two she had already set aside, but another one revealed a locked safety deposit box and a bunch of sealed manila envelopes with a series of numbers and letters that meant nothing to Kitty. It felt like they were full of photographs and cds. She shoved that one over to the side with the other two. Where had all this stuff been stored when she was living in the apartment? Or was this stuff Gray had intentionally left there and had packed to look as if it belonged to her? Her stomach turned over. She knew he was not above implicating other people in his shady business deals, but she never thought he would turn on her. She had enough information on him and how he kept his "books" --- or so she thought. Was all that only a ruse, too?

She ripped open the rest of the boxes and did a quick scan. Her own clothes, several of Gray's golf outfits, and a few plastic bags with her cosmetics and perfumes mixed in with Gray's shaving equipment, some odd plates and mugs that were not part of the furnished apartment's kitchen equipment, seemed to be all that remained. She pulled all of Gray's things out and put them in one of the empty boxes Jack bought when they were cleaning out the house. She used strapping tape and sealed up every edge of every box that belonged to Gray. She didn't want anybody tampering with any of it, and it would be more than obvious if they did. She wouldn't put it past Gray and his companions to sneak in here and take it all away. In fact, she kind of hoped they would. Because if they did, she would no longer be implicated. She'd be free. But how could she explain that to Jack?

JACK WAS on the phone when Kitty came into the house. "When could we meet with you, Emily?"

Who was he talking to? His back was turned, and he didn't hear her come in. She tiptoed to her room and put the box she was carrying on the bed. Then she went into the bathroom and closed the door. She had to collect herself before she went out to face him. She could no longer pretend, even to herself, that all of this was going to blow over without consequence. She knew Gray too well, and she knew he would stop at nothing to get what he wanted, even if it ruined other people's lives. He only protected himself. He would have thrown his wife over long ago if he had a way to get his hands on her money, though. He certainly talked about it enough. Maybe she found out about some of his risky behaviors and business deals and was now jerking him back into line. Either that, or the police finally caught up with him. *Bloody hell, if I could only have a drink right now.*

She stripped down and stepped into the shower, trying to think of some way to stay centered and focused on keeping Jack on her side. If she lost his support, she knew she would fall back into living on the edge. She'd be back to bouts of drinking with one sucker or another until she found someone like Gray. That's what always happened. No wonder her daughter didn't speak to her. Her life until now had been one long series of lies, and her daughter so often the collateral damage.

She stayed in the shower until some of the anxiety and dread drained away, along with real tears of regret and shame. She didn't know how to put that all behind her, not yet. And if Jack knew her whole story now, he'd back away and she'd be alone, again. Was she too old to change? Could he forgive her? She began to realize that until he knew the whole story, there could be no kind of lasting relationship. But that wasn't like her, anyway. Did she want a real relationship? Could she face the scrutiny that would inevitably be coming her way from his daughter? She sounded like she was hard to please.

This wasn't the time to unburden herself. She had to stay strong, at least until Deena had gone home and it was just Jack in the house. She'd tell him then, come clean. But for now she had to maintain the fiction that she was just down on her luck and had been badly treated for a few more days.

Chapter 61

THE DAY HAD GONE from cool and overcast to hot and sunny. Deena was glad her hair was in a braid and out of her way. And she was grateful that the air conditioning in Mike's car was working. He must have had it fixed since the last time he gave her a ride. She had to sit in the back seat so she could put her leg up, but that gave her an opportunity to admire the back of his neck and his strong profile. He wasn't one to turn around to look at her when he was driving – and he couldn't see her face in the rearview mirror. She made sure she was looking out the window when they stopped, so he wouldn't catch her staring. Was she an idiot to think he could be interested in her except as a friend? She knew he was twenty-three, and she had only just turned eighteen. But five years wasn't that much of a difference, really. Was it? Maybe it was because he seemed so much older that she thought the idea impossible.

"So which way do I turn?"

"Turn right at the next corner and then you'll see it. Can't miss the landmark they've put up."

He turned onto a dirt road lined with pepper trees. "Is this where you fell?"

"Yep. Those pepper berries can be like walking on tiny marbles – it's easy to slip. There on your left you can see the Colony Springs!"

"I thought it was an actual spring of some kind, you know, like a hot spring?"

"Nope. We have a lot of those around here, but this one is entirely man-made. Or woman-made. Can't remember who built it. I was just a little kid when it first went up. But sometimes they fill it with water and it makes an interesting sound if the pump is working. The birds love it."

"That's quite a project! Must have taken a long time to collect all those bits and pieces and figure out how to put them together to make anything that resembled a work of art. But it's really quite something. I like it. I'd love to see it working. Does the city take care of it?"

"No – it's entirely up to the artists who live around here. They didn't exactly have any kind of permit to put it up in the first place. Grampa helped build the firepit and delivers a load of wood every now and then. They have concerts, and poetry readings, and storytelling sometimes. There's a local theater group that puts on plays on summer evenings, too. If you want to do a performance, or even give a speech, you can sign up in the little General Store over there."

"This is fantastic. It's just the kind of gathering place that I'd like to see in the complex I'm planning to build someday. Everybody gets invested in making it happen, and everybody helps maintain it. That's community!"

"They have a big garden, too. They run the local corn stand where Grampa gets a lot of in-season produce. The corn we had at lunch was from there. If you drive around to the right we can see it."

The community garden was on at least an acre of land. Rows of corn lined one side and climbing pole beans and peas ran along the opposite fence. Ripening pumpkins, squash, and watermelons sprawled everywhere. Strawberries were spilling over the sides of a raised bed. Marigolds in bright yellows and orange made random dots of color, along with chard and purple kale.

"I know it doesn't look very organized, but apparently they plant things that do well side-by-side or provide natural protection from hungry bugs."

"It's fantastic, Dee. Reminds me of what my grandparents used to talk about from the sixties. Communes that were completely self-sustaining. I never got why they failed. Seemed like a good way to do your life if you liked to be independent."

"I know, right? I've done some reading about why they failed, but I still don't fully understand it. It seems like they had a lot of good things going for them, but some were susceptible to cultish behaviors that prevented sensible health care and that could have had a negative effect. Personal greed or a free and easy attitude towards drugs and sex had an impact, too. I'm not against personal decisions about any of that, but when it becomes a kind of enforced lifestyle, I think that's not good for anybody."

"You have given this some thought!"

"I want to do something that puts us all back on a more sensible track to protect one another and the earth, but I don't think dropping out or dropping acid helps. Does that sound too simplistic, Mike?" Deena felt like she had just shown him a part of herself that she rarely shared with anyone. Her peers at school wouldn't have understood it, and her parents never seemed interested.

"Not at all! I couldn't agree more. That's exactly why I'm interested in creating communities with something for everyone, space for all that helps everyone to thrive and contribute. My professors say I'm naïve – interestingly enough, some of them have had experience on communes and eventually were completely disillusioned. But I'm talking about something completely different."

Deena breathed a sigh of relief. "I thought people would call ME naïve! You're braver than I am, Mike."

"I'd like to hear more about your dreams for the future, Dee. Let's go find someplace where we can get something cold to drink and you can rest your leg."

"Okay. Turn around and go back the way we came. We can go the Snowbird. They have a real soda fountain, and they also have old-fashioned booths where I can put my leg up. Maybe they'll give me a bag of ice to put on my knee. It's beginning to swell again. Probably the heat."

Mike and Deena sat down for a cold drink at the Snowbird, and when they looked at the clock, it was almost time for dinner. "I've never been able to talk about my ideas – my dreams – like this with anyone, Mike. I'm sure I've monopolized the conversation."

"Hey – I loved hearing every single word. You and I are on the same page, just with slightly different goals. I can tell your heart is in the green spaces and recycling in a way that makes really good sense. I'm interested in building living space that provides for maximum use and maximum community – as well as workplaces so people can give up their long commutes." He paid the bill and helped Deena with her crutches. "Just let me use the restroom, and then we can go. Can you call my Grampa and let him know we are on our way?"

"Sure. Can you put the number in for me? I don't have it."

Chapter 62

KITTY PULLED her hair up into a band and put on the blouse and skirt she'd bought the day Jack took her to the grocery store. The day had turned out to be so hot she would have preferred to stay in a tepid shower, but she knew she'd have to show her face eventually or Jack would worry and come looking for her. There was a pile of clothes she had brought in from the garage to wash, too. They smelled of cigarettes and Gray's cologne. She picked them up and headed to the laundry room. She put her things in the washer and went to check on Jack. He wasn't in the house, so she decided he must have gone out to check on Carlin. He was on his way back when she caught up with him.

"So, things going well?"

"Yep. So much faster than I expected. Things are going VERY well." He gave her a thumbs up, and winked.

"When are you expecting the kids? I thought they'd be back by now."

"So did I. Maybe they'll call and let us know what's happening."

"There is a message on the machine – I saw it blinking when I was in the kitchen."

"By the way, I talked to my attorney friend. She would like to meet with us to see if there is anything she can do to help. So how about meeting her for lunch on Wednesday? We can drive to the campus and eat at the faculty center."

"Um – okay. I don't have a lot of money, you know, for an attorney."

"She runs the Women's Center at the University and does quite a bit of pro bono. You can let her know a bit about your circumstances – I don't have to be in on that by the way – and she'll let you know if she can help."

"I see. Even though I'm not connected with the University she'll be able to do that?"

"She can. She helps a lot of women in the community who have no connection with the University. That's one of the reasons it exists. To help women who couldn't afford to get help elsewhere."

"It can't hurt to meet with her, I guess. Sure. Let's do it."

"Good. I already told her we'd be there!"

He was pretty sure of himself. But what else was she going to do? She was without resources or any other kind of option. And a clean break with Gray was absolutely what she wanted and needed. The sooner the better.

Jack saw Kitty's hesitation when he said he'd already confirmed the appointment with Emily. He told himself that he was giving her an opportunity to resolve some issues. An opportunity she might not otherwise have had, but he knew it was coming across as controlling. He had no right to assume that she would be okay with any of this, and yet he had gone ahead and put things in place. She could just pick up and run at any time. She did have access to some money, now, and he wanted very much to keep her here, keep her safe, keep her with him. "I'm sorry, Kitty, if I took it for granted that you would want this. We can cancel, of course."

"No, I'm grateful. I wouldn't know how to proceed without some legal advice. Let's keep the appointment and see what she has to say." *And let's see what I decide I can tell her, too. I know there is an attorney-client privilege, but who knows how strictly they adhere to that.*

The answering machine told them that Mike and Deena were on their way back.

"How about we have a glass of wine before the kids get here?" Kitty was afraid Jack would say no, but he agreed without any hesitation. "Red or white?"

"I'd prefer white. Something that's not too sweet."

"I think I've got a bottle of sauvignon blanc in the garage refrigerator. Why don't you fix a plate of cheese and crackers?"

Jack was afraid to push Kitty any more for details about her predicament. He could sense he had gone as far as he could without having her shut down completely. They would just have to wait until Wednesday to see what could be done. He trusted Emily's judgment completely – as well as her discretion.

Kitty went to the kitchen to organize some cheese and crackers, her thoughts about how to get through this next step with legal advice spinning in her head.

I'm so stupid. I never should have gotten in this far. I'm not good at being sensible or balanced. Or good at being good. And I could drink that whole bottle just fine all by myself. Why didn't I get out before I was so far in? I like Jack a lot, more than anything, though, I trust him. And I'm about to blow all of that if he finds out about my life before we met.

Kitty put the plate of food on the table, wiped her eyes with the back of her hand, then smiled broadly as Jack came back with the wine.

"You okay?" Jack put his hand on her shoulder.

"I'm fine. I was thinking about next week and dreading it.

I'd like to just disappear sometimes. I have made a mess of things."

"Anyone who has had any kind of life at all has made mistakes. I know I certainly have. But people can change, make different choices."

"Do you really believe that? Because I don't think there's much evidence of it in my life."

"I do believe it. I've seen it happen. I don't believe it's easy, though." He offered her a glass of wine and poured one for himself. "In any case, right now there is no point in worrying about it. You won't be alone going through this, Kitty. Not unless you want to be."

She raised her glass. "Here's to change, then. Maybe it isn't too late."

Chapter 63

THE AFTERNOON HAD SOFTENED, and a breeze lifted the long branches of the pepper trees, and then was gone. Jack thought about Lily and all the choices she had made, they had made. He saw them very differently, now. Lily was capable of a kind of joy that Jack had never trusted. Her moods were too volatile. Joy could lead to a manic state that resulted in a paranoid hysteria, followed by a deep depression that brought on destructive, suicidal behavior. He always felt as if he were her guard rails, keeping her from going too far one way or the other. And yet it had never worked. The cycles had become more extreme as the years passed. Sometimes he wondered if she would have been happier, less volatile, with someone who could match her ups and downs. Her extremes cornered him, almost immobilized him, until he was forced into action to protect her. It would mean another hospital stay – another medical evaluation – another attempt at medication, which she hated to take. The toll it took on Jenny had been huge. Neither one of them were available to her after she was about ten. She had to learn to fend for herself. That was when Lily really started to exhibit behaviors that couldn't be called normal. There were so many sleepless nights, so many spoiled holidays, so many times when the house had been in chaos. Jenny was on her own a lot. No wonder she left home when she was so young.

"Are *you* okay, Jack?"

"Oh, sorry. Just thinking about some of the mistakes I've made over the years."

"I didn't mean to put you in a funk! You're right. Let's just forget about next week and enjoy tonight with the kids. I think I heard the car."

"I'll start the barbeque." It was funny how natural it sounded to him when Kitty said 'with the kids.'

"Can I take them out back and see what's been happening with the farm house?"

"Of course. Good idea. See what you think! Still some work to be done, but it's looking good."

THE FARMHOUSE WAS, indeed, looking good. The floors had turned out beautifully. There was a big sign propped up against the door that said DO NOT ENTER. WET VARNISH ON FLOORS. There would be no close inspection tonight. But they could see quite a bit through the windows.

Mike was impressed. "I've always wanted to live in one of these little bungalows. They seem so efficient, with all those built-in cabinets and drawers. No need for a lot of furniture. I like that."

Deena was amazed at the transformation. "I thought it would be days before this much could be done!"

"Carlin is amazing – and he's in a hurry to get to another job he contracted. Looks like they've taken up the floor in the bathroom – they took out all the fixtures! Too bad, I loved that

Victorian tub." Kitty realized she sounded proprietary, and quickly said, "It just seemed to fit the style of the whole place."

"That can be replaced, I'm sure. So many different designs available these days." Deena was balanced on one leg, one hand shading her eyes so she could see through the glass. Mike stepped closer to her, ready to catch her if she started to wobble.

"How was your trip to Colony Springs? Did you get to see all of it? Jack told me they have a wonderful garden. I'd like to see that, for sure."

"Yes it's quite the thriving little community. We brought some strawberries back." Mike placed his hand on Deena's back, steadying her.

Kitty looked at the two of them standing there, Mike so protective, and Deena trying not to look flustered -- but her cheeks were pink, and she was a little breathless.

"You guys hungry? Shall we go back and see if we can help get dinner on the table? Maybe we can set Deena up so she can slice the strawberries."

"Good idea! It's about time she did something to earn her supper!" Mike winked.

"You sounded just like Grampa, then...what are YOU going to do to earn YOUR supper, Mike?" Deena laughed.

"Oh I'll probably crack open another one of those beers and help Jack with the grill. Unless you have some other task in mind."

Kitty wondered if she were doing enough to earn HER keep. She'd been working hard, but was that enough?

Chapter 64

MIKE HAD BROUGHT a little portable speaker that allowed him to use his phone to stream music. Deena mentioned that her Grampa liked big band music, so he opened a new station on his Pandora account and put it on a shelf by the kitchen window so they could hear it outside. He picked up a couple of beers from the refrigerator and took them outside. "You want one of these Jack?"

"Yes! Thanks."

Kitty's face lit up. "You hear that Jack? Dance music!"

"I sure do! Amazing what you kids have available these days. We would have had to carry a record player and an armload of records if we wanted music. That's great!"

Deena called from the kitchen, "I think Kitty might like a beer too, Mike."

"No – I'm fine. I'll have a glass of wine with dinner. You need any help in there?"

"I'm all done with the berries. I'll be out in a second."

Dinner was a success. Jack grilled vegetables as well as

chicken, and Kitty put together a watermelon salad with sliced red onion, Deena's strawberries, feta cheese and balsamic vinaigrette.

"Could I have a little glass of white wine, Grampa? Dad lets me have it on special occasions. Mom doesn't know, though. She'd hit the roof."

"Sure, kid, go ahead. Why not. You're certainly not driving anywhere! And as far as I'm concerned at eighteen a glass of wine isn't going to cause you any harm. Just as long as, you know, you keep it at one."

"Yeah – I think I've learned my lesson the hard way on that one," she blushed.

Mike poured her a small glass and refilled Kitty's. "Canyon Springs is really quite the place, isn't it? Deena and I have ideas about how to carry those concepts into the future, don't we Dee?"

"Yes we do! What did you think about communal living when you were younger, Grampa?"

The discussion over dinner ranged from a brief history of archeological and anthropological analysis of community life from thousands of years ago to the experiments begun in earnest in the 1960's. By the time the grill was cold and their plates were bare, the sun was setting.

"Jack, let me help you clean up." Mike started picking up plates and stacking them.

"Sounds good to me! Actually why don't you girls go in and settle down in the living room. Mike and I will clean up out here and load the dishwasher. Or would you rather have a fire and sit here under the moon?"

Kitty looked at Deena and they both said at once "Under the moon!"

Jack had already laid the fire. It caught immediately with a little shower of sparks from a couple of pinecones he'd used for kindling.

"I'm going to get a sweater, Deena. You want something? It's getting a little chilly." Kitty put her wine glass down as she got up from the table.

"Yes, please. There's a sweater in my room, I think."

The cleanup didn't take long. Jack and Mike returned with a container of ice cream, bowls and spoons, and the last of the strawberries.

"Grampa this is the best time I've ever had here. Really. I feel for the first time like I'm really part of the party! And Kitty, you've been so kind – almost like a grandmother – not that you seem old enough!"

The kitchen door opened and they all jumped. Who would just walk in and come through?

"Jenny! What a surprise!" Jack got up and went toward her.

"Never mind about that, Dad." Jenny put her hand up to warn him off. Her face was contorted into a smirk. "Is that how you really feel, Deena, that Kitty is like a grandmother? You've only been with her for what, two days? Nice to know my mother is so easily replaced."

"Mom! I didn't mean that at all! It's just that she's been very kind and helped me a lot since I hurt my knee. Really."

"Good thing I showed up when I did – looks to me like you've been drinking again. Dad how could you let her do this?" Jenny grabbed the wine glass out of Deena's hand.

"Jenny—calm down! Come into the house for a minute and let's talk. This will accomplish nothing. And I have guests."

"Yes – you've got MY daughter, and I think I have a right to know exactly what's going on here. Let's see if you can explain everything to me so I'll calm down like a good little girl." She slammed back into the house, Jack following her.

Deena burst into tears. Mike rushed over and put his arm around her. "Oh Dee, it's all right. Everybody has weird parents. Don't worry about it. She'll probably calm down and come back out and apologize."

"I doubt it. You don't know my mom. She starts one of these tirades and there's hell to pay until she gets through it. I'm so sorry you had to see this, and Kitty I'm so, so sorry to you, too."

"Don't worry kid, I've seen much worse. I think I'll just go around to the side patio and let myself in so I'm out of the way. If you need me, I'll be in the guest room." She patted Deena's hand.

Mike said "I think we'd better stay put and let your Grampa handle your mom. No need to complicate things. Here, you want to finish Kitty's wine?"

"No. I wouldn't enjoy it now."

The music seemed intrusive. Mike pushed the remote and changed the station to classical music and turned the volume down. There was no sound from the house. Jack and Jenny must have taken their argument into the front yard.

They sat together, Mike's arm around Deena, and just watched the fire. After a few minutes, Deena said "I really hate my mom sometimes."

"I feel the same about mine, sometimes."

"How can someone who is supposed to love you be so mean? She doesn't treat my brother that way. But I come in for a lot of this drama. I always have. Dad tries to protect me, but sometimes she just lashes out for almost no reason. Like tonight."

"It sounded to me like she was not only angry but scared. Is that how it always sounds?"

"I guess I never thought about it before. What do you mean, 'scared'? She just sounded like Mom screaming again, to me."

"Maybe scared isn't the right word – threatened, maybe?

Defensive? Did you see the way she kind of pushed your Grampa away?"

"She pushes everybody away, sometimes. Except my brother. Even my Dad gets a big dose of it. Sometimes I wonder why he sticks around. I think she's different at work, though. Everybody seems to think the world of her there."

They heard a car start, saw headlights flash against the side of the house as it backed out of the driveway. Then it took off, scattering gravel.

"Sounds like she left. She does that at home sometimes when she and Dad have been fighting."

Jack came out the back door. "Where's Kitty?"

"She went into her room through the side patio. She wanted to stay out of the way in case Mom came back out, I think. Thought she might be complicating things."

"Your Mom decided to drive down tonight without telling anyone. She wants to go to your appointment tomorrow so she can talk to the doctor herself. Then she'll take you home. She's booked into a B&B in town for tonight. They'll figure out a way to pick up your car later this week."

"But I don't want to go home! I want to stay here until I'm able to drive home myself! After all, I am eighteen! I can make decisions myself. She can't force me to go!"

"I know, Deena. But think about it. Do you really want to make this into THE big thing? You know your Mom, you fight her and this will get worse. You'll have to wait for a better time to assert your independence. A time when you are in a better position on a lot of levels."

"Sometimes it feels like I will never be in a better position, a better time. I always have to give in to her, even when I know I'm right. It's not fair."

"No, it's not."

Mike looked at Jack. "I think you're right, Jack. This isn't the time to make a big break. And you and Kitty have some things to take care of this week, too, Deena tells me."

Deena shrugged. "All right. I'll go with her. But I'm going to figure out how to exercise some power, too. I have to get through to graduation until I can leave – and that's going to be months away – so I'll just have to stay out of her way until then. Right now I'd like that glass of wine, please."

"I'll get it." Mike picked up the ice cream bowls.

Jack put another log on the fire and sipped his beer. "I know how hard this is, Deena. And I'd love to keep you here. In fact, once you've figured out how to get through school and into the rest of life, you'll always have a home here. That little farmhouse we're fixing up would be just the kind of place a person starting out might need, right?" he smiled and winked.

"Oh Grampa, I do love you! Yes. That would be perfect. And it will give me something to hang onto. A kind of a dream that might come true!"

"I checked on Kitty – she wants to call it a night. She said she'd see us all in the morning."

The three of them sat in silence, sipping their drinks, until the fire was nothing but embers. Deena stretched and yawned. "Guess I'm more tired than I thought – it has been a pretty big day. Too much drama! I'll head in to bed too. I think Mike's bunking on the couch, right Grampa?"

"Kitty put out a blanket and a pillow for you Mike – you said you have a sleeping bag?"

"Yes. I'll be fine."

"If you want to take a shower, Mike, you can use the one in my room. I'll wait out here until you're done. I just thought of something I want to ask Grampa. Towels are in the cabinet in there."

"That would be great. I'm feeling a little grungy. I'm fast. Be right out."

Deena waited until he had closed the kitchen door before she spoke. "So, Grampa, I want to ask you a question and if it is too personal, or you don't want to answer, I'll understand."

"Okay --- shoot!"

"Was Grandma like my Mom? I mean did she fly off the handle when you least expected it? Because I'd like to understand where Mom gets this. It doesn't seem quite normal to me. Sometimes there is just no talking to her. Even Dad can't talk her down."

Chapter 65

It took Jack some time before he could answer. He didn't want to seem disloyal to either Lily or Jenny – but there were realities that Deena really did need to know, especially now. He got up and poked at the fire, put on another log. This could take some time.

"Your Grandma had what I liked to call an "intensity of personality" when I first met her. She was the life of every party when she was in the mood. But she also had long, moody periods when she was anxious and worried. She would fret about what she thought people were saying about her, how her own mother was treating her, then when your mother came along, I thought things were going to be better. For a time, they were. But once Jenny started asserting her own personality things went, well, haywire."

"Haywire? What do you mean?"

"Things got worse, in terms of her highs and lows. We managed, your mother and I, to weather the storms until she was about thirteen. Then all hell broke loose. Your Grandma began exhibiting behaviors that really were unbalanced more than just mercurial. She would go for days without sleep –

starting projects she never finished – writing things down on slips of paper and leaving them everywhere – wearing odd clothes, almost like costumes. She'd forget to cook dinner, and when she remembered she would bake a cake and serve it at midnight; or put a whole watermelon on the table and expect us to sit down and eat. I often brought food home so your mother could have a decent dinner at a normal time, but that also made your Grandma furious. I eventually arranged for your Mom to stay with one of her friends while I tried to figure out what to do. It was clear Lily needed more help than I could give her. It took me weeks to get her to a doctor, and then to get her into the hospital, we had to convince her that they needed to do more tests. It was a long nightmare, Deena. I still don't know how I managed to keep my job – luckily all of this happened during summer break, so I didn't have many responsibilities at the University. She had to sign herself in to the hospital, so we had to cook up a reason that had nothing to do with her mental state. She wouldn't admit there was anything wrong with her." Deena looked frightened. "Has your mother never told you any of this?"

"She's told me that she and Grandma had issues – which I could see for myself when they were together. But I had no idea things were that bad."

"That wasn't even the worst of it. You sure you want to hear this?"

"I think it's time I did. Don't you? It sounds like Grandma was bipolar."

"How would you know anything about bipolar?"

"I've studied psychology Grampa – and I have a couple of friends who are on that continuum who take medication to keep them stable. I know about bipolar!"

"In those days they called it 'manic-depressive'. Which gave it more of a stigma, I guess. And it wasn't until sometime in the

70's that they found the right medication for Grandma. That first time she was hospitalized they gave her a series of electroshocks to help bring her back to normal. They were brutal, and she hated them. Anyway, when she was in the hospital your mom came back home and we were able to put the house back together and maintain a regular schedule. Your mom did the shopping and most of the cooking during the week – all while she was going to high school. It was a pretty heavy burden for her but she never once complained. When your grandma came out of the hospital things were very tense between them. She was angry that Jenny could run a household and go to school. It made her feel terrible that Jenny had to do that." He sighed. "You want a little more wine? I'm going to get another drink."

"No, thanks. Just some water?" She could see Mike moving around in the kitchen. "Could you ask Mike if he needs anything while you're in there?"

Jack stopped at the storage shed to retrieve his bottle of scotch before he went into the kitchen. Mike was winding the power cord from his speaker when he came through the door. "You need anything Mike? Deena wants to know."

"No – I'm okay. Just taking my speaker and phone down. I'm going to check some e-mails and then hit the hay. Thanks, though. Looks like you and Dee are going to have a nightcap!"

"Well, I am. She's going to have a glass of water. It's a good time for us to talk. She'll be in before too long."

"What time is her appointment tomorrow?"

"Nine o'clock. Are you planning on coming?"

"I thought I might just take her there. Since Jenny will be there too, I thought maybe it would save the two of you some tension. Is that okay?"

"Very sensible. Maybe Jenny will let you drive Deena home, which I know she would like very much. Make sure you get her books and things in the car before you leave."

"Of course. I'm so sorry about all the drama you have right now, Jack. Seems like you could have used more time to deal with each issue on its own."

"Boy, isn't that the truth. But we'll just have to get through the best way we can. I appreciate you being here for Deena. It makes a big difference to have a friend you can rely on."

"I'll always be that for her. She's pretty special to me."

"I know – I think I understand how you feel about her. And I can see you have the good sense not to push things. That would be hard for her right now, and confusing. She's so vulnerable."

"Yeah. I get that."

Jack put ice in two glasses and poured scotch into one, water into the other. "Help yourself if you want a nightcap, Mike."

"No thanks – I've had enough beer for one day! And scotch really isn't my drink."

"Suit yourself. There's a TV in the living room if you want to watch something. The girls have got it all set up!"

"Not tonight. I'll see you in the morning. Good night."

Chapter 66

JACK WATCHED Deena for a moment before he took their drinks out. She looked so like Lily out there, watching the fire. But there was a calmness about her that Lily never had. She had listened to everything he said about her Grandma and it was as if he were talking to someone much older – someone who listened with her heart as well as her mind. If only Jenny had a bit of that. But who knows – maybe she did. Maybe Jack had just never given her the opportunity to show it. He had needed her to fill in the pragmatics of his life, and sometimes to pick up the pieces when he was at the end of himself. She had done that for him. She had no patience with her mother, but she seemed capable of doing anything he asked of her without complaint. And in the end, he had to ask her to move out. The tension between her and her mother was only making things worse. She was too young to be on her own, but if she didn't get out while she could still make a life for herself, she would be trapped. Trapped just as he was. He certainly didn't want that for her. And she had risen to the challenge. She had worked her way through college, met Kevin and married him, settled into her own life with her own family. It had been a big risk, and he lost sleep many nights worrying, but in the end he was right. She was better off.

"Here you go kid, just as ordered. Water with a little ice."

"Thanks, Grampa. You know I was wondering – do you think mom has some of Grandma's mental issues? I know you can inherit bipolar syndrome."

"I think your Mom is volatile, no mistake about that. But usually she calms down and is able to be a little introspective and apologize. Isn't that your experience?"

"I guess. But boy, when she blows, she blows!"

"She's lucky to have your Dad – he seems pretty even-tempered. And I know how much he loves her – and you and Ben. You can see that."

"Yes. Dad is the rock at home. He's always there, always calm, always rational."

"That's why your Mom was attracted to him in the first place, don't you think?"

"Probably."

Deena put her glass down. It was still mostly full. "I'm so tired. I think I'll just fall into bed. Will you wake me in time for my appointment? I charged my phone, but the battery seems dead already. Probably need to replace it."

"Of course. Try not to think about this kerfuffle, or Kitty's, either. Things will get sorted. None of it is your worry, really. Mike's going to take you to your appointment and your mother will be there too. Then I guess you'll be going home. Call me and let me know what the doctor says. Promise?"

"Of course. And Mike will probably bring me back down to pick up the car as soon as I can drive."

"Plan to stay and visit when you do that – come on a weekend?"

"If we can. Thanks for everything, Grampa." She kissed him and made her way across the patio and into the house.

JACK WATCHED the fire until it had almost burned itself out. Then he put the spark screen over the pit, picked up his drink and the bottle of scotch. He returned the bottle to the shed and locked it. Was Jenny really as balanced as he had told Deena? He often wondered if she had inherited her mother's psychosis. But she didn't have the mood swings, and even though she was hot tempered and occasionally moody, it didn't seem outside what was normal. She did have a good head on her shoulders, and she could be introspective. In fact he often thought maybe she was overly introspective. But he understood why that might be. Her own fear probably mirrored his. He sighed deeply and went off to bed.

Chapter 67

THE NEXT MORNING Jack fixed a couple of egg and cheese quesadillas for Mike and Deena, and after a second cup of coffee, they were ready to leave. Kitty was still asleep. "You guys have everything? Deena's books? Computer? Phone?"

"Yes – we're good to go, Grampa. Please tell Kitty good bye. It was fun getting to know her. I hope she will be here when we come back to pick up the car."

"I think she will be – at least I hope so too! Good luck with your Mom, Dee. I'm pretty sure she will have calmed down a bit by now. Let's hope she got a good night's sleep."

"Oh – and keep us posted on the progress on the farm-house! I can't wait to see how that turns out!"

"Of course. And you remember to call me and let me know what those x-rays reveal about that knee!"

Jack gave Deena a kiss and waved them off.

KITTY HADN'T BEEN ASLEEP. In fact she barely slept at all. She was thinking about just leaving and finding a place to stay where Gray couldn't track her. But all of her things were here, and she couldn't leave Jack with that mess. Especially since she had no idea what some of it was. Maybe they could return those boxes that had Gray's things to the storage facility. He had to have paid for at least a month for that unit. She could just say that some of the things they cleared out didn't belong to her, but to the guy who rented the space. Would that work? Then she'd be freer to make a move herself. Maybe she could at least make a phone call and find out. But she'd have to finish going through all the boxes to make sure there was nothing else of his mixed in with her things. That would probably take the better part of the morning. And she didn't want Jack around while she was sorting through everything. How could she get him out of here without making him suspicious?

She took a quick shower and pulled on her jeans and a t-shirt. Maybe she could send him on an errand that would take him out of the house for a while.

If he went as far as Riverside, that would take him at least an hour out and an hour back. What about that thrift shop that was near the University that was raising funds for scholarships? She'd seen that when they went to the Credit Union the other day and thought he might agree to take some of the boxes they had sorted and labeled "donate" – in fact she had mentioned that to him at the time and he thought it was a great idea. Maybe, just maybe, she could get him to take those over there today. They needed to get them off the patio anyway. And if she asked him to get a receipt, for tax purposes, that would take him even longer. They'd have to open the boxes, go through things, and estimate value. It was worth a try.

"Any coffee left?" Kitty asked. Jack was sitting at the table in the kitchen, trying to focus on the crossword from the paper. She could tell he was agitated.

"Sure – I made another pot. You sleep well?"

"Well enough, I guess. You?"

"Pretty well. Just couldn't stop worrying about one thing and another. I'm so sorry you had to see Jenny at her worst. She can really let it fly."

"Oh, come on Jack. I've seen worse. And I understand. She's worried about her kid, she's worried about you. I'm sure seeing the house so changed upset her, too."

"Yeah. She mentioned that. She's the one who wanted to make order out of my house. I think she's miffed I allowed someone else to help me. But I needed to do things in my own time, and in my own way. And you've made that possible. We're a good team."

"I think so too. And since we still have a lot to do, I was wondering if you might be willing to take a load of things you decided to donate over to that thrift shop we saw in Riverside. I know it's a long drive, but it seems like a worthy cause – and it looks like the people running it know what they're doing. They would be able to give you a receipt that reflected actual value, which could be good come tax time. What do you think?"

"I guess we could do that. I have some checks that came through that I need to deposit at the Credit Union, too."

"There you go! Oh – and maybe you could bring back some of that good rye bread from that little bakery near where we ate when we were there?"

"Me? Just me? Won't you go with me?"

"I want to get through the rest of those boxes from storage today. It's kind of driving me crazy until I know what's there and what may not be. So I think I would like to stay here. If that's okay?"

"Well – I guess. You sure you want to stay here on your own?"

"I'll be fine, Jack. Have you had breakfast?"

"No, I fixed some for the kids – but I was waiting for you."

"Good! Why don't we go over to the Snowbird and get their special? My treat."

"Sure. I'll take you up on that!"

Chapter 68

JENNY PACED UP and down the doctor's office waiting room. She was still upset. She also hated the fact that she couldn't be with Deena in the doctor's office. But she was eighteen, and old enough to go in alone if that's what she wanted. And that's what she wanted. Jenny was upset at herself for losing it, last night -- especially in front of Mike and Kitty. That would be an embarrassment she'd always regret. But when she saw the changes that had been made in her mother's house, jealousy kicked in. Her Dad would never have let her do what Kitty had been able to pull off. He was so protective of the way things were – and the snail's pace he was going drove her nuts. He moved the TV into the living room – that was startling. And the furniture was arranged so the room really was appealing. But it didn't look like home. It didn't feel like home. When she looked into the room she usually stayed in, she could see that Kitty was using it. And Deena was in the room she had used when she was a little girl – but there were no boxes or bags of whatever it was her mom had stored there. In fact it looked like a very welcoming bedroom. Wildflowers on the dresser – Deena would love that. *Who was this woman, really? And why had she taken such liberties with mom's things? They all certainly looked very cozy out on the patio – all drinking together. Well, it can't be undone now.*

Deena came out to the waiting room with a brace on her knee. Mike looked up and smiled. "No more crutches?"

"Nope. Just this brace. And, I have to see a sports doc when we get home so he can make sure I'm doing the exercises I need to do to heal. But NO broken bones!"

"Oh, Deena – that's great!" Jenny stepped towards Deena, her arms out. But Deena drew back. She was clearly still seething about Jenny's outburst from the previous evening.

"Yeah, I'm okay Mom. You really didn't need to drive all the way out here."

Jenny started to say something, then thought better of it. She picked up her purse and walked out to the parking lot. Mike and Deena followed her.

"I'm going to go straight to the office, since you obviously don't need me, and have a ride home, I'll let Dad know. I assume you two are going straight there?"

"That's the plan. Mike has to get back to work."

"Good. Drive safe." Jenny got into her car and drove off.

Mike opened the door for Deena, holding it while he waited for her to get in. Deena watched her mother's car leave the lot.

"I wondered why mom had her business clothes on when we went to the doctor this morning. She looks so unhappy."

"She's got a lot on her mind – that argument with your Grampa last night, your knee, and who knows – maybe something's going on at work."

"She's got plenty of people to sort work out. She just can't stay away. Takes responsibility for every little detail. Must drive her employees crazy. Talk about a micro-manager."

"Let's get you home. You going to call your dad?"

"I'll text him. Can we stop and get some coffee or something? I'm still hungry. Breakfast seems like a long time ago."

"Sure. We can stop for coffee. And maybe a pastry?"

THE PHONE RANG and Kitty jumped. Jack laughed. "It's only Deena calling to let me know the results of her x-ray!"

"Hi Grampa – I'm fine. No broken bones as far as they can tell. The doctor says to check in with a sports specialist when we get home. He thinks physical therapy will be all that's needed. So that's a relief. They gave me a kind of walking brace, so I don't need the crutches."

"Oh I am glad!"

"Okay. Well, mom's already taken off. And Mike and I are going to stop by Starbuck's and head out. Thanks for everything! Tell Kitty good bye."

"Will do. 'Bye."

"Sounds like she's okay?"

"Yes. No breaks. She may need some physical therapy – she's going to see a sports injury doc when she gets back home. Thank goodness."

"Phew. I was worried. I still feel so bad about the whole thing – and responsible."

"Nonsense! Now let's go get some of that breakfast you promised me before we get our day going."

JENNY CALLED Kevin to let him know they were on their way home, and that Deena was okay. He didn't pick up, so she left a message. Then she called Peter at work. He picked up immediately. "Jenny? I'm so glad you called. You coming in soon?

Everything is okay, but they were only able to do a temporary fix of the plumbing and need to talk to you about shutting down the facility for a couple of days to replace some major pipes."

"Great. That's all we need. Yes, I'm on my way in but I won't be there for another two hours, at least. Is everyone situated for today?"

"Yes, I think so."

"Well don't just think so, Peter! Find out!" she hung up.

Why did everything have to fall apart at once? She bumped up her speed to 80, risking a ticket to save some time. She knew she couldn't push it too far, but at least for this stretch of road she could gain a few minutes. She would gamble. Poor Peter. He'd already covered for her this morning. He didn't deserve to have her snap at him. She'd have to take him a goodwill offering to smooth things over. She slowed down when the highway started to curve, remembering that for some reason traffic slowed way down whenever that happened. Nothing really in the way, but when people couldn't see too far ahead, they tended to be more cautious. Maybe that was her problem. She couldn't see far enough ahead for comfort. She couldn't see if her Dad would make good decisions and stay healthy and safe. She couldn't see if Deena would learn from her bad experience with alcohol and not make that mistake again. She couldn't see where Deena was going with this Mike. She liked him, but he was clearly too old for Deena. Especially now. Maybe in five years, not now. But she didn't have a window into five years from now, either. She'd just have to slow down. Develop some trust. She felt anything but trust right now. She was sure Kitty was up to no good although she had no proof of that. Her Dad could so easily be taken in by a woman who could manipulate him and make him jump through hoops to keep her happy. That's what her mother had done, and people get used to things. She knew that. Maybe she could do a background check on Kitty. She certainly had access to that process at work. But she would need a last name to do that. Maybe Deena would know. Was Kitty as crazy as her mom had been? Was she cuckoo? She certainly seemed like a cuckoo to Jenny – settling in someone else's nest.

The road straightened out, and traffic sped up. Jenny moved into the fast lane. Time to deal with all of this later. Right now she had to get to work. Work issues were easier.

Chapter 69

AFTER BREAKFAST AT THE SNOWBIRD, Kitty and Jack went home and loaded the truck with boxes of items identified as "giveaways". They were able to clear off both patios. Jack looked a little hesitant after the last one. "You having second thoughts, Jack? Are you sure you really want to get rid of all this stuff?"

"Oh, I'm just thinking that once it's all gone I'll hear from Jenny about how she wanted this or that."

"We did put aside things that you thought she might want. Remember?"

"Yes. But given her mood last night I wouldn't be surprised if she accused me of giving away everything she REALLY wanted."

"We can put it all back, Jack. I thought this was what you wanted."

"You're right. It isn't hers, in any case. And if she had wanted any of it, I'm sure she would have taken it by now."

"There are a couple of boxes of keepsakes and jewelry we set aside."

"I know. But I do feel so much freer now that all of that stuff is out of the house. Okay – I'm heading out."

"Remember to get a receipt! There's so much you're donating, it could help you out on taxes."

"Right. Well – I probably won't make it back here until two or three. You sure you're okay here on your own? You could come with me."

"I'm sure! I want to get the rest of my own stuff sorted so we can make another trip with what I don't want to keep. Go! I'll be fine. And I won't be alone – isn't Carlin going to be working today?"

"Oh – that's right. Actually I think he's already here. So if you do need help moving anything, you can ask him."

"Of course. See you when you get back!"

The drive to Riverside was uneventful, but painfully slow. Jack had a lot to think about, and this was a good opportunity to do that. What was Kitty's past, really? He sighed. Maybe Emily would be able to get more out of her – in fact Emily would HAVE to learn more or she wouldn't be able to help her. But then there was that attorney-client privilege – and he knew Emily would never reveal anything Kitty wanted to keep private. He would just have to be more patient. In good time she might just open up. But he knew it wouldn't be until she felt really free of Gray. Hopefully that would come soon.

What could possibly be so terrible that she couldn't share it with him?

THE REST of the boxes from storage were full of Kitty's clothing, books and personal items. She didn't find anything else that belonged to Gray. But when she opened her jewelry box, she saw that several good pieces were missing. *What a shit.*

He made sure to get everything of value. Why am I surprised? He never willingly gave anyone anything. He would pretend to be the magnanimous, generous, benefactor – but he always got something in return, and always more than he had given one way or another. How could I have been so desperate? What was it about the high-life that was so compelling?

As if I don't know. I loved the attention I got when I was with him – the star treatment because I was on Gray's arm, or at Gray's side, or in Gray's bed. He was royalty in the closed world he had created of people who were rich and never worried about rules. I am so much better off without him. Even if I am practically broke. The jewelry was never more than an illusion of a kind of financial security, really. He told me it was worth thousands, and he was probably right. But it's all gone now.

She put everything that was beaded or sequined in a box to sell. Then she pulled out the business clothes and put them in a box to donate. She didn't want any part of that life. If she had to get a job it would be something honest, something she could feel good about. Maybe there was a way to keep doing what she had been doing for Jack for other people – sorting out the unnecessary and organizing the things that were wanted.

I wonder...does Jack really want me? I know I've been useful, and sometimes he looks at me with such sweetness... I want something real this time...with somebody I can trust, who won't just take what he can get and then leave. Or, to be honest, I don't want to take advantage of him and be the one who runs off, either. I'll have to be careful or I'll blow this. I've got more than all these boxes of stuff following me. And the interview with that attorney on Wednesday...it's too much.

The trip to Riverside took longer than Jack thought it should. He had no idea how thorough the thrift shop would be when he asked for a receipt. His experience before with donations had been that he handed over the boxes, and they handed him a receipt after filling in how many and a general description of "household" or "clothing." But this place must have been run by some very detail-oriented volunteers who had to examine each box and determine approximate worth. It was a good thing Kitty had insisted on separating things that were new or almost new from those that were truly used. Obviously, these were people who knew exactly what the "good" stuff was. In fact, he saw them setting aside many of the items as they were sorting.

He was hungry and tired by the time he was headed back, and he hoped Kitty had thought about putting something together for dinner. There were some leftovers from yesterday's barbeque, and that would suit him just fine. That and a nice glass of scotch.

Chapter 70

Mike held Deena's door open, but she didn't get in. She looked at him and said "I hate that nothing is ever really resolved with my Mom! We walk around in denial for a few days until we're worn out from it. Then we go out to dinner or something and everybody just breathes a sigh of relief. I'd like to know more about what she's thinking, how she's processing. I never get that."

"Maybe she doesn't get it either? Some people are terrified of confronting their own messy lives. My family's a lot like that too."

"Mike, as long as we are friends let's promise to talk about everything. I mean everything that matters. Deal?" She stuck out her hand to shake on it.

Mike grabbed her hand and pulled her to him, gave her a quick hug. "Sure, Dee. Absolutely."

For one moment she thought he was going to kiss her – then he squeezed her hand and pushed her gently away. She ducked her head, her cheeks burning, and turned to get in the car. Mike closed the door and let out a long sigh as he went around to the driver's seat.

He started the car and turned to look at her. "So in order to keep things straight about this friendship – for me at least -- it feels like more than just friendship. There I've said it. And it's true."

Deena felt herself blush. "Yes. It is for me, too."

"I want to take it slow, Dee. I want to be sure. This feels too important to treat like an ordinary thing, know what I mean?"

"Yes. I do. And I agree."

They drove in silence until they found a coffee shop. When they pulled into the parking lot, Deena turned to Mike. "Just kiss me, Mike. Kiss me here, in this parking lot ..." His lips were on hers before she could finish the sentence. It wasn't the first kiss for either of them. But it was the best. "I feel like I've wanted to do that my whole life, Deena."

"Me too, Mike. My whole life."

Is young love the best love? Is it the rosebuds we gather or scatter, that we remember? Is it the courtship full of glances, teasing, seducing, that outshines the misunderstandings and disagreements when we look back? Can romance outshine friendship, should it? Is it even possible for romance to be honest, to be true, to be fair? Or will it always be just a little bit deceitful, just a little bit unfaithful, just a little bit jealous or opinionated?

Deena and Mike had no template. They knew what they didn't want more than what they dd. Could you build a relationship that was balanced and sound? That would be the journey. That would be the challenge. And it would all have to be done with a chorus of voices surrounding them. But in that one moment, in that one kiss, everything seemed possible.

DEENA AND MIKE sat talking in his car for a long time after they got home. Kevin finally went out and asked them to come in and have something to eat. Mike looked at Deena, and she smiled at him and said "Please?"

"You probably should put that leg up, too Dee. You've been in the car for a long time." Kevin opened the passenger door.

"Yes. You're right. I probably should."

Jenny was on the phone with her Dad when they came in, and she obviously had been crying.

"Mom, are you okay?" Deena whispered.

Jenny nodded at her and took the phone into the backyard to finish her call.

―――――

KEVIN PICKED up Deena's backpack and computer. Mike excused himself, saying he needed to get home and get ready for work.

"Sorry you couldn't stay for something to eat, Mike. Looks like Mom is pretty upset. Call me later?"

"Of course. You take care. Put that leg up! And you know you can call me, too!"

Kevin looked at Deena. She seemed tired. "Why don't you make your way upstairs? You look like you need to stretch out. I'll bring your stuff up."

"Thanks, Dad. Could you just bring my computer and books up? Clothes in my backpack need to be washed, so leave that down here. I am kind of tired."

She lay on her bed, watching the afternoon light dappling the maple tree outside her window. It wasn't long before she drifted off.

Chapter 71

JENNY CALLED Peter again from the road. She was now stuck in traffic. "Hey there. I'm not going to make it before noon, I'm sure. There's an accident or construction or something, and traffic is at a dead stop. Anything I need to know before I get there?"

"The contractor doing the repairs has some questions, but that will wait until this afternoon. He needs to do more work than he thought, which is going to bump up the cost."

"Great. Well, I don't see how we can NOT fix it. Did he tell you how much it was going to add to the cost?"

"He thinks it will run another five or six grand."

"WHAT? My god, what is he going to have to do?"

"I'm not entirely clear about that, but apparently it involves tearing out some flooring and part of a wall. In the meantime, the center can't be open. We'll be okay in the offices, but the facility is going to have to stay closed. I've called around to see if we can find some space somewhere temporarily, but so far I haven't had any luck."

"Great. Well --- give him the green light, but make sure he knows that it needs to get done quickly."

"Will do. I thought I might call some local churches and see if we could use one of their community rooms. What do you think?"

"I think that's a great idea. See what you can find out and let me know. In the meantime, let's get some extra help for the facilities handling our people from the flood. Jeez – sounds biblical, doesn't it?"

Peter laughed. "Yes – too bad we can't find an ark! I'll call the groups who've volunteered to help before – maybe we can get some free services before we hire temporary staff."

"I like the way you think. Traffic is inching along now. Talk to you later."

The traffic felt like another personal attack. Another kind of boxing in, not giving her room, impeding her. It made her angry, and it made her sad. She'd felt trapped so long by her mother's illnesses—mental and otherwise—even after she left home. The relationship she craved from both her parents kept eluding her. And now, just when she thought she might have a chance at building something with her dad, there was another needy woman in his life. Somebody else with a claim on his time, his focus, his emotional energy. Would Jenny ever get to be the focus? Even for an hour? A minute? Deena seemed to enjoy the company of both of them. They all made quite the merry little group – and Mike fit in well also.

She leaned on the horn until other drivers turned and glared at her. She couldn't make the traffic move any faster by blasting it with sound. She couldn't make her dad respond by yelling at him, either. Not in the way she wanted. Why was that still so important? She had a husband who loved her, was patient with her moods and distractions. She had two great kids. Why wasn't that enough?

The radio sent out strains of Beethoven's Ninth, and she angrily pushed the button to a jazz station. Classical music was one of the things her parents used to argue about. Her mother hated it, felt depressed by it. Jenny thought it was beautiful; maybe because her dad loved it. She thought by choosing classical music, as he had, it would be a point of connection she could keep. Maybe she needed to break off that connection entirely. Would he even notice? Would he care?

She grabbed for a tissue – her face was streaked with tears, and her nose was running. Why was she crying for god's sake? Nobody had died, here.

Except her mother had died. She had died and left Jenny feeling relieved but orphaned. Glad that her mother was finally at peace, sad that there still was something she wanted and now could never have. Never.

But these tears felt like another kind of grieving. It was as if now she had lost her father, too. Although he was still living and breathing – healthy – he was more remote than ever. More out of her reach. More caught by someone else. Why couldn't she have had just a month or two of his attention, his engagement with her family?

At least Deena had some of that even though Kitty was there. Maybe because Kitty was there, even though apparently Kitty had been the cause of her accident. Jenny could see they had formed a connection. Deena laughed with Kitty, she'd heard that before she even got out the back door. And Deena's beautiful hair in that French braid? She knew Deena hadn't done that. Kitty was already that comfortable that she would do Deena's hair. *Best put it aside. Think of the work problems. Think of Kevin, and Ben. Anything. Anything else but that unsatisfied longing for connection, any connection, with my dad.*

Chapter 72

JACK'S CONVERSATIONS with his daughter were exhausting. She was always pushing for more information. She wanted something from him, but he had no idea what it was. *She has a full life with her own family – what does she still need from me?* It was a mystery he could not unravel. It felt like the same kind of insecurity Lily had exhibited, and it scared him. Had she inherited a tendency to paranoia and mood swings? So far she seemed stable enough. She certainly had a responsible job and was well respected. But sometimes he felt that those closest to her were struggling. Deena's issues could be chalked up to her age, but Kevin had shown signs of tension and a kind of exasperation too. He dialed Jenny's number, hoping it would go to voicemail.

Jenny answered. "Dad? Oh thank goodness. I was beginning to get really worried. I've been calling all day! Where have you been?"

"I've been running some errands and I've been out back helping Carlin in the farmhouse. I'm okay! How are you? Was traffic bad going home?"

"I wish you'd carry your cell phone with you!" Jenny sounded angry.

"Sorry if I worried you. I didn't have it on. I only keep it in the car for emergencies. So – everything okay your end? How's Kevin? How's Ben?"

"They're okay."

"Did you go to work today?" Jack hoped he had deflected her anger.

"Yes – I had to. One of the facilities had a big plumbing problem over the weekend, and I really should have been there yesterday."

"Deena get home okay?"

"Yes. They just pulled in."

"Mike seems like a nice guy."

"Yes, he does. He's a bit old for Deena, though. I'm not sure I'm comfortable with that relationship." Jenny sounded sad.

"Parents seldom are. As I recall, I wasn't too keen on Kevin. She's a good kid, she's got a good head on her shoulders. It was nice to have her here. Just sorry about her fall."

"I'm sorry about flying off the handle the other night. I don't know what gets into me, sometimes."

Was she crying?

"Well, you've got a lot on your mind. Hope you get your work problems sorted out without too much hassle. And don't worry about Deena, Jenny. She's going to be fine. Really."

"I hope so. She's pulling away from me." Jenny said.

"She's supposed to. She's not a kid anymore, Jenny. It's hard to let go when they're ready to fly. I know. But you and Kevin have done a great job with her, and she's going to soar." Jack waited for her response.

"I hope so, Dad. Call me again soon? I really do worry about you too."

"I will. Right now I've got to go. I've got steaks on the

BARBEQUE. I'll talk to you again tomorrow. Have a good evening. And stop worrying about me!"

"I'll try. Enjoy your steak. 'Bye."

Jack went out to the patio where Kitty was waiting for him. He stopped for a moment and watched her pinch a few brown leaves off a geranium plant. He smiled. *She feels at home.*

Chapter 73

Deena's appointment with the Orthopedist went well. He looked at her x-rays, saw what her range of motion was with that knee, and said that everything looked fine. He wrote out a referral slip for physical therapy and told her he would see her in six weeks. She was free to go back to school but should wear the brace unless she was home--start giving that leg a little practice but protect it when she was out. He reminded her to use her good leg to lift when she was going upstairs so as not to damage the injured knee.

It was good news that she could take the brace off at home. Her leg felt fine, but she was still reluctant to put too much pressure on it. One thing she did learn from Dr. Jock (as she would always remember him, now), was that soft tissue takes longer to heal than a break. She could expect it to be a full six weeks before her leg was back to normal. But it was okay for her to drive. Lucky it was her left knee, and not her right.

She was tired when she got home. The ride to and from the doctor with her mother had been cordial, but frosty. Her mother was obviously still unhappy with her and her Grampa. She wouldn't even talk about it. She did ask some leading questions about Kitty, but since Deena didn't really have any information beyond what Jenny already knew, she couldn't answer them.

Deena had to protect herself from her mother. That had been true since she turned thirteen. There was a wall between them that hadn't been there before. Sometimes her mother would open a crack from her side and try to connect, but Deena was cautious. She'd been burned too many times by giving up too much information or saying something her mother considered rude or inappropriate. It was better to keep her own counsel. She often felt as if her mother were observing her as if she were a science project, or a sociological experiment. It was creepy. She longed for the old connection she'd had as a child, but that didn't seem possible now.

On the other hand, Kitty had treated her like a friend. Like family, even. And they had been able to laugh together and enjoy each other's company. She hoped she could make that connection again, that Grampa would stay in touch with Kitty for a long time. Maybe even let her rent the farmhouse! That was a great idea. Kitty needed a place to stay, and it was almost ready. She could send her some links about furnishings and décor and they could stay in touch that way.

She was looking at retro furnishings when her mom opened her bedroom door. "What's up Dee? You want to come have some lunch? I've made a Waldorf Salad with chicken. You like that, right?"

Deena jumped – it wasn't usual for her mom to just walk into her room. "Um – sure, Mom. I'll be right down. Just want to save this link."

Jenny waited while Deena bookmarked the link and asked her if she needed any help with the stairs since she wasn't wearing her brace.

"No. I'm okay. The doctor said to take it slow, and not put

stress on my left knee, so I step down with my right leg every time. I can do it. It'll take me awhile, but I'll get there. You go ahead."

Deena reminded herself to be careful. Not only of her knee, but of any probing conversation that might be the real reason for her mother's offer of lunch together. Usually she would rush right back to work after a doctor or orthodontist appointment, telling Deena to fix herself something.

After a few polite exchanges about the salad, the questions started again. Jenny was relentless. Deena sighed.

"So, tell me again about this Kitty? How long is she going to be there, did they say?"

"I don't know Mom, they didn't say."

"Do you ever remember your grandma talking about her?"

"No, but why would she talk about an old friend with me? Maybe they went to high school together or maybe even elementary school?"

"Well, sometimes people talk about how they're connected – especially if they seem to come from nowhere – from out of the blue."

Deena could hear the edge in her mother's tone. This was going to be tough.

"She seems like a very nice lady. She makes Grampa laugh. And she has really made a huge difference in the house. It's more like a home than a storeroom. You saw it, right? At least the living room?"

"Yes. I saw it. I don't understand why she has the right to take everything in my Dad's life and rearrange it. He wouldn't let me do it, that's for sure." Jenny stabbed at a piece of apple with her fork.

"He seems to appreciate everything she's been able to accomplish. And he's cooking again, which is good for everybody. After Grandma died, he was eating tuna out of a can. Remember?"

"Which is why I thought he should just sell the place and move up here, closer to us. Closer to me."

"He's happy where he is, mom. And he's remodeling the old farmhouse. I think Kitty might wind up renting it from him. It would be good for both of them."

"WHAT? I can't believe it. He's spending more money on that broken-down hovel? He must be losing his mind."

"It's NOT a broken-down hovel. It's actually in good condition. And his friend Carlin has been repairing and refinishing and bringing the wiring and plumbing up to date. And isn't that what you wanted? For Grampa to have company and not live all alone?"

"I certainly didn't want him taking in someone we know nothing about!" Jenny picked up the empty dishes and banged them down on the counter. "I've got to get back to work. Since your knee is so much better, you do these dishes." She slammed out the back door, muttering to herself.

Deena sighed, rinsed the dishes and loaded the dishwasher. She could tell that difficult times were ahead with her mom. She'd seen it starting when Jenny showed up at her Grampa's last Sunday. She remembered her Grandma's moods and how they had impacted the whole family. *Why can't Mom see that she's doing the same thing? And how does Dad manage to stay so even-tempered through all of it? Sometimes that's a little maddening too! Why couldn't he make her see the pattern and help her step out of the loop?*

Deena made her way back upstairs. She'd send Kitty the link to the retro fixtures website, and text Mike; then maybe do some studying and figure out what to wear to school tomorrow. It would be so good to get out of this house again.

Chapter 74

JACK HAD AGREED he and Kitty would meet Emily at the University Faculty Club to talk about Kitty's options to protect herself from Gray. They would leave after the morning traffic had subsided. Kitty had said almost nothing during the drive. She was thinking about the serious conversation they were going to have. They got there before Emily did and were considering the menu when Emily came through the front door. He stood to greet her and pulled out a chair.

"Hi Jack! You look pretty good for an old retired guy!" she smiled. He felt a sense of relief when he realized she still greeted him with an affectionate tease. It had been at least a year since they had connected. She sent flowers and a card when Lily died, but Jack wasn't good at keeping in touch. It didn't seem to matter to Emily. Here she was, warm and friendly as ever.

"How are you doing? You look pretty good for somebody who is still working!" Jack said, and Emily laughed and looked at Kitty.

"This is Kitty, Emily."

"Nice to meet you. And thank you so much for taking the

time to talk with me." Kitty put out her hand and Emily took it in both of her hands.

"It's what I do! Hopefully there will be something that I can tell you that will help." Emily sat down and picked up her menu.

Kitty fidgeted with her napkin, then excused herself to use the restroom.

"So, Em, how are things going here?"

"Jack, you got out just in time. Things have gone south since you left, at least in terms of support for programs that matter. Still battling with the administration for more funding and chasing grants all over the place."

"Ah yes, I remember that all very clearly. At least the Women's Center is still up and functioning?"

"Yes, happily. We got a pretty hefty windfall from some anonymous donor who designated the Center as sole beneficiary of their estate. That came to us last year and means we can operate without too much worry for the foreseeable future. Now it's just a matter of protecting those funds from the busy little number crunchers who have ideas about skirting around the provisions of the trust to benefit other programs. Fortunately, we are well-protected. But they keep trying!"

"I remember that game, too."

Kitty returned to the table looking a bit more composed, and the waitress came to take their order.

Kitty decided on a salad and a glass of iced tea. Jack chose a ham on rye and asked for coffee. Emily just wanted a cup of potato soup.

After the waitress left, Emily looked at Kitty. She could tell that Kitty was nervous.

"You know that whatever you tell me is protected information, Kitty. But I think I do need to hear the whole story, not just a piece of it."

"Yes. I know, and I won't pretend that this is easy for me. I've gotten myself involved in something bad, but I'm not clear about all of the pieces." Kitty picked up her water glass with a shaky hand.

"I've been doing a little nosing around, Kitty, and I know that you were working for Gray Carmichael and that you were seen out and about quite often at one casino or another. Right now I understand he's under investigation for fraud and money laundering, and a possible connection to organized crime. I think you are going to need more than just a restraining order at this point. Especially after that confrontation at Jack's the other night."

Kitty's eyes widened, and she looked at Jack. "Gray is the one who threw me out of the apartment I was living in, and then drugged me and left me in a homeless shelter. When I finally realized where I was, I felt trapped. Left the place to clear my head, and that's when Jack found me. I'd blown a tire on the bike I had 'borrowed'."

"And so Jack, you, being you, offered to fix it for her. Am I right?" Emily smiled.

"Well, yes. I did. She looked so vulnerable – and then I offered her a place to stay until she got herself sorted. She agreed, but only if I'd let her work to earn her keep. So that's what she's been doing. And up until last week everything was fine. Then Gray showed up, drunk. He'd had a private investigator track her down. That's when I called you."

The waitress returned with their food, and they waited until she left to continue their conversation.

Emily said, "So now Gray is facing an investigation. And from what I've learned about him and his reputation, he will take very little blame for whatever he's involved in. He has a knack for setting people up and making them take the fall. So now that he knows where to find you, we need to make sure you have some good protection."

"I knew he cooked the books for his business; but is there something else going on too? It sounds so much bigger than I could imagine. Tax fraud, maybe, but money laundering and connection to organized crime?" Kitty hadn't touched her salad. "I've still got a bunch of his stuff in Jack's garage. We picked it up from the storage unit Gray moved my things into. I thought it was only my things. But I opened the boxes yesterday, and there are some papers and locked strong boxes, too. I sealed them all up. Should we turn those over to the police? Is that what he wanted to talk to me about?" Kitty picked up her tea, her hand still unsteady.

"Do you think he could show up again at my place to try to get those things?" Jack looked shaky himself.

"It's hard to say. I'll see that your place is put under surveillance. If he does attempt to do that, he can be stopped. He has no right to anything that is on your property without your permission. But I do think you should arrange to turn over those boxes to the police just to be on the safe side. We want to make sure you are not implicated as an accomplice. From what I've learned, this is a very big investigation that involves more than just Gray and whatever he tries to do to implicate Kitty. The agents investigating will need to be sure you are willing to cooperate with them, and I think that's your only way to get the protection you need. You did know Gray was married, Kitty?" Emily looked at Kitty, and Kitty looked back, but couldn't hold Emily's gaze. She felt cheap, dirty.

"I knew he had an arrangement with his wife. He told me it had only been a marriage of convenience." Her voice was barely audible.

"Yes, well, his convenience, not hers, obviously." Emily said, tersely.

Chapter 75

EMILY PULLED a gossip magazine out of her briefcase. And there was a photo of Gray, with another woman, under the headline 'PHILANTHROPIST ADA CARMICHAEL SUES HUSBAND FOR DIVORCE"; followed by a story suggesting that Gray had been siphoning off Ada's money and living the high life. The story also suggested that a pre-nuptial agreement would leave him penniless if there was a divorce. Ada's money didn't belong to Gray, nor did the string of car lots spread all over the inland empire.

"If Gray or his dicey companions decide you know too much and might give evidence against Gray or any of the others implicated, they'll want to make sure you stay silent." Emily looked at Jack. "She's in real danger, Jack, and now you could be too. These are nasty, clever people. And none of them has a conscience. My sources tell me that the Feds suspect drug trafficking, also. Do you see why I'm worried? And particularly worried because we don't know what those boxes contain?"

The color drained from Jack's face.

"You need to turn state's evidence, cooperate fully with the investigators, Kitty. Tell them everything – everything you know. I don't see any other way out for you, and Jack's role as an accomplice, unwitting though it is, makes this situation dangerous for him too. So, we need to make sure the two of you are protected. I'm going to speak very plainly, here. The two of you are going to have to go into hiding. I'm very serious about this. It's the only way I can protect you, Kitty. And you too, Jack. You are vulnerable if you stay at your home. They clearly know where you live. And these people are ruthless."

Jack looked at Kitty. She had gone very pale. He covered her hand with his.

"I have a facility that I work with when I need to be sure my clients are protected from spousal abuse or elder abuse. I want you to go there. At this point, you need to be out of harm's way."

"My god, Emily, do we have to enter a witness protection program? You're scaring me."

"You should be scared, Jack. This is big time stuff you've both fallen into. I'm not blaming anyone, but we need to make sure you are safe, and get those boxes off your property. Are you willing to be interviewed by the District Attorney's office Kitty?"

Kitty looked at Jack, and he nodded. "It's your only option, as far as I can see."

Kitty said, "Yes. I will do whatever I can. Especially if it will help to protect Jack. He really is innocent in all of this."

"Good, because I've arranged with the DA's office for you to be interviewed as a witness for the prosecution a week from tomorrow. But between now and then I want to make sure you are safe and that those boxes wind up in the hands of the authorities. So the first thing you both need to do is pack a bag. Then put those boxes in storage, and move to the facility I've mentioned. Okay?"

"Can I let Jenny know I'm going somewhere?" Jack said.

"No. You can phone her and tell her you will be out of town for a few days. Then disconnect your house phone."

Jack had lost all interest in his sandwich, and his coffee. He sat there, staring at Emily.

"You have only done what decent people always do, Jack. Tried to help someone in need. It's not foolish, or naïve. You're a brave man, and you're going to get through this. So is Kitty. We are going to use, as they say, 'an abundance of caution,' to keep you both safe. Now try to finish that sandwich before you go back home and pack your bags and load those boxes." She patted his hand and motioned for the waitress.

Kitty's face was streaked with tears. "I'm so sorry, Jack. Really. You should just leave me along with those boxes. I should have to deal with this on my own. I'm the one who landed myself in this position, and I must face that."

"Don't be silly, Kitty. We will get through this together. Besides – Gray is just the kind of man Emily would love to see behind bars. She's defended abused and battered women her whole working life."

"He's right, Kitty. It's not going to be easy, but I am ready to take this on, and if we all work together, we'll see Gray gets what he so richly deserves."

Jack paid the bill, and hurried Kitty out of the restaurant. Emily stayed behind to finish her lunch and make a phone call.

Jack and Kitty were silent for a long time, both nervous about what was next, and worried for each other. That was a new feeling for Kitty. She normally was only worried about herself.

Jack marveled at Emily's understanding of the situation. She had really done her homework. But then, she had years of experience sorting out legal entanglements and dangerous liaisons as attorney for the Women's Center at San Fernando University. She had seen it all. And had saved so many from the despair of abusive relationships and legal entanglements. He really couldn't have anybody better on his side. He hoped Kitty understood how lucky she was, too. Although in her current circumstances he was sure she didn't feel anything but pain and regret for ever having gotten involved with Gray. How was he going to keep all of this from Jenny?

Emily had handed him a slip of paper with an address on it and a key ring with a couple of keys as they were leaving the Faculty Center. She also gave him an address of a storage facility and told him to take all the boxes that belonged to Gray and leave them before they left town. She said there was a unit under the name of Dan Sinclair, that she had arranged. They should leave the boxes there and turn the key in as well. Then they should go straight to the safe house. It was only about an hour out of Hemet, up near Idyllwild in the mountains. It was an area he was familiar with, where he and Lily had gone many times foraging for wood. And Jack was more than eager to get away and to a place where he and Kitty could be safe, for now.

But what did the future hold for the two of them? He felt like he was suddenly in strange and foreign territory, without a map or compass.

Chapter 76

WHEN THEY GOT to the ranch house, they packed quickly. Jack unplugged the phone, locked all the windows and doors, and set the security alarm that he usually didn't bother with. He knew Kitty didn't have anything that would be warm enough for cold nights in the mountains, so he pulled a couple of warm jackets out of the closet and threw them in the truck. When Gray's boxes and their overnight bags were loaded, he went back to the farmhouse to talk to Carlin.

"Hey there – where have you been? I was hoping to see you earlier, but no luck. It's pretty damn quiet around here, except for the noise I'm making. It kind of gives me the creeps."

"I've had some things to do. Listen, Carlin, Kitty and I are going out of town for a bit, so I set the security alarm in the house. Haven't used it for years, but I still pay the monthly bill and it is connected to the Police. You're listed as a contact, so if you get a call, could you deal with it?"

"Oh my god. I knew this Kitty was nothing but trouble. What's going on, Jack?"

"We are going to be fine. Just need to sort out a few business things back in San Bernardino. I want to be sure the place is secured, that's all. Will you talk to the Police if you get a call? Tell them we are out of town?"

"Well, sure I will – but is there any way to get in touch with you Jack? In case something does happen? You going to take your cell phone?"

"I'll check in with you every so often, Carlin. I'm not sure my cell will take a charge anymore; it's been so long since I've used it. But I'll take your number and I promise to stay in touch."

"Well, I'm pretty much done here. Won't be around after tomorrow – starting that new job soon. You want me to get some security set up out here too? I could get a cheap system and link it to my phone, temporarily."

"That would be great – please do that. Please. I'd appreciate it. You and I will have a long talk after I get back, I promise – and I'll be able to fill you in. But right now I'm in a hurry."

"Well, best not to take any chances, especially since I've done so much work on this place! Besides, if you do rent it out, you'll want security out here anyway. Things aren't like they used to be, gotta lock everything up!"

"Thanks, Carlin. We okay to settle accounts when I get back?"

"No problem. But hey – check in while you're gone, okay? I worry about you old son!"

"Will do. And thanks again – for so much."

"When you going to be back?"

"I'm not sure. I'll probably be gone for at least three or four days."

"Well go on then. I'll secure everything here before I go. I just want to finish this tile, and then I'll pack up and be out of here."

"Okay – I'll give you a call when I can." Jack turned and headed for his truck.

"You do that, now, hear?" Carlin shouted at Jack's back.

Something didn't feel right about the whole thing. Carlin shook his head, and went back to setting tile. *No, it doesn't feel right. Jack and Kitty going off. That's not like Jack at all. Not one little bit. He never runs from trouble, and this feels like trouble to me.*

THE DRIVE UP the mountain was taking longer than Jack remembered. But it had been years since he'd come up this way. They used to approach Idyllwild on Highway 10 from San Fernando, which was pretty much a straight shot. The route from Hemet on the 74 was full of twists and turns, and not as well maintained as the more heavily traveled 10. But it was a pretty drive, when he could take the time to glance out the side windows. He had already passed through the shrubs and grasses on the lower levels of the San Bernardino Mountains and was starting a shady drive through taller growth. Pines, juniper, and oak lined the highway. He rolled down the window. It was a cool day, and the air was scented with sage. Or was it something else? Lily would have known. She would recite the names of wild plants and tell him how they were used by the natives in cooking or to cure ailments. She spoke with such authority that he never questioned her seemingly vast knowledge of which plant was which – but he often wondered if she made some of it up, just to keep him entertained. He had studied botany when he was getting his degree in anthropology, but he'd forgotten most of it by now.

This area was all new to Kitty. She'd never been one to

spend much time in the mountains – or anywhere outdoors. It was like going through a door to a whole new world.

The directions took them off the main road and down into a little valley. They had to travel for some time on a dirt road, and Jack was beginning to think he'd made the wrong turn. Then he spotted a cluster of small cabins protected by a huge, large-leaf maple in a clearing at the bottom of the canyon. He wondered if he'd get any cell-phone service down here. He may not be able to stay in touch with anybody. That could be a problem.

He pulled up in front of the largest cabin, assuming it was where they should check in. There was a small sign above the door that said "Welcome Traveler. Come in and abide with us before you continue your journey." He grimaced. He hoped Emily had not sent him to some kind of religious organization. That would require too much togetherness, too much interaction to suit him. She knew him better than that. Maybe this wasn't the right place.

He parked the car, noticing there was only one other vehicle in sight. An old beat-up van sat at the far end of the clearing, cobwebs visible underneath the carriage. Obviously, it hadn't been moved for a long time. They got out of the truck, stretched, and went up to the door. Before he could knock, it opened, and someone pulled them inside. "Heard your car comin' down the road. You Jack and Kitty?"

"Yes, we are."

"I'm Sister Helen. Emily sent you here?" Sister Helen was of indeterminate gender, so Jack was grateful for the name. She wore overalls and a flannel shirt, and her hair was cut short.

"Yes. She said we could stay for a few days. She thought we needed to be in a 'safe' house, or something." Jack was beginning to feel foolish. He wasn't sure this was at all necessary now that he was here.

"Well then, you've come to the right place. Hardly anybody

knows we're here, and we've given refuge to many when it's been needed. If Emily sent you, she knew what she was doin'. You brought any luggage or anything?"

"Just a couple of overnight bags. They're in the truck. Emily gave me some keys when she sent me. Do I need them here?"

"Oh yes, yes you do. Don't want anybody to find your own car here. If you must go out again, you'll be takin' the van that's parked over there."

"Does it work? It looks like it hasn't been driven for a long time – all those cobwebs and the tires look pretty low."

"Don't let that fool you. Those webs can spring up overnight. And we've got an air compressor out back so you can fill up the tires if you do go anywhere. Now pull your car around behind this cabin. You'll find a garage back there. Park your car in there and bring your bags back here. Be quick about it! I didn't see anyone following you, but you never know."

Jack and Kitty did as they were told and returned with the bags.

"You get any cell phone service up here? It doesn't look promising."

"Oh, we're better set up than we look. Yes. We've got internet service and wifi and anything else you want. Don't ask me how it all works, but we've got everything you'll need, for sure. But if you've got one of those fancy smart phones, you'll have to turn off the tracking. Somebody could sure find you if that thing's on."

"No, my phone isn't that sophisticated. Just a flip top."

"You hungry? This is where you'll take your meals. We have a kitchen here and all our guests eat with us. It's kind of a rule. We don't want to lose track of anybody, like to make sure you're all here at mealtimes. Dinner's almost ready. We eat every night at 6."

"How many people are staying here? I don't see a sign of anybody. No cars, no noise."

"We're a quiet community here. Some people come just for the silence. We've got two other guests, and you may see them at dinner."

"Is this a religious community? I mean, you call yourself 'Sister,'" Jack asked.

"Not so far as I'm concerned it isn't. I left all that behind years ago. No the Sister just kind of stuck I guess, because I used to be a nun. But not anymore. I married an ex-priest years ago and lived to regret it. No need to go into all that. You can go put your things in the cabin directly behind the garage and up that little rise. One of the keys Emily gave you fits that lock, and the other one goes to the van out there in the front. Come on back at 6 for dinner. Got that?"

"Yes, yes. We will. Thank you."

Jack, like Kitty, felt they had entered another reality. He carried the overnight bags back to the cabin and unlocked the door. There were two identical rooms, with a bath between them. The bath had a toilet and a shower, the sinks were farm sinks with countertops, and stood just outside the bathroom doors, one in each room.

"It looks like this cabin could accommodate a whole family, Jack."

"I suppose they have to be pretty flexible to provide whatever's needed."

There was a fireplace in each room, with a neat stack of wood and kindling. The double beds had brightly colored quilts. There was a small closet, and tables in each room with four chairs.

Chapter 77

JENNY GOT no answer or even the message machine when she called. Where could her dad be and why wouldn't he have the machine on? Should she be worried? She decided to wait and try again when she got home from work. Things had settled down, the plumbing problems had been solved, and all the programs were back online. Peter had things well in hand.

She settled down to do some planning for staff training. It was a requirement that staff take continuing education courses each year, and she liked to make them available on-site if possible. It cost a little more, but it gave her more control. She liked being in control. Her programs were specialized, serving the needs of seniors with various abilities and interests. So, the training for staff should fit in with what she wanted to offer. She had a large community room, and if she offered training on a weekend, she could open it to others as well as her own staff and cut the costs. And, that way, she could offer a few enticements to make the training go down well. Crafting classes, basic painting skills, and gardening tips were always popular. *Always good to offer an incentive to fulfill a requirement,* she thought.

She pulled out the file where she had accumulated course

offerings and was deeply engrossed in putting together a day that would not only educate, but also entertain, when Peter came in with a message. "Hey, boss – don't like to bother you, but this one looks urgent."

"That's okay. I'm almost done here anyway. Let's see it." Jenny read the message, then looked up at Peter. "Oh my god! I have to leave. Sorry. You were right, it is urgent."

"Of course. Don't worry, I'll hold down the fort. Call me later?"

"Yes, sure."

Jenny grabbed her purse and her coat. *What could have happened? Why was Kevin's message so cryptic? 'Get home as soon as you can. It's urgent.'* She was calling him on her cell phone while she was walking to her car. No answer. Shit. Deena and Ben would be at school. If he was home, why wasn't he answering the phone? She tried his cell. It went straight to voicemail.

Traffic was maddeningly slow, and she tried again to get Kevin on the phone. Still no answer. She pulled into the driveway and saw his car and a big Cadillac parked at the curb.

Kevin was sitting in the living room with a woman Jenny didn't know. He looked up and said "Oh good, you're home Jenny! This is Mrs. Carmichael. She's the wife of the man Kitty is running from. She wanted to see if we knew where Gray might be."

Jenny felt her heart do a flip and then a burst of adrenaline. She sat down abruptly. "No, how would I know where her husband would be? I don't know anything about this woman Kitty. She just showed up at my Dad's claiming she needed a place to stay. He tells me she's an old friend of my mother's. I have no way of verifying that because my mother died six months ago. I can tell you I was pretty upset when I found that woman so comfortably dug in at my dad's house. How did you know she was staying there?"

"I've had Gray followed for some time, and I knew he was at your father's last week. It wasn't hard to discover where you lived. I'm sorry to have upset you." Mrs. Carmichael said. "I just wanted to warn you that if Kitty is involved with your dad, he had better be careful. Gray can be violent when he's upset, and he's likely to be very upset right now."

"So you think my Dad may be in danger?"

"I don't know, but you should tell him to be careful. The police are investigating my husband's business and his associates. If Gray tries to get to that Kitty again, and shows up at your father's again, there's no telling what could happen." Mrs. Carmichael picked up her purse and stood to leave.

"I will let him know." Jenny opened the front door.

As soon as the front door closed, Jenny turned and glared at Kevin. "Why didn't you pick up the phone? I called you the minute I got your message! I was terrified something had happened to you or the kids!"

"I really didn't know a good way to handle it without making you so upset you couldn't drive safely. I knew you were already really worried about your Dad."

"Did you tell her Deena was there this weekend? I don't want her involved in all of this. She's got enough on her plate."

"No."

"I need a drink." Jenny went into the kitchen and poured herself a glass of wine.

"Are you sure that's what you need? Don't you want to call your Dad and see if he really is okay?"

"I've been trying all day and there was no answer. The machine didn't even pick up. And his cell phone is never on. You know it's bad enough when your kids get involved with people you know nothing about. For him to get involved with someone like Kitty at his age is insane."

"He's lonely, Jen. He's lonely and he has always had someone to take care of his whole adult life. Can't you see why Kitty might have been just what would attract him?"

"Hah! She sounds like a manipulative opportunist to me. Everything I know about her points to the kind of woman who takes advantage wherever she can. And she found somebody who is so vulnerable. Even the idea of my dad getting involved with someone like that makes me sick." She poured herself another glass of wine.

"Sometimes you have to take risks to find happiness, Jen. He's trying to rebuild his life. Maybe he's making some mistakes along the way, but at least he's trying. You have to give him credit for that."

"Do I?" Jenny picked up the wine bottle and her glass and went out to the patio, slamming the door behind her.

Chapter 78

Kitty lit the fire in her room and lay down on the bed. She was asleep almost immediately. The previous night had not been a restful one, and the day had worn her out.

Jack opened his overnight bag and pulled out the bottle of scotch he'd brought. He poured a drink and took it out to the front porch of the cabin. The air was cool, with the clean smell of pine and juniper and he could smell the fire burning on Kitty's side of the cabin. He sipped his drink, wondering if Sister Helen would object to alcohol. His cell phone was getting a strong signal, so he punched in Jenny's home phone number. Maybe he could just talk to Kevin and not have to deal with Jen.

"Hello?"

"Hi, Kevin! It's Jack. Just calling to check in. Wanted to let you know the house phone is out of order, probably won't be working for a few days. Carlin's doing some work. So I'll keep my cell on if you need to get me. How are you? How're Jenny and the kids?"

"We are all fine, Jack. But we had a visit from someone claiming to be the wife of someone Kitty may be involved with?

She said you may be in danger, that this guy can be violent. Jen is pretty upset. In fact, she's out on the patio with a bottle of wine. So you know how that will go."

"I'm so sorry, Kevin. I just didn't want to worry you. Thought I could keep all of this off your radar."

"Nothing happens without ripples, you know?"

"Yes. Yes, I do know. Kitty and I are staying out of town for a few days. Just to be on the safe side. My friend Emily, I think you've met her – I know Jenny will remember her – is helping me sort all of this out. She's an attorney and seems to have things in hand. Please don't worry. And tell Jenny I'm okay and I will call her every day."

"I will – do you want to tell her yourself?"

"No, I think it's probably best that you handle it, especially if she's drinking. Find the right moment, you know?"

"Yes, I know. You take care, Jack. We <u>are</u> worried about you."

"I will. I've got everything I need here, and I'm going, for once, to let the experts handle things. It's all out of my field of expertise, whatever that means."

"Good. Time to let other people take care of you for a change. Talk to you soon?"

"Yes. 'Bye."

Kevin put the phone back on the charger and went out to the patio to give Jenny the news. He grabbed a glass for himself on the way out, hoping that she'd left enough wine in the bottle so he could save her from drinking the whole thing.

"You GOING to share any of that?" Sister Helen was coming up the path towards Jack.

"Sure. I'll get another glass."

"Great! I'll take a double." She sat down in the other rocker.

"At this rate my supply isn't going to last very long!" Jack handed her a glass.

"No worries there. I've got some on hand if you get desperate." She sipped her drink. "You look like you've got a lot on your mind. Something besides Kitty's problems maybe?"

Jack looked at her. Was she a mind-reader?

"I was thinking about how hard this whole thing is going to be for my daughter. I just left a message with her husband, but I know she's already frantic about what's happening. She hasn't really been able to let go of worrying about me since my wife, Jenny's mom, died."

"Oh yeah? How long ago did she die?"

"Six months. Jenny kind of went into a tailspin. Lily had been ill for some time – mentally unstable long before she got cancer – and those last few years were pretty hard on all of us."

"Does your daughter live with you?"

"No, she has her own family. They live in Los Angeles. But Jenny just can't let go of her anxiety about me. She seems obsessed, to the point that I don't think she focusses on her own children or husband."

"Ah. Was she close to her mom?"

"No. They fought a lot."

"That doesn't necessarily mean they weren't close, you know."

Jack looked up from his glass. "I guess it doesn't. But they never did get along. Not since Jenny was little. Seems like the more independent she got the more they fought. About everything."

"That's tough. For all of you."

JACK SWIRLED the scotch in his glass before he took the last swallow. "Yes. I don't think I handled any of it well."

"It isn't like you won't have another chance at getting it right. Now hand me that bottle. I'm going to keep it up at the office under lock and key. You come ask when you want another drink. We just don't allow alcohol in the cabins. But I'll keep you company any time."

He handed her the bottle, feeling she was treating him like a child.

"I'm not doing this to control what you do, Jack. But I have others to think about, and some are here to avoid this kind of temptation. I don't want to make it harder, not at this point in their recovery. Dinner in ten minutes. Come on up as soon as you can. You won't want to eat it cold."

Chapter 79

JACK COULD SMELL something delicious cooking, even from the cabin. It reminded Jack of a dish from his childhood but he couldn't quite identify it. Then, as he got closer, he recognized what had to be a combination of dried peas, onion, celery, and a ham hock – his grandmother's "artsoppa" or pea soup. He hadn't had it in years. Lily didn't like it, so the recipe stayed in the box. He wondered if Jen had liked it. Would she even remember? Why didn't he know that? He should know that. He'd have to ask her.

"Smells so good. Is it time for dinner?" Kitty asked from the door to the porch.

"Just about! I think that wonderful aroma is pea soup. I haven't had it in years. Lily didn't like it, so the recipe stayed in the box. We better not be late according to Sister Helen. You'll want a jacket or a shawl – it's chilly out here."

There was a warm loaf of Swedish rye bread, as well as a plate of cheeses. A fire was crackling in the fireplace, as only a pine fire can do, and places set for three people. Sister Helen came through the swinging door from the kitchen with a soup tureen.

"It's just us tonight. There may be more checking in tomorrow, I never know for sure. But for now it's just us."

"Pea soup? Am I right?"

"You are right. And there's an apple pie in the oven for dessert."

"I may just be in heaven! My grandmother had a great recipe for what she called 'Artsoppa'."

"Good old-fashioned peas porridge! Can't waste a good ham bone on anything else as far as I'm concerned. Unless maybe it's lima beans. Either of you like lima beans?"

"Gosh – yes! But I haven't had those since I was a kid!" Kitty said.

"Ummmm I'll pass on those." Jack made a face.

"We eat pretty simply around here. So you just may have a chance to try them Kitty. We'll give Jack a crust of bread. Now dig in. We don't want cold peas porridge!"

A CAR ROLLED IN JUST as Sister Helen was ladling a second serving of soup. She handed Jack the ladle and went outside to see who it was.

"Emily! I wasn't expecting you tonight! Was I?" Sister Helen looked confused.

"No, Sister, you weren't. But I decided I needed some time with Kitty and Jack, and I thought this would be, well, convenient!"

"Right you are. You hungry?"

"Yes, and that soup smells wonderful."

"Good to see you, Emily. Thank you so much for sending us here. Kitty and I are so grateful, for all you're doing. Really." Jack helped Emily with her chair.

"Glad you found the place before it got dark! I almost missed the turn myself, and I've been here many times."

Sister Helen brought out another place setting and Jack ladled soup into Emily's bowl. Kitty passed her the bread and butter. "This 'safe house' is nothing like I expected it would be. It's more like a retreat."

"It is different, that I'll admit!" Emily smiled, gave a little chuckle. "I do sometimes make a retreat here myself! Maybe the two of you can return under happier circumstances one day."

Kitty felt her face flush. Jack patted her hand and said, "Maybe!"

Sister Helen brought out the apple pie, hot from the oven. "Don't suppose anybody would like ice cream with this?"

Jack and Kitty said, almost in unison, "Cheddar cheese?"

"Me too!" Emily laughed.

"Well I'm going for ice cream. Help yourselves to the cheese, there's some on the platter there. I'll never understand why people would rather have cheese than ice cream. Seems sacrilegious to me...."

Even before she'd finished her apple pie, Kitty was yawning. She excused herself.

Jack pushed his chair back and walked her to the door. "I'll be there in a bit. I want to talk to Emily." He handed her the key to the cabin.

"Of course. I'm just beat. Dinner was great, Sister. Thank you."

Sister Helen made her excuses while she cleared the table and disappeared into the kitchen.

Jack looked at Emily. "You look like you could use a drink."

"Yes. Please. It's been a chaotic kind of day. Let me get you something. I know where she keeps the booze."

"Oddly enough, so do I. She must trust me." Jack laughed.

"You've been given a very good reference!" Emily went to the liquor cabinet and returned with a bottle of scotch. "You also know where she keeps the glasses?"

"No, but I bet I can find them." He got up and made his way to the kitchen. He brought three back, in case Sister Helen returned.

"I see you know that Sister Helen isn't above a bit of a tipple, herself."

"Yes. We had a drink on my patio this afternoon."

"But she confiscated your bottle, right?" Emily poured Jack's drink and then her own.

"Yep. However, she also filled me in on the rules, so I'm in good shape."

"She does like to keep tight control. Here's to 'getting away from it all' as I like to call it."

"I will drink to that, for sure. I'm not sure I'll ever be ready to go back to what we've left behind. Pretty unnerving."

"I heard from my contact in the police department. It sounds like Gray's wife is going to make sure he's hit with everything. Apparently, she has exercised her premarital agreement and taken over all his business holdings. She's had auditors going over the books, and what she discovered links him tightly with a money laundering scheme. I'm not clear about the details, but she also seems determined to leave him without one penny. The police are watching his every move. I don't think it will be long before they arrest him."

"I'll be glad when we know he's in jail. I certainly don't want to see him again, nor would Kitty!" Jack sounded angry. "Speaking of his wife – she came to see Jenny this afternoon.

Jen's pretty upset about it. I talked to Kevin not long after I got here."

"She's probably trying to find out about Kitty's connection to Gray in all of this. Has Kitty told you anything?"

"She's said enough for me to know that Gray is one of those people who finds someone who is needy, makes them dependent and then uses them for his own ends. But I doubt she knows much beyond the fact that he liked to drink and gamble, have a pretty woman on his arm who didn't ask questions and was available whenever he called. Obviously the apartment she was living in was a convenient place to stash drugs and money."

"She knew nothing about what he'd put in those boxes you moved from storage?"

"No. When I left that day, she told me she was going to start going through the boxes. I never had a chance to even go into the garage after I got back."

Emily was staring into the fire, swirling the scotch in her glass before taking another sip. "How much do you really know about Kitty, Jack? Has she talked about anything from her past over the last few weeks?"

"Not a lot, no. We've been pretty busy clearing out the house. You know what a packrat Lily was, and I was overwhelmed by the task. Kitty just dived right in and helped me sort and organize. She's even made sense out of the living room, and you'll remember how that looked! She wanted to earn her keep, I guess. And I didn't press her for information. I know she was in a shelter for a few days, sleeping off a bender. She did tell me about that. I offered to fix the bicycle tire, as you know, and things just sort of .... I mean, I was concerned that she.... wasn't...." he trailed off, staring into the fire.

"You decided to take her in and help her out. I know you, Jack. You're a guy with a big heart. But this is a person you know nothing about!"

"Yeah. And still know very little." He looked at Emily. "I've been so lonely, Em. And she is good company. There's something about her that reminds me a bit of Lily, when Lily was having a good day. She's got an easy laugh, she loves my cooking...she's even got me watching old movies. Deena was out last weekend and they really got along. Did my heart good to see the two of them together."

"I'm sure. But Jack, you need to be careful here. She's got a past, and some of it isn't very pretty. I've done my homework. I had to if I was going to help her at all. She's moved in edgy social circles for quite a while. And although she's never done time herself, she's had a few interventions, from people who can pull strings, to get her out of some tight situations. She's been lucky. But she's not an innocent, by any stretch of the imagination."

"I know. I sense that. But you know what, Emily? I don't care. I don't care what anybody thinks about her or what her past has been. I haven't been this happy in a long time. I'm not saying this is anything permanent, I don't know if she has any feelings for me, really .... but I want to give her a place to stay until she's figured out a better life for herself without people like Gray. She's got a lot of life to live, and I do too. I don't know if we'll live it together. But for now, it's good. And I just want her to be safe, feel safe, as much as possible."

"I can see that. But you'll have a lot of work to do to ever get Jenny to accept her. You know that too, right?"

"I do. But, you know, I'm thinking about myself for the first time in a very long time. And this, for now, is what I want. I really don't care what Jenny thinks. She needs to focus on her own family, not be so worried about me and my life."

"She cares about you, Jack. You're her father."

"Don't you think I know that? Of course I'm her father! And I always will be. But that doesn't mean I have to live life the way she wants me to!" He stood up and slammed his glass on the table. "I'm so tired of trying to figure out what it is she wants from me. I doubt I'll ever know what it is, really."

"I doubt she knows, either. But our focus for the next few days must be on clearing up whatever is left that impacts you, and that involves Kitty. You both may be seen as accomplices, whether or not you were aware of what Gray was doing or storing in those boxes. I don't think they can make any of it stick for you, but Kitty has a history of connections to Gray and his cronies. That's going to be harder to resolve."

"Can we talk about all this tomorrow? I'm exhausted." Jack rubbed his face and looked at Emily.

"Of course. I'll be here until late tomorrow afternoon. Let's talk in the morning when Kitty is more rested. After all she's been through, I can understand why she is exhausted. Good night Jack. Try not to worry. I'm sorry if I upset you."

"I appreciate your willingness to help. More than I've let you know, Em. Good night."

Emily knew there was a complicated legal battle ahead, especially for Kitty, and she had discovered that some of the connections Gray had were not only powerfully wealthy, but some also held prominent political positions that forced extreme caution. If she could manage to have Kitty and Jack exonerated that would be one thing, and it was her primary focus. But if she could take out some of the people who thrived on the misery of others while lining their own pockets and pretending to be virtuous law-abiding citizens in public service, that would be icing on the cake.

She contacted the DA's office and told them it was time to confiscate the sealed boxes in the storage unit. There was no time to lose.

Emily was not always patient with the process. She knew it and saw it as her biggest fault in uncovering all the relevant details that might help her clients. As a consequence, she became even more diligent and thorough, schooling herself to wait for all the information to come out. Sometimes she thought she might have been better off in another profession, one where there were immediate, tangible results. But her heart had called her to this work. Advocacy for women who could not speak up for themselves, who had been beaten into submission and betrayed into commitments for which they paid dearly in so many ways. Women who had given up on themselves and resigned their children to misery because they saw no way out. She provided a path through the darkness, a tunnel into a better reality, a bridge to a new life. And she would go on doing it for as long as she could. Retirement was something she thought about, but then got caught up in the realities of a case and realized she wouldn't consider it any time soon.

Chapter 80

JACK STEPPED out into the cold. It smelled like rain was on the way. The pines were swaying, whispering as the wind caught at their branches. He shivered and opened the door of the cabin. Kitty had lit the fire, and the room was warm and welcoming. The door to her side of the cabin was closed. He took off his shoes and jeans, and slid between the sheets, grateful for the heavy quilt. It didn't take long for him to fall into a deep, dreamless sleep.

KITTY SIGHED AND TURNED OVER, but she wasn't awake. She was dreaming.

The summer was ending, but the evening air was still warm enough to run barefoot through the sprinklers as the sun was going down. The manicured lawns in the front yards of all the houses in the new tract had been freshly trimmed. It was Saturday. Kitty could smell the lighter fluid from recently lit backyard Barbeques, could hear the laughter as families gathered around outdoor tables, glasses clinking. But not from her house. There would be nothing much on her dinner table, and she'd be sitting there alone, her mother and father already well into their bottle of scotch, staring at the television. She was always the last one in, the last one begging her friends for just one more game of tag, or statue-maker. She dragged her toes through the wet grass, her footprints drying on the warm cement as she slowly walked home. Her mother would have put something on the table for her dinner before she started her evening cocktail hour. But usually that was the last coherent thought she had for the evening, and Kitty was on her own at the kitchen table. She longed to be part of one of the families who were eating around a picnic table, laughing and talking, eating ribs or chicken or even hamburgers and hot dogs. She was invited, sometimes, but when invitations weren't returned, most families stopped including her. This evening she banged the screen door as she came into the kitchen, hoping someone would notice. No one did. She wondered if she was alone, if this time they had not only shut her out but had actually left her alone. Her heart beat faster, and she ran into the living room where the television was blaring. No one was there. She ran to their bedroom. It was empty. Even the furniture was gone. She ran to her room but couldn't find it – her room had disappeared completely – there was the bathroom, there was her parent's bedroom. But where her room had been there was nothing but a dark void. She stepped forward and found herself falling, falling into the deep blackness. She grabbed out and tried to scream, but she couldn't make a sound....

"Kitty! Kitty! It's okay, you're having a bad dream, you're okay. You're okay."

Jack had his hand on Kitty's shoulder, trying to reassure her. She opened her eyes but couldn't place where she was. It was a minute before she recognized she was with Jack, that she was safe.

She sat up and put her arms around his neck, sobbing. He

just held her, recognizing her sobs as those of a child. After a few minutes she took a deep breath and reached for a tissue.

"Nightmare gone? You okay?" Jack looked at her, his eyes full of concern.

The room was dim. It all felt so other-worldly that she wasn't sure whether she was still dreaming or if the flickering fire and Jack were real. She reached out and touched his face.

"You are real, then? It felt for a moment like I was still in a dream."

"Yes, I'm real, and I'm here. Can I get you a glass of water? Should I turn on a light?"

"No. But could you sit with me a little longer? The firelight and some company is all I want right now."

"Of course."

He sat on the bed until she finally drifted off. Maybe she would tell him about her dream in the morning if she remembered. Lily used to have terrifying dreams, too, but could never remember them. But this wasn't Lily, it was Kitty. He shivered, and went back to his own bed, leaving the door open between their rooms in case she needed him again.

The sound of rain woke Jack just before dawn. He loved the rain and the peace it brought. Was it an omen? Would there be a cleansing, an opportunity for new growth, a quenching of the long drought he felt he'd been living in for so long? He smiled, turned over, and went back to sleep.

Kitty heard the rain too and was soothed by the patter it made on the roof, by the drip drip from the clogged gutters. She opened the window over her bed just a crack to be sure she wasn't dreaming again, and the scent of wet pine needles filled the room. A few drops hit her face, and she closed the window and snuggled into the blankets. She felt safe. It was a new experience. She listened for a few minutes, and then dropped into a deep, dreamless sleep.

Chapter 81

KEVIN TOLD Jenny to wait for her Dad's call. He knew if she called and he didn't answer, she would take it personally. She had already finished the bottle of wine when he went out to join her, and started on another. He sat with her while she rambled on about her dad, and how he had abandoned not only her, but her whole family. She finally went up to bed. She slept fitfully, sometimes crying out in her sleep. When she woke in the morning, her head was pounding. The phone rang, and she picked it up.

"Dad? Are you okay? We had a visit from some woman looking for Kitty yesterday! She claimed her husband was having an affair with her?"

"I'm fine, Jen. Don't worry. And I'm safe. I can't tell you where I am, but I am absolutely okay."

"This is terrifying, Dad! How could you let yourself be drawn into it? Sounds like Kitty is in a lot of trouble, and because you've taken her in, you may be too!"

"I told you, Jen, I'm fine. And Kitty is not the problem, here. She was mixed up in something that had nothing to do with her. In any case, I don't want to discuss any of this on the phone with you. Not now. I promise you I will stay in touch. I'll call you every day. Please, just let me handle this. I have some expert legal help, and all of this should be sorted soon."

"Are you serious? Why can't you tell me anything? Don't you want my help? And Kevin's? We could be there in two hours!" Her knuckles were white clutching the phone.

"No, Jen. I don't want your help or Kevin's help. And I'm not at home, as you would know if you'd been listening. I'm safe. That's all you need to know, and I'll call you every day. Your job is to take care of your family. And your job is to stop worrying about me. I'm an adult. Just let me handle this."

"Really? Is that what you think? That I treat you like a child?!!"

"Yes. Sometimes you do. And one that's not too bright." He could tell she was crying. "It isn't that I don't appreciate your concern, honey, but it's time for you to focus on your own family and let me figure out my own life. I love you. I hope you know that."

"Fine. If that's how you feel don't bother calling." She ended the call without allowing him to respond.

Jack stared at his cell phone for a minute, wondering whether he should call her back, try to calm her down. He sighed and decided to let her be.

BREAKFAST WAS A SIMPLE AFFAIR. The coffee was hot and strong, the cinnamon rolls fresh out of the oven, and the bacon crisped to perfection. A warming dish with scrambled eggs stood next to a platter of fresh fruit. Emily was at the table having her second cup of coffee when Jack and Kitty walked in. She had a couple of legal folders and was scowling at her computer screen.

"Good morning!" Jack said as he handed Kitty a plate from the stack on the buffet.

"Oh, good morning! Hope you slept well!"

"Yes, thanks. The rain sort of calmed us down. We are so glad you arranged that!" he winked.

"Oh sure – all part of Sister Helen's regular accommodation. She's gone out, by the way, so we have the dining room to ourselves for the next couple of hours. And we have a lot of work to do. So eat up, and let's get busy!"

EMILY HAD SEEN all of this before, in one guise or another. Gray was not unique. A man or woman with a strong personality, a pleasant and engaging manner, finds someone who can be used to further his or her own needs. And those needs were not always financial. Sometimes it was to gain complete control over another person. Sometimes it was to get the victim to provide sexual favors or to offer up continual accolades, adoration, or loyalty to satisfy a ravenous ego. Often it was to find someone attractive and witty who would act as a social ticket or gateway to situations that would otherwise be unavailable. The ability to lure a victim in was always the same. Promises of safety, financial support, access to a life-style previously out of reach, devotion, implied commitments, security, were effective lures for those who were vulnerable. And another quality these men and women shared was the ability to immediately spot a victim who would be easy prey.

Unwinding the subtle, tough threads that bound the victim to the abusive person, to the circumstance, was never an easy task. Someone came to her for help and often decided it wasn't worth the struggle. They gave up, gave in, went back for more abuse or simply walked away giving up money, property, even children because they were too defeated to continue to fight back.

Emily worked for months recently to extricate a young mother and two children from the emotionally and physically abusive, controlling man she had married. But the woman was terrified of trying to make a life on her own. Her parents were urging her to reconsider, reconcile, with her husband. How often she had heard that from those who were only interested in keeping the appearance of normalcy, of family harmony, over rescuing someone who was clearly suffering.

And now here she was, back at it again, because of Jack. He was a good friend for so long and had suffered so much through Lily's illnesses. He deserved someone who could make him happy. And as unlikely as it seemed, Kitty just might be that person. Emily was reserving her final assessment on that, however, until she saw whether or not Kitty would hang in there through what was looking to be a difficult and painful process of extricating herself from Gray's fraud and corruption.

"I've made a list of the things Gray is up against, Kitty, and unfortunately some of them may implicate you. We'll have to see. But could you look at this and tell me what, if anything, you know about them?" Emily pushed the paper over to Kitty.

"You need to know that this isn't a comprehensive list, though. It's what I could glean from police reports and newspapers. So if there is anything else, anything at all, you'll need to tell me about it."

Kitty picked up the paper and started to read the list. Halfway through, her hand began to shake. She looked up at Emily, her eyes wide. She was clearly terrified.

"It's okay, Kitty." Jack put his arm around her. "Whatever it is, it's over. We will deal with it."

"It's not going to be easy, Jack. Kitty can see that. But if she is willing to cooperate with the police investigation, and clearly, she is, we work towards some kind of plea bargain. One thing you can be sure of, Kitty, is that Gray is not getting out of prison anytime soon. They arrested him yesterday, and they have enough evidence already to keep him where he is for months while this is sorted. And with your help, maybe even longer. His wife certainly wants to keep him there permanently."

Kitty pushed her plate away, leaving most of her breakfast untouched. She stood up and dropped the sheet of paper Emily had handed her on the table. "If you'll just excuse me, I think I need to get some air..." She stumbled a little on her way to the door.

Jack jumped up and said "I'll come with you..."

"No, I need to be alone. Thanks Jack, but no," and she closed the door.

Chapter 82

"It's okay, Jack. It was going to be a shock to her no matter how she got the news. She's been involved for some time with a ring of money-launderers and drug dealers. And although she is once removed from the actual crimes, she probably does have enough information to know that something illegal was going on. The police have had Gray under surveillance for over a year, and his wife has had a private detective on his trail as well.

Jack picked up his coffee cup and took a sip. "I had no idea. I knew she was badly treated, but this is unbelievable. How could she be that involved with someone like that? She's a good person, I know it. I've seen it."

"Women can be vulnerable to someone like Gray. Big spenders, high rollers – with all the glamor and bling that goes along with the life style. And he did provide her with some security. From her own history, it looks like her life was pretty unsteady before she got involved with him. Has she told you anything at all about it?"

"Not much. I know she's estranged from her daughter, and

that she's had some financial difficulties, but beyond that I guess I really don't know much at all."

He stood up and started to pace back and forth in front of the fireplace. "How can we get through this, Emily? Will we? Will she have to go to jail? I couldn't stand that. Truly, I couldn't. And it would kill her, I know it."

"Don't jump to the worst conclusion, Jack. She's got some things to answer for, that's true, but there is also the fact that she turned over everything in those boxes to the police. Gray will have a lot to answer for once they've gone through everything, and I doubt much of it will implicate Kitty beyond the fact that she had them in her possession unknowingly. My guess is there will be other witnesses who will turn on Gray as well and will provide evidence that Kitty was an unwitting accomplice."

"I hope so. How long do you think it will take before she is in the clear? We can't stay here forever!"

"I just wanted to be sure you weren't in any danger before you returned home. We should hear something in a few days, and then we'll see. And I didn't want Kitty to run. She has a history of that, and if she does run she'll give every appearance of being guilty herself. So you and I need to keep her close."

"Should I go check on her?"

"Yes, go and see if she'll come back in. We need to get started on prepping her for her statement."

KITTY HAD to face what was ahead of her. There could be no more running away. For years she had suspected that Gray was involved in something illegal and dangerous. She certainly knew that he was an abuser, not just of alcohol and drugs, and that he was a compulsive gambler. Now she was face to face with the fact that he had gambled with not only his own life, but hers as well without a thought to consequences for either of them. She walked back to the cabin she was sharing with Jack and sat down in one of the rockers on the porch. She had endangered Jack. Would he be subjected to prosecution simply for holding whatever was in those boxes that belonged to Gray? Even if he had no knowledge of what was in them?

Her feelings for Jack were different than anything she had experienced before. He was such a good, kind man. He risked involvement with her and her problems without hesitation. And he brought in legal help when he knew she was without resources. Would he be disgusted by what could come to light in the course of preparing for whatever she was facing? There was so much she regretted, so much she wanted to leave behind, but now it would be dragged out for all the world to see.

She pricked her thumb on a pinecone she picked up from the porch and gave an involuntary cry just as Jack was coming up the path.

"What happened? Are you okay?" he hurried to her.

"Oh, just a prick from a pinecone, it surprised me. That's all."

"You're bleeding! Let me get you a band-aid. Come in and wash your hand."

He helped her up and guided her into the cabin. They stood together at the sink and he washed her finger, dried it, and found a band-aid in the medicine cabinet. "You know, Kitty, that I wish the next few days were going to be as simple and straightforward as putting a band-aid on your finger. But you and I both know that's not going to be the case. I just want you to know that no matter what happens, I'm going to be right there with you for all of it. No one should have to face something like this alone. Especially you."

"Jack. You are so good, so kind. But I'm not who you think I am. You are going to learn things about my past that I had hoped to bury forever; that I have been trying to run away from for years. I wouldn't blame you if you just let me go."

He held her hand, then lifted it to his lips and kissed her wounded finger. "I'm not afraid, Kitty. I know we will get through this and when we do, we can both start off on a new adventure. I'd given up on ever having one at this point in my life, but you give me something to look forward to. We have things to finish! I hope you will be staying around for that. We could make a good life together. I feel it."

"I think we have to get through this mess with Gray before we make any plans for the future. You may feel differently when you learn more about my past."

"I'm not worried about that. Truly. Now let's go back and talk to Emily about what's next. You need to eat something. You never touched your breakfast."

Chapter 83

EMILY SPENT an hour going over what Kitty and Jack might expect based on what Gray's boxes contained. The investigators had been sifting through them and were compiling a list of evidence to use against him. Fingerprints as well as video cameras at the storage facility made it clear that Kitty and Jack had both handled them. But it was also clear that Kitty had not been present when the boxes were packed and moved out of the apartment. There was a statement from the storage company and the signature on the paperwork was clearly Gray's. And there was video tape from the apartment security company that showed Gray removing boxes from the trunk of his car and telling the movers to add them to the load. It was careless on his part, but he seemed rattled and unsteady. "Probably high and/or drunk," said Kitty when she heard the report. "His wife must have been hot on his trail."

"I'm not as concerned about what was in those boxes as I am about some of the business deals he pulled with the car dealerships. From what I can understand, he seems to have had quite a large money-laundering operation going on for some time." Emily pulled out a spread sheet and handed it to Kitty.

"I've never seen this." Kitty said.

"Are you sure?"

"Yes, I am sure! It doesn't look like the reports I worked with at all. The formatting is different – and the codes are off. Even the dealerships seem to have different designations. This one only dealt with new cars, and only top of the line. It was the premier showroom. But here on the spreadsheet it says there were used cars moving in and out as well as rentals. I don't get it. We didn't do rentals at all. He would provide top clients with loaners, but he kept those transactions separately and off the books. He told me it wasn't necessary to track them."

Jack and Emily looked stunned. Emily said "Not necessary to track brand-new vehicles that were 'loaned' out? Did that seem like a good business practice to you?"

"He told me he knew exactly where they were and who was driving them. And that some of his clients preferred to deal directly with him rather than go through the accounting department. I didn't ask questions. Nobody questioned Gray."

"But how were these cars accounted for when it came time for an inventory? Did he ever lose track of any of them?"

"He never had more than four or five out at one time. And when they came back he would have them detailed and adjust the odometer so that they still could be sold as new. I didn't question that either – he said it was just routine and that everybody did it. I guess I was willing to believe him."

"So no rental operations were happening at that facility?"

"None. He didn't like the older cars to be anywhere near that lot. It was strictly brand new. Any trade-ins were transferred the same day to the Hemet lot. But they didn't rent cars there, either. It was strictly sales at all his dealerships. That's why I'm so sure there were no rentals at the new car lot."

"Did Gray ever ask you to deposit large sums of cash?"

"Yes, he did. But I thought that was because he'd sold a car to someone who preferred to pay by cash, for whatever reason. That's not illegal, is it?"

"Did you ever see any paperwork to account for that cash transaction?"

"No. He always handled that himself. When there was a large amount of cash he didn't trust anyone at the dealerships with it. He always brought it to me and I took it to the bank."

"And that didn't strike you as odd? Forgive me, Kitty, but I have to ask. I must know how much you knew about this odd arrangement and what, if anything, you suspected. It's the only way I can help you." Emily looked grim.

"I never questioned Gray. He ran the most successful car dealerships in the entire inland empire – he was famous! You've seen the ads, the commercials! Why would I have reason to suspect anyone in his position would do something criminal?" Kitty was clearly upset.

"He was apparently running the most successful drug dealership in the inland empire as well, Kitty. And he was laundering the money through his business accounts. That's a serious criminal act, for sure. And he was also supporting his gambling addiction that way too. He finally managed to bring the business to the edge of bankruptcy and he is facing over five hundred thousand in gambling debts. He had been spiraling downward for some time, according to his wife."

"How could I not have known? I never suspected anything. Did anyone else who worked there?" Kitty was on her feet, pacing.

"The books you kept were for tax purposes and were fake. He's a sharp dealer, that's for sure, and he had another system entirely for tracking the huge amounts of cash that flowed in and out. You weren't the only one he 'trusted' to take cash to the bank. He had accounts everywhere, and he had other willing and unsuspecting women who made those runs." Emily looked grim.

"Is there any evidence to incriminate them?" Kitty asked.

"Some, yes. The investigation hasn't been completed yet, but you are not the only victim of Gray's criminal behavior. He liked to use other people as much as he could to do his dirty work. And to implicate them should he be caught. It's going to be a long, messy trial. They have correctly identified him as a flight risk. I learned today that they picked him up and he had an airline ticket booked to South Africa."

Kitty sat down suddenly, twisting her napkin back and forth. Jack covered her hands with his and looked at her. "You are going to be okay, Kitty. You have me, you have Emily, and we are going to see you through this nightmare."

"I'm so scared." The color had drained from Kitty's face. "I've been such a fool."

"Then let's get ready for what's coming next. You are going to have to give an interview in a couple of days, and I want you to be prepared. I don't think they are going to throw anything at you that you can't answer, but just in case I want to make sure you are completely cooperative and willing to tell them every-thing you know. But before your interview we will negotiate as few consequences as we can for you. We'll just have to wait and see what they offer." Emily reached into her briefcase and pulled out a sheaf of papers.

Kitty looked at Jack. "What have I gotten you into? I think you should just leave me to face whatever comes. Keep your name out of it, keep your family out of it."

Emily said, "It's too late for that, Kitty. Jack is implicated. Probably as an unwitting accomplice, but nonetheless you will need to clarify that for the prosecution. A good share of the evidence they have was found on his property."

"See, Kitty?" Jack said. "I'm involved too. Like you. Not a

willing participant; an unwitting participant. And I'll have to face any consequences just like you. We will get through this, I promise."

Kitty saw a copy of a news article that Emily had uncovered when she looked at the papers Emily had pulled from her briefcase. She picked it up and saw the caption under the picture. "THIS is a picture of Judge Berquist? Really? I met this man on several occasions – I'm sure it's him – with Gray. He called himself Ron MacPherson! He's a Judge???"

Emily looked at Kitty and said nothing for a long time. Kitty was pale, but she held Emily's gaze. "You know this man?"

"Yes. I do. I know him too well."

"How, Kitty? How do you know him?"

"Gray used to host these parties down in Tijuana. They'd start off at a casino near San Diego, then hire a couple of limos to take everybody to an exclusive, gated community across the border. Things could get pretty wild." Kitty was hyperventilating, her hands shaking.

"It's okay, Kitty. I know about this Judge – he's been skating on very thin ice for a long time. But no one has been able to prove anything against him, not yet. If you know anything, anything at all about him, it can only work in your favor as the prosecutors build their case. I want you to calm down, and then tell me all you know, everything you can remember." She poured a glass of water and handed it to Kitty. "This may change everything, in terms of what we can negotiate with your testimony."

"Could we talk privately, Emily? I'm not sure Jack would want to hear any of this, and I'm not sure I want him to hear it, either." She looked at Jack and gave him a weak smile.

Emily looked at Jack, and Jack said to Kitty, "I know your life was very different before we met, Kitty. It doesn't matter to me what happened then. I only care about what happens next. There is nothing you can say that will shock me or make me think less of you."

"Maybe – maybe not, Jack. But I will think less of myself if you know these things now. Can you understand that? You need to give me some time. I know that's selfish, but we don't know how all of this is going to turn out – and until there is more certainty about the future..." she started to cry.

"It might be easier for you both, Jack, if you let Kitty talk to me on her own. Just for now."

Jack sighed, patted Kitty on the shoulder, and said "Alright. If that's what you want, Kitty. I'll go for a walk. I'll be back in an hour or so."

"Thank you, Jack." Emily handed Kitty a tissue.

Chapter 84

Kitty went to the window and watched Jack walk up the path. When she could no longer see him, she started to pace. "You must know by now, Emily, that my life before Jack was not anything I could be proud of. Right? You've seen the police reports, the credit reports, everything. You must have, with all that research you've done. Have you shared <u>any</u> of that with Jack?" She turned and faced Emily, tears still streaming.

"No. Kitty I haven't told him anything you haven't already shared when he was in the room with us. He knows you've had a troubled past. He doesn't care. He's told you, again and again. I know Jack. And I know he means it."

"I just can't believe that. When you hear what I have to say about those parties, you may not want to keep me as a client. And I wouldn't blame you."

"I doubt it's possible to shock me, Kitty. I've been privy to too many stories over the last thirty years from women like you. Women who have been used, abused, been complicit in their own captivity, and who didn't want that life any longer. I've heard from women who turned a blind eye to the abuse and use of their own children. Whatever happened to you then, whatever you did, would you want to return to that life? Ever?"

"NO! Never." Kitty was angry now. "I just don't want to drag Jack down or hurt him—can you understand that? Wouldn't it be better for everybody if I just disappeared?"

"That's all I need to hear. The worst hurt you could give him at this point would be to give up on yourself. If you do that, it might destroy him. I can see how much he cares for you. However that resolves or grows or changes – at this point if you give up, he'll give up too. Is that what you want, Kitty?"

Kitty sank into her chair. "No. I don't want him to give up. Not on himself, not on me." She reached for another tissue. "So – do you want to take notes or make a tape of what I have to say? How do we do this?"

"Just tell me what you have to say. I'll decide what's next when I hear your story."

"I think it might be easier for me to talk if I had a drink."

Emily got up and went to the kitchen. She came back with a stiff pour of bourbon and handed it to Kitty.

"Thanks." Kitty's hands were shaking as she lifted the glass to her lips. "I met Gray about six years ago. He only had three showrooms, then, and he wasn't as well-known as he is now. No billboards with that flashing smile. I came to his office looking for a job. I was desperate. The last relationship I'd been in turned sour. I was depressed, and about to be evicted. I mean, I was completely broke and in debt.

Gray looked at me, then at my resume. I could tell that his assessment of my looks was more important than any work experience or expertise I claimed. So I made the most of it. I flirted with him. I admit it. He hired me, and then took me to lunch. After a week, I was in his bed every evening. I knew he was married. I didn't care. He took me to a furnished apartment – I assumed it was one he kept for just such occasions. Again, I didn't care. When I told him I was about to be evicted, he told me to move in there until I could sort things out. So I did." She took another sip of her drink.

"I worked in the office for about six months, and then he decided it might be more 'convenient' if I worked from the apartment. He slept there a lot – came for lunch a lot too. Eventually, I wound up with expensive gifts, clothes, and on his arm when he wanted a long weekend away to 'play' with his cronies. I started drinking heavily. Sometimes I lost days in an alcoholic blur. But I could always maintain the party-girl illusion. He loved that. He wanted me to take drugs, but I never did. Told him I'd drink with him any time, but drugs were out. I made my regular runs to the bank and kept what I thought were his private accounts straight. I really did not know they were fake, that the receipts and justification for all that cash I was depositing were lies. I didn't want to lose my job, my jewelry, my clothes – the roof over my head. I didn't do much thinking about any of it. Didn't want to.

I know it's no justification for how I lived, for what I did. But that's the truth. It wasn't until he started taking me to Baja that I began to want out. And I didn't care at that point when he slipped something into my drink to make me 'forget' what was going on. It was horrible, Emily. I started hating him first, then I hated myself for staying." Her face was streaked with tears.

"I know it's hard, Kitty, but I have to know what happened —especially if it involved Judge Berquist. It may be the thing that solves more than your own puzzle, but a host of them for a lot of people. What happened?"

"Well, as I understand it, this Judge—Ron as I knew him— owned the property in Tijuana. It was a really exclusive compound, up on a hill, gorgeous views of the ocean. Every kind of luxury was available there. It was the ultimate spa and the ultimate entertainment playground. Huge gambling room, lots of luxury suites, fancy food, non-stop drinks. Ron – the Judge – had taken a fancy to me and was after me all the time. Gray encouraged him. I think he liked to feel he had some competition – you know, two men trying to win the favor of one woman. It was crazy. It's not like I'm some young, fresh thing. But whatever was on their minds, it made me very uncomfortable when we were down there all in one house. But I thought I could handle them. I was wrong. One afternoon Gray and Ron had a long conversation on the patio – I couldn't hear what they were saying, but it seemed that Ron was threatening Gray and that Gray was pleading his case. Eventually they calmed down and things seemed to settle." Kitty stopped, looked at Emily, and drained her glass.

Emily got up and went into the kitchen. She returned with another glass and the bottle of bourbon. "I'll join you."

Kitty was silent for more than a minute. Emily just waited. She knew that silence was the best way to get more of the story than any questions.

"That night Gray and Ron wanted to gamble. The winner would get some kind of prize that the two of them had agreed on earlier in the day. I guess as a result of the conversation they'd been having on the patio, that was all I could figure. So they played Black Jack for more than an hour. Gray kept pouring more drinks for me. I wanted to go to bed, but he insisted I sit and watch. At some point I think he put something in my drink because things got really hazy. All I can remember is that later that evening I was in bed with both of them and they were all over each other and then all over me.

I finally passed out, and in the morning, I woke up in Gray's bed, alone. I was bruised everywhere, and I could smell semen in my hair, on my hands, could taste it in my mouth. I struggled to the bathroom and threw up, again and again. My slimy, torn underwear lay on the floor. I picked it up and put it in the plastic liner of the wastebasket. There was a patio off the bedroom, and I put the bag deep into the dirt of a huge potted palm using my bare hands to make a hole. I didn't want anyone to discover my underwear – even in the trash." Kitty finished her drink in one gulp, stood up and walked to the window. "I suppose it's still there – but no one will ever know it's mine if they find it." She turned to look at Emily.

"You must think I am the worst kind of woman."

"You have been through terrible trauma, Kitty. No one deserves what was done to you. No one. And I do not think you are the worst kind of woman. Only a very vulnerable one who was treated horribly by privileged, powerful, men. Men who thought they could use you and abuse you and never suffer for any of their actions. And you and I are going to prove them very wrong. And they *will* pay.

"We have a lot of work to do. Why don't you go and freshen up while I get some coffee for us. Then we can begin to put what's in the past where it belongs — and start to build a new beginning."

Chapter 85

WHEN KITTY CAME BACK into the room, she saw that Emily had found some pastries and fruit to go with the coffee. Kitty took a bite of an apple and had a sip of coffee. She kept her eyes on the table, ashamed to look at Emily.

"Kitty. It's alright. You can look at me. Don't you believe what I told you?"

Kitty looked at her and found Emily was smiling. "I can't really believe it, Emily."

"Yes. You can. Now let's get to work." She pointed to the papers on the table.

"The first thing I need to ask you is whether or not you saw a doctor after that terrible assault in Tijuana. Can you remember?"

"I was such a mess. I can remember being so cold and feeling so alone, even though someone was trying to help me. I learned when Jack took me to the clinic, that the doctor there had seen me that awful night. She remembered me, but I didn't remember her. She was so kind. She gave me a pretty thorough examination and had some blood drawn. She prescribed some antibiotics. I told Jack they were for the blisters on my feet, but it was really because she was worried about infection from some of the injuries I had gotten in Tiajuana. He doesn't know any of this, Emily. And I hope he never does."

"We may need to contact that doctor and get the medical records she has. Would you permit that?"

"If it helps, yes. But please, do we have to involve Jack?"

"No. All of this is your secret, Kitty. Not mine or anybody else's. But what those records show may help to further the case against both Gray and Judge Berquist. Or 'Ron' as you know him. Read through these questions I've put together for you." Emily handed Kitty a sheaf of paper. "Then go back and answer each one as fully and as accurately as you can. If there is something you can't remember, just note that as well. I've got some other things to attend to today, but I'll be back before dinner. Anything you need while I'm out?"

"If I'm honest, I'd like to get some Valium or Ativan. I've got some anxiety issues, and believe me – they are kicking in, big time. But I know that's not possible."

"Sister Helen can give you whatever you need. She's an M.D. She will make you go through a little screening first, though, so you'll have to agree to that."

"Of course. It's not that I take medication often, but when I need it, I need it."

"I understand. Just talk to her and she'll take care of you."

Jack knocked on the window and pointed at the front door. "OK to come in now?"

Emily picked up her briefcase and coat and went to the door. "I'm headed out for a bit. I'll be back for dinner. Kitty is getting started on the paperwork I've given her. You need anything in town?"

"A way to speed up time? I'd like to get through this as quickly as possible."

"We all would. You can help Kitty work through that list of

questions. Might be an opportunity for you to understand exactly what she's up against."

And it might let you know what you're up against, too. This woman does have things in her past you should know about before you get in much deeper," Emily thought.

"I'll let Helen know I'm off – and she'll let you know when she's got lunch on the table. Now get busy, you two. You've got some homework." She closed the door quietly behind her.

JACK LOOKED AT KITTY, but she was deep in thought. When he put his hand on her shoulder, she jumped. "Sorry, Jack. I was a million miles away. Want some coffee?"

"Sure — but let's take it back to our cabin. I think it might be easier to work in there, don't you?"

"If you are sure you want to be that involved with this horrible process. I would understand completely if you'd rather just take a walk — or a nap."

"I've told you, Kitty. I'm with you. I'm with you all the way. No matter what. Now let's get started."

JACK AND KITTY sat at the pine table in their cabin with paper and pencil, working through Emily's list. The simple fact of having something to do calmed Kitty down.

Now Jack was the one who was a bit shaken, a bit anxious. He began to see patterns in Kitty's past that were troubling. It wasn't just the frequency of moving – lots of people did that. It was the series of relationships that led up to her involvement with Gray that was upsetting. Over the last twenty years she had moved from one job to another, one man to another, lasting no more than one or two years in any one place or with any one man. She had been with Gray four years, longer than with anyone else. Why? Did he offer her something she couldn't find with all the others?

"You look miserable, Jack. Are you going to be okay?"

"Yes — I'm fine. I'm just overwhelmed by what you have had to endure. But we'll get through this. Together."

"We both need to be careful. You can see from my past, I'm not one who looks before they leap. But I want to change what I can. I want to build on something solid."

He covered her hand with his.

She smiled, and they went back to work.

They worked steadily for another hour, until Kitty put her pencil down and said "I'm whacked. I've got to lie down for a bit. My head is spinning."

"That's a good idea. You be okay here on your own? I think I might take another walk."

"Yes, of course. I'll be fine. We can start again when you get back."

Jack pulled a jacket on. "You sure now? That you'll be okay? You still seem pretty shaky to me."

"Jack. I'm fine. I promise. Don't worry, I just want to rest a bit."

"I won't be gone long, And I'll let Helen know you're resting."

Jack stopped by the lodge to let Helen know he was taking a walk and Kitty was resting in their cabin. He knew it probably wasn't necessary, but he felt someone else should know Kitty was on her own. "That's okay, Jack. I'll keep an eye out. Maybe take her some tea in a little while just to check on her. You take your walk, clear your head. I doubt she's going to try to run away. I have a feeling she knows that if she tried to do that things would get even worse for her." She looked at Jack, smiling. "I also think she really cares about you. She won't want to let you down."

"I won't be gone long. I saw a trail sign that points the way to a lake?"

"Yes – that's about a mile and a half – not too far. And not too difficult. There's a bit of a downgrade, which means you'll have some uphill work to do on the way back, but it's easy enough. Let me get you a bottle of water – it can be thirsty out there."

The rain the night before had settled the dust, and the air was clear and cool. So cool that Jack was glad he'd brought a jacket, but when he'd walked for five minutes, he was plenty warm. He was always on the lookout for something that Lily would like when he got into the woods like this. Funny, he hadn't thought about her much at all since Kitty came into his life. And, as difficult as life had been with Lily, he didn't want to erase her memory or forget about the things they had shared. After all, she was the mother of his daughter, grandmother of Deena, and had been a faithful wife for over forty years. It was only a little over six months since she died. No time at all. Why was he hoping to rush into this new relationship that looked more and more perilous?

His eyes welled up when he noticed a patch of yellow wall-flowers. Lily would have been thrilled, and no doubt would have picked some. Not really a permitted thing these days. That was then.

Suddenly he felt very tired. He sat on a fallen log next to the spikes of early winter flowers and wept. The tension of the last few weeks reminded him of the times with Lily when he was powerless to help her fight either her mental illness or the ravages of cancer. He could only stand by and pick up the pieces, only give support the best way he knew. Was he setting himself up for that same kind of relationship again with Kitty?

Would he always be standing between her and whatever disaster she was facing? Did he want that?

Patterns are hard to break. He knew that. But the feelings he had for Kitty were weighing so heavily in the balance. He hadn't felt this way about anyone since the first time he met Lily. Was he too old to change? Was Kitty?

He sat there for a long time, reflecting. If he'd been a praying man, he would have prayed. Perhaps this was a kind of prayer. He was laying out his hopes, admitting his own weaknesses, and trying to find guidance from his deepest, truest self.

Chapter 86

WHAT KITTY really wanted was to sleep. The bourbon and the emotional outpouring of her experience leading to the homeless shelter had exhausted her. But her mind was full of self-recrimination and doubt. Emily's questions were hard to answer without access to some of her records. That would have to wait until she got back to Jack's. And she could only hope that the personal files she had kept were still there somewhere in the boxes that belonged to her. Would Gray be THAT vindictive and mean-spirited that he would destroy EVERYTHING that could help her make a new future? She had letters of recommendation from previous employers, certificates from training she had taken, and of course her own personal tax returns. Not to mention her birth certificate, marriage licenses, and divorce papers. All of those things were probably replaceable, but what a nuisance that would be. At least she still had a driver's license and social security card tucked into her purse.

She was discovering that reconstructing a life from memory alone was not an easy task. And she was seeing patterns of her own behaviors that she had refused to think about until now. It made her feel small. And mean. And self-indulgent, self-centered.

Was it because she had stopped drinking so much, stopped taking so many pills? Was it because she now was having to look at her life through other people's eyes – people who needed to know everything in order to help her? She had never been able to admit how scattered and thoughtless her life had been. If she ever had a self-doubt in the past, she had been able to brush it aside and look for something to distract, something to dull the pain. But now she was being held to the task. If she wanted to survive this and make a new life, she would have to stick with it.

And there was Jack. She admitted to herself that at first she saw him as another potential meal ticket, a bridge to some-where or something else. She was shocked when she discovered she liked the settled, calm way he lived his life. To her surprise she was content with coffee in the morning across the table from someone who looked at her with kindness instead of avarice; of encouragement instead of cold calculation. She loved sitting by the fire with a glass of wine or watching a movie. Something had slowed down inside her. Instead of looking for another high, another hit of glamour and buzz, she found she was looking for just another day of making her life mean something to someone. Of accomplishing a simple task, bringing order out of chaos. Maybe that was it. Her own life had been so chaotic she was finding peace in sorting out someone else's.

She longed to get back to the tasks they had left behind. Work on the cottage was almost finished, and her ideas for decorating and furnishing that sweet little space often occupied her thoughts before she drifted off to sleep. A home place, is how she thought of it. Whereas before she had only ever thought of her living space as just that. A place to live, a roof and a bed.

But now she was faced with the straightforward questions Emily had laid out. She had to work through them carefully before she was ready to undergo the questions that would be asked by the prosecuting attorney. Sleep finally came, and she slept, dreamlessly, for an hour.

"Knock knock!" Sister Helen didn't wait for an answer but opened the door and stepped over the threshold. "Hope I'm not interrupting too much – but I thought you might like a cup of tea and a biscuit. Just made some wild blackberry jam that goes down pretty well!"

Kitty startled awake when the door opened, thinking maybe Jack's walk had been shorter than he intended. Then she realized it was Sister Helen. "Oh, no, I was just taking a little nap – I could use a little something. I didn't eat much breakfast."

"So I heard. You feel okay otherwise? Emily told me you might want to talk to me about some anxiety medication?"

"I think I am okay. Having something specific to focus on seems to have calmed me down. But I appreciate the fact that if I get into trouble, I can come to you."

"Yes. You can. How are you doing with all that paperwork? Looks quite intimidating!"

"Emily is very thorough. She doesn't want any surprises. It's becoming an eyeopener for me, too."

"Oh? How do you mean?"

Helen sat down at the table and buttered a biscuit for herself, adding a large dollop of blackberry jam. She poured out two cups of fragrant tea, pushing one towards Kitty.

"I'm seeing some patterns in my past that make me cringe."

"I doubt there's a person living who couldn't say that about themselves, Kitty."

"Maybe. But I feel so bad about dragging Jack into all this current mess."

"Really? He's a big boy. I think he can take care of himself. He has a clear head and a pragmatic sense that should get him through. I wouldn't worry about <u>him</u>."

She buttered a biscuit for Kitty. "Jam?"

"Yes, please."

Kitty sipped the tea and took a bite of the biscuit. She was glad Helen had shown up. She needed someone to talk to. "I feel like I am on the edge of something so much bigger than myself. Like I'm being pushed along by a wind or pulled by a riptide and could tip over or be dragged under at any time. But I'm also experiencing a kind of peace, too. It's crazy to me."

"Facing your past means for a time you aren't looking to the future. That can feel pretty edgy. You can't go back to the past, but you have to look at it. And you can't go forward until you do. I think you have what it takes to do that, and I sense a kind of resolve in you that always brings with it a sense of peace. You are looking for a good life. And by that I don't mean a privileged life, I mean a life of value, of worthwhile work and connections. I think you will have that. But I also don't think it's going to be easy."

"In spite of this calm and kind of peacefulness, I'm still fighting the old pattern of simply picking up and running away."

"Hmm. Do you really want to do that?"

"It's tempting. But deep down I know I couldn't get far. And I know that whatever I face now won't be as bad as what could happen if I do cut out. I'm just saying that the impetus is still there."

"Old patterns, familiar patterns...no matter how comforting or easy it might seem to follow them...sometimes they just need to fall away of their own accord and be absorbed like leaves on a compost heap. Food for the new things growing, you know?"

Kitty smiled. "Yes, I get it." She sighed and took another bite of her biscuit.

"I'll leave you to finish up here. Lunch soon. And dinner will be a little later tonight. I have a sense Emily won't be back until seven. She'll be fighting commuter traffic until she gets into the foothills. So, you have some time after lunch to keep working. Come on up to the Lodge if you need anything."

"Thanks. I will."

Chapter 87

JACK CONTINUED DOWN the path to the lake. He needed to consider carefully how he was going to support Kitty through this and still be honest about his concerns. He didn't want to give her reasons to hope that he was ready to commit to anything more than friendship, although he wasn't entirely sure there was anything more than that on her side, either. But making promises, real or implied, that he couldn't keep was something he would not do. Dealing with his own feelings for her was another matter. He wanted her. He had to acknowledge that to himself if he was going to act with any integrity.

He sat on an outcropping of rock overlooking the lake for a long time before he headed back up the path.

KITTY FINISHED ANSWERING Emily's list of questions. She was exhausted by the effort of trying to recall details of her life with Gray, and her history before she met him. But that wasn't nearly as bad as coming to grips with the mental picture that exercise provided. There was so much she wanted to forget. So many bad choices, so much self-destruction. She'd been a drifter, even a grifter – and she felt sick at heart. God, what she wouldn't give for another drink. Or a bottle for that matter.

She lay down on Jack's bed and wept until sleep overtook her.

BY THE TIME Jack returned to the cabin the sun had almost set. The room felt damp and cold. Kitty was curled into a ball on his bed, probably to keep warm. He pulled a blanket over her, wishing he could lie down beside her and hold her in his arms. He stood looking at her for some time.

Did he recognize who she really was? He sighed and moved as silently as he could to build a fire. When it caught, he put the fire screen in place. He realized he hadn't called Jenny as he had promised. He picked up the cell phone, grabbed his jacket, and went outside to make the call. No answer. Relieved, he left a message telling her he was fine.

It was time for him to get back home. He needed to talk to Jenny face-to-face. And he and Kitty needed to figure out their future. He wanted so much, so very much, for it to be a future with her in it.

He went to find Sister Helen. Had they missed dinner? He didn't see Emily's car, so he knew she wasn't back yet.

A LOUD 'SNAP' from the fire woke Kitty. The room was dark except for firelight – how long had she been sleeping? She went to the sink and washed her face, wondering where Jack was.

She pulled on her jacket and picked up Emily's folder. In spite of all the drama and tension, she was quite hungry and hoped she hadn't missed dinner. She turned on the porch light as she left, hoping it would give her enough light to find the path back to the Lodge.

She needn't have worried. Just as she pulled the door closed, she saw Jack coming with a flashlight. Good. He was back. Her heart gave an extra beat and she suddenly felt a bit of a glow – a glimmer of happiness? Surely not, in all this trouble? But there it was.

"Kitty! You finally woke up! I was coming to get you. Dinner is on the table. Did you have a good nap?"

"Yes, I guess I did. I don't know how long I slept – I only wanted to rest a bit. Did you light the fire?"

"I did. It was chilly when I got back from the lake. That's a beautiful walk, by the way. We'll have to take it together, tomorrow, if you're up to it."

"Of course!"

Jack took her arm, to help steady her on the uneven path. Neither said anything, but both felt a connection that was comforting, a welcome warmth neither one of them expected.

EMILY SPENT the day in her office sifting through case law and drafting a preliminary statement of defense for Jack should it be needed. Kitty might possibly be charged as an accomplice in one or more of the charges filed against Gray, but Jack was clearly an unwitting accomplice. She had to admit that was her first concern; getting Jack cleared. She had never known anyone less likely to get involved with any kind of questionable behavior. In fact, he was honest to a fault, as she had seen many times while they both were on the faculty at the University. He put himself in harm's way for other faculty members and students on more than one occasion and risked his own reputation to do so. She knew he was involved with Kitty because that was who he was. Always defending the defenseless, helping the helpless. But the fact that he had known her for such a short time would work in his favor. The criminal activity the police were concerned about had happened long before Jack came to Kitty's aid on that back road.

Kitty's situation was different. She had been involved not only in a personal relationship with Gray but was in a working relationship with him as well. She had facilitated money laundering and fraud. She could face some time in prison. It all depended on what she could provide as a witness that might help the prosecution. If she were a cooperative witness, then she had a chance to make it through this without serving time in jail.

Chapter 88

EMILY WAS ALREADY SITTING at the table when the two of them walked in. Sister Helen brought in a casserole of lasagna. She looked at the two of them. "You two look pretty happy with yourselves – considering what you're facing!"

Kitty blushed, and Jack laughed. "I guess we're just glad dinner's on the table."

"That's a good sign. Come on, take off those jackets and sit down. Since there is no one here but us, I've opened a bottle of wine. Anybody object to that?"

"No, no – of course not!" Jack pulled out Kitty's chair, and she sat down.

Emily watched the two of them closely. She knew how vulnerable they both were, and she could tell that something had shifted over the last few hours. They looked less wary, more connected – content, even. She hoped that the drama that had drawn them closer would come to a swift resolution, a happy resolution. But she wasn't at all optimistic. "Let's agree to save any business until tomorrow. Let's just enjoy dinner. I don't have anything new to tell you, so we can set all of that aside. Agreed?" She lifted her glass.

"Agreed!" they said and lifted their glasses.

The lasagna, a green salad, and a basket of garlic bread were passed around. The bottle of chianti, shared between the four of them, was soon empty. Helen produced another one, and they each had another glass. It was good to relax. Kitty was learning about Jack's life at the University as he and Emily reminisced, and she filled him in about current collegiate drama. Most of their mutual friends were retired, but it seemed the same old politics and turf wars were still operating at full steam, only with different players. It wasn't easy to change a culture that had been in place for so long.

"How are things going at the old canyon adobe! Is the native plant project still in place? Did they ever restore the old structure?"

"You know it has become quite the pride of the Environmental Studies Department. And they have a program that sells native plants and seeds to local growers that brings in an astonishing amount of money. All the upscale homes in the San Fernando Valley are going native with their gardens, and of course they want the best!"

"Is the adobe still used at all?"

"You mean for other than illicit trysts for young lovers?" Emily winked at Jack.

"No! I mean did they restore it so it could be used to support academic studies? And Emily, I don't think there is such a thing as an "illicit tryst" anymore! Is there?"

Emily laughed. "Of course! That's what makes it interesting, you old stick-in-the-mud! They did restore it, and that was quite a project. The purists in the Native American Studies Department insisted it be done as close to the original as possible, taking into account the need for sound structure. It took three years, but they finally got it done to everyone's satisfaction. It's a real jewel. They have furnished it with found period pieces from the Sacramento archives, so it's like stepping back 150 years in time. You should come see it!"

"Do they use the building? Or is it just for show?"

"They use it for special occasions – rent it out for weddings, and so on, and the University uses it for fund raising. They put on quite the spread – and they have authentic music and dancing. They were able to build an outdoor kitchen complete with clay ovens. The food is amazing."

"I'm sorry I haven't kept up. I'm surprised Jenny hasn't mentioned it – she still stays involved with the Alumni Association."

"She probably knew you had other things on your mind, Jack. And she did too."

"Yes. Yes. We had other things going on." A shadow passed over Jack's face as Sister Helen got up to clear the plates.

Kitty looked at Jack and he gave her a weak smile. She picked up the bottle of wine and poured him the last few ounces. "You've been through so much, Jack. And now here I am putting you through this mess."

"No, no – you mustn't mind me. I'm fine. And we aren't to talk any business here tonight, remember? How about some music?" He got up to choose an album. "Feel like Frank Sinatra or Jefferson Airplane?"

Emily laughed and Kitty said, "How about some instrumental? Got any Mantovani?"

Sister Helen said "Oh, no, please not Mantovani – I had someone here last week who would listen to nothing else. How about some Chopin piano solos? Not too loud?"

She disappeared into the kitchen and returned with warm chocolate brownies and coffee. "In case any of you old folks are worried about caffeine this late at night, the coffee is decaf. So drink up!"

They spent the rest of the evening listening to music and

chatting. When the plate of brownies had disappeared, and the last cup of coffee had been drunk, Jack stood up and stretched. "I think I need to head to bed. All this fresh air and that long walk has worn me out. You ready, Kitty?"

"Absolutely." She reached for her jacket.

Helen said, "Just a minute. I have something that will help you sleep, Kitty, if you need it. You don't need to worry – it's all natural, but it's very effective. Don't take it unless you need it."

"The way I feel right now, I think I'll be okay. But thank you. I will keep it on hand."

Emily excused herself too. "I'm beat. Thanks for the lovely evening, one and all!"

"That was a wonderful meal." Jack opened the door for Kitty. "Good night, all!"

"Oh, Emily – here's the information you asked me to provide. I think I've answered everything." Kitty handed her the sheaf of questions and her answers.

"Good. I'll look it over in the morning. Good night!"

Chapter 89

Jenny picked up the message on her cell from her Dad just as she was about to leave the office. She didn't recognize the number when the call came in, and didn't answer the phone when it rang. *So he's fine. Well good. I'm glad he's fine. I can't imagine how he's going to get through the mess that woman has gotten him into, but if he says he's fine, he must be fine. I'll give Emily a call tomorrow and see just how fine he is. But I won't call him. He can be fine without hearing from me, I'm sure.*

She got up from her desk and walked out to see Peter. He was on the phone. She motioned that she was leaving, and he nodded. It was almost four o'clock, and she had to get out of the office. Maybe stop somewhere for a drink. It wouldn't be the first time.

Deena was out with Mike and Ben was working on the float when Kevin got the call from the hospital. Jenny had rolled her car on Sunset just off Sepulveda. No one else was hurt, but she hit a tree. The officers who showed up at the scene gave her a breathalyzer test, and she was well over the limit. The hospital wanted to keep her under observation for twenty-four hours. She was going to face a DUI when she was released. Kevin turned off the oven and drove to the UCLA Emergency Room, his heart in his throat. He called Deena to let her know she would have to pick up Ben and give him dinner.

"Okay – Mike and I were just going to get a burger, but we'll go get Ben first and he can come with us. What's up, anyway? Where's mom?"

"Mom's not coming home until later – something came up at work."

"Why can't you pick up Ben? I mean we can do it, but weren't you going to go get him?"

"I know it seems odd, but this can't wait. I've got a project due tomorrow and there's something's come up that I'm not clear about. I need to revisit the construction site. I won't be too long. Call me when you get home and maybe I'll be able to let you know when I'll get back. Sorry, honey, but this can't be helped." He hoped she'd buy that. "There's a meatloaf in the oven – turn it on when you get home, 350, and let it go for another hour. We can have it tomorrow."

"Are you sure everything's okay? You sound kinda weird."

"I'm just ticked that I have to run out. I'm fine. Call me later."

"Well, that's very odd." Deena slid her phone back into her purse. "My dad says I need to pick up Ben and get him some dinner. He has to run out to some construction site – and mom, of course, is stuck at work. Sorry to drag you into this...if you want to just drop me off at home I can get the car and go get Ben."

"No, that's fine! More time to spend with you is a plus for me – even if we have Ben along. I'd like to see how they're doing with the float, anyway. Haven't been over there lately."

"Thanks, Mike. I'm glad. Dad sounded tired – and worried. That's not like him. I get the feeling whatever is going on is serious. Can you stick around this evening? I'd like the company, and I know Ben would too."

"Sure – yes – did you hear me? I said more time to spend with you is a PLUS." He pulled her close and gave her a kiss. "Besides, it might just piss off your mom, and I somehow think that wouldn't bother you at all...."

"Hah. You know me too well. Why can't she EVER be around when we need her!?"

Kevin was pacing the waiting room when the doctor came to find him.

"She's badly concussed. And she's broken her collar bone. She'll need to stay here under observation for the next twenty-four hours, and when the swelling has gone down, we will have to do some surgery to set that break. She's also got some bruised ribs. We've sedated her, and she may not be awake when you see her. I just wanted to prepare you before you went in there."

The doctor put a hand on Kevin's arm. "You feeling okay? Why don't you sit here for just a minute. I'll have someone bring you some water." Kevin had turned pale.

"No, no I just want to see her. I'm okay. Is she going to recover?"

"She's going to be fine, but it may take her some time to heal. And she may be pretty uncomfortable with that broken collar bone. I'm sure you're aware that she had more alcohol in her system than the law permits. I'm not saying she was way over the limit, but it was enough. Good thing no other cars were involved."

"Yes. Can I see her now?"

"Of course. Follow me. She's got a small cut on her forehead, but it was deep and it bled quite a bit. We've given her a few stitches, but you need to be prepared to see some blood. We haven't had time to clean her up yet."

Jenny wasn't conscious. The nurse checked on her vitals, and said she seemed stable, but her blood pressure was still a little high.

"She'll probably be out until tomorrow morning. Let's see if there is a room for her close to the nurse's station." The doctor picked up her chart.

"Can you see if there is a private room? She would rest better, I think." Kevin was holding Jenny's hand. Then maybe I could stay with her overnight? And keep an eye on her myself? If she wakes up, I'd like to be here."

"Of course. But first there's a police officer wanting to see you in the ER waiting room. We'll see what we can do and come and get you once we've moved her." The doctor glanced at the nurse. "See what you can do?"

"Right away. We're going to need this bed soon, in any case. The waiting room is full." She looked at Kevin. "You may want to take the officer to the cafeteria. When the waiting room is busy, that's no place to talk. Do you have a cell phone with you? We can let you know when she's settled."

Chapter 90

JACK HAD A RESTLESS NIGHT. He was dreaming. Lily was searching for bird nests. He was following her with a basket, trying to keep up with her as she ran from one tree to another, catching the nests as she tossed them towards him. The basket was getting full, and he could see Lily was getting more and more manic. When she started the upward swing she was so scintillating, so seductive, so full of an electric happiness that he was selfishly enjoying the day. It made him feel young again, newly infatuated with this gorgeous, energetic woman. She was so engaging, so warm. But there was also a deep anxiety, knowing that the turn was coming. She would flame out and begin to hallucinate and lash out at anyone who tried to temper her mood or control her behaviors. She stumbled and fell. He ran to her, dropping the basket of nests. She was face down, she had tripped on a fallen log. He turned her over and it was Kitty, not Lily. "Can we go home, Jack?" He woke in a cold sweat.

Was he involving himself with Kitty just because there was something about her that reminded him of Lily? Could he trust himself this time? Or would he be back in a relationship that had him trapped in an endless circle of drama and situations he had no power to resolve? Was Jenny right? Did she see what he couldn't? How could she? And over the last few weeks he had seen something in Kitty he never saw in Lily. Kitty had focus for the task at hand, she was a hard, organized worker – and that was something Lily could never master. Kitty also was ready to admit her mistakes, her weaknesses, and wanted to change. Lily had no desire to engage in self-reflection, and certainly no desire to change her behavior.

He got up and walked out onto the porch and realized it had been raining. But the rain had stopped and there was a cool breeze. The moon was bright enough that the wet trees were dripping silver in its light. The path to the cottage was littered with pinecones and debris, some of it had blown onto the porch. He turned to go back in and there, at his feet, was a bird's nest. It held two white eggs with dark spots at the large end of each. And one grayish-white egg with gray streaks. Two different birds laying eggs in the same nest? He took the nest inside and placed it carefully on the window ledge next to his bed. Lily would have been so excited to find an intact nest with eggs. A miracle, really, that they hadn't been lost when the nest fell from the tree. But it was unlikely that they were viable. This wasn't breeding season, was it? Maybe Sister Helen could explain. Odd that he had been dreaming about nests, and about Lily, and Kitty. He shivered and crawled into bed, pulling the comforter tight around himself.

EMILY SPENT the next day working on Kitty's defense. She found out that there had been a large quantity of high-grade cocaine as well as bottles of oxycodone in one of the boxes they retrieved. And Kitty's fingerprints were all over the boxes, as well as Jack's. That would be reasonable, considering they had moved them out of the storage unit and into Jack's garage. But if any prints were discovered on materials inside the boxes – that would be a different matter. One or two of the boxes had been opened and obviously resealed. Did Kitty take anything from inside – or touch anything that might have preserved her fingerprints?

There was a long list of very valuable jewelry also. Was it stolen property? The police were following up on that possibility.

Emily realized that the sooner Kitty was interviewed by the DA's office, the better. And now the date for her interview had been reset to Friday. That gave them a few more days to prepare. Hopefully that would be enough time.

At least she now understood the magnitude of Gray's crimes. Money laundering was one thing – drug trafficking something altogether different. How did Kitty <u>not</u> know what was going on? That was going to be the question asked. And her answer would have to be truthful as well as believable. Tricky business when Gray's attorneys were undoubtedly willing to spread the blame around. But she'd seen this before – a man trying to implicate a woman for his own bad behavior. All too common.

Emily snapped her briefcase shut and closed the office. She had a lot to think about.

KITTY WOKE before Jack on Tuesday morning. She washed her face and pulled on her jeans and the sweater she'd worn on the day Jack picked her up. She lit the fire and Jack still didn't stir.

His face looked peaceful, happy. She heard him mumble a couple of times in the night – like he was having a bad dream. But he looked content enough now. She noticed the bird's nest on the window ledge. He must have picked it up on his walk. She smiled and quietly closed the door. Breakfast would be waiting, and she was hungry.

It was chilly – the sun just appearing through the pines. She hurried up the path to the lodge and was glad to see the fire was lit there, too. She stood before it warming her hands. Helen came through the kitchen door with a coffee cake still hot from the oven.

"Honey, you must be freezing in that little thin sweater! Don't you have anything warmer?"

"I left a heavier jacket in the cabin. I didn't realize how cold it was until I was halfway here!"

Kitty picked up a plate from the buffet. The coffee cake had been cut into big squares, and she cut one in half before she lifted it to her plate. She poured coffee into a mug and sat down at the table.

"What about the two of you, Kitty? You and Jack? Are you more than just friends?" Sister Helen put a plate of scrambled eggs on the sideboard.

Was Sister Helen able to read her mind? Kitty blushed. "No. Just friends. We haven't known each other very long. And I'm feeling terrible about all the trouble I've caused him."

"Life brings everybody different challenges, doesn't it? Emily told me Jack lost his wife not too long ago."

"Yes. I don't know much about the details, except that she died last year."

"That's a hard time to take up a new relationship. You'll want to go carefully." Helen poured herself a cup of coffee and sat across the table from Kitty.

"I know. And it's been a crazy time in my life too. This is the first time I've felt any kind of security with someone, really, for the right reasons, and I don't want to spoil that."

"Just go forward with as much honesty as you can. That's

always best. You want another piece of coffee cake? I noticed you only had half of one! That's not enough in this cold weather! And how about some eggs?"

"I guess I would like more – seems like I'm hungrier than I thought. Where's Emily? Is she up yet?"

"She left about an hour ago. Wanted to get down the mountain and into her office as soon as she could. She said she had a lot to sort through today. She'll be back for dinner."

Jack came in, bringing some of the cold air with him. He was holding the bird nest in his hand. "How long ago did you leave the cabin, Kitty? I never heard a thing!"

"You were out cold. Seemed so peaceful I didn't want to wake you. I did wonder about the bird's nest! Were you out in the middle of the night collecting things or did you find that on your walk yesterday?"

"Just stepped out onto the porch for a bit in the middle of the night, and there it was. I had a troubling dream."

"I thought so. You were talking in your sleep."

"Morning Helen! I wondered if you could identify these eggs? The nest was blown onto the porch – and I've never seen this kind before."

"You a birder, Jack?" Helen took the nest. "Looks like you've found a nest that belonged to a yellow-breasted chat! But that odd, small brownish egg is a brown-headed cowbird's. Our local 'cuckoo' if you will.... supposed to report them if you find them. They're crowding out native species. But you don't have to worry about this – obviously these eggs won't be hatching. Odd that you would find it on your porch, though. They don't build their nests in trees – usually underbrush is where they tuck them in." She put the nest on one of the bookshelves. "Come on Jack, you and I need to wash our hands. Hot water and soap! I'll deal with the nest later. There's a nature reserve not too far away, no doubt they'll use it for one of their exhibits."

Kitty looked inside the nest. She wondered which birds yellow-breasted chat birds cared for. Did they notice the difference when a cow bird laid an egg in their nest? It must be a good strategy for the cowbirds if the area was now overrun with them. Clearly, they had no parental responsibilities.

Chapter 91

DEENA PICKED up her Dad's call on speaker phone, so Ben and Mike heard the news about Jenny's crash too. "Oh my god, Dad! No!"

"Is Mike still there with you?" Kevin asked.

"I'm here, Kevin! Helping Ben with some Algebra homework."

"Is mom really okay? She has to stay in the hospital?" Deena asked.

"She's going to be okay, but she has a broken collar bone and a concussion. They say she will have to have some surgery to set the bone but they won't do that until sometime tomorrow. They want to keep her here for a few days just to be sure there is no brain injury other than the concussion."

"Brain injury? Have you talked to her? How does she seem to you?" Deena was pacing now.

"They've given her something and she's asleep. I haven't been able to talk to her yet. They are moving her to a room and I want to stay here overnight."

"Of course. Don't worry about Ben and me – we'll be fine. Maybe Mike will stay over. Would that be okay?"

"Actually, I'd like him to. Just so you guys aren't alone. And Deena – he sleeps in the guest room, okay?"

"Yes. I know what you're saying Dad. It's okay."

"Mike, could you bring me a change of clothes and my shaver? They'll give me a toothbrush. And maybe my robe?"

"Sure. Deena can pack what you need. Shall I come right away?""

"You can wait until Ben's finished his homework. I've got to talk to the police about the car and grab a bite to eat. I'll probably be in the cafeteria when you get here. Thanks Mike. Look out for my kids!"

"Will do, Kevin. No worries there."

"Dad, kiss Mom for me when you can. I love you. Oh – shall I pack some things for Mom, too?" Deena was already headed towards the stairs.

"I don't think so, not at this point. They've got what she'll need for now."

"I'll just put a few things together she might want. Just so she knows I'm thinking about her."

"If you want – I'll give Mike an update when he gets here. Ben? Take care. I'll see you tomorrow. And don't worry, if you can help it."

"Sure Dad. I'll be okay. Tell Mom I hope she feels better soon."

Deena knew exactly what she would pack for her mom. She'd want her moisturizer and her hairbrush, and probably her earbuds and her iPad. There was one she used for movies and music that she usually left at home. She took a deep breath and suddenly burst into tears. Mike put his arms around her.

"She'll be okay, Deena – she's in good hands. Don't worry."

"I feel so guilty, Mike. Like I kind of caused her to crash.

We've been angry at each other for so long, and even though she drives me nuts I do love her."

"You didn't cause this, Dee. She was in an accident. Accidents happen. Now let's do what we can to make her comfortable while she gets better."

Deena looked at Ben. He said, "Can I go with Mike when he goes to the hospital?"

"No. I think it's best if we do what Dad said, and just have Mike drop some things off. We can see her tomorrow, I hope."

She looked at Mike. "Should I call Grandpa and let him know what's happened? Mom said he's not at the house and I don't think I have his cell number!"

"Don't worry about that tonight. He can't do anything right now, he's too far away."

"I guess you're right. Maybe she has the number in her cell and we can call tomorrow."

"Let your dad handle that, Dee. You don't need to try to fix it."

Chapter 92

EMILY REVIEWED the charges filed against Gray and made some notes. More and more information was coming forward about Gray's money laundering and drug dealing. And with Kitty holding the dubious title of "Personal Accountant" Emily was afraid she would be implicated as a co-conspirator. Although she probably was innocent of any personal involvement in the drug deals, she had to have known that something was very wrong. As she was also known about town as the "other" woman, with newspaper photographs to substantiate that, the fact that she was willing to be in that role and accept free rent, a car, and a generous clothing allowance as a benefit, had to figure into any decision the DA's office made about how she should pay for her involvement.

What she had learned about Gray revealed him to be mean-spirited, calculating, and willing to take anybody down with him. How his wife got involved with him in the first place remained a great mystery. He must be one deceptive and conniving character to have involved anyone who had a modicum of self-respect. Kitty was obviously easily manipulated; but his wife seemed to have a solid head on her shoulders. It was her salvation that her father had locked up her money so Gray couldn't touch it. Which probably led to Gray's manipulation of finances and drug dealing. He wanted to live the high-life, and he needed funds to do that. Why hadn't his wife blown the whistle on him long ago? The ways of the human heart and the need to maintain a façade of respectability! Emily had to admit that was something she would never completely fathom. So many women had one thing in common, the nearly inexhaustible hope that the abuse would stop if they found some way to change either themselves or the abuser.

But the connection to Judge Berquist was the thing she felt held the key to solving this whole mess. If she could get to the right person in the DA's office, deliver some real information about the Bergquist connection to Gray and all his money-laundering and drug dealing, she might just win not only this case, but take the judge down too. And that would be a very satisfying conclusion. Very satisfying indeed.

She sighed – and reached for the phone and punched in the number for her contact in the DA's office. During the process of discovery, a connection had been made between Gray, his money laundering and drug dealing, and, as she suspected, Berquist. Now Kitty held a pretty powerful hand if she could corroborate some of what they already had in hand. And the evidence that could prove very difficult for Berquist to explain or deny, was still very much available at his property across the border. How to retrieve it would be a different matter. But it wasn't an impossible task for the District Attorney, not at all.

Emily put the notes she'd made in her briefcase, closed up her office, and set out to get to Kitty as soon as she could. She would like to share the news with Jack, too. He needed a ray of hope as much as any of them.

Kitty's interview had been postponed again because of the

new evidence that was being collected. There was enough to consider Gray a flight risk, and he had been jailed pending trial. This would buy them all some time to rest and recover. Jack and Kitty could go back home, and so could Emily. It was funny how, when she got involved in a case, she almost forgot that she had a home, too, and a life of her own.

"How did Dad seem? Was there any news about Mom's condition?" Deena went to the door as soon as she heard Mike's car pull into the driveway.

"He's really shaken up. I think it's best he stays the night. For his own peace of mind and yours too, Dee. No new information on your mom. She's sleeping and they'll be able to do a fuller assessment tomorrow. At least she's in a private room, and the fact that she's not in intensive care is a good sign. Is Ben asleep?"

"Yes – he hit the shower and crashed with his iPad right after you left. He didn't have much to say."

"Poor kid. Probably time you hit the hay too – and I'm ready to turn in. You need anything?"

"No. I should be asking YOU that! You want a beer or something? There's a few in the refrigerator."

"Not really. I just want to take a quick shower and get some sleep."

"Sure – I put some towels in the bathroom off the family room. I'll say goodnight then. Thanks, Mike. I'm so glad you're here."

"Hey – me too. I'm very glad I'm here. You going to kiss me goodnight, or is it just this polite hostess thing you're going to do?"

Deena laughed and then started to cry. Mike put his arms

around her. "Hey, it's alright, Dee. Your mom's going to be okay."

She let him hold her for a long time, then turned her face up to his for a kiss. It was several minutes before he finally took her by the shoulders and looked at her. "I wish things were easier, Dee. I think maybe you need go to bed and... I need a...shower...!"

She smiled and pecked him on the cheek. "See you in the morning."

Before he fell asleep, Mike started thinking about Colony Springs. He couldn't stop imagining the possibilities for that place. Deena's suggestions, not to mention her sheer enthu-siasm for such a project, had inspired him. Colony Springs was ideally located for what he envisioned. He wasn't even concerned about property ownership or zoning restrictions. Everything was there already – access to wind, solar and water – a farming community with livestock – all of it waiting and ready for someone with a vision to bring it all together. The creative process was the fun, really, and even if it turned out to be an impossible dream in that place and in this time, the plan-ning and mapping out of space, buildings, and communal areas would be something he and Deena could work on together. He needed a project like this, just to prove to himself that what he had in his head could become a reality. He fell asleep thinking about how he could get it all on paper, so Deena could see all of it as clearly as he did.

Chapter 93

Sister Helen had laid the table, and set up a buffet of roast chicken, garlic potatoes, and dilled green beans. There was a mixed green salad, and a cheese plate, as well as two bottles of chilled chardonnay. A crusty loaf of sourdough bread had just come out of the oven, and a blackberry cobbler was waiting in the warming oven. Emily drove up just as Helen was going to let Jack and Kitty know dinner was ready.

"Oh good, you're right on time for dinner. Listen, Emily, I've got some things to do this evening and I think you three have a lot to talk over without me hanging around. So I'm going to head on out. Everything's ready, all you have to do is eat and if you're up to it, maybe clear things away. I'll be back later and can take care of washing up, but I'd appreciate it if you put any of the leftovers away."

"Of course! I'm glad you haven't had any other guests, Helen. This would have been so much harder to handle with other people around."

"Well, that's the thing. I've got a family coming in tomorrow. In fact it's going to be a pretty busy time. So I hope that you all won't have too much trouble doing what you need to do."

"No, no — not at all. We'll stay the night and be out of your way tomorrow. We've got some breathing space now, and I'm glad. The person who had threatened Jack and Kitty is now safely in jail, thankfully. And now that we know Jack and Kitty will be safe back at their place, we can all go home. Thank you so much for all you've done. You know how grateful we all are."

"Oh that's all fine — without you, Emily, I wouldn't even have this place. So I am glad to do what I can." She patted Emily's arm. "I'll see you at breakfast and say good bye then."

DINNER TURNED into a kind of celebration. After Emily told Jack and Kitty that Gray had been arrested and that Kitty's interview had been postponed for at least a few weeks, they all felt a wave of relief. So, food and drink were enjoyed, and they all helped to clear up the dishes and store the leftovers. Jack and Kitty even did the dishes, feeling like something mundane might give them a sense of normality again.

Emily left them on their own to finish up. She was exhausted and fell asleep almost as soon as she pulled up the covers.

JACK PUT his arm around Kitty as they walked back to the cabin, pulling her close. She felt protected, safe, and put her arm around his waist. They slowed their pace a bit, neither of them wanting this connection to end. When they got to the cabin door, Jack turned to face Kitty. "I want to kiss you, Kitty. So much."

"I know. I wish you would."
And so, he did.

Chapter 94

Two MESSAGES on Jack's phone, both from Kevin. Both timestamped yesterday. Jack reluctantly hit 'call'. If Kevin was calling, there must be something going on with Jenny or one of the kids. He wasn't sure he was ready for any more bad news. The call went right to voice mail. He didn't leave a message but called Deena to see if she was alright and maybe figure out why her Dad had called.

"Grampa? Everything ok?"

"Yes, yes. But I was calling to see how you are doing? How's the knee?" He was pacing up and down in front of the cabin.

"Oh I think it's better, actually. Did Dad call you about Mom? He said he would."

"I guess he tried to, but I didn't see that he had called until this morning. What's up?"

"She's going to be okay — but right now she's in surgery. She was in a car accident yesterday and broke her collar bone. She also has a concussion."

"Oh no! That's terrible. Why surgery?"

"To set the bone, I guess. She'll be in a cast for some time.

So far they think it's just a mild concussion. They said she would have to stay in the hospital a few days to make sure."

"Do you think I should come there?"

"Um — well, the way things are with her right now, what do you think? Maybe wait a bit?"

Deena was right. He'd just add to the confusion at this point. But Jenny would also have something to say if he *didn't* go, he knew that well enough.

"I suppose waiting is best. Would you tell your Dad I called? And ask him to let me know how surgery went as soon as he can. I'll keep my phone on."

"Sure. You still away from home?"

"We are headed home today. Should be there this afternoon. How's Ben?"

"Ben is good. Mike took him out to pick up some subs for lunch."

"I'm glad Mike is helping out. So, I'll talk to you again soon."

"Grampa, you sound tired. Are *you* ok?"

"Yes, yes. I'll feel better when I know what's going on with your Mom. Give her my love when you talk to her. Bye"

He slipped the phone into his back pocket and went in to tell Kitty about Jenny. She was almost finished packing.

"What's up? I saw you out there on the phone — you upset about something?"

"It's Jenny. She's been in an accident and is in the hospital. I don't have the details, but she's in surgery now for a broken collar bone."

"That doesn't sound good! Shouldn't you be there? For Kevin and the kids?"

"I don't know. Deena thinks it might be better if I wait a bit. Given the fireworks the last time I saw Jen, she's probably right."

"What hospital is she in? Don't you want to send flowers or something?"

"I don't know. It's hard to figure out what will help and what will just upset her. I'll think about it. Kevin is supposed to call me when the surgery is over." He looked lost.

"Let's get going as soon as we can. Maybe by the time you're back home there will be some news. Then you can make a plan." She started folding his clothes, putting them in his case.

"I'll finish up here. Why don't you go up to the lodge and get some coffee? I'll bring the bags up when I'm done."

He picked up his jacket. "Thanks."

He looked smaller, and older. Kitty watched him through the window until he was out of view. She sighed. One more thing for him to worry about. Maybe she should just leave him to deal with his family. It wouldn't be the first time she had to deal on her own with her messy life.

Chapter 95

THE LODGE WAS EMPTY, but the pot of coffee on the sideboard was full, and hot. Jack poured himself a cup and stood by the window, watching for Kitty. If they left now, they should be able to miss traffic and get home before three. He was ready to be back there. And if he was honest, he'd be glad to not have to worry about Kitty's problems for a while. He knew that Emily had things in hand, and he almost felt like a break from the drama would be welcome. *Kitty's in good hands, isn't she?*

Why was the news about Jenny such a blow? I feel as if the wind has been knocked out of me. Of course it was a serious accident, but she's getting good care, and she has Kevin. Should I leave everything and go there? Is there a right way for me to handle any of this?

Maybe Jenny was right. Maybe he was heading into dangerous territory with Kitty. Maybe he was just another old fool taken in by someone who seemed to need him.

He drained his cup just as Kitty walked through the door. She saw the look on his face and realized that something was wrong. He looked angry, determined.

"I'm ready if you are." She put the bags down by the front door. "But do I have time for a cup of coffee first?"

His expression softened. *She looks so vulnerable. What was I thinking? She's not trying to change my life, I am trying to change hers. Maybe she feels uneasy about that.* He smiled at her. "I'll get it for you. But let's not dawdle. I want to get on the road."

He poured coffee for both of them. "I'd like to be back there by three, at the latest. Don't want to face all that rush hour traffic."

"Good. We can probably do that if we leave now."

"I'll go get the car while you finish your coffee."

Kitty couldn't finish her coffee. She was finding it hard to swallow. She had a lump in her throat and was very much afraid she was going to cry. Jack was all business now. His focus was on his family, and no longer on her. Which was as it should be. But it hurt. And she was beginning to feel she was once again in free fall.

Chapter 96

Anxiety can motivate, or it can debilitate. Kitty had fought the debilitation it caused her for most of her life. She distracted herself with alcohol and sometimes, if she was lucky enough to have some, with tranquilizers. She knew if she started down that road now she could lose everything. Jack already knew alcohol was hard for her to manage, and he had helped her with that during the short time she'd been with him. Now she was beginning to feel a distance from him, a setting aside of his focus on her. The free-floating anxiety was returning, and she knew if it got a grip on her, she would be helpless to fight it.

Sister Helen had given her some herbal supplements when she couldn't sleep, and she hadn't taken all of them. Maybe if she tried those she could manage. It was something. But they were going back to Jack's house. She wouldn't have Sister Helen's medicine cabinet there.

She walked into the kitchen. It was empty. She couldn't hear a sound. Holding her breath, she opened the door into the storeroom. There was a locked cabinet against one wall and a shelf of bottles labeled with names she couldn't decipher. Which ones would help? Which ones might hurt? She had no way of knowing. She tried to pull the cabinet door open in case the lock hadn't been fastened. It didn't give. But the metal cabinet made a sound when she pulled on the door.

Helen came up behind Kitty and said "Were you looking for something Kitty?"

Kitty jumped and turned around, blushing. "Oh there you are! I wondered if you had any more of that stuff you gave me to help me sleep? I am feeling pretty unsteady — and to tell you the truth — I'm feeling helpless against my anxiety. I've had trouble with it my whole life, and I have to face a lot once we get back to Jack's. I need help. And I don't think using alcohol is going to get me through this. I need to be able to think. With a clear head." She was breathing fast, her heart was pounding.

"I see. Come on back to the lounge. I'll bring you some tea. We can talk, and then I can find something to help you."

Kitty went out to the lounge and sat at the table, her hands shaking, fingers beginning to tingle. Helen handed her a paper bag. "Take a few minutes and breathe into the bag. Have you done that before? Usually works pretty fast..."

"Yes. I know how to do that. Thanks."

"I'll be right back with some tea. When you feel a little better, you can take a few sips. Okay?" She patted Kitty's shoulder. "You're going to be just fine. It's no wonder you're edgy. You've been through a lot, and you have a big challenge before you. But you're surrounded by people who care. And you're not alone, not anymore."

By the time Helen returned with the tea, Kitty was feeling better. She heard the car pull up in front of the lodge, and the door slam.

"You feeling okay, Kitty? You look pale." Jack stood in the doorway, holding the door open.

"I'm okay. Just feeling a little panicked about what's coming next. I think it all finally caught up with me. And I'm worried for you and Jenny. And I'm so, so sorry that I have dragged you into all of this." She was crying now, tears sliding down her cheeks, nose running.

Jack closed the door and grabbed some paper napkins and handed them to her. "It's true, everything seems to have fallen apart for you, and now I'm looking at some of the damage I need to repair for myself in my own life. We've been dropped in it, Kitty. No mistake. But I need you, Kitty. To be my support. And I hope I can be yours, too."

Kitty looked up at him, a shaky smile breaking through her tears. "Yes. Yes. I want to help. And I need you, Jack. Maybe more than I've needed anyone."

"Well then aren't we lucky? We found each other by chance, and now here we are, facing some real challenges — but not alone, together."

Helen brought in a mug of tea. It had a strange, medicinal smell. 'Oh Jack, good. Kitty has asked me to give her something for her anxiety, so I've put together a blend of herbs that should work well for her. She needs to be careful about how much she takes, though, or they could have the opposite effect. I've written out the instructions and I want you to help her monitor when she takes them. They need to be mixed in hot water and measured as directed. She's sipping some now, and we'll see how that goes before you leave. You want a cup of coffee or tea while we wait?"

"Just water, please. Then we have to get on the road. Thanks so much." He sat down next to Kitty and covered her hand with his. "Now sip that tea, and let's see how you feel when it's finished. It certainly smells like it should work!"

"Actually, it doesn't taste too bad. Kind of like licorice. Do you think it's safe?"

"Yes. I think it's safe. Helen has been using herbal remedies for years, according to Emily, and whatever secrets she has, she's kept them to herself. And no one has been poisoned!" He winked.

"Here's your water, Jack. How you feeling, Kitty?"

"Actually, I feel pretty good. I'm surprised. Do I have to drink it all?"

"Yes, you have to drink it all! And when you have, we'll wait a few minutes to make sure you are still feeling pretty good, then you can get on your way."

"I'm so grateful. I felt I was going into a full-blown panic attack."

"And no wonder, all you've been through. But I do believe you'll be steadier now. And you have Emily and Jack to see you through the worst of what's coming. I'm always here, too, if you need to come back."

THE DRIVE down the mountain to the valley was uneventful. Barely any traffic, until they hit the flatlands. The heat surprised them both when they got out of the truck. Mountain air and valley air were never the same. But they were both glad to be back at Jack's. They talked a bit about the farmhouse and agreed they wanted to see that before they unpacked.

They didn't even unload the truck until they had gone back to check. Then Jack remembered that the farmhouse would be locked, and security in place. So he called Carlin and asked about access.

"Guess we'll have to wait until he calls me back. Let's go back and unload."

Kitty was trying to see through the windows, but the light was fading, and it was too dim to really see anything. The porch had been swept, though, and a tub of bright red gera-niums was next to the front door. It looked like heaven to Kitty.

And she wanted nothing more than to move in and make it her own. But was that what Jack would want? Time would tell.

———

THERE WERE three messages on Jack's answering machine, all of them from Emily. She had been trying to reach them all afternoon. Kitty was to call her as soon as she got in. There had been some major developments and the testimony Kitty was ready to give needed to be entered into the record as soon as possible. Emily wanted to see them both, preferably tomorrow morning. They had no time to waste.

"It's too soon! I thought we had more time before I had an interview. I'm not ready — I'm not!" Kitty was beginning to panic.

Jack took her by the shoulders and looked at her frantic face. "You are fine, Kitty. Yes, it's upsetting. But you are up to this. You have to be. There is no going back. And the sooner you can put this all behind you, the better. Right?"

"Right. I know. Maybe we should eat. I'll call Emily. You need to check on Jenny, Jack. That's where your attention should be right now, not on me."

"See if Emily can drive out here tomorrow. The two of you can meet here, and if I need to go to L.A. to see Jenny, you won't be alone."

"I'll ask, but if she can't do that, I think I'll be okay to drive myself."

"No. If she can't, then I'll take you. Jenny is in good hands, she has Kevin and the kids. And who knows, this may not be a good time for them anyway. But I will call after you've talked to Emily."

Chapter 97

EMILY PUT THE PHONE DOWN. Her conversation with Kitty had been a bit unnerving. Kitty seemed so shaky, so unsure. That would never do if she were to be a credible witness. She had agreed to meet with her at Jack's place the next day. All she could do was hope that after a good night's sleep Kitty would feel stronger. She sighed.

I think I'm getting old. This whole thing has worn me out. I need a good night's rest too — and after this is all over, maybe I should think more seriously about the kind of cases I agree to take on. This would be a good one to go out with, though, if we manage to win. That scumbag judge should have been locked up years ago.

She sat down at her desk and started going through her notes. She would need to keep things as simple and straightforward as she could tomorrow. She didn't want to frighten Kitty. But the evidence Kitty might be called to corroborate would undoubtedly be traumatic for her.

Jack had unloaded the car, and Kitty was putting lunch together when Carlin called.

"Jack! Glad you are back home! Sorry I didn't leave more information about how to get into the cottage. I left the new key on the hook in your kitchen - did you find it?"

"Oh! No — but I see it now! Thanks. And the code for the security pad?"

"It's the same as the one you have for the house. Thought that would be easier for you. And you can change it anytime if you want. Why don't you look around when you can later today and let me know what you think? If it's all good, I'd like to pick up a check tomorrow. I'm getting a little short here and I've got two more jobs coming up real soon."

"Of course! That's fine! Kitty will be here if I'm not — and she can give you the check. But I'll talk to you later today, in any case, and make sure I've got the numbers right!"

"Good. Talk to you then."

Kitty put a plate of ham and cheese sandwiches on the table. "Ready for lunch?"

"Thanks. Carlin left the key and the code is the same as the one for the house, so that's easy. After we finish here let's go take a look at what he's been able to do! What did Emily have to say?"

"Oh - she can come here tomorrow, so it's fine for you to go to L.A. if you need to. She said we could do what we needed to do here, and then the actual interview will be on Friday. It's sooner than we expected, but I guess there has been some new evidence brought forward and the DA's office wants to move quickly."

"Wow. That's a lot earlier than we expected! I thought we had another two weeks!"

Kitty looked at her plate. "I know. I'm so sorry. Especially with poor Jenny needing you."

"Jenny will be fine. I'll call her later today and see what she wants me to do. She may not want me there at all until she's home from the hospital. We'll just take it one step at a time. Kitty — look at me. Breathe. Come on — bring your sandwich and let's go take a look at the farmhouse!"

It was the hottest part of the day, and there was no breeze at all. The plants around the patio drooped, and even though Kitty wasn't much of a gardener and usually didn't notice such things, she said, "We need to water out here! Things look pretty tired."

Jack smiled. "Yes — but not until it cools down a bit. It can be hard on them if you try to water in the heat of the day. We'll do it when the sun's moved a bit lower in the sky."

The farmhouse was shaded by two big maple trees, and when they opened the door they could feel the cooler air inside and smell new wood and new paint. The Franklin Stove sat on the blue and yellow tile, and the refinished wood flooring had a warm glow.

"Is it okay for us to walk on this? Is the finish dry?" Kitty hesitated at the doorway.

"Yes. Carlin said it was fine. Been dry now for several days."

"Oh, Jack it's just beautiful! Better than I could have imagined!" She ran her fingers over the window frame by the door. "I love the way he used the colors we suggested. The off-white walls with the beige trim is such a clean, classic look!"

The kitchen area looked surprisingly efficient, with a tiled surface for appliances and a large farm sink. Carlin had used ceramic tiles — mostly in a dark midnight blue, and a few vintage, random tiles he salvaged from another one of his projects.

The bathroom was the biggest surprise, though. A white claw-foot tub with bright brass fixtures had been installed, and the small vanity had an oval shell-shaped sink dropped into a cabinet topped with the same tile as the flooring.

"Did Carlin build that cabinet, Jack? It's beautiful."

"No. It was something I had in the shed — used to keep odds and ends in it. But it was a solid piece, and he said it would be perfect to use as a vanity — so I told him to go ahead. He really did a great job on it. Looks like he just sanded it though — it's going to need some paint."

"It is a beautiful piece. Maybe all it will need is a coat of varnish? It looks good just as it is, don't you think?"

They walked back into the living room. "Yes. It's beautiful. Lots of beautiful things in here, actually." Jack looked at Kitty thoughtfully, and then pulled her into his arms and kissed her. And for a few minutes, life felt comfortable, joyful, with the two of them, standing by the window, looking at all the possibilities for that little space and the home it might become. It was simply uncomplicated, and complete, with no pretentious airs, no secrets, no expectations that it be anything but exactly what it was.

Chapter 98

JACK CALLED Kevin when they got back to the house. He learned that Jenny was still in the hospital, and probably would be there for a few more days.

"Would she like a visit from me? Should I call? I know she's upset about Kitty, and what happened to Deena when she was here. I don't want to make her even more uncomfortable."

"It's hard to say, Jack. With Jenny sometimes no matter what you do it's the wrong thing. She's still angry, yes. But she's also on some pretty heavy-duty pain killers, so who knows what she'll feel once she's back to herself. If I were you, I think I'd just send her some flowers and a note at this point. Then wait a few days and give her a call. She knows I have been keeping you posted."

"Thanks, Kevin. I'll do that. Maybe I'll check in with Deena later too. She doing okay?"

"Yeah. You know kids, they bounce back quick! She's been doing her therapy and is pretty much back to normal. But give her a call! I know she'd love to hear from you. How are you doing? You back home? Everything okay?"

"Yes. We are fine. Still some things to work through. We're

glad to be back. Promise to fill you in soon. Take care, Kevin. And do let me know if there is anything you need or anything I should do."

HE'S SO RIGHT — it's hard to figure out what Jenny needs. Have to hand it to Kevin for hanging in there. But then I guess I did that with Lily, too. Through thick and thin. Kevin does a better job of being there for his kids than I did with Jenny, though.

"What's the matter, Jack? Is Jenny okay? You look so sad!" Kitty handed him a cup of coffee.

"What? Oh — no she's mending. Still in the hospital. I was just thinking about how hard it is for Kevin to cope with Jenny's moods sometimes. She's not like her mother, but she can get pretty prickly. Well, you saw that when she came to check up on Deena. She smolders and then she blows. Unpredictable."

"Yes. I did see that. Must have been hard on you to manage the two of them when she was living at home."

"Actually, she never was a problem then. I look back on that time and Jenny was the one who tried to keep things together. At least as much as any kid could, under the circumstances. There were some really hard times, and I'm afraid Jenny suffered more than she ever let me know. At least then. She's making up for lost time now, though! Seems to have no trouble telling me exactly what she thinks. I'm not good at figuring out how to deal. I just kind of back away and let Kevin take care of it."

Kitty put her hand on Jack's arm. "It must be tough. God knows I haven't figured out how to have any kind of relationship with my daughter. Not that she gives any sign of wanting one. I miss her sometimes—-at least I miss the little girl she was. They grow up though. Have their own minds about a lot of things. I think you are handling all of it well, Jack. You stay in touch even though sometimes it's hard. And it's clear that Jenny does still want you in her life."

"You think so? Sometimes I wonder."

"Deena doing okay too? How's she managing with her knee?"

"Kevin says she's getting around great. Almost finished with her physical therapy. You know kids, they heal quick." Jack drained his cup, then looked at Kitty.

"I feel like we've been in lock down. It would be fun to go somewhere. You feel like dinner out?"

Kitty hesitated a minute wondering if it would be safe. She still felt like they should be in hiding. "I guess so. You think it's safe?"

"Oh I think so. Gray's behind bars, so that's no threat. And we can go someplace close. There's a little Mexican restaurant near Canyon Springs. Thought we might go there. They usually have music and they serve the best handmade tortillas. I think you'll like it."

"Let's make it an early night, though. Emily said she'd be here at 9:30 tomorrow morning."

Chapter 99

EMILY DID SHOW up as promised at 9:30. Jack had coffee waiting and Kitty fussed around the kitchen, unable to sit down. She found a package mix for blueberry muffins and busied herself making them. She hadn't touched a bite of her breakfast.

"You two look very domestic! Smells great in here. Something in the oven?"

"Yes — nothing fancy. Just some blueberry muffins from a mix." Kitty gave her a weak smile.

"Sounds good! Where do you want to work today? Here at the kitchen table?"

Jack said "Why don't you two use the living room? There's a big table there where you can spread out if you need to, and there's an internet connection. Might be kind of cramped in here. And that will give you some privacy if you need it. I'll stay out of your way."

Kitty looked at him gratefully. "That would work best, I think. I'd like you to be there, but on the other hand, it might be better if Emily and I slogged through this together. You have things to do around here, I'm sure — and didn't you say Carlin was coming over?"

"You're right. But just let me know if you need anything. I'll be out back in the Farmhouse. I've got plenty to keep me busy. Those muffins sure smell like they're done. I'd pull them out of the oven if I were you!"

"Thanks, Jack. I'll just go get set up in the living room. Bring some of those muffins in, Kitty? We should get started. There's a lot to go through," Emily smiled and walked into the living room.

She put a chair for Kitty on one side of the table, and she sat opposite with her notepad, files, and a tape recorder. Setting things up as close to the way they would be at the interview would help to make the whole process a bit easier. Knowing what to expect made a difference.

"Oh wow. This looks very formal!" Kitty put the plate of muffins down. "It's kind of intimidating, isn't it?"

"We just need to get you familiar with how things will work on Friday. It will be pretty cut and dried, I think, but you and I have a lot of things to cover so that you are not caught out or intimidated by the process. The DA's office has discovered some critical evidence and the prosecution is going to want to know as much as you can tell them about what they have."

"Oh my. Do you know what this new evidence is?"

"I think you can guess, Kitty. They were able to find the things you buried in that pot on the patio of the bedroom where you were staying."

"Oh my god." Kitty blanched, dropped the muffin she was holding. "How?"

"Apparently, they've had the place under surveillance for some time. I don't know how they work out all the details when it comes to investigations on the other side of the border, but I think there must have been undercover work going on. The information you were able to provide gave them something tangible. More pieces of the puzzle. And now it all seems to be falling into place. Your testimony is going to be critical. That, and the evidence they uncovered in some of those boxes you turned over to the police. It will certainly be to your benefit to give them all the information you have, all the corroboration of evidence they have put together, in order to extricate yourself from whatever Gray is trying to pin on you. Let's hope so."

"Yes. Let's hope so."

They spent the rest of the morning going over how to answer difficult questions. It was hard work, and Emily posed some theoretical questions that were tricky enough that Kitty was bewildered — afraid she'd say too much or too little. But she was a quick learner, and Emily drilled her, was tough enough, that Kitty was beginning to feel some confidence in her answers.

When Jack told them lunch was ready, they were more than ready to stop and take a break.

———

THERE WAS a pitcher of iced tea and a platter of fruit sitting on the table outside. Jack had grilled some chicken and corn. "You must have gone shopping!" Kitty took a grape off the table and popped it in her mouth.

"Yes. Got a lot of things done while the two of you were working. Carlin has come and gone. So how did you guys get on?"

Emily sat down at the table. "Kitty's going to do well. She's been drilled for two hours straight, and I threw her some pretty tough questions. One more session after lunch and she should be thoroughly prepared."

The day was hot, but the table was in the shade and there

was a bit of a breeze. There wasn't much conversation. Kitty and Emily had talked all morning long, and both were tired. But the silence was companionable. Emily excused herself when she had finished. She needed to make some phone calls.

Jack poured Kitty another glass of iced tea. "You feeling better about this, Kitty?"

"Yes, I think so. I'm not quite as intimidated by the whole interview thing now that Emily has taken me through what is going to happen. You know you see all these TV and movie dramas where the questions come pretty hard and fast and wonder how you'd be able to respond. But she's assured me the process is a lot more civilized, and fairly prescribed. And she will be there with me, so that's really good — the best in fact. She thinks my corroboration of the evidence they have may give the prosecution enough that I may not have to be at the trial."

"That's good to hear. Will you know anything more after your interview on Friday? About what happens next?"

"No. That, she says, will take a while. There will be negotiations based on the evidence. She says it is possible there will be more arrests. So, it's going to be some time before I'm out from under this mess. She doesn't think they have enough evidence against me directly to require jail time. I can't believe I just said that. Jail time. Jack my life is such a mess! And without your help now I don't know what I would do..."

"We've all gotten wound up in things that we didn't think through, or things that other people dragged us into without our full understanding. You're not alone, believe me. We can get through this. I know we can. People like Gray and that Judge will not prevail. No matter how much money or power they think they have."

The question still remained about what would come after all of these legal processes were over. She felt she was in her home place when she stepped into the farmhouse. No pain, no regrets, no manipulation, or dread lingering in any of the corners, no questions about her past. Only the smell of fresh paint and new wood. Furnishing it would be so much fun. She'd already picked out a few good pieces that were stored in the shed that should work beautifully. There was a small bureau that could hold table linens, and a round drop leaf table with four chairs. All of it was in need of a good cleaning or paint, but that was easily done and would give her the opportunity to choose colors that pleased her. If, if ... she was going to live here. Jack seemed to think that question was already settled. But how could it be until all she faced her troubled past?

Kitty sighed. She should probably focus more on what remained to be done in the main house so that if she had to leave, at least Jack would have some benefit from her having been here.

Tomorrow was the day of the interview. She should go help Jack with dinner and make it an early night. She closed the door of the farmhouse and walked back through the pepper trees and Albizias. The air was still, and full of sweetness. She felt relaxed. Happy. Even though tomorrow was full of the unknown, she knew she was not going to be alone.

"I DON'T UNDERSTAND. What do you mean you have more evidence? Does this still mean the interview is going forward tomorrow?" Emily was pacing up and down her office, glaring at her speaker phone.

"Based on what we found at the compound in Mexico, we are tabling the interview for now. This case has turned out to be much more than we thought and has given us evidence that we have wanted for months. I do need to ask you one question. Did your client see a doctor when she returned from that weekend? From what you told me, she was pretty beat up."

"Yes. But not until she was in the shelter."

"Good. If she did see a doctor, and she gives us access to those medical records, we may have another important piece of evidence to add to the prosecution of not only Gray, but Judge Berquist. And the evidence your client has already provided should make sure he is removed from office and jailed."

"I will. I'll talk to you when I have something...if I have something more."

"Thanks, Emily. I know this case has exploded beyond anything you expected. I appreciate your willingness to assist us. I'll talk to you tomorrow, then."

Emily sighed. She picked up her coffee cup and walked to the kitchen for a refill. The detective was right. This case had exploded. But to have the chance to put both Gray and the Judge where they belonged, in prison for a long, long time, would make everything she had done in her professional life matter more than she had ever dreamed. Between them they represented everything that was wrong with people who think they have the right to use and abuse women and feel secure that they are above the law. Having a part in bringing them to justice felt good. And, she was fairly sure Kitty's willingness to cooperate would mitigate any of the consequences she might have had to face.

All in all it had been a good day. She decided against another cup of coffee and poured herself a glass of wine. Then she called Kitty to tell her there would be no interview tomorrow, but that she would come down so they could talk in person about new developments. She hoped Kitty could remember more about the weekend in Mexico but knew that was a gamble.

Chapter 100

JENNY WAS FINALLY OFF MOST of her pain medication. The doctor told her she could go home. They had set her collar bone and provided her with a sling that kept her arm immobile while it healed. He told her it was going to take at least six weeks, and that she had to be faithful about wearing it.

Her concussion was a bit more complicated. It might take longer than six weeks for the headaches and dizziness to subside. But if she followed his directions carefully, she could expect to make a full recovery.

"You are going to have to let your husband carry the load for the next couple of months, Jenny. I know you have a busy life, but the consequences of this accident are going to take some time to resolve. Not only for you physically, but you have other legal consequences to face. You're very lucky no one else was involved when you hit that tree." He signed her release form and handed her some prescriptions. "And best not to drink while you are taking these medications. Not even a little." He patted her hand.

"I understand. Thank you. Shall I make an appointment to see you again soon?"

"I have already talked to your husband about that. He'll bring you to my office in two weeks unless you need to see me earlier. And do be careful. Is he here to take you home?"

"Yes. He's already taken my things to the car."

"You're all set then. I'll let the nurse know to come take you down to meet him."

Jenny sat on the bed. The nurse had helped her dress, putting on a pair of lounging pajama bottoms and shirt that fastened with velcro on the side with the sling. Thank god Deena had been able to find something online. Orthopedic clothing was available, it seems, but certainly not very stylish. She felt like an old woman. It wasn't pretty, but it would have to do for now. *Just what I deserve. I guess I had this coming for a long time.*

I just want to be home.

Chapter 101

DEENA WAS DEEP INTO MIDTERMS, studying until late at night, spending hours at the library doing research for papers, and trying to keep to her physical therapy routine so she could gain full recovery of her knee by Thanksgiving break. She and Mike had talked about taking a trip that weekend to visit her Grampa and Kitty, and she was determined to be able to show them both how fully recovered she was. And it would be fun to see what had happened with the farmhouse. The restoration of that little corner of her Grampa's world seemed significant to her, not just in and of itself, but as a promise of a brighter future with a steadier life. She hoped Kitty would be a part of it.

"Deena could you come in here for a minute?" Jenny called from her bedroom. "I need some help, honey."

Honey? Deena couldn't remember when her mother had called her that. Normally she wasn't one for pet names. "Sure, mom, I'll be right there."

Jenny was sitting at her desk, her arm now in a regular sling. "Could you open that bottom drawer for me? I'm looking for something, and I can't quite get in a position to pull it out."

"Should you even be doing that, mom? I thought you weren't supposed to do anything that would put pressure on your collarbone!" Deena pulled out the drawer. "What are you trying to find, anyway? Can I help?"

"I think my diaries are in there. The ones I kept when I was about your age."

"Why?"

"I've had a lot of time to think, lately, and I want to check in with my younger self, is all...." Jenny smiled and pushed a lock of hair off of Deena's forehead, tucking it behind her ear.

"You sure you want to do that?" Deena looked concerned. She knew a lot about her mother's troubled past.

"Yes. I'm sure. See if you can find the one with a green leather binding."

Deena pulled the journal out and handed it to her mom. "This one?"

"Yep. That's the one. And would you mind bringing me a cup of tea? And maybe one for yourself?"

"Okay..."

Deena closed the desk drawer and went downstairs to make tea. She wondered if her mother's current interest in her journals had anything to do with the long letter her mother had received from Grampa.

That letter had come a couple of days ago and was obviously more than just get well wishes. Her mother had taken it to her bedroom to read it, and when she finally came back downstairs, Deena could tell she had been crying. But she was smiling, too, which was puzzling. She had patted Deena's hand, and gone out to the backyard with the letter in her hand.

Chapter 102

EMILY ARRIVED at Jack's before he and Kitty had finished breakfast. She accepted the offer of coffee and took it into the living room where she and Kitty had worked the last time she was there, giving them time to finish eating. And it would give her a chance to set up her computer so she could take some notes.

She looked around the room, realizing that she hadn't noticed how changed it was. Lily always had a clutter of knick-knacks and ruffles. She couldn't imagine how Jack lived with that, knowing how meticulous he was about his office at the University. But Lily had a spark and a vitality that could be compelling, and most of the time, quite charming. Kitty was different, but there was a kind of exciting edge to her personality, too. Certainly, she had had a very complicated and dangerous past. But whereas Lily was vulnerable and dependent, Kitty had a worldly wisdom about her, and a toughness that Lily did not. Still, they were both women who needed rescuing, no matter their personalities. Jack did have a penchant for rescuing stray students, stray causes. She knew that well enough.

"Would you like more coffee, Emily?" Kitty had the pot in her hand. She looked a bit vulnerable, standing there with an apron over her jeans and a long-sleeved t-shirt. She was pale, her eyes puffy and smudged as if she hadn't slept.

"Oh yes, please. Thank you. I don't mean to rush you, Kitty. Please take your time with breakfast. I know it's early. I can keep myself entertained!"

"Jack's clearing the dishes. I'll just put the coffee back in the kitchen."

Emily could tell Kitty was nervous, in spite of the fact that they weren't going in for the interview. Last night when Emily told her she had a few more questions about her weekend in Mexico, Kitty had sounded hesitant. But she agreed to tell Emily all she could remember. Wondering what else Emily was trying to discover had kept her awake most of the night.

The kitchen door opened and closed, and Kitty reappeared. "Jack says to excuse him. He's going to run some errands. Are you ready for me now?"

"Yes. Hopefully this won't take long, and I'll be on my way! I am sorry we have to go into all of this again. But there is some good news. They have discovered more evidence that may mean you will not have to testify and may not face much in terms of consequences from your involvement with Gray."

Kitty's face lit up. "Really? What? Do you know? Does it involve that Judge?"

"Yes. And they have been after him for years. If this case breaks the way the prosecution hopes it will, he and Gray will be going to jail for a long, long time. So let's go back to what happened when you got to the Casino. I want to make sure I have all the details."

"Had a drink, of course. And then another. I still had the key to the room Gray used at the Casino and I just went there and passed out. I have no idea how long I slept, but when I woke up Gray was there and told me to clean up and come with him to the bar. Said he had some important contacts he wanted me to meet. I tried to tell him I was too ill to move, too ill to clean up, too sore to even move. But he wouldn't listen. He threatened me, then he poured me another drink and took me to the bar. That's the last thing I can remember until I woke up at that shelter.

"The woman there told me a doctor had seen me, but I didn't remember that. She gave me a number to call because the doctor wanted to follow up, but I didn't think anything more about it. By that time I was with Jack, and he took me to a clinic to see about the blisters on my heels. And it's funny, because that doctor at the clinic said she had been the one to see me the night I was brought to the shelter."

"Oh good! That's very good, Kitty! Did she do any medical tests or..."

"Well, she kind of did a bit of a physical and had me do some blood work."

"And why would she do that?"

Kitty looked terrified. "Does Jack have to know anything about this?"

"Not if you don't want him to. But if you have anyone who might have witnessed the damage done to you, especially a doctor, it might turn this case on its head."

"I told the doctor that I had been on a date that went wrong, and that I'd been given something to drink that knocked me out, and that put me in the shelter. I told her I didn't remember what had happened to me but that I had some bruises and soreness. And some bleeding. You know, vaginal bleeding. That's why she did the physical. And did a blood test."

"Would you be willing to give access to your medical records from this doctor to support your statements that you've already given to me about what happened? Because with that evidence, I think we can make sure these men are locked up. You know they found your underwear, which of course has all the DNA they need to make the connection to the two of them. They told me they have had an investigation going on for a long time at the Berquist compound in Mexico."

"Yes. I would give permission to the doctor to share whatever information might help. Of course I would. She put me on antibiotics, you know. I told Jack they were for my blisters, but that's not the truth. She was afraid I was developing an infection, one that might affect my bladder and my kidneys."

"How are you now?"

"I think I'm fine. But I should probably do a follow-up visit with her. Should have done that a few weeks ago. I've put it off."

"Well, make that appointment as soon as you can and tell her that you are giving me access to your medical records. She'll have a form for you to fill out. In fact, if you want, I could come with you and perhaps talk to her then?"

"I wouldn't want Jack to know."

"I understand. Well, get that appointment made as soon as possible. Can you get there on your own? Maybe I could meet you there?"

"Yes. He's given me the keys to his wife's car. I can make some excuse. I've been encouraging him to go visit his daughter. Maybe I can suggest he do that on the day of my appointment."

Chapter 103

JACK HAD TAKEN his time writing to Jenny. They had spoken on the phone a couple of times since her accident, but the exchanges had been perfunctory and short. He knew she was healing well, and that she still had some difficult things to face when she was fully recovered. He wanted to be sure she was clear about how much he loved her, and how much he supported and admired her, no matter what. Kitty and her problems had taken up so much of his time, and he knew Jenny was concerned about his involvement with someone he had known for only a short time and under such strange circumstances. He tried to put his feelings for Kitty into a structure that would make sense — not only to Jenny — but to himself. He had started to write the letter when he was still hiding away with Kitty at Sister Helen's, and when he finally finished, he waited a few days before sending it. He was tempted to read it, or parts of it to Kitty, before he mailed it but decided that this letter was better left as it was for just Jenny to read. He couldn't worry about a response because he had no reason to expect one. His daughter had so often been pushed aside for some crisis with her mother. He knew how much of a threat this new relationship must be for her. But it still was, after all, his life. And she had one of her own.

THE WHEELS of justice are often agonizingly slow to turn, but turn they do. Jenny faced up to the fact that she would have to go to court. The doctor was right, of course, she was lucky her accident had not involved anyone else. And her injuries certainly would prove a reminder of her behavior for months, maybe even years, to come. The judge had been lenient. It was her first offense. But she had to pay a stiff fine, and damages to the city for the tree she hit. Her license was suspended for six months, and she also had community work to complete, but that could wait until she was released from her doctor to return to normal activities. And she would have to go through a program for alcohol abuse, something she was truly dreading.

She was thankful she had Peter to rely on, or the community center she ran would have had to shut down. And she was thankful that now she could at least relieve some of his burden, at least in terms of paperwork. She had been released by her doctor to do deskwork, but no travel for now. She could work from home. The members of the board of directors were still, thankfully, unaware of the cause of her accident.

She phoned her dad and asked him to come visit when he could. She did not pressure him, or whine about how other things always took his attention. His letter had made her think about what they both faced during those long years of her mother's illness. And her accident had made her grateful for all that she had now, with her own family, in her own life. But she needed to have that conversation with her dad. The one where they might come to some understanding of each other as adults. They had the rest of their lives to live and she wanted to make a new beginning. She knew, from his letter, that was his hope as well.

Chapter 104

Kitty needed something to occupy her, make her feel productive, while she waited for her appointment with the doctor, and the outcome of her involvement with Gray's shady business deals. She longed for a resolution that would set her free, would take her out from under the fog of uncertainty and insecurity. It had only been a few months, really, since everything fell apart with Gray, but looking back on it now she could see how fragile her whole existence with him had been from the beginning. He used people to get what he wanted, and she knew she wasn't alone, wasn't the only victim, when his whole empire began to crumble. One thing that gave her comfort was that in some small way she might be able to help put him behind bars. She made her way out to the farmhouse.

"What are you doing out here, Kitty? I wondered where you were! I thought we might take another load to the thrift shop and maybe get some lunch." Jack looked worried. "You all right?"

"Yes, yes — I'm fine. Just admiring this wonderful little home. Fantasizing about how it might look when it's furnished!

Are YOU all right? You look worried. Was that phone call from Jenny?"

"Yes — she does want me to come visit, so I thought I might plan to go up there soon. But it's not urgent. No, I was just wondering what happened to you. Couldn't find you in the house." He smiled.

"Jack, wouldn't it be fun to furnish this little place? Maybe Deena could stay here when she visits you!"

"Well yes. I kind of thought the two of you had plans to do that together!"

"We have sent each other a couple of pictures of things that might work. But she's so busy with school right now. We haven't messaged each other for a while. I'm kind of feeling like I need a project to keep my mind off what's happening with the inquiry. Could I clean up some of the pieces from your storage shed?"

"Of course, you can make this your project! And maybe we will find some things at the thrift shop — that is if you want to make that run today?"

"Sure! Let's do it. Maybe stop for lunch first? I'm hungry!"

THE SNOWBIRD WAS ALMOST EMPTY. Only one couple sat at the counter. A bit early for the lunch crowd. They chose a booth in the corner. The menu listed a special of a hot turkey sandwich with cranberry chutney. Pumpkin pie was the featured dessert.

"Wow. Isn't it a bit early for Thanksgiving?" Jack asked the waitress.

"Not really - first sign of cold weather and that's what people start thinking about. And we've got a new chef. He's trying out what he calls "pub grub", whatever that means. So far, it's been thumbs up. We'll see how much he can change things around here." She winked.

"How about some pub grub, Kitty? You want to take a chance?"

"How could I resist cranberry chutney?"

"Ok we'll take it! And some coffee. Might was well get a jump on the holidays!"

The coffee arrived, and Jack took a sip. "Uh oh. They've flavored the coffee with something!" he made a face.

Kitty sniffed hers and took a sip. "Oh it's pumpkin spice! I like it. But obviously it's not your thing," she laughed.

The waitress appeared with two empty cups and a coffee pot. "I'm sorry, I poured your coffee out of the pot we're testing. Jack, I'm pretty sure you won't want flavored coffee. Am I right?"

"You are SO right. But I think Kitty likes hers, so she'll keep it!"

Being with Jack, in that place, feeling so free and easy, relaxed and happy, made Kitty realize how empty her life had been. And how full her life could be. Not with big events, or even holidays, but just in the act of sharing a cup of coffee with someone who simply wanted to be with you. Someone who wasn't out to get anything from you or expect anything except the pleasure of your company. She sighed.

Jack looked at her. "Something wrong? Were you serious about the coffee? Do you want to change it?"

"Nothing's wrong, Jack. Everything, right now, feels perfect. That was a happy sigh. How about you make that trip to see Jenny next week? Spend a couple of days with her? Emily said things are under control, and she wants to meet with me again to go over some details on Tuesday. You wouldn't need to be here. And, if I needed to go anywhere, you've given me keys to the car. But rest assured, I would not go farther than into town!" She smiled at him and reached for his hand.

Chapter 105

JENNY WAS a little nervous about her father's visit. She asked Kevin to give them some space, so he took himself out to a job site before Jack got there. Before he left he made sure there was coffee ready. Jenny was still operating with just one good arm, so he wanted to make sure they had what they needed.

Jack was nervous too, but optimistic. Jenny's tone on the phone had been sweet, not sharp or angry. It was a relief to hear her without her usual edge. He hoped he would be able to give her what she needed. But he knew he wasn't good at judging what that might be. Kitty was right, she told him to just let Jenny talk. Listening, she said, was maybe the best gift one person could give to another.

He had left early on Tuesday, to beat the traffic, but it had still taken him almost three hours to get to Jenny's house. He was ready to get out of the truck and move around a bit. He stretched and walked around to the back of the truck, pulled out a box of things that had been Lily's that he and Kitty thought Jenny might want.

Jenny heard the truck pull into the driveway and was

waiting at the front door. "Wow! Is it Christmas already? Did you bring me presents?"

"Hah! No, these are just some things you might want to keep, things that your mother treasured. Thought you might too. But if not, no worries. You can pass them on or donate them to charity. Not much of value here, except maybe there's some good memories connected to them. Where shall I put this box until you have time to go through it?"

"Why not bring it in to the family room and we can go through it together. I'd like that." Jenny smiled.

"Oh? You want to do that now? Okay. Lead the way!"

"Want some coffee Dad? Kevin made a pot before he left."

"Oh? Kevin's not here? I thought he'd be here." Jack looked nervous.

"No, he's got to do a site visit for a project he's on. I think maybe it's better, anyway, if just the two of us have some time to talk."

"Well sure, if that's what you want. And yes, I'd love some coffee."

Jenny had a calm about her Jack hadn't seen before. She seemed different, more centered. Jack was encouraged that maybe this visit would not be as awkward as he had feared.

"You'll have to come out to the kitchen and get your cup, Dad. I can pour, but I'm still not very good at carrying."

"I'm just glad to see you up and about and looking so perky! You've been through quite a lot, kid. I've been worried."

"Perky? Now there's a term I haven't heard in a long time! Well Dad I've been worried about you too. But it seems to me like you are looking pretty perky yourself!" Jenny laughed.

It had been Kitty's idea for Jack to bring the box of things. She thought it might be a good way for them to sort through what was worth keeping and what could be let go. And in so doing, perhaps figure out what those things might be in their relationship, as well. She was right. It proved to be a valuable afternoon full of tears and laughter, and the start of a new beginning for them both. There was no anger, no lashing out, only a sharing of their pain over the past, and their hopes for a better future.

Chapter 106

KITTY MET Emily at the doctor's office. They were able to get a copy of Kitty's medical records and have a frank discussion about how the doctor had assessed Kitty's condition at the shelter and during her visit to the clinic. The doctor had the wisdom to put together what information she could and carefully preserve the lab work in case it was needed should Kitty decide to file charges. Kitty never indicated that she had been raped, but from what the doctor had seen, it was clear that whatever had happened, was against her will.

Emily wasn't shocked by the information, much to Kitty's relief, only saddened and horrified that she had been subjected to such abuse. She was grateful that she had seen a doctor who had thoughtfully recorded her observations. It would go a long way toward validating the evidence the investigation had uncovered in Mexico. She had all the necessary paperwork so that the doctor could release what she had to the police department's forensic lab. Now they just had to wait for the final compilation of the evidence by the District Attorney, not only against Gray, but also Judge Berquist.

"I am glad that your blood tests came back with everything

looking normal, Kitty. It must have been one more thing for you to worry about," Emily said as they walked to their cars.

"To tell you the truth I didn't give it much thought. I guess I thought it was a minor inconvenience considering everything else I was facing. But thank you. And thanks for coming today."

"Of course. So now I have all the medical records, and soon the forensics lab will have the results of the evidence they've obtained. Our work here is done! At least until we hear from the prosecutor's office about a possible interview date for you. Which I don't think will happen for at least another week. So try to take a break from all of this. If you can. I think I'm going to try to do that too!" She squeezed Kitty's hand.

"I will try. I do have some things to do back at the house, and that should keep me out of trouble until Jack gets back! Hope his visit to Jenny proves to be a good one. He was really nervous about it."

"I have a good feeling about that too, Kitty. I think they may finally find a way forward to a happier relationship."

Kitty wanted to get home and fix dinner. She knew it would, at the very least, have been a long day on the freeways for Jack, but he had made it clear that he was returning this evening. Whether the visit with Jenny had worn him out remained to be seen. She stopped at the Farm Stand in Canyon Springs and picked up fresh corn, tomatoes, and a large pumpkin to mark the beginning of the holidays.

It would be the first time in a long time that she looked forward to celebrating anything, but now she was hopeful. And she was happy.

Chapter 107

JACK WAS LATE LEAVING for home. The visit with Jenny had been a good one. She seemed to have softened, and as they discussed some of the shared pain from their past, she opened up about her reactions to her mother's illness and how it had affected her as a child and teenager. It wasn't really new information for Jack, but it did bring into the light how much pain she had to contain to protect him, and to protect herself. He began to see her anger as a coping mechanism rather than an annoying personality trait. She told him that she recognized how much he had to cope with, and she gave him credit for being so protective of her mother. But she didn't let him off the hook when it came to how it had impacted her life. She revealed times when she really needed him to be there for her but felt she could never trust that he would be because her mother had taken all the care and attention he could give.

He didn't try to explain anything away. He just listened. She let him read some passages from her journal, and he was on the verge of tears by the time he finished.

"Oh, Jenny. How I wish things had been different for you. You didn't deserve any of this. You were always such a remarkable child, and you seemed to grow into a competent adult way before your time. I wish just saying 'I'm so sorry' would erase the trauma of the past and allow you to be free of it. But I don't think that would be enough. I hope you find some peace, and that all of this won't continue to weigh you down."

"I'm okay, Dad. Really. I think my accident created an entirely different kind of focus for me. And I have resources now that I didn't have before that I know can help me."

They spent some time going through the box of things he brought. They remembered some happy times, and some sad times. And they shared with each other how they had felt about all of it.

It was toward the end of the day that Jenny brought up her concerns about Kitty. Jack wondered when that would happen and had been surprised that wasn't the first topic she wanted to talk about. He steeled himself when she said, "So Dad, now that we've cleared the air a bit, and have some understanding about the past, I want to let you know my concerns for you now."

"Oh?" Jack got up and started to put the things he'd brought back into the box. "Shall I put these things somewhere to get them out of the way?"

"No, Kevin can do that. Don't try to change the subject, Dad. Let me have my say."

Jack sat down again. "OK. Shoot."

"It's Kitty I'm worried about. And I want to tell you why, and then I want you to understand that if you aren't worried about any of my concerns, I can let that go. But I need to tell you what I think. Just in case there is something you haven't thought of or considered."

So the conversation went on for some time, with Jenny talking again and Jack listening. She recounted all the things he already knew about Kitty's troubled past. He was glad she didn't know everything, but she knew enough. She also reminded him how vulnerable he was to someone who was in need, and how concerned she was that he might be replacing her mother with someone who was equally needy and dependent. And she was frank about how Kitty might take his attention away from her and his grandchildren. She forecast a gloomy future where they were only in his life when he remembered to send a birthday card, or a holiday present. She wanted more from him, and for herself and her children.

He listened and held back any of his objections until she finished. But then he said, "Thank you, Jenny, for your honesty. I do understand your concerns about Kitty. And I want you to know that those concerns are not far from my thoughts, either. But you also need to know how lonely I have been. Not just in the last six months since your mother died, but for a very long time before that too. And yes, Kitty might be risky business. But I have seen so much in her that she herself has not recognized. She's strong, she's good company, and she has been forthright about all her past mistakes over the time we've been together. I'm sure that there is still a lot to learn about her. I also want you to know that I am not going to make any rash decisions about any commitment to her. I don't think either one of us wants that. What we want right now is to support each other, be good company for one another. You haven't wanted me to be alone. And now I'm not! I think she is going to move into the farmhouse once her legal problems are resolved, and that way I will have someone. I won't be alone. She'll have her own space, and I'll have mine. We will share meals when it's right and spend time together. We will take it very slow. And who knows? It may turn out that once she is feeling strong enough, she will move on. I know enough about myself that if she does that, I will be sad. But I won't hold her. I am hoping you can come to see that she is not going to be a threat to my relationship with you and your family. In fact, in many ways, as we have sorted through the house, she has helped me understand how important those relationships are to me."

Jenny smiled. "OK then, Dad. But you know I'll be checking in regularly to see how things are going, right? That won't bother you?"

"No! Of course not! I hope you will come and visit often so that you can get to know her and see that there isn't much of a threat there. She isn't your mother, Jenny. She's different." Jack took Jenny's hand and kissed her forehead. "And now I really do need to get back on the road. I'm probably going to hit some pretty heavy traffic."

"Call me when you get there?"

"Yes. I will call you when I get there. I promise."

Chapter 108

JACK CALLED the house phone when he was about half an hour away. It went to voicemail. Kitty was restless and had gone out to the farmhouse to distract herself from watching the clock. The sun was low in the sky and bathed the farmhouse porch in a pattern of light and shadow from the pepper tree. It was quiet, except for the chattering of a flock of finches as they picked at seeds from a patch of wildflowers. Kitty sat on the steps and watched them until she heard Jack's truck pull into the driveway. She heard the door slam and hurried to get back to the kitchen before he went looking for her.

"Kitty? Kitty? Are you here? Why didn't you pick up when I called?" Jack sounded worried.

"I'm here – I was just out at the farmhouse. Sorry I missed your call!"

"Oh thank god! I suddenly had this vision of you being hurt or kidnapped – I think I was on the verge of panic!" Jack sank into a kitchen chair.

"It's no wonder you're on edge. You've been gone a long time, and I would bet the drive home was terrible." Kitty handed him a glass of water. "How did it go with Jenny?"

"Pretty well. She seems to be a bit more balanced, a bit more in control. She's still not able to use her arm, so she's not able to do too much. But I think this time to rest and think has done her good. Terrible thing to go through, but she seems to be putting a brave face on it. We had a nice visit. I am glad you encouraged me to go. It was right, and it turned out to be good for both of us."

"I'm glad. Was she happy about the things you brought her? Did she want any of them?"

"Yes! I was surprised, but she seemed to want all of it. So that turned out well too. Gave us a chance to do some reminiscing."

Kitty opened the oven to check on the casserole she'd made for dinner. "Did she ask about me? I know she's been worried about me being here."

"We talked a bit about you, yes. She's worried that you might come between me and her family. I assured her that nothing could be further from the truth."

"No, I would never want to do that. I hope she believed you, Jack." Kitty pulled the casserole out and set it on top of the stove.

"That smells wonderful! What have you created?"

"Nothing fancy, believe me! Just a kind of Mexican dish with green chiles, corn, tortillas, and cheese. I made a salad, too. Are you ready to eat? Or do you want to wait a bit and have a drink?"

"Let's have a glass of wine on the patio. Will your casserole keep warm?"

"I'll just pop it back in the warm oven. It will be fine."

Jack opened a bottle of red wine and Kitty followed him out to the patio carrying two wine glasses.

This feels so normal, I wonder if that's true for Jack as well.

He looks so tired tonight. Kitty put the glasses on the table and went back into the house to get some napkins. Jack watched her go, wondering if everything she was facing would be resolved in a way that meant she could stay with him; that meant she would want to stay with him. His reaction when he thought she had disappeared told him that he wanted that more than ever.

———

EMILY CALLED the next morning and asked if Kitty would be willing to come into the DA's office for her interview the next day. "I know this interview has been pushed off calendar and back on again too many times for anybody's comfort, but since they feel they have everything they need to proceed, it's probably in your best interest, Kitty."

"I understand. To tell you the truth, I'd like to get it over with. I'm ready to move on, and whatever the outcome, I need to see this through. So of course, I'll be there. What time?" Kitty looked at Jack and gave him a weak smile.

"You'll need to be there at 10, and of course I will be there with you. I'll send you an email with directions to the office. I think you are well prepared. And hopefully, this won't take long. The evidence you can provide should be pretty straight-forward."

"OK. I'll see you tomorrow." Kitty hung up the phone.

"What's up? You have to be somewhere tomorrow?" Jack looked worried.

"This is it, Jack. The DA's office wants to interview me tomorrow at 10 a.m. I guess we should find out what I face pretty soon after that, from what Emily says." Kitty was twisting the dishtowel in her hand. "I doubt I'll sleep much tonight."

"Even if you don't, getting this interview behind you will be a big relief, I'm sure. And I will drive you. No fighting me on this one. I want to be there when you're done."

Chapter 109

Mike and Ben were putting the finishing touches on the hydraulics for the float they'd been working on for months in preparation for homecoming at Ben's school. The hydraulics Mike helped with were working smoothly, and the oversized football it would lift would made a nice arc from one end of the float to the other. Now it was time for the decorations crew to start covering the structure with paper mâché and crepe paper flowers.

"That's amazing, Mike. I never thought we could actually get this to work! Maybe I'll consider studying engineering when I graduate." Ben was grinning from ear to ear.

"Well keep going with those math courses, and you'll have a good foundation for doing just that! You seem to have a real talent for mechanics, too. I watched your technique with those tools, and I think you're a natural!" Mike snapped his toolbox shut. "You want a ride home? I didn't see Deena here today."

"She had a physical therapy appointment. I think it's her last one, though. She said she could pick me up after that. But we finished here early. So yeah, a ride home would be great! I'll just text her and let her know."

Mike grinned. There might be a chance to see Deena, after all.

"You want to pick up some tacos on the way home? I think we could use a snack." *And maybe Deena will be home by the time we get there, if we take our time...* Mike put his toolbox in the trunk of his car.

"Sure! I'm always hungry, so that suits me fine!"

By the time they got to the house, Denna had come home. Mike had timed their arrival perfectly.

"Come in and say hi to Deena, Mike? Pretty sure she'd like to see you..."

"Sure. I'd like to see her too! And I did bring her a taco..."

"Yeah. I kinda noticed that!"

Mike and Deena went out to the patio, and Ben headed upstairs to start his homework. He wanted to tackle his Algebra while Mike was still here in case he needed some help. No sense in wasting that opportunity, and he knew his sister would want to visit with Mike without him hanging around.

Kevin was in his office, and Jenny was napping. The house felt settled, calm. Mike noticed that Deena seemed less edgy.

"My physical therapist said I have completed my course, and that as far as she's concerned, I should be free to return to all my normal activities without any further restrictions. I'm so glad to be done! She would push me pretty hard sometimes! I have one more appointment with the doctor just to be sure. But she seems to feel I'll get the green light from him too."

"That's great news! You should let your grampa know, and Kitty. I think they will be relieved to hear that too."

"Yes, I will. In fact, what would you think if we planned to go visit them soon? We had a good time the last time we were there, in spite of all the drama, and wouldn't you like to go back and pay a visit to Colony Springs too? We could maybe walk around a bit, talk to some of the people there, and find out more about what they're planning for the future of that place?"

Deena had finished her taco. "I'm thirsty – you want something to drink?"

"I would like something to drink, and yes I would like to go visit your grampa and Kitty again and Colony Springs! I'm working this Saturday, but maybe we could go the following weekend?"

They went to the kitchen, and Ben came down the stairs with his Algebra book. "Hey Mike! You got a few minutes to help me with this problem? I've tried to figure it out, but I'm really stuck."

Mike looked at Deena and smiled. "Sure, Ben. Let's take a look."

When Kevin came into the kitchen, he found the three of them at the table, Ben and Mike bent over the Algebra book, and Deena sipping her drink, dreamily staring out the window. They never noticed him. And when Jenny came downstairs to check with Kevin about dinner, he motioned her into his office so as not to disturb the little tableau at the table.

Chapter 110

THE INTERVIEW TURNED out to be sworn testimony at the DA's office and went on much longer than Emily thought it would. Emily had said she thought it would last about two hours, but they needed to continue after they took a lunch break. The three of them went to a café across the street, but Kitty was too nervous to eat. She sipped her iced tea, and picked at her salad, but clearly, she had been pretty upset by the intensity of the interview and the scope of the questions she was asked to answer.

"Am I doing okay, Emily? Have I said too much or too little? Sworn testimony seems so much harder than a simple interview."

"Kitty, I have rarely seen anyone do a better job. You are doing just fine. But I really think you need to eat something if this is going to continue for another hour or so after lunch. You'll need to keep your focus and doing that on an empty stomach isn't easy."

"I'm trying, but ... maybe I should have ordered some soup."

Jack motioned to their waiter. "What soups do you offer today?"

"Tomato bisque and split pea, and we always have our house potato cheese."

"Any of those appeal to you, Kitty?" Jack asked.

"Maybe the potato cheese. But just a cup."

"Good choice, Kitty. That should get you through! And remember, I'm not going anywhere. If you have any hesitation about any of the questions, you can always look at me and I will give you whatever you need." Emily took a bite of her sandwich.

Kitty nibbled on a piece of bread until her soup came, and then managed to eat most of the soup and a few bites of her salad. She drained her iced tea glass and seemed to settle a bit. She excused herself to use the restroom, and Jack asked the waiter to refill her glass and ordered a slice of apple pie.

"She's doing so well, Jack. No matter how nervous she looks now, in the interview she seems calm and collected. I'm amazed, really, how she is keeping it together. None of the questions she's being asked are presenting her with a pretty picture of her past with Gray and Berquist. Hopefully they will only keep us in there for another hour before it's over. I think they are getting what they need. And because she has been so open and cooperative, I think we will be able to get her home. She has been granted immunity in this case, in return for her testimony. But that doesn't mean she can't be called again if additional charges are made. I wish I could say differently. It's unlikely she would be called as a witness for the defense, since her testimony has been so credible for the prosecution, though."

"We are so ready to move past this, and with some assurance that none of it will follow her into the future. Will she have community service or probation or anything else?"

"She may be ordered to take some kind of ethics in

accounting course, especially if she wants to continue to do that kind of work. But we'll see. I have a hunch that there might only be a probationary period, which means she will just have to stay in touch with her probation officer for a few months."

When Kitty came back to the table, Jack was able to get her to eat a few bites of apple pie and drink a little more tea. She was well fortified for whatever the next few hours would bring.

Kitty was quiet on the ride back home, and eventually fell asleep with her head against the passenger window. It had been a long day. The interview went on for another three hours after lunch. But as Emily said, it was better to get it all done in one day if at all possible. And she had found out that the DA had at least three other witnesses who suffered some of the same treatment as Kitty, who had agreed to come in and give their testimony. So the case was building and not just on Kitty's testimony. Emily felt certain that Kitty and Jack, even as unwitting holders of hard evidence found in Gray's boxes, were not going to be charged with anything. Gray was going to spend a very long time in jail, possibly for the rest of his life. And Judge Berquist had been arrested and held without bail because he was definitely a flight risk. His days on the bench were over, and he too would find himself incarcerated possibly for the rest of his life, given the additional evidence they had uncovered.

When Jack turned into the driveway at the house, Kitty woke with a start. "Oh wow! I slept all the way home?" she rubbed her neck and looked at Jack.

"Yes, you did! I'm not surprised. Let's get you in the house and get you settled. I'll put some dinner together and we can have an early night. I think we are going to need it!"

There was a voicemail on the machine when they got in. It was Deena asking if she and Mike could come visit the weekend after next. Kitty's face lit up when she heard it.

"Oh tell them yes, Jack! It would be so nice to have that to look forward to, wouldn't it? We could make a real party, couldn't we? Maybe we could even decorate a bit for Halloween and make some pumpkin pie?"

Jack smiled. "Decorate for Halloween?? Well why not! Let's just pull out all the stops and celebrate! Who knows? Maybe we could even get the whole family down this way for Thanksgiving. And by that time, maybe the farmhouse will be furnished and ready for occupancy! You and Deena can talk about that when she comes."

"A home place. We've made a home place, Jack. Haven't we?"

"Yes. A home place. That's what it feels like to me, too. Both here and out there in the little farmhouse. We did it. Together."

Acknowledgments

"Have our thank yous been said?" they asked.

"Let me do that here," said the author. "Over the last ten years and many drafts and iterations of characters, there has always been the support of my family. Ken, Jonathan, Heather, and all the extended family connected to them. Particular thanks to my beta readers Ken, Jonathan, Melanie, Sandy, and Myra. All of them have gone over the manuscript with a keen eye and with literary sensibility and I can't thank them enough. My granddaughter Gwendolyn has done a beautiful design for the cover, incorporating all the details I requested, and I am so grateful for her talent.

Many thanks also to the members of Let's Write! They know who they are. Encouragement from that group has kept me going at every turn, blind alley, and point of distracted frustration." I replied. "And also thank you to the MFA program at Antioch University Los Angeles, where I gained the courage to put this out into the world."